A Killer in the Family

By the same author

She Lies in Wait
Watching from the Dark
Lie Beside Me
Little Sister

A Killer in the Family

GYTHA LODGE

MICHAEL  JOSEPH

PENGUIN MICHAEL JOSEPH

UK | USA | Canada | Ireland | Australia
India | New Zealand | South Africa

Penguin Michael Joseph is part of the Penguin Random House group of companies
whose addresses can be found at global.penguinrandomhouse.com

First published 2023
002

Set in 13.5/16pt Garamond MT Std
Typeset by Jouve (UK), Milton Keynes
Printed and bound in Great Britain by Clays Ltd, Elcograf S.p.A.

The authorized representative in the EEA is Penguin Random House Ireland,
Morrison Chambers, 32 Nassau Street, Dublin D02 YH68

A CIP catalogue record for this book is available from the British Library

HARDBACK ISBN: 978–0–241–47100–5
TRADE PAPERBACK ISBN: 978–0–241–47101–2

www.greenpenguin.co.uk

Penguin Random House is committed to a
sustainable future for our business, our readers
and our planet. This book is made from Forest
Stewardship Council® certified paper.

For Benji.

I'm heartbroken that I can only imagine your insightful, hilarious thoughts on this one. You are so very much missed.

New Year's Eve

Lindsay was laughing – really, genuinely laughing – for the first time in months. And possibly even for the first time in years.

This wasn't the kind of thing she did. The car. The man. The intoxicated flight through crowded streets.

She hadn't been out on New Year's Eve for decades. Not since Peter. And, even then, it had only happened in the early years. The year that they'd met, at a party neither of them had quite wanted to go to. And for three or four years afterwards as they'd each forced themselves to go out of love for the other, with a babysitter booked to look after the child they hadn't planned on but both of them adored.

They'd each eventually admitted that the kitchen table and a game of Risk with each other held more appeal than the fireworks and the crowds. And from then on they'd stayed in, with Dylan always begging to stay up until midnight with them. He made them party a little, at least. He'd persuade them to get the Twister mat out or dance around to Pink Floyd.

And then, after Peter's slow dwindling and loss and Dylan's departure for university in Dublin, it had mostly been Lindsay alone. Her not even forty, and left to ring in the New Year with a jigsaw, and the TV, and a lot more wine than she was used to. Every year had been the same: a flood of memories from that first night, when she had fizzed with the hope that Peter might kiss her at midnight, and a sense of profound loss that she was moving into a new year without him.

It might have been easier if Dylan had chosen to stay

within easy visiting distance. But he'd met the woman of his dreams and decided to start a new life in Dublin. And so each New Year's Eve before this one had been marked, for Lindsay, by aching loneliness.

She wasn't sure what had changed tonight. Any other year, she would have been out for the count by now, numbed into oblivion by wine. She wouldn't have been in an unfamiliar car, going to watch fireworks with a man she barely knew.

She glanced over at him, this other man, who had been as tentative at first as she'd been. A man so clearly as full of hope, but also of anxiety, as she was.

She watched the intelligent, attractive lines of his face as he manoeuvred the big vehicle past a crowd of revellers that had spilled onto the road. And she felt a sense of the serendipity in everything.

She had gone for a long, hard walk until dusk. It had left her tired but also, somehow, enlivened. She'd showered and gone in her dressing gown to pour herself a glass of wine, and realised that she had somehow run herself dry. And it had seemed the right thing to do, tonight, to put on her nicest black sweater and jeans with the heeled boots she hardly ever wore, and walk to the wine shop on South Parade.

Those decisions had sent her straight into his path. And him into hers. There had been no question in her mind that this was what was meant to happen: for her to meet someone on another New Year's Eve, somewhere else she'd never really intended to go, and for the two of them to be the obvious outsiders. Clear soulmates.

Lindsay didn't know exactly where they were driving to, and it didn't worry her. He'd told her he knew where to get the best view of the fireworks, his voice full of energy and a delight at sharing this, and she believed him.

She felt a wave of joy at the trust she felt towards him. At the fact that she'd at last, *at last*, felt that same warmth and willingness she'd felt towards Peter. A hot, gut-deep excitement. A feeling of wanting to give someone else control.

'Here,' he said, as he pulled up at a temporary traffic light. He was holding a small thermos flask out to her, and she took it with a smile. Tipped it back without needing to think.

'Spiced rum and apple,' he said. 'Is that OK?'

'Definitely,' she said. It was strong but comforting. She could feel the heat of it spreading down and into her stomach, adding a sense of comfort to the jubilant feeling that had built in her all evening.

She glanced out of the car at a ruckus going on. There was a group of twenty-somethings on the pavement, drinking out of cans and yelling at each other instead of talking. On any other night, she would have felt irritated by them. Threatened maybe. Whereas tonight, she was part of an exuberant whole. She raised the flask to them, and drank again, more deeply.

He grinned, and said, 'I might have some soon. If you're OK to stay out a while so I don't have to drive for a bit.'

'I am,' she said, without hesitation. And this, again, wasn't the Lindsay who had spent the last seven years making excuses to be alone. This was the Lindsay of her past life. Perhaps an even bolder version.

He lifted his hand from the gearstick and squeezed her fingers just as the lights changed. They moved off, away from the hubbub. The bypass was quiet as they joined it and began to fly past illuminated houses. Just their car and one further ahead.

It wasn't far off midnight, and everyone who wasn't spilling out of pubs was at parties or on sofas; on riverbanks or clustered in gardens.

She realised she should send something to Dylan, before

the mobile networks jammed up. Her son would scoff at any suggestion he was sentimental, but he would mention it if he didn't get a message from her tonight.

She pulled her phone out of her jeans pocket, and found it surprisingly hard to focus on the screen. It made her laugh.

'God, can hardly read,' she said.

'Are you calling someone?'

He asked it lightly. Without jealousy.

'Just messaging Dylan.'

She glanced over to see him smiling and was glad when he said, 'I'd like to meet him sometime.'

'He'd love you,' she said. 'You're just his kind of person.'

And then her focus was on the screen for a few minutes as she laboriously typed:

Happy New Year! Hope you're all having a great time.

She scrolled for a while until she'd found a few celebratory emojis. They weren't in her most frequently used list, something she found herself thinking firmly, happily, that she was going to change. She was going to be the sort of person who was excited, happy and celebratory again. She'd never believed in New Year's resolutions, but she was making one now.

And then, in a determined move, she turned the phone off. The rest of the night was going to be about her, and him, and nothing else. She could catch up with Dylan in the morning.

By the time she looked up again, they'd left the town and were driving between trees, the road dark on either side. She squinted out through the windscreen, disorientated, until she recognised a junction. They were already at Ashurst. Had it really taken her that long to write the message?

They turned a slight bend in the road, and Lindsay's phone slid off her lap, and down into the gap between the seat and the central console.

'Bugger.'

'What's up?'

'My phone is . . .' She waved, her hands feeling only vaguely connected to her. God, she was drunk.

She reached over to get it, just as he lifted his arm to look underneath it, and her head collided with his elbow, hard.

'Eesh,' he said.

Lindsay found herself laughing. 'Sorry.'

'You shouldn't be apologising.' He shook his arm, glancing at her. 'That must have hurt. You OK?'

'I'm fine,' she said, grinning at him. 'I can't even feel it.'

'Good,' he said, shaking his head slightly as he looked back at the road. 'You're clearly tougher than I am.'

She reached down for the phone again, her fingers finding it, but not able to grasp it. She succeeded only in shoving it backwards, until it was pushed into the rear of the car.

'Sorry. Hang on.'

She pulled on the seat belt to give herself more room, and half turned in her seat. Twisting her right arm, she could just about reach down to where the phone now sat.

In this contorted position, she could see into the rear of the car, and at first it meant nothing to her: the neatly bound piles of wood wedged front to back, one of which stretched out towards her. The can of kerosene. They were just things. The sorts of things people had in their cars sometimes.

But then she found herself thinking about a woman, and a murder, and a bonfire. A lonely forty-something woman whose photo had appeared again and again in the papers and online. A woman who had reminded Lindsay of herself in painful ways. A woman whose killer hadn't yet been found, though everybody had tried.

And the happy, detached contentment suddenly shifted. She felt it for what it was: a fog of confusion that was descending, and overtaking her, as he drove her god knew where. And with it came the most crushing sense of dread.

He's drugged you, she thought, furious with herself. Though the fury was hard to hold onto in the haze that was wrapping itself around her. *You shouldn't have had the drink.*

And then she thought about the three drinks she'd already accepted from him. And she realised that he might have been drugging her for hours.

She briefly imagined the other woman, Jacqueline, drinking with him too. Getting into the car with him and taking the flask. And then being unable to defend herself as he dragged her out into the middle of the woods.

And still there was a part of her that wanted to let him kiss her. That hoped she was wrong.

No. You have to get out. You have to get out now.

The thought was almost enough to keep her focused. She needed to do something to make him pull over.

But she might not be able to make him stop. She needed the phone. It was her one chance to call for help. And if he knew she'd done that, then maybe she'd be safe.

She reached further, ignoring the kerosene and the wood – a piece of which pressed into her head as she turned – and stretching out with her fingers. She could feel how close he was to her now. How vulnerable she was. It was no longer exciting.

But somehow it was hard to hold on to her fear. Even to concentrate. She found herself staring into nothing, even while her body was twisted uncomfortably, her arm out towards the phone.

'You OK?' he asked, his voice rumbling close to her. It jolted her, kicking a little fear back into the haze.

'Just trying to reach it,' she said. And she tried to laugh. And then she found herself laughing for real, for some reason. It was so stupid, not being able to get her hands on the bloody phone. What a ridiculous way to end up dead.

The tips of her fingers slid on it, barely able to grip. She'd only shoved it further away.

'It's OK; we're nearly there,' he said.

She became aware that the car was jolting now. That it was tipping and rolling over something bumpy. The phone slid beyond the touch of her fingers.

She put a hand out to the wood to steady herself, but the nearest piece wasn't very well tied. It started to come out of the bundle.

She found her hand gripping it as she faced forwards again, and tried to remember to be afraid as she saw that they were driving down a high, open track over heathland.

'We'll get a great view up here,' he said.

She saw that he was smiling. It was a surprisingly warm smile.

You need to get away, she thought. *Get away from him, Lindsay.*

She sure as hell couldn't fight, with her limbs feeling loose and her thoughts foggy. And she wouldn't have stood much chance anyway. As fit as she was, he was clearly stronger, his muscles used to activity.

There was a stand of gorse ahead of them, suddenly, and he swung the car round to park next to it. They were on the brow of a hill, looking out over woodland below. And it was familiar to her. Lindsay had walked here.

'Lyndhurst Heath,' she said, out loud, unclipping her seat belt clumsily and letting it slide across her.

'I love it up here,' he said, turning to her.

He looked as though he might kiss her. And for a moment a surge of longing made her hesitate.

What if he meant everything he said? What if he really feels this?

But even through the haze, she saw a flicker of something

cross his face. Something anticipatory. Faltering. Something that wasn't adoration.

And suddenly Lindsay wanted nothing less than his kiss. She pointed past him, and said, 'Look!'

As he turned, she pulled the piece of wood free and jabbed it at him as hard as the confined space and her loose-feeling arms allowed. She felt it jar as it connected with the back of his head and heard him cry out.

She didn't wait for him to react further. She dropped the wood and opened the door. She slid out, and then she ran for the trees, down a path she knew well.

She heard the car door opening a way behind her. And then there was another shout. It was angry this time. She hadn't injured him; she'd only pissed him off.

She just had to make it to the trees. That was all. Get there, and hide.

She looked up at them, their shadowy shapes seeming close but also impossibly distant, and she could feel the fuzziness closing in further. Her legs were almost entirely without feeling as she ran, every bump in the ground sending her bouncing over it.

'Lindsay!'

He was behind her, and he was closer. So much closer.

Lindsay tried to focus on the blurring trees, fighting the exhaustion, and the part of her that told her to give up.

No, no, no, the stronger, more stubborn part of her repeated. And as she tripped, and stumbled to her knees, it was that part of her that let out a howl of fury at the unfairness of it all.

PART ONE

I

1 January

He'd watched them ever since that first fire back in October. Followed their little team from scene to scene as they tried to unpick it all.

He'd been with them, in an ironic sort of camaraderie, while they'd walked it over, and attempted to work out who had been burned to ashes in the forest. Though none of them had seen him. He was good at being invisible when he wanted to be.

He'd been with them, invisibly, for most of the three months since. Always watching them. Always unseen. He'd followed them to the victim's house, and on visits to bars and shops and cafés. He'd followed them as they'd gone to interview possible suspects, and smiled to himself as he'd seen them leave with expressions of frustration.

He hadn't just watched them, of course. He'd read about all of it, in print and online. He'd known the moment they'd identified the victim as forty-six-year-old Jacqueline Clarke. He'd read all about her lonely life in Brockenhurst, as viewed through the eyes of a journalist.

He'd cut round each photograph of striking, sandy-haired Jacqueline and kept it. And each photograph of the team too.

One of the local press had used the term 'the Bonfire Killer' in a follow-up piece, and even though it hadn't been picked up on elsewhere, he'd liked it and started using it privately.

Two weeks after Jacqueline Clarke had been found, he'd

watched them rush to a second pyre, this one still burning. He'd seen them douse it, even though it was abundantly clear that there was no body on it this time. And then he'd smiled to himself at their confusion. Their consternation.

He knew what they were thinking. He was too far away to hear most of their conversation, but he could read their expressions in the harsh lights that arrived with them.

They think it might happen again, he told himself. *They're expecting another Jacqueline Clarke now. Another Bonfire Killer victim.*

The little team had begun to travel further afield, as they tried to tie in other crimes, and he'd followed them. Many of them had been laughably dissimilar, but as some of them had picked over the burnt remnants of a house in West Gradley, where a woman of Jacqueline Clarke's age had died, he'd enjoyed their angst. Their uncertainty about whether to investigate it further.

Their agitation had been clearer still at the next two sites. Two more fires, each without a victim. And at each one their movements had been faster, like ants disturbed by a stick. He'd found it all amusing.

The thing he hadn't expected to feel, however, was an increase in his own sense of camaraderie towards them. Somehow, in watching them all work, he'd developed an odd sort of affection for them. For DCI Jonah Sheens and his wry thoughtfulness. For DS Domnall O'Malley and his warmth.

Maybe even for DS Ben Lightman, whose model-handsome good looks had produced an immediate revulsion in him. As though he was some Hollywood actor pretending to be a police officer. He'd hated him on sight.

But it had been hard to keep up the same level of distaste when he'd seen Ben Lightman pull on wellingtons and wade through mud, and then stand in drizzle for an hour and a half at an extinguished pyre. That hour and a half of standing in the rain was an experience the two of them had shared, despite Ben Lightman not knowing it.

And then, of course, there was Juliette. He thought of her as Juliette, not by her title. She was different. So easy to watch. To be drawn to. He found himself watching her even when the action was elsewhere. When more interesting things were going on.

Things shifted for him after the third pyre, too. He'd left before the team, heading back to the four-by-four he'd hired for the occasion using a fake driving licence. He'd parked it back up the track, to be out of sight, and as he walked back to it he'd passed Juliette's little Nissan Micra which she'd parked off to the side of the poor-quality road.

The Micra was clearly, profoundly and irretrievably stuck in the mud. Something Juliette was going to discover when she tried to drive it away.

He looked at his watch. It was almost midnight. She'd be making that discovery at close on one a.m., at a guess.

He went to the car and tried the door. It was, he realised with a shiver of excitement, unlocked.

And a strange, thrilling thought had run through him. He could actually help her. He could help Juliette. Do something kind for her. And if he did it right, she might suspect that it had been him, but never know for sure.

He'd glanced back towards the lights of the crime scene, way back down the track beyond a locked gate. They were half a mile away, and most of the forensics team would be there for hours.

Without any further hesitation, he'd gone to get the rental four-by-four with its steel-cable pulley, attached it to the Micra's tow bar, and pulled it clear of the mud. He'd done it with his lights off, and the revs low, and his gaze half on where the police might return from at any time. But by the time he'd dragged the car back onto the stony road, nobody had come.

With a smile to himself, he'd unhitched the cable and driven away, feeling a bond connecting the two of them that he'd not expected. A strangely satisfying one.

Now, today, as he dressed carefully, he thought of the help he'd given her. It warmed him as he pulled his shirt on in the chilly bedroom.

He wondered, idly, what she'd think of his outfit. Though what he really wanted to know was what she would think of the little surprise he had in store for her today.

2

The best thing about not going out on New Year's Eve, Aisling had decided, was how much nicer it made the bank holiday. Gone were the days where she would wake up at ten, her head full of pain and a vague sense of shame and regret hovering. Admittedly, she still had a slight headache from the bottle of Chablis she'd drunk most of on the sofa. But she was confident that would be gone after a few hours and a couple of ibuprofen.

It was so much better to really enjoy a morning spent with her boys, even if Ethan was clearly struggling with a monster hangover. Her older son had managed to make it out of his war zone of a bedroom at ten, his face pale, and his mop of blond curls standing up like it had been backcombed.

He'd given monosyllabic answers to Aisling's cheerful greetings. This was out of character enough for her to say, 'Aww, good night, was it?'

Finn, by contrast, had been up since before Aisling, and was now almost offensively full of energy. He bounced around the kitchen, fetching ingredients for their customary eggs benedict and keeping up a stream of chatter about all the big events from the night before. Aisling hadn't really been following, but the main gossip seemed to be his friend's girlfriend deciding to switch her attentions to the friend's older brother.

'I mean, in all honesty, he might be a really decent guy,' Finn told her, at the point when she had zoned back in, 'but I just can't see how that's ever worth it for either of them. I mean, Pete's completely bruk, and can't even look at his brother, and Lauren's now basically lost her whole fam.' He heaved a big sigh. 'I know people think it's love, and you can't help it when it's love, but you have a choice, right? I mean, there were points where both of them could have gone, "You know what? I'm not going to flirt with, like, my brother's girlfriend," or whatever. I just – I can't see Marian doing that. Or Ethan being happy to go along with it either.'

'Definitely would,' Ethan called from the table.

Finn just grinned at him. 'You'd have to start doing some exercise to be in with a chance. Marian's not massively into the whole layabout rock-star thing.'

'That's just what she tells you,' Ethan retorted.

Aisling turned to shake her head at him, and realised that he was slumped almost entirely onto the tabletop. He looked rough, and like he was in the throes of proper hangover depression too. His attempts at their usual banter were not matched by his expression at all.

God, how much did he drink? Aisling wondered. *Was he sick?*

At nineteen Ethan was technically old enough to look after himself, but he had a thoughtless streak that made him in many ways more of a worry than his seventeen-year-old brother. This was attested to by the number of times he'd set fire to things in his room, or thrown away objects he'd then needed, or ended up stranded after not considering how he would get home from an impulsive trip. It didn't help that he was by nature a people-pleaser, and would sometimes agree to do ridiculous things just to avoid killing the vibe.

Finn was a very different person. Despite being two years younger, he was a great deal more definite about what he wanted, and always had his eye on the long game. He was hard-working, responsible, and dead set on a career in professional tennis. Which meant he was never going to get himself so drunk that he was sick, or call her at three a.m. from a car park in Lymington.

'What time did you crawl in?' she asked Ethan, wanting to go and ruffle his hair but unable to leave the eggs at the critical stage of poaching.

Ethan gave a shrug. 'Don't know. Two? Something like that?'

'Did you leave your car at Matthew's?'

'Er, yeah.' Aisling stayed looking at him long enough to see that he glanced towards his brother. 'I'll pick it up after rehearsal.'

'I'd suggest *much* later,' Aisling said. 'Like, maybe to-morrow.'

'I'll be OK once I've eaten something,' Ethan said a little tetchily.

Aisling decided to ignore this rare bad humour. She finished cooking, and served up two plates of eggs. She let Finn add bacon and dribble his home-made Hollandaise sauce over the top.

'You two start,' she said. 'Mine'll only be a minute.'

She watched Finn pick the plates up to carry them to the table, and saw that he'd got what looked to be a fresh bandage on his left leg.

'Did you cut yourself last night?' she asked, waving the egg spoon at him.

'Oh, no,' Finn said, with a slightly brittle laugh. 'Just from running the other day. I trod on a stick, which jumped up and bit me.'

'Poor stick,' she said with a grin.

'Marian says "Happy New Year", by the way,' Finn said, dumping the plates and picking up his phone.

'Tell her the same back,' Aisling told him. 'When's she coming to stay again?'

'Probably not until February realistically,' Finn said with a short sigh. 'Too many weekend commitments for both of us.'

Aisling felt a squeeze of sadness for him. She had never pushed him to excel at tennis. The drive came purely from within, but it didn't always make his life easy. And falling for another very driven tennis player who lived halfway across the country didn't help much, either.

She served herself and joined the two of them at the table. Finn had already managed to eat half his four-egg plate. Ethan, by contrast, was looking at his barely touched food with a slightly queasy expression.

She was about to ask him if he needed painkillers when he pushed the plate away and said, 'Mummo, have you seen that Amazon package that came for me?'

'No.' She started eating. 'Hasn't crossed my radar. What's in it?'

'Plectrums.'

Aisling raised an eyebrow at him. 'I gave you some for Christmas. Can't you use them?'

'I can't find them either,' Ethan said, with a slightly sheepish look. 'I'm going to need some for rehearsal later. I owe Dan a couple too.'

'Of course you do,' Aisling said. 'How big is this package?'

'It's like . . . A5?' He gestured with his hands.

'And it definitely arrived?' she asked.

'Yeah, it was in the hall.'

'Where presumably you decided it would now live until you needed it.' She shook her head with a half-smile. 'Did you ask your brother? Finn, have you seen this Amazon package of your useless sibling's?'

Finn was doing a good job of ignoring them both as he

ate, but he paused long enough to say, 'Oh. Yes. I put it in your room.'

'Ah, Jesus,' Ethan said, with only a trace of humour. 'I'll never find it now.'

'True, that,' Finn shot back. 'You could lose actual small countries in there.'

Barks, their miniature schnauzer, rose from his basket at that point and climbed delicately onto Ethan's lap. Ethan, who usually made a huge fuss over the dog, didn't seem to notice.

Aisling looked at her older son more carefully, wondering whether he was just hungover, or whether he was actually unhappy. He'd been to his so-called friend Matt's house for a party, but Aisling knew full well that that friendship was extremely unreliable. Matt could be a full-on arsehole at times, though he was mostly just irritating. Ethan sometimes had to rely on him to step in and play when they were a band member short, but she still didn't see why he spent time with the guy beyond that.

Though, in fact, most of Ethan's friends were a little grating. Aisling couldn't help preferring Finn's sweet if hopelessly posh friends to Ethan's self-absorbed musical ones.

'Ooh,' Finn said suddenly, leaning forwards onto the table with his phone in his hand. 'There are loads of police on the heath. Look.'

He held his phone out towards Aisling, who peered at a photograph that had been shared on Twitter. It showed an elevated shot of the far end of Lyndhurst Heath, towards the woods. Right by the treeline was a cluster of police cars and vans, and there were two figures in white who looked like forensics officers.

'Is that from today?'

Finn nodded. 'Yeah. I might run over that way. Go and see what's going on.'

'Don't be a ghoul,' Aisling said. But then she found herself pulling out her phone and googling for articles about events on Lyndhurst Heath. Nothing came up.

It was unsettling to think about something happening so close by. Forensic teams implied something serious.

She'd always thought of the New Forest as safe, at least from serious crime. But that had changed three months ago, when a lonely forty-something woman had been murdered not far away. An ordinary, average person named Jacqueline who could so easily have been Aisling herself. She felt a little skip to her heartbeat at the thought that this might be another woman dead. Another murder. Was there really nothing online about it yet?

She tried searching a few different terms, but only came up with articles about the original murder. Which might mean it was unimportant, or simply that nothing had made it into the press yet.

Ethan rose to make himself coffee, and Aisling turned her phone over. She shouldn't be thinking about murders. She should be focusing on her sons. On today.

She found herself watching the two of them, for a moment, with a strange sense of nostalgia. Almost as if this scene was already done and she was looking back on it with longing.

She often felt a hint of sadness at the dawn of a new year. It had to do with saying goodbye to all the festivities and time with her boys. But the New Year was always spiced up, too, with a back-to-school feeling. A forward-looking determination to shake off the booze and the indulgence and get to work.

But right now that energised feeling was absent. She felt, instead, a sense of loss. Perhaps, she thought, it was because they might only have one more Christmas together in this house. If they were lucky.

She almost wished she could trust her sons with the truth of their financial situation. It would have been such a relief to share the burden of it, but that wasn't something she was willing to do to either of them. Ethan had none of the skills necessary to help, and Finn had the right to a proper childhood and adolescence, free of the worries of adulthood.

Which meant it was Aisling alone who knew the reality facing them. Her sons assumed that with one mega-hit game under her belt and a steady stream of work coming in, Aisling was very comfortable. She'd never admitted to them how little she'd actually made from *Survive the Light*, or how many things she'd gone without to keep them at their public school. They didn't know how much juggling she'd had to do to keep up Ethan's touring with his band, or Finn's tennis lessons and tournaments.

She'd sometimes asked herself if she was mad trying to send them to a public school when she had nowhere near that kind of money. The whole idea of Hanyard House had come from Stephen, her charming but ultimately selfish ex-husband, who had chosen to walk out on them when the boys were two and four rather than face up to his responsibilities as a father. She suspected now that he had sent them there in the hope that they might start boarding, freeing him from most of his parental obligations.

Pride had made Aisling settle for far less in the divorce than she should have done. It was clear to her now that she should have demanded support for their school fees right up until they turned eighteen. But, of course, she hadn't been sure she *wanted* them to stay at that school. So she'd decided, for continuity, that she'd just stick with it while they were in junior school. Make her sons' disrupted lives as easy as possible by letting them stay at the place they were used to for the time being.

But they'd each, in turn, been put forward for scholarships to the senior school and won them. Ethan had been awarded a huge music scholarship, and a small academic one, and Finn had followed that up with almost half his fees paid by a sports scholarship with more offered for his academic ability.

It had made Aisling feel duty-bound to send them there. She felt as though they'd earned it, and she'd vowed to somehow manage the five thousand a year she still had to find for each of them.

She'd done it too, but only by using up her full inheritance from her mum, and then by gradually sinking further and further into overdrafts and loan debts. There had been heart-stopping moments, like when she'd been refused an increase on a loan to bridge a gap and had looked around frantically for a solution with a feeling of impending doom.

She'd felt incredibly alone then. With no parents to turn to, and no partner, and with a friendship group that consisted entirely of parents who had no concept of financial issues, she'd known that it was all on her.

Her biggest fear had been of losing the house. She'd worked so hard on this little place to make it perfect. To make it *theirs*. It had been a tired, depressing building when they'd moved in, and she'd sunk hundreds of hours into stripping off old wallpaper, painting, and creating perfect lighting.

The place was beautiful now, she thought. Comfortable and airy. And it made the most of the view out onto the fields behind too. She could sit in her kitchen and gaze out at them whenever she wanted, and it had made a lot of things better over the years.

Even now, with her sons all but grown-up, the thought of having to move out broke her heart. Though she knew it would solve a lot of their financial problems. She could sell the house at a significant profit and start again, buying another fixer-upper somewhere promising, and slowly making it hers. She'd be able to reduce their mortgage and her debts all at once. But it would still tear her up to do it.

But I might not have to, she thought, as breakfast turned into a good-natured argument over the washing-up, *if I can sell* SINN.

SINN was her new game. Her secret, cherished project. She'd worked at it for the past year. Around all the board-meetings for the start-ups she'd sat on. Around the management of her house and her sons.

She knew it was brilliant. That it was as good or better than *Survive the Light*. It was just about convincing Sony, and getting them to pay her what it was worth this time.

As Finn bullied Ethan into helping wash up, she pulled her phone out of her dressing-gown pocket and looked through her emails again, uncertain why she was checking. Sony weren't going to reply to her message now. It was New Year's Day. She just had to wait until the right people were back from leave, and then they could set a date to meet. She knew that she'd piqued their interest already.

She found herself glancing through the few emails that had landed between Christmas and New Year. She hadn't really looked at any of them. Most of them were threads about the new start-up she'd joined the board for, a very enthusiastic little developer based in Holborn called VePlec.

She found herself sighing over the ambitious tone of their emails. Aisling usually loved that aspect of start-ups. The way their enthusiasm hadn't yet had a chance to meet hard-hitting reality. She loved the way their ideals meant more than money.

But the founder of this company was full-on arrogant. He seemed to think he was Steve Jobs crossed with Elon Musk, when he was actually just a fairly ordinary nerd who'd teamed up with the right people. He also had a habit of annoying potential investors with blithe statements about how much better this game was going to be than everything that had gone before.

She shook her head over the most recent thread. The CEO suspected someone was sharing concepts and code with a rival developer. An idea Aisling thought about as likely as Sony sitting in on their first board meeting.

> There are clear signs from recent Adelpho announcements that they are imitating details of our new game platform in ways that go beyond coincidence.

Except, Aisling thought, that when he went on to list them, they were so vague as to sound indeed like coincidence. And, in fact, like another firm developing another slightly retro platform game.

'Oh my god,' she said out loud, with a grin, as she read on. 'The founder of this start-up is nuts. He thinks someone's stealing the IP of a game nobody's ever heard of. He's even hiring a private investigator to *go undercover* in the firm.'

'Oh, that's great,' Ethan said, looking animated for the first time this morning. 'They could hire me. I could totally get away with being a developer for a week. A lot better than some PI who knows nothing about games. And I can always tell when someone's sneaking around.'

'I'd hire you,' Aisling said, and then, reading on, added, 'Ahh, shame. They already hired someone. Your big break, ruined.'

She scrolled down through the email, intending to read out the name of the PI so they could all have a laugh about it. But instead she found herself looking at one sentence, over and over, her heart squeezing in her chest.

Jack O'Keane, from O'Keane and Ross, will be working undercover within the firm.

She found herself remembering, in a sharp rush, a fifteen-year-old boy with dimples and a tolerant smile. Him taking her hand. Him laughing at her as she spun off the track in *Mario Kart*. Thoughts of his breath mixing with hers on a cold night.

They were memories she had never really allowed in. Not for thirty years. And they left her heart speeding like she'd run for miles.

3

The wind over Lyndhurst Heath was cold. Unforgiving. It ripped at exposed skin, and Jonah felt an urge to cover the woman they'd found lying here. But the blueness of her skin was more than simple cold. It would never warm back up to a healthy colour.

McCullough was here, of course, though as Hampshire Constabulary's in-house forensic scientist, she wasn't meant to be. They had a chief forensic officer who was nominally in charge of the process of gathering evidence. But Linda McCullough was obsessed, hyper-conscientious, and incapable of trusting anyone not to spoil the samples that would go to her for analysis. She had also taken scene of crime training specifically in order to feel qualified to interfere.

She did at least restrict herself to the serious crime scenes. Which meant that Jonah was entirely used to meeting her at places like this. At places of murder. Of violence. Of suffering that had grown cold with time.

They had their roles mapped out precisely. Well, McCullough had them mapped out. Jonah's role as DCI and senior investigating officer was to take a cursory glance and then keep well out of the way. She and the forensic science team would secure the scene and get to work. Jonah would watch, perhaps drinking coffee, while they photographed, took samples and discussed among themselves their findings. With a murder like this, a pathologist would also be brought in. Once they were ready, Linda McCullough would run Jonah through it all, letting the chief forensic officer listen in if he or she were lucky.

Jonah stepped further away from the scene, trying to keep his hastily pulled-on trainers out of the patches of standing water that were scattered around the heath. He hadn't been prepared for this today. He'd woken at nine, thinking about a bike ride and then cooking a roast, possibly while also trying to entertain Milly. At almost six months old, she was nothing if not demanding.

He'd been looking forward to eating and then collapsing in front of a child-appropriate film with Milly and his partner, Michelle. Some genuinely nice time together, in contrast with what had felt like fleeting, practical interactions for the last three months.

But there were some calls you couldn't ignore, and this had been one of them. It had set up a dull, beating thrum in him the moment he had answered it.

Forty-six-year-old woman . . . Body left on a pyre . . .

That's what they'd said, but what he had heard, insistently, was the phrase: *Serial killer. Serial killer. Serial killer.*

They had known they might find themselves here. Ever since October, when Jacqueline Clarke's barely recognisable remains had been found on a pyre near to Longbeech Campsite. And increasingly, as they'd chased empty pyre after empty pyre across the New Forest.

They'd been desperate to stop it happening, and they had failed.

He'd seen the same knowledge in Domnall O'Malley's eyes as his sergeant had arrived on scene. The heavy tiredness. The feeling that this was their failure.

'Found by a dog walker,' Jonah told him. 'He's over by the squad car, being given tea. He looks freezing and fed up. Want to put him out of his misery?'

O'Malley had nodded, pulling out his iPad in order to take notes. Jonah could have spared the dog walker a few minutes in the cold and talked to him before O'Malley arrived, but he'd felt instinctively that this was a place for his friendly detective sergeant. For O'Malley's warm, mates-together banter and his Kilkenny brogue. Not for a senior officer who would be the focus of his irritation and complaints.

O'Malley had headed over to the witness and Jonah had been left with a rapidly cooling takeaway cup of coffee rustled up by a constable. That, and his thoughts, many of which were bleak.

The sound of a car engine reached him a while later, and he saw Juliette Hanson's Nissan Micra arriving at the top of the hill, making heavy weather of the bumpy track. His detective constable parked close to Jonah's own Mondeo, and climbed out. She was still several hundred metres away, but it was as far as any car could go without some serious tyres and four-wheel drive.

Jonah went to meet her at the bottom of the slope. He was relieved to see that she had changed into hiking boots, though they looked a little odd with her knee-length black-and-white dress and thin wool jacket. It made him feel all the worse about dragging her away from the funeral.

She nodded to him. 'Chief.'

'Sorry about this.' He tried to read her expression. 'How did it go? Was Ben . . . ?'

'He did perfectly, of course,' Hanson said, with a wry smile. 'Amazing speech, everything organised flawlessly. The wake was lovely too. Country pub. You know.'

Jonah gave a small smile. He could well imagine. Ben, the fourth member of their team, was one of those people who seemed to achieve perfection without trying. From his movie-star good looks and athleticism, to his absolute self-control and organisation, he was a model officer. But he was also, Jonah had long suspected, someone who struggled to be open about the feelings that bubbled away underneath, and the death of his father couldn't have been easy on him.

He wanted to find out more, but it wasn't the time. Instead he asked, 'Have you got more layers with you?'

'Umm ... I might have something in the car,' Hanson offered. 'I can have a dig around if we're here long.'

'I would. I'm freezing even in my big coat. I'll talk you through and then you should layer up as much as you can.' He glanced up towards the hill, and realised that there was someone standing up there, close to where Hanson had parked. A twitcher, by the looks of it, in a woolly cap and wax jacket with a pair of binoculars. He might not have been exactly invading the crime scene, but with binoculars he'd be able to see a lot of the activity from up there.

'Hey,' he called to the closest pair of uniformed constables. 'Can you move him on?'

The two officers nodded, and started up the hill, but the twitcher turned and ambled away of his own accord. Hopefully, Jonah thought, before he'd had time for a ghoulish look or to take a photo. The thought of a high-quality image appearing before they'd had the chance to contact the victim's family made him feel decidedly uneasy. But there was only so much they could do in a very open public space.

He turned back towards the cluster of white suits, and Hanson followed. 'OK,' he said. 'So she was found at eleven.'

'Another pyre?' Hanson made an effort to tuck her blonde hair out of her eyes. It was being whipped around by the wind, and she was wearing it loose today. Part of her funeral look instead of her practical policing one. 'We think it's the same perp?'

'Yes,' Jonah agreed. 'And yes. But it didn't burn, this time.' He felt, all over again, the same rush of incremental yet tainted hope he'd felt when he'd first arrived at the pyre. 'For reasons that aren't clear, it looks like he or she doused the fire just after it began to catch. There's a fire extinguisher been used. The body is untouched.'

He glanced at her. 'And there's blood. It doesn't look like it's the victim's.'

'So there's a chance of DNA?' Hanson asked.

'Maybe,' Jonah said. 'Though I haven't been close enough to the scene to know.' He gave her a wry grin. 'McCullough's been on the warpath.'

He watched Hanson's reaction, seeing that same, complex reaction he'd had. The deep-rooted anxiety over this being, almost without doubt, a serial killer at work would have hit her too. Hanson would know, as he did, that this second death made a third enormously more likely. Although there was no absolute pattern among serial killers, the step up from one killing to two was often like the breaking of a dam. The killer found confidence. They felt powerful. It made everything they did far more important, and every mistake potentially a fatal one. And that made all of them feel huge pressure.

But fighting with that pressure would be the hope that this second killing might give them the evidence they needed to solve the first. If they could just do it before anyone else became a victim.

Jonah heard Linda's voice from close by before Hanson could answer. McCullough was approaching, her mask raised now as she moved away from the crime scene.

'There's definitely blood,' she told him. 'And it isn't the victim's.'

Hanson turned to look at her with her mouth slightly open. 'We might have the killer's DNA?'

'Yes,' Jonah agreed. 'We might.'

4

Jack O'Keane.

The name kept repeating in her head, as Aisling went to shower and get dressed, and then to steal laundry from Ethan. She'd heard the name's rhythm as she'd made a mug of tea and settled herself in the kitchen with her phone to do some New Year's scrolling.

She'd been half listening to Ethan and Finn as they made food. Ethan was creating some bizarre sandwich to take to rehearsal while Finn was making vegetable-rich pasta to eat after his run. She found herself wanting, badly, to break into their conversation and tell them about Jack. But this was one thing she couldn't mention to either of them.

They'd always been so open about everything. So honest with each other. At least, they'd *become* honest, after Stephen had walked out to pursue his affair.

With him gone, she'd felt suddenly that it was the three of them against the world. That they had to be a team now. She'd tried so hard to have a relationship with them that was imbued with honesty. She'd been truthful about why Stephen had gone, and clear that it was absolutely his own fault and not theirs. And if she'd stopped short of telling them that their father had gone for a twenty-two-year-old intern in the biggest cliché in the book, she'd told them everything else.

She'd learned to admit, when they'd seen her crying over a memory of their previous life, that she *was* sad. But that being sad was OK sometimes. She'd told them, truthfully, about her need for space from them sometimes. And when they'd begun asking questions about sex, she'd been honest about that too.

She supposed it was only natural that they'd decided to become an active part of her dating life. Not that she'd planned it that way exactly. Ethan had seen a Tinder notification on her phone a couple of years before, and had demanded to see her profile. It had made her cringe. But when you'd engendered an idea of total openness, you had to practise it.

'Why haven't you mentioned gaming?' he had asked indignantly, having grabbed her phone off her. 'I can't believe you've said you like long walks, but haven't mentioned how much you like playing *Halo*. Or that you actually design games for a living, like.'

'Look, I'd quite like to meet a grown-up,' she'd said. 'And I feel like most of those are going to be put off if I say I like shooting the shit out of stuff on screen.'

Ethan had shaken his head. 'You want to attract people who are actually *fun to hang around with*. If you put that long-walks-and-nice-wine stuff up, you're going to get a bunch of twitchers and socially inept bankers.'

That had made her laugh, of course. And she hadn't protested very seriously when the two of them had composed a new profile.

Her sons' version had, in fairness, sounded a lot more like Aisling than her own efforts. It was warm, silly, and game-orientated. It was also firmly against hook-ups.

'What if I *do* want hook-ups?' she'd asked them indignantly.

'Oh my god, Mum,' Finn had said, appalled. 'You are not allowed to say that to us.'

'You're the ones interfering in my love life!'

'It's for your own good,' Finn had told her. 'And ours too. We don't want sleazeballs walking in here.'

'Or some boring bastard coming round, talking about to-
mato growing and pensions,' Ethan had added. 'Actually,
we'd better help you pick who to swipe on.' To her noisy
protests, he had started viewing potential matches. 'I'll let
you choose which way to swipe,' he'd allowed magnani-
mously. 'But you clearly need our feedback on them first.'

Unlikely though it sounded, scrolling through Tinder profiles with her teenage sons had turned out to be hilarious.
Mostly because a lot of men had no idea how to choose
photographs.

'There's another one with a finger up his nose!' Finn had
yelled through the hysterics at one point. 'What is *wrong* with
them? Do they think women actually go for that?'

'Maybe we're the ones who are wrong,' Ethan commented.
'Maybe nose picking is a massive turn-on to some women.'

'Oh my god,' Aisling had said of the next one. 'Is that a
photograph from his *own wedding*?'

That particular photograph had made her laugh so hard
she couldn't breathe.

'Who does that?' Ethan asked, once he'd stopped laughing
enough to talk.

'Well, I mean, he had dressed up for the occasion,' Finn
said. 'Shame to waste a good suit.'

From then on, the worst examples of Tinder pics had become a regular source of entertainment for the three of them.
Aisling had started taking screenshots to send her sons, and
even passed on some of the cringeworthy messages she'd
received. She would occasionally tell the boys about the nice
guys she met too, but that was distinctly less fun.

She'd kept the edited profile they'd written, as well, and
had ended up getting their help choosing images. The result
had been a lot more matches than she'd had before, even if
she hadn't clicked with anyone yet. She may not have picked

up a boyfriend, but she had met three new online gaming buddies, and Ethan and Finn sometimes squadded up to play with them too.

Openness and honesty, she thought, as she watched Ethan dump his laundry into the machine. *Honesty and openness in everything. Except one thing . . .*

Because there was one area of her life Aisling had excused herself from talking about. The piece of her past that she had glossed over.

She'd never actually *lied* about it. About Maimeo and Daideo Cooley and why they'd left Ireland. About how little she wanted to think about any of it. She'd never said anything that wasn't true. But she'd never volunteered anything about it either. And she knew, in her heart of hearts, that she was guilty of lying by omission.

If she told them about Jack O'Keane now, and why his name meant so much to her, she'd have to tell them about everything. About all of it. And she couldn't. Not without admitting to her two sons that she had a past that she'd never revealed to them. One that made her feel nauseous to recall.

At two a car swept aggressively onto the drive, breaking into the fog of Aisling's thoughts. She was already in the hall, and went to open the front door. She was unsurprised to see Ethan's friend and occasional band member Matthew Downing emerging from his BMW. He seemed to do everything assertively, ploughing a path for himself in the world as definitively as he'd ploughed two tracks into the gravel. You'd think, to meet him, that he was going places.

Except that he never quite did. Determination and a lot of his father's support had never quite made up for lack of any perceivable musical talent. At twenty-eight he had ten years of solid failure behind him, despite multiple chances coming his way. He'd had meetings with big record labels. Talent scouts in his audiences. He'd entered countless battles of the band . . . and lost them all.

In other people she might have felt it was simply about luck, but with Matthew – whose wealthy father had tried to manufacture him all the luck in the world – she was positive that it was about not having what it took. Though, of course, that was never the problem according to Matthew. The issue was either the provincial nature of Southampton audiences, or the backward attitude of record labels and their fear of anything new.

Ethan had initially looked up to him, but now just relied on him to step in if he was lacking a bass guitarist or drummer thanks to illness or injury. It was better, Ethan said, than cancelling. But she'd seen her son's disappointment after more than one ragged performance caused by Matthew's failure to keep properly in time.

Aisling tried to paste on a smile as Matthew emerged from his car. His nearly handsome face was amused. He seemed convinced that she found him desperately attractive, which made her feel uncomfortable. She *had* found him strangely appealing when he'd first come to one of Ethan's parties. Something about the heavy eyeliner, skinny jeans and absolute self-belief of the guy had drawn her in. Right up until she'd seen one of his gigs.

'Hi, Matthew,' she said. 'Are you giving my reprobate son a lift?'

'Yeah, it's no bother, Mrs C,' he said, lifting his arms in a stretch as though he'd just driven fifty miles instead of one. 'I'm coming to rehearse anyway in case Nick's wrist isn't mended. I didn't really drink last night, so I'm good for it.' He looked past her into the hall. 'Guessing Ethan's a little . . . fragile.'

'A little,' she said noncommittally. Matthew would take any

opportunity to mock Ethan in front of her, all in the name of apparent humour. Her best response was no response.

She looked towards the stairs, hoping to see Ethan emerging before she had to invite Matthew in, but there was no sign. With a feeling of resignation, she asked, 'Do you want to come in while he gets his stuff?'

'Sure.'

Matthew followed her to the kitchen, somehow managing to occupy most of the large space. It was a talent that her ex-husband had also possessed. An automatic assumption of ownership over everything he surveyed.

'Did you have a good time?' she asked Matthew. 'At the party?'

'Yeah, it was a great night,' Matthew said, leaning back against the countertop. He gave a small smile, one of those smiles of his that implied he knew a lot more than he was saying. 'I mean, some great social time, but some great inspiration too. I managed to record quite a lot of footage for my new video, actually.'

There was a rushed, stumbling thumping, and Ethan erupted into the kitchen, breathless. His hair was still wet from the shower and he was attempting to pull a jacket on.

'Sorry,' he said. 'Didn't hear you come in.'

Matthew cut his eyes from Ethan to Aisling, and gave a very small smile. 'No problem,' he said. 'Just chatting to your lovely mum.'

'Shall we get going?' Ethan said across him, almost before he'd finished speaking, and Aisling found herself looking at her son more carefully. At the tightness in his body. The brightness of his eyes. He seemed ill at ease.

She watched Matthew amble out slowly behind her son, pausing at the door to give her a lazy, self-satisfied wave. And then the door closed behind them and she was left staring at it, with a sudden weight of sadness. Everything about that interaction told her that there was something Ethan didn't want her to know. And that Matthew, whose motives she trusted about as far as she could shove him, knew all about it.

Had Ethan embarrassed himself? Had he kissed someone he shouldn't have? Vomited? Taken something very illegal? Trashed something?

The restlessness she'd felt since reading Jack O'Keane's name morphed into real anxiety. She wished he'd just tell her. She might be able to help.

Openness and honesty . . .

She felt her mouth curling wryly. Had she been kidding herself about all of that? And was it even fair of her to expect her sons to tell her everything? When she'd never been really, truly honest with them?

She found herself moving into the living room, and then away from it. Away, even, from her study and the distraction of work. She climbed the stairs, wondering whether she could somehow share some tiny part of all this with Finn.

But even as she thought this, she heard her younger son's phone ring in his room. He answered with a slightly uncertain, 'Hello?' And then, after a pause, he said, more quietly, 'Oh, hang on a sec,' and a moment later, he appeared briefly in silhouette as he very quietly but firmly closed the door. And just after that, she was certain she heard him say, 'No, I didn't tell her anything . . .' before he moved further into the room and his voice became an indistinct murmur.

She felt her heart squeeze. There was secrecy here too. Finn had clearly closed the door so she wouldn't hear what he said. But he'd never been too embarrassed to talk to anyone in front of her. Not to his girlfriend, or to any of his friends for that matter. He'd always been happy to chat away as he moved around the house with the phone to his ear, occasionally passing on a 'hello' from whoever it was. But the sounds coming from the other side of the door now were murmurs. The unmistakable sounds of someone who was trying not to be overheard. Whoever Finn was talking to, he didn't want her overhearing.

Was it Ethan? Had Ethan called to make sure Finn didn't tell her whatever it was that he'd done?

Or, worse, were there two secrets in their house? Two secrets being hidden from her, that might be nothing, or might be something genuinely awful?

Three secrets, her own mind shot back at her. *Two of theirs, and one big, big secret of mine.*

5

Hanson was chilled through by the time she made it back to the station. It had been seriously cold out on the heath, and her sheer tights had been as good as no protection at all from the wind.

It would have been a lot worse if she'd had to survive with the clothes she'd brought. By the time she'd even walked around the scene, she was shivering with cold, and she'd known she had nothing more than a running top in the car. Nothing like enough to keep the chill out.

But as she'd approached her little Nissan Micra, she'd seen a coat sitting on the bonnet. A warm, dusty-red Rab coat with fleece lining. It looked almost brand new.

She'd glanced around at the closest constables, and guessed that one of them must have left it for her on the chief's instructions. She hoped, as she shrugged it on, that it hadn't been left by accident.

The coat enveloped her and immediately stopped the shivering. Zipping it up, she felt as though she might last the distance in spite of the cold wind on her legs. Though when she'd mentioned it to the chief, he hadn't seemed to know anything about it. And nor had O'Malley or any of the constables. Whoever had left the jacket for her, it hadn't been any of them.

And then she'd thought back to the night at the second pyre, when an unknown person had moved her car. She'd seen the tracks where it had been dragged back onto the road, and realised that it would have been stuck in the mud if they hadn't. Someone had chosen to help her.

And then she'd remembered the twitcher, or a man who had looked like one, loitering close to her car. She'd suddenly felt a little uncomfortable, as though the jacket might be contaminated somehow. But it was clean and comfortable and surely harmless.

Unless, she'd thought, *it's Damian.*

The man she'd seen at a distance could have been him. She'd been vaguely aware he'd looked tall and reasonably strong. Damian was both those things.

She hadn't heard from her ex-boyfriend in more than a month. His campaign of harassment had seemed to fizzle out as the date for the court case had moved and moved.

Damian was awaiting trial for arson with intent. He'd been caught on camera throwing a Molotov cocktail through her kitchen window in what had been the crowning glory to his campaign of vandalism and harassment. He'd been stupid enough to believe that he could do it without being caught, reckoning without her hidden security cameras.

Faced with the sudden reality of up to life imprisonment if intent to kill was proved, it had been hardly surprising that her narcissistic ex-boyfriend had chosen to defy the restraining order placed on him and do his best to make Hanson's life a misery. Section 4 stalking was a drastically lesser crime in comparison, and Damian clearly saw the upcoming threat of the trial as her fault.

But over time, the anonymous emails, phone calls and damage to her car had tailed off. She'd guessed he'd grown bored, but had they now been replaced by some weird form of helpfulness? By a pretence at being kind to her? What was the endgame if so? Was he trying to unsettle her, or was this about trying to make her like him and not testify against him too harshly?

She hated to admit that it *was* unsettling her, almost as much as the harassment had, but she'd been glad when the time came to leave the heath, and she'd been able to take the jacket off. Having checked again that it didn't belong to anyone from the force, and wondering whether she ought to discuss this with the chief, she'd hung it carefully on a protruding branch from a gorse bush. She left it there as she drove away. If it *was* Damian's, he'd have to retrieve it for himself, she decided.

Back in CID, she took a few minutes to shrug on the spare trousers and shirt she kept under her desk. She packed away thoughts of the coat, and her car being towed out of the mud, for now. They were due a briefing, and it wouldn't be long before all hell broke loose with the press. Her own concerns could wait until later.

The victim on Lyndhurst Heath was officially unnamed, but scene of crime had called through with a name taken from a driving licence found in her clothing. And although it wasn't certain, it was highly likely that she had been a Totton resident named Lindsay Kernow. O'Malley was at work now, confirming the ID.

The presence of that driving licence was another indication that the killer had been rushed. Interrupted somehow in his burning of the evidence.

Hanson was bracing herself now to find out about Lindsay's life. About the family she'd left behind, and the things she would never get to do.

Three months ago, Hanson had been waiting to find out about another woman's life. They'd been called to the discovery of a body not far from Longbeech Campsite on the fourth of October. It had taken four further days to confirm that the victim was Jacqueline Clarke, a woman of forty-six who had devoted her life to the care of animals.

Hanson was now planning what she would say to Jacqueline's daughters about this second victim. Although Pippa and Rosie weren't Lindsay Kernow's relatives, informing them before any media coverage happened was important. They needed to know, before the world did, that their mother had been the first victim of a serial killer.

Hanson hoped that the public were still unaware of the second pyre. The crime scene on Lyndhurst Heath must have attracted some attention, and it might not take long for someone to start drawing their own conclusions.

With that in mind, she found herself searching Google, Twitter and Facebook for mention of the police presence on the heath. She was relieved to discover that there was nothing specific so far. Nothing but a Twitter post from someone with a grainy, very distant photo of the police vans, taken from further up the hill. That was good news at least. It was almost three p.m., and scene of crime had the bulk of their work done now.

Not that getting the press involved was in itself a bad thing. There would be people out there who knew the killer. Who would have seen them in the preceding days, and perhaps on the day itself. Who had sold them the kerosene and perhaps the wood.

The best way of reaching those people was through an appeal for information. Hanson was in full agreement with the chief that, handled correctly, the media could be their best ally. Though, of course, when things went the other way, press intrusion could be a disaster.

She spent a while setting up alerts on her phone for search terms like 'bonfire murder', 'Bonfire Killer' and 'New Year's Eve murder' and then went to the kitchen, where she found O'Malley already in possession of three mugs of tea.

'Here you go.' The older sergeant handed her a mug.

'Legend,' she said. The tea was a good, strong shade of

orange, and she was pleased to note that he'd used her *Kind of a Big Deal* mug. Though from the look of the stain down the side, he hadn't actually washed it before reusing. O'Malley was a big fan of the vague rinse and a good-natured remark about the dangers of a sterilised life. But she was willing to accept what were technically last year's tea stains in order to have strong tea ready to drink.

'Have you confirmed the name?' she asked him, after the first mouthful.

'Yeah, looks like it,' O'Malley said. 'There's no answer at Lindsay Kernow's house. Her car's at home too, along with her wallet. Scene of crime only found cash on her body.'

'I'll deal with next of kin,' Hanson said impulsively. 'After the briefing. You found a son?'

'Ah, it's a difficult one,' O'Malley said gently. 'Only one son, and he's in Dublin. I can check with Passport Control whether he happens to be over here, but it looks likely we'll be informing him at a distance.'

'Oh.' There wasn't much to do about that. It was far from ideal. It would be better for one of them to help break the news for many reasons. One was that the family might be involved in Lindsay's murder; another, that being there in person showed respect.

The only option in this instance would be to ask the Gardai over in Dublin to inform Lindsay's son on their behalf, and to offer assistance to him here in Southampton if he wanted to come over.

'The DCS is going to sit in on the start of the briefing,' O'Malley said, his words cutting across her thoughts.

'Ooh, OK.' Hanson felt a rush of nerves. She guessed it was inevitable that more senior officers would now be stepping in. There was always going to be a big difference in response to a serial killer.

The last time she'd spoken to the detective chief superintendent had been in a formal interview over the chief's handling of a murder investigation. The case had not gone perfectly for DCI Jonah Sheens and his team. It had been a messy situation, and the DCS had asked hard questions over how the team had conducted its investigation, as had the Independent Office for Police Conduct.

She'd got the impression during the inquiry that DCS Wilkinson was scrupulously fair. She could tell that he liked the chief but wasn't going to let that get in the way of judging him objectively. And, while laudable, that objectivity was also quite an intimidating quality.

DCS Wilkinson arrived a few minutes later, expensively dressed and looking trim, tanned and undeniably upper class. Wilkinson was one of a handful of genuinely posh officers who'd been fast-tracked into management positions during the nineties, having come from expensive schools.

Hanson watched him greet the chief at his office with both warmth and a trace of sombreness. A perfectly pitched attitude for the discovery of a serial murderer. The DCS had the political side to his position totally sorted, Hanson thought. Probably the kind of thing you learned at Eton. Though it occurred to her that he might just be the sort of person who did it naturally. An empathetic type of man.

She turned to say something to Ben about him being a proper grown-up, and then remembered that Ben was still at the wake. So instead she muttered to O'Malley, 'Look at that glorious tan. Wonder where he went for Christmas. Barbados? The Maldives?'

'Oh, I know this,' O'Malley answered. 'The chief mentioned it . . . The Seychelles.'

'God,' Hanson said, with a slightly desperate feeling, 'I'd

kill for the Seychelles. Actually, I'd kill for anywhere warmer. Don't care if it's the south of France or Ibiza.'

'Wouldn't you love to see the DCS in Ibiza, though?' O'Malley asked. 'Imagine him hitting the clubs.'

Hanson was still laughing at this image as the chief came to get them for the briefing, and to his raised eyebrow she offered, 'Trying to make ourselves feel better about the DCS's tan.'

'Let me know if you manage it,' the chief said with a rueful grin.

'I just want to begin,' the chief said, from his position next to the whiteboard, 'by running over the basics of both Jacqueline Clarke's murder and what we now know about today.' He nodded towards DCS Wilkinson, who was sitting back in his chair with a relaxed posture. The DCS was on the other side of the table to Hanson, making it easy for her to take furtive glances at him, but also easy for him to watch her if he wanted to.

The chief nodded to the DCS, then pressed a button on the data projector remote, and brought up an image of the crime scene close to Longbeech Campsite. It had been taken from the other side of the small clearing to where they'd found Jacqueline Clarke's remains, and showed the pyre, with the blackened bones just visible amid the white ash.

'Jacqueline Clarke died during the night of Friday the third of October,' he said. 'Her remains were found in the woods north of Longbeech Campsite the following lunchtime by a picnicking family who'd come for the weekend.'

Hanson saw a flicker of a reaction in the DCS's expression. She felt like telling him that it wasn't as bad as it sounded. Jacqueline's body had been so thoroughly burned that it had been unrecognisable to the kids. A display of carbonised bone that had looked more like a Halloween decoration than a woman.

The chief scrolled to an image of Jacqueline herself, taken at her daughter's twenty-first. Her sandy ringlets and startlingly blue eyes were as striking now as they had been the first time Hanson had seen them. Jacqueline looked savvy, and striking, and together, and in no way helpless. As little like a victim as anyone could.

'Jacqueline was forty-six and worked at a Southampton animal shelter not far from the city centre,' the chief said. 'She lived alone outside Brockenhurst in a house with its own drive, with only a dog for company. She was a divorcee and mother to two grown-up daughters who each live at some distance.'

Hanson nodded, thinking that this didn't tell the full story either. That Jacqueline had been abandoned by her husband for a much younger friend of hers, and had been unable to move on from it. That it had ruined her relationship with her daughters and left her profoundly lonely. So much of it had a parallel with Hanson's own, slightly older mother's story that she had felt deeply saddened, and grateful that the two of them had become a strong team instead of almost strangers.

'As far as her daughters or her colleagues at the animal sanctuary can tell us,' the DCI went on, 'Jacqueline wasn't dating anyone at the time of her death, or in contact with any particular friends. Her phone records show only messages to her daughters and occasional brief communications with staff at the shelter. None of them were close to her, which made it difficult to work out her movements on those last days. She was only reported missing four days after the event when a neighbour a few hundred yards further down the Lyndhurst road complained of insistent barking from her house.'

Hanson knew that the barking dog had been a springer spaniel named Merlot. He had been Jacqueline's closest friend and truest love. 'She was totally soft-hearted,' her colleagues had said. 'But only towards anything with fur,' they'd added.

Merlot had waited four days for her to return. For her to shower him with affection, and to walk him out in the forest. Hanson had found it impossible not to feel broken-hearted at that thought.

Though it had been something else that had hit her hardest. The only things to survive the blaze had been two molten fillings and a pacemaker. The serial number on the pacemaker had finally confirmed that they had the right person, and for some reason the fact that this life-saving device was all that was left of Jacqueline had been a gut punch. It had driven Hanson away from her desk for a while, out into the car park, where she had breathed in cold air and tried not to think of her own mum and what she might leave behind.

'Jacqueline's car was still parked at her house,' the chief carried on. 'There were no signs of forced entry, violence or other disturbance at the property. The gravel driveway didn't provide any indication of tyre marks, but it's possible that the killer picked her up in a vehicle and transported her to where she was killed.' He paused. 'Unfortunately her neighbours don't share a driveway with her and don't remember seeing or hearing anything, so we're basically guessing.'

He changed the photo to an aerial view of Jacqueline's house, showing exactly the problem. It was set amid trees some distance from its nearest neighbours, a good way back from the road, and down a single lane driveway. He changed the image again, showing the front of the house this time. A pretty, well-tended house with white paint and climbing plants.

'The last time her phone pinged any masts was on the

afternoon of the third as she was leaving work,' the chief added, 'which suggests that it was off after that point. Her daughters informed us that this was pretty normal. Their mother saw her mobile as a device for emergencies and only used it at work when she had to. She did her communication using the landline.'

Which was still, Hanson thought, one of the weirdest sides to it all. That a woman of only forty-six could have so completely rejected the world of smartphones.

The chief went on for a few more minutes, detailing the leads they'd followed. The appeals for witnesses. The door-knocking. The fruitless CCTV searches. The ruling out of her ex-husband, who had unquestionably been in the south of France at the time, and the daughters themselves, who could be placed variously in Aberdeen and Loughborough.

The process sounded simple, but it had been unending. It made Hanson tired just thinking about it again.

The team had worked themselves ragged trying to pro-duce witnesses to either the murder or the disposal of the body, and had found none. No vehicles had been spotted in the surrounding area, and the dry ground of the nearest track to the clearing had offered up no recent tyre marks. Walkers and pony trekkers had left prints over several damper preceding days, but they didn't seem to overlay any footprints, and there was nothing to show for sure how the killer had brought Jacqueline Clarke there that night. And no sign, either, of how they had transported the wood and kerosene used to burn her. Though the sheer fact of a woman having been taken into the woods and laid on a pyre made them ninety-nine per cent certain that they were looking for a male suspect.

Hanson, O'Malley and Lightman had thrown everything

at the investigation, and the chief had pushed them to do ever more. To go beyond the usual.

There should never, of course, be a hierarchy to the investigation of murder. Hanson knew the chief believed that as strongly as she did. A gangland shooting should be as urgently investigated as the assassination of a politician. And yet they had all felt the same feverish urgency in their need to find Jacqueline's killer. An urgency that had gone beyond a desire to bring her daughters a sense of justice.

They had all of them felt the same fear that this might be the start of something rather than the end of something. That fear had been triggered by the flawlessness of the crime scene. The ritual nature of the pyre. And then by all the other fires that were to come after. The profoundly unsettling, empty pyres they still didn't understand.

The first one had been found on heathland out towards Hale Purlieu, five miles from where Jacqueline's body had been burned, and nobody had seen anyone setting it. It had been built late at night and reported by a pair of lads on the way back from an evening of drinking and barbecuing on the heath. They'd seemed a little disappointed that there hadn't been a body. Hanson and the team had felt the opposite.

Two other fires had sprung up and burned themselves out since, the furthest of them at Kingston Great Common, ten miles from where they'd found Jacqueline. The other had been south of Milkham car park, a mere three miles away. Each one had been perfectly built. Each had been accelerated using kerosene. And at none of them had there been anything left to identify the person responsible. No clear tyre tracks or footprints. No detritus or dropped items.

It wasn't clear why each one had been set. It was possible that they were deliberate taunts, or that the killer had set them up and waited for a victim who hadn't emerged. But whatever the reason, the team had shared a sense of foreboding. A constant worry that whoever was responsible was going to kill again.

They had dug out every report of a past murder or attack, of course, searching for similarities to their killer's MO. They had raked over the ashes of house fires; of arsons; of car explosions. They had looked at missing persons information, and at troubled young (or not so young) people who had harmed animals. Or who had burned objects or buildings. But there had been nothing conclusive. Nothing that seemed an exact match, and nothing to lead them towards a particular individual.

It was their failure to catch the culprit that had brought them here. To a cramped meeting room on New Year's Day, when they'd all supposedly been on leave.

'Today's victim has now been informally identified,' the chief said, his tone more sombre. 'Her driving licence is in the name of Lindsay Kernow, a resident of Totton who is not at home, and hasn't been seen by neighbours since yesterday. Lindsay was a widow. She has a son in Dublin who we'll need to notify in order to make a formal identification.'

The chief brought up an image taken from social media. It showed what was to a certain extent the same face Hanson had seen on the pyre earlier that day, though it was in some ways very different. Not just because the hair was longer in this photo or because Lindsay had been wearing glasses in it. It was different because everything slackens so much in death, the face hollowing out. Becoming a mask.

'There are numerous similarities between both the two crime scenes and our two victims,' the chief said more loudly. 'Lindsay was forty-eight, only two years older than Jacqueline, and worked as a self-employed book editor. She lived alone, though she seems to have a cat rather than a dog. She also has grown-up family at a distance, and lived in a house that isn't overlooked.'

He brought up an image of an odd little cottage, jutting into what must have been one of the remaining clumps of woodland around Totton. A second image showed that access to it was via a private paved driveway.

'The driveway comes off a side road that runs along the A35. There are only three houses along it, and Lindsay's is the furthest out. I'd say that talking to the neighbours there will be a key starting point.'

'And I suppose we don't know anything about any friends yet?' the DCS asked.

The chief glanced O'Malley's way, and O'Malley sat up to say, 'Not much. Pretty inactive social accounts with poor engagement when she posts. No images of Lindsay with particular individuals to help us there. Her phone is missing too. Though we're onto her network provider for any location data from it.'

There was a tap on the door at that point. Hanson glanced around and then found herself half grinning. Ben Lightman was letting himself into the room, still wearing the light grey suit he'd worn for the funeral of his father and looking, of course, movie-star perfect.

'Sir,' he said, with a brief nod to the DCS, who was looking at him with a raised eyebrow.

'Ben,' the chief said, and Hanson was amused to see that he looked momentarily lost for words. He clearly hadn't expected his second detective sergeant to come in, even allowing for the fact that it was Ben, and Ben seemed magnetically drawn to work.

Working was, Hanson had come to learn, Ben's coping mechanism as much as anything else. She had only learned recently that the driving force behind his self-discipline – and behind his determination never to let on what he was feeling – was rooted in some incredibly difficult events in his childhood. In trauma essentially.

But he'd at long last started having therapy, spurred on in part by the additional pain of his father's illness, in part by having to work on a case that had brought it all very much to mind, and in part perhaps by just having reached the point where he was ready for it. Hanson hoped that talking to a psychologist about it might help him talk to her, too. Though she no longer felt hurt when he didn't.

'I . . . There's really no expectation for you to be here,' the chief was saying, as Ben paused just inside the doorway. 'I mean, you're always welcome. But if you need to be with your family . . .'

'I – could do with not being with them now really,' Ben said wryly. 'According to them.'

He glanced over at Hanson, who shook her head, but smiled and tucked her chair in so he could get to one of the free seats.

'OK,' the chief said, nodding. 'But if you want to leave, you don't need to give an explanation. Just head.'

'See?' Hanson murmured, as Ben settled himself into the chair next to her. 'He's trying to get rid of you too.'

'Good thing I'm thick-skinned,' Ben muttered back.

The DCI nodded at them both, half smiling, and then went on, 'So, what we have today in the murder of Lindsay Kernow is a similar MO and a similar victim to Jacqueline Clarke. That's one whose isolation might make her difficult to trace. Worse still, we're looking at trying to find her on New Year's Eve. It goes without saying that it's likely to be challenging. It's the one night of the year where nobody is where they usually are, and most people who are out and about are the worse for wear.' He gave a short sigh. 'But the one thing we do have, which marks this scene out from the last, is DNA.'

He scrolled to a close-up image of part of the pyre, with Lindsay's bare arm visible on one side. Across both the timber and the woman's skin there was a spray of blood.

'Hmm,' the DCS said, as if this had finally broken through his veneer of polite interest. 'Presumably not the victim's?'

'No sign of any injury, and a quick profile shows male DNA,' the chief said.

Hanson found herself sitting up slightly at that. They'd been all but certain that they were looking at a male killer, and this, she felt, made it all the more likely that they had the killer's blood.

'As soon as a full sample's ready, we'll be running it through our database,' the chief went on, 'and looking for a match. If that's negative, then we'll be doing everything we can to identify suspects. And then we'll be attempting to match them.'

Hanson felt a mixture of excitement and wariness at that. Even in the few short years she'd worked as a DC, she knew that the chances of a match with an existing suspect were small. And narrowing down a suspect pool in order to cross-reference could take months of painstaking work.

The one really good thing, though, was that it all but guaranteed a conviction if they could do it. Few cases were decided on non-physical evidence now. If they could find a suspect who matched that DNA, and they did it right, they were looking at a strong likelihood of the culprit being put away for this murder – and for Jacqueline Clarke's too.

She found herself wondering how their careful, methodical killer could have left such an obvious trace behind. Had the blood been part of some sort of a ritual? Had there been blood at the first scene, which had been burned to the point of total erasure? Though perhaps the bigger question was why the pyre hadn't been burned this time.

If someone came along and spooked them, Hanson thought, *then that person knows something too.*

'We have to bear in mind,' the chief added, 'that there are other possible explanations for the blood being on the pyre than it being the killer's. Although scene of crime are confident that the blood ended up there after the pyre was set and the victim laid on it, we do know that the killer was interrupted. It's possible that whoever interrupted them was the source of the blood. But in the absence of that individual coming forward with any information, it seems overwhelmingly likely that the blood is the killer's, and in either case, we need to find whoever left it there.'

In the short silence that followed the chief's words, Ben Lightman said, 'Sir, there's something I'd like to suggest.'

Hanson glanced over at him, surprised that he was fully engaged in this. She had expected him to be only partially present, trying to distract himself from the loss of his father. But Ben's cool expression was as together as usual, and he seemed, if anything, almost enthusiastic as the chief nodded to him.

'In the event that the DNA isn't a match with anyone known to us,' Ben said, leaning forwards and resting his arms on the table, 'I'd like us to consider whether there might be other avenues we could explore.' He cleared his throat slightly. 'I was listening to a podcast a while ago, and I think we ought to try this the way they've been doing in the US.'

6

Forty-eight hours had passed since the discovery of Lindsay Kernow's body. Forty-eight hours during which, Jonah was keenly aware, they had made no convincing steps towards catching a serial killer.

And yet, in that time, a lot had changed. At six p.m. on the day they'd found Lindsay, Jonah, the DCS and the deputy chief constable had called a press briefing to explain that they had found the body of a woman on the heath. By that time they had informed Lindsay's son and Jacqueline's daughters. They didn't name Lindsay in their first briefing, however. They would make no move to announce it until they were sure they had reached all of Lindsay's family.

The DCS had explained to the assembled press that this killing might be linked to Jacqueline Clarke's. Jonah had then been the one tasked with advising the public to stay in touch with their relatives, particularly females living alone, and to make certain they knew to be cautious.

'As yet, we have no firm evidence as to how the killer approached his or her victims,' Jonah told the assembled press. 'We've ruled out any connection between the two women. The victims seem to have been targeted separately, and though we don't believe they incited this in any way, we would advise caution while we work to apprehend the killer or killers.'

A mere twenty minutes after the briefing, the *Herald* had

run an article online about the discovery of a second body with the title:

Bonfire Killer strikes again

The journalist must, Jonah realised, have been following the developments closely, in spite of the apparent lack of media interest after Jacqueline's death. The reporter's article included details of three empty pyres they'd investigated since the first murder, and the picture she drew was chilling. There was a stalker out there, she told her readers. A hunter lying in wait. And nobody could ever really be safe.

With that article and the 'Bonfire Killer' name, things had taken on a whole new life. It wasn't just the Southampton press who were interested now; the story was picked up and run by the nationals, with reports of women who had been placed 'ritualistically' on a series of pyres.

The effect on everyday life was immediate. By eleven that night, when Jonah refilled his car at a petrol station on the way home, he could see clear anxiety in the two women who were refuelling alongside him. They both looked impatiently between the fuel gauge and each of the men on the fore-court as they filled up, and both rushed inside to pay.

He saw some of that same worry in the groups of women he drove past on his way out to Ashford too. A noticeable huddling together, despite all of them having clearly been out drinking.

He found himself torn at the sight. He wished, if any-thing, that they would be more careful. That none of them would go out at all until he'd found this killer. That nobody else would risk becoming a victim. But they all had lives to live, these women of all ages. They had break-ups to get over or birthdays to celebrate. They had a right to be out on the streets without being threatened, and it made Jonah angrier than he wanted to admit to himself that he couldn't guarantee them that.

As much as he didn't want the killer to cut short another life, he didn't want him to stop the women on his beat living their lives either. The bastard did not have that right.

He'd carried his fear and anger home to a half-cut Michelle that first night, and found the fear gradually winning out. Michelle was a year younger than Jacqueline Clarke. She was a striking woman, as Jacqueline had been, though Michelle was dark-haired like Lindsay Kernow instead of sandy blonde like Jacqueline. His partner was also going out drinking in bars several times a week now that she'd rediscovered her social life.

Michelle might not be going alone, but Jonah had worked so many cases where a group had become drunk and lost track of someone. And his partner would generally arrive back alone in a cab. He didn't trust the process that got her to that point.

The post-mortem results were strongly in his mind as he watched Michelle stagger around unsteadily with a glass of wine she'd somehow thought she needed after a skinful out on the town. As well as confirming that Lindsay had died as a result of asphyxiation, the report showed that she'd had a high dose of ketamine in her system. Enough, the pathologist said, to render her unconscious. Which made Jonah suspect all the more that the process of abducting her had begun at a bar, with a first spiked drink that had led Lindsay to get into a car with a man she should never have trusted.

But he couldn't talk to his partner while she was drunk, he thought, watching her stumble slightly and then laugh. He would talk to her in the morning. He'd ask her to stay in for a few nights. Just for a week or so, until he'd had a chance to bring this guy in. She would understand, he thought. She would surely be happy enough to put her rediscovered social life on hold in order to stay safe.

But it had become strangely, depressingly clear to him as he'd got up the next day and fed Milly that this wasn't a conversation he could have with his partner right now. She was hungover, and a little haggard, but was talking about the night before and what she and the girls had got up to with real animation. He couldn't ask her to give up the one thing that was making her feel like herself, just when she most needed it.

As afraid as he was for her safety, he was more afraid of asking her to stay at home, he realised. He was afraid of tipping her back into the depression that she'd had to fight her way out of. Afraid of angering her. And afraid, if he was honest with himself, of making her resent him.

And so he smiled when she told him, just before he left, that she was going to the Wheatsheaf to watch comedy with Sabrina later on.

'Sounds great,' was all he said. 'Just keep an eye on each other.'

Michelle rolled her eyes. 'Big scary murderers out there, hey?'

Jonah could only nod, but his partner was already turning away to go and get dressed.

He'd hugged Milly, handed her over to their live-in nanny Rhona, and then climbed into the car. It had been a relief to shrug his purely work persona back on during the drive. To think only about the morning's press conference.

He had named Lindsay Kernow as the second victim that morning. He'd also revealed that she had most likely been drugged, and had asked for anyone who had experienced drink spiking to get in touch too. Any events that might have been an aborted attempt over the last few months to drug another victim.

It had produced a deluge of responses within hours. Far too many, in fact, for Jonah's team to handle. It was unclear whether drink spiking was hugely on the rise now, or whether it had always happened, but the number of reports alarmed him. He'd found himself slowing as he passed pubs and bars each time he made a journey that day, irrationally trying to look into them and catch someone in the act of drugging another victim.

He knew that, as much as the urge was irrational, it came from a very rational conclusion. Their killer wasn't done. That much he was sure of. It was clear from the second victim, and from all those fires he had laid in the New Forest since. Although serial killers could, and did, go through fallow periods or stop altogether, he was convinced that the Bonfire Killer was only just getting going.

The thought made him push himself and the rest of them ever harder. Keeping on top of the investigation overall would have been impossible with just his team of three but the super had granted him a team of constables, and the DCS had approved the co-opting of a few of the Portsmouth area detective constables from DCI Acharya. He'd set them all to work investigating each instance of alleged drugging or concerning behaviour, many dating back months.

What Jonah had immediately formalised with the DCS at that point was a ring-fencing of his own team to look at the most promising leads. In particular, to investigate Lindsay Kernow's movements. They'd been the ones to start tracing her through her mobile phone on the day she'd been found, and to interview all those who knew her best. If other lines of inquiry bore fruit, they would be the ones to pick them up from the other co-opted officers.

As Jonah had warned his team in his first briefing, the biggest difficulty in finding Lindsay's killer lay in her being murdered on New Year's Eve. It was always a night of chaos. He knew from experience that it was incredibly difficult to get reasonable accounts of events at bars and celebrations, and on New Year's Eve very few of the folks out and about would have been sober. Bar staff and taxi drivers who *were* hopefully sober were likely to be confused by the numbers of people served, driven or witnessed, rendering them far less likely to remember individuals.

With all that in mind, Jonah had urged his team to move fast. The phone mast data they'd received confirmed that Lindsay had been in Totton until at least five past ten, and given that her phone had pinged further out at almost eleven it seemed likely she had been in Totton for that time. The first mast her phone had pinged had been further into town than her house, and the azimuth of the ping suggested that she could have been at one of several pubs, or a wine shop, or one of two seven-elevens at that point. But forty-eight hours on, they hadn't found a single staff member or regular from any of those establishments who'd remembered seeing her, and they'd failed to discover any friends who lived in the area of the ping who she might have visited.

While the team worked, Jonah had been in the background, smoothing their paths and completing Community Impact Assessments to ensure that the general public were safe. Despite his belief in the importance of both these roles, he had felt a keen sense of impatience to be getting on with what he did best: with solving this, and stopping the threat entirely.

Two days had passed since they'd found Lindsay, and they needed the killer off the streets. Which was why he was glad to have a video call lined up with a forty-something American woman named Cassie Logan.

Despite not being a police officer, or even specifically qualified in the science of crime, Cassie had been directly responsible for bringing in some of the highest-profile killers in the United States in recent years. She'd done it not via ordinary detective work but by using DNA matching and a global ancestry site. She'd started out as an amateur, and ended up as the East Coast's foremost expert on forensic genealogy.

The UK had been lagging behind both in terms of forensic genealogy and the laws that allowed its use. There was technically no legal use of such techniques in bringing killers to justice. But with the recent creation of UK-based ancestry site Globalry, which stipulated that its data could be used in this way, and with a CPS genuinely interested in a test case, that could all be about to change.

Their own case might provide the perfect test. But only if the chief constable was sufficiently convinced to push for it.

Ben Lightman came to knock on his door at midday, a good time to catch Cassie, who was based in Saratoga and running five hours behind them.

'I've got the Teams call set up and Cassie says she's ready to go,' Ben said.

'Thank you,' Jonah told him, rising with a feeling of actual optimism. 'Let's hear what she has to say.'

Fifteen minutes later, Jonah was feeling less enthusiastic. It seemed as though fast-talking, smart Cassie Logan might be offering no more than a distant match. A fourth or fifth cousin that would give so many possible results that they would be no further forwards in their search.

'I get the feeling the chief constable won't go for the idea of a test that produces vague results,' he said apologetically, having listened to what Cassie had to say.

Cassie smiled at him on-screen, and shook her head, making her brunette waves bounce. 'A relative being distant isn't the same as the result being vague,' she said, her voice clear and decisive over the connection. 'It's all about reading the data correctly. Look, if we prep the DNA you have and upload it, and we get a match with two people who are only distant cousins of your perp, but those two people are essentially unrelated because one comes from the perp's mother's side and one comes from the father's, then it'll take no time at all to pinpoint the very few common relatives. It doesn't matter that they're third or fourth cousins. The one point of overlap is the thing that helps us. If it's an only child, that would give us just one person.'

Jonah grinned, glad he'd managed to hang on to what she was saying. Cassie's torrent of words was as relentless as it was enthusiastic. 'All right,' he said. 'But what happens if we have only one match? Or a match with two people on one side of the family?'

Cassie gave a small, unconcerned shrug. 'Then it's more fun. The Globalry test tells us the closeness of the relationship they hold to the perp. Cousin, second cousin, half-brother . . . So my job is to find out the exact make-up of their family through the site. I then contact members, and zone in on where each person lives. You're looking at a serial killer, so if we find someone who's the correct relation to your DNA match who lives near the two murder sites, then you'd obviously want to look at them pretty closely, right?'

Jonah glanced around at his team, who were all trying not to smile. It was obvious that Cassie had talked to police officers before and knew how they worked. 'Sounds pretty sensible to me,' he said after a moment.

And, in fact, it sounded more than that. The more he thought about it, the more it sounded like the direction that policing should be moving in. With so many people voluntarily uploading DNA onto sites that tested large parts of the sequence, using it could save huge numbers of lives and bring closure to the families of victims.

What the DCS had made clear already was that if his team found results from a DNA match, serious care would need to be taken in progressing the investigation to avoid jeopardising any prosecution. The match would have to provide, in the first instance, nothing more than a pointer for them to investigate someone. The case would then need to be built independently of the DNA match. They would have to provide conclusive reason to prosecute without reference to it. And the crown prosecution service would have to accept their process.

All of which had to be weighed against the fact that time was against them. That the longer they let this killer roam free, the more chance there was of him taking another woman's life.

'What if the family won't talk to you?' O'Malley asked, tapping his pen on his knee. 'It's not like you can bring them in for questioning.'

'No, but I hear there are some police around who can do that . . .' Cassie replied with a laugh.

Hanson grinned at O'Malley. 'You know how they've signed a disclaimer on the site saying their DNA can be used this way, right?'

'Ahhhh, the small print,' O'Malley said good-naturedly. 'I never read that.'

'That's why I put all the stuff about how Globalry works in a big font in my report,' Ben said drily.

'I never read those either,' O'Malley said airily. 'Wouldn't want to bias myself at the start of an investigation.'

'I'd just like to disown responsibility for my entire team,' Jonah said to Cassie.

'Hey,' Hanson protested. 'I have an actual question!'

'Fire away,' Jonah said through a half-smile.

'You said you needed to prep the DNA,' Hanson said. 'How long would that take if we sent it to you?'

'With blood? A couple of hours in the lab,' Cassie replied. 'Hair and other forms take longer.'

Hanson glanced Jonah's way, her expression eager. He nodded. 'I'm happy to go ahead. If we can get documents signed off by you in the next hour or so, I'll arrange to get some of our sample shipped to you express. Should be guaranteed to arrive within forty-eight hours.' He paused thoughtfully. 'Unless you know of a friendly lab over here who will do it?'

Cassie gave a slow smile. 'You know, I just might.'

7

Aisling had been consciously ignoring the spare room and everything hidden within it for two days. It was an island in the middle of her frozen lake of deliberate forgetting, and Aisling had felt the ice cracking under her feet as she'd moved around it. Had felt herself slip at times into the freezing water of everything she had tried so hard not to think about. Had felt herself consumed by memories, even while everyone she encountered day to day was preoccupied with a very present fear.

It was strangely hard to hang on to the fact that there was a serial killer on the loose. Everything else that she was trying to hold at bay seemed to make it impossible to remember that fact as well. Walking into the Co-op on the second of January, she experienced a jolt as she saw a headline about it in the *Daily Mail*, and realised that this was something the whole nation was interested in. And yet somehow she'd still forgotten by the time she'd got to the checkout, and experienced the same jolt of shock as she heard the woman in front of her mention it to the assistant, her voice low and full of fear.

She found herself looking around at the man in the queue behind her, then, wondering. She had to try to hold onto this somehow, and be careful. What was wrong with her? It was like she'd forgotten how to function. But even after that thought, she found herself in the car without any memory of how she'd got there, aware that she'd been as open to attack in the early twilight as a child.

It had been Jack O'Keane's name that had broken every-thing open. His name, and the fact that, on Monday, they'd both be in the same building. That she'd almost certainly see him.

Knowing that she'd have to face him, and perhaps even to explain, had driven through that carefully formed barrier be-tween her and her past. It had made it impossible for her to keep it locked away.

Though she'd tried. On that first day, she'd made every effort she could to pack it all back up and keep functioning. Not least because her older son seemed withdrawn and even bad-tempered in a way that was so unlike him it made her ache.

Ethan had returned from his New Year's Day band re-hearsal in a foul temper, driving his own car this time instead of getting a lift from Matthew Downing. But she'd wondered whether Matthew had been the cause all the same. He might have disrupted the rehearsal, or – more likely, she thought – given Ethan a hard time about whatever had happened on New Year's Eve.

It was so unusual to see Ethan glowering that she'd gone, instinctively, to hug him, and felt hurt when he'd brushed her off.

'I need some food,' he'd said, and she'd nodded and grinned, and decided it was just the end of his hangover.

Except that the dark mood had lasted. It had suddenly been like having a sulky teenager in the house. She and Finn had been the ones keeping the conversation going over din-ner, despite her distraction, while Ethan had sat in largely sullen silence. And in the end it had been Finn who had pointedly asked his brother if he could be more communica-tive. It had produced a small response at least. A little effort for the next twenty minutes.

Two days later, Ethan still seemed depressed. Angry, even. Aisling knew she should be trying to get to the bottom of it, but she was seeing it through a fog. Because as much as she wanted to be present, she kept finding herself thirty years ago, back when Jack and her parents had been part of her life.

To her bewilderment, she found every memory clean and sharp. It was as if she'd hidden them away carefully in some attic room, lovingly wrapped up, so that they were now as fresh and as jewel-bright as they'd been on the day they had happened.

Memories of Jack. Of school. Though the ones that took her breath away most of all were the ones of her father.

Her gentle, adored daddy. The man who had defended her against the harshest of her mother's judgements and been a friend to her as well as a parent. The looming, bearded figure who had hugged and comforted her as her mother never had, and who she had thought perfect – right up until their lives had fragmented. Perhaps even until he'd left them, in an act of unspeakable callousness.

She'd been unable to make herself sift through her parents' belongings after her mother had died. It had all been too hard for her. She'd paid a solicitor to sort probate, and had blindly signed every document that had been sent to her. She had paid removal men to pack away the portable possessions, of which there were remarkably few, and asked a charity to come and take the furniture. And then she'd packed every remaining box away, into the spare room, where she had tried as hard not to think about it as she'd tried not to remember her daddy's hugs, or her mammy's endless heartache.

But she'd known, during all her circling of that room, that she would find her way in there in the end. And the time had now come. She needed to face the pain of it, as well as the fierce nostalgia for a life she'd lost. And so, at one o'clock on the third of January, she poured herself a large glass of wine and made her way up into the spartan little room. She pulled every box out of the wardrobe, and sat herself on the bed to begin going through them.

The first box she opened was full of carefully wrapped items that she guessed were china ornaments. She left them where they were for now and pulled the next one out, which proved to be full of photograph albums.

It was sad and painful to be confronted by her old self within them. Her as a baby. As a girl. Photograph after photograph of her growing up. Her with her father. Her standing stiffly next to her mother, often at church or at church-related gatherings.

She looked through them all with a strange, heartbroken hunger. And then she moved on to another album that was full of later pictures. These had all been taken after they'd moved to England. Mammy's eyes and mouth were tighter. Grimmer. And Daddy was no longer smiling. His face was weary, and his eyes distant. He was a man who looked broken.

Aisling tried not to look at herself in the photographs she appeared in, but even so, she sometimes found herself caught by the haunted look of her. At sixteen and seventeen she had become a melancholy, distant-looking creature.

She could feel tears on the skin of her cheeks by the time she'd finished with those albums. Beneath them were simple packets of photographs: images that had never made it into an album. She knew what these were.

With a sense of enormous resistance, she opened the first one up to see the photographs she had taken. They were from the years after Daddy had walked away and never returned. Soul-wrecking pictures of Christmases without joy. Of summer holidays spent simply passing the time. A scant few of Aisling, but in all of them, her mammy. A woman who had still French-pleated her hair every day, and worn freshly ironed floral dresses, but who seemed to have lost her heart and herself in every other way.

Aisling found herself moving from those to the other boxes. What began as an almost reluctant curiosity became a burning need to see.

It was only after a good while, and a second glass of wine, that she was able to admit to herself what she was looking for. She was trying to find, almost thirty years later, some evidence that her father really had loved her. Something she'd missed before. Some message or note or memento from him, sent after he'd gone. Something her mother might have chosen to hide from her, as a result of her own pain.

She finally stumbled on a box full of letters, and there, right on the top, making her breath catch, was the last letter she'd read from him.

My darling Dymphna and Aisling,

I'm so sorry to both of you. But I have to leave. I love you deeply, but I can't keep living this duplicitous life. I have to make a choice. And every fibre of me is telling me to go.

Your
Dara and Daddy

She put it aside quickly, knowing that she might cry over it and not stop if she didn't move on. Beneath that letter sat the deeds to the house, which her father had transferred wholesale to her mother, his one kind act. Aisling shoved the deeds aside. She had no idea why she'd kept them. The house had become hers on her mother's death, and then someone else's entirely.

She started to pick other letters up instead, looking at every piece of paper in a box that was full, desperate to see some sign that he'd written to her later. Or if not to her, that at least he'd salved her mother's misery before her death. That, she tried to tell herself, would be better than silence.

But the end of the box came, and there was nothing.

With increasing desperation she looked at the objects her mother had kept in her dresser, but none of them were her father's. And she recognised all of them from her childhood.

There was, in fact, nothing but harsh reality to find after that. It was contained in the neat documentation from her own solicitor detailing the inheritance granted to her by her mother's death twenty years ago. She looked at her own, neat signature on one of the pages and wondered how she'd managed to write so clearly.

And that was the end of it. The end of what was here.

She found herself staring into space. Realising that she could have done more before now. That she needed to do more.

She climbed up off the beige carpet, where she'd ended up sitting awkwardly surrounded by boxes. She went to her study and there she loaded up the desktop.

Somewhere in the back of her mind, she was half remembering an article she'd read recently about the newest British ancestry site, Globalry. Despite not remembering much of what the article had said, she typed it into Google and then clicked on it.

We offer our own testing, and a platform that allows people to share their data from every other ancestry site . . .

She read it, and scrolled onwards, finding out about the nature of their tests. About how many parts of the sequence it would look at, and how confident it could be about correctly identifying relatives.

She was on the point of clicking to register when she heard Ethan returning from his shift at the record shop. She heard his call and shouted back, 'Hey! Just working, but I'll be finished up soon.'

She could just tell him, she realised. She could tell him and Finn, and let them be part of this. She could break through the ice entirely.

Maybe talking to him about her own past would help Ethan open up about whatever was bothering him. It could be the right thing for all of them.

But to do so would mean telling them *everything,* and she had to acknowledge at last that she still wasn't ready to do it. Even after thirty years.

8

Jonah woke with a rush of hope, and struggled to identify what lay underneath it until he remembered Cassie Logan's offer of help, and the lab which had taken delivery of their sample by a same-day courier.

They had now uploaded the DNA from Lindsay Kernow's body to Globalry. It meant that even if every other part of the case went nowhere, within two weeks they should have a list of any related individuals who appeared on Globalry. The materials needed for Cassie Logan to weave her magic.

He blinked at the clock on his side of the bed. It was almost seven. Milly had slept in for once. She would do this, sometimes, without warning and without frequent enough repeats: suddenly forego her usual five-thirty demands for food, and sleep right through till breakfast time. Though breakfast was, in fact, still another bottle. She was still just shy of the recommended age to start solid foods.

He thought about staying in bed until Milly woke. It was such a rare opportunity to lounge around. But his mind was working already, mulling over Lindsay Kernow. Jacqueline Clarke. His own home life.

Michelle had stayed in the night before, drinking on the sofa while minding Milly. Their nanny, Rhona, had been on one of her nights off, and there had been no way Jonah could leave work to look after his daughter. Not this week.

Rhona was sixty-one, and a grandmother whose family now lived overseas. She was also a lifeline. Capable, unflappable and doting, she gave Milly all the attention Jonah wished he could give and more. He knew that having her there was the right thing for his daughter, but he wondered, sometimes, whether she was closer to Rhona than she was to either of them. Whether she'd learn to say Rhona's name first.

But this was the nature of the job. There were quieter times, and there were times like this: when everything was put on hold for an urgent case. A serial killer was as urgent as it got.

At four the previous afternoon, they'd finally found someone who'd seen Lindsay Kernow: a barman at a Totton pub. His thoughts on her arrival time matched the information from her phone, and he'd seemed together and not prone to fabrication. But he unfortunately had no recollection of seeing her leave.

'I only remember her coming to the bar once,' he'd said apologetically. 'It was just after we'd opened, in that really quiet bit on New Year's Eve when everyone isn't out again yet. She was definitely on her own, sitting at a corner table for a while. But then it got busy, and I didn't see her again.'

So Jonah's team had mobilised, going variously to the bar and to surrounding CCTV points to try to pick Lindsay up on camera. At ten they'd eventually suggested that he go home and see his partner, promising to call if anything firm came up. Given the silence of his phone, it looked like nothing had.

They would all be in the station again today; he was sure everyone would be in early. But they'd agreed to reassemble in the big meeting room at nine, which gave him time for breakfast with Milly. A small consolation prize for the many nights when she was asleep by the time he made it home.

He glanced over at Michelle, watching the way she slept. She was always so hard to wake at this time of the morning, despite being an incredibly light sleeper in the middle of the night. For some reason he wanted her to stir this morning, despite how protective he'd become of her rest in recent months. He knew lack of sleep could contribute to the post-natal depression she'd slid into.

In some strange ways, those early weeks after Jacqueline's murder had been a blessing. His gruelling schedule had made it unquestionably clear that they needed a nanny, and that had finally freed Michelle from the feeling that she had to be the one to look after their daughter. She'd gone back to work full-time too, without feeling any guilt about it. Taking the pressure of constant parenting away had also freed her from numerous feelings of inadequacy about neither enjoying it as she thought she should, nor being able to do it as well as she'd hoped.

The initial effect on their relationship had been positive. He'd seen in Michelle the woman he had once proposed to. She'd been upbeat. Confident. She'd started to talk about all the things that fascinated her once again – work or news articles about science or astronomy or medicine – and she had rediscovered a social life. It had felt as though their relationship might be back on track, in spite of all the difficulties they'd been through.

But somehow things had then stalled. Michelle now seemed less inclined to talk to him once he made it home in the evenings. And the physical side to their relationship, including basic touch, had not resurfaced. Or at least, not yet.

Jonah was determined to make more of an effort. To compliment her more, encourage her to dress up and go out – because, his friends Roy and Sophie said, she probably felt like little more than a milk and motherhood machine right now. He was also making sure they got time together, however busy work was. He was determined to fix whatever the problem was. To solve it.

But today, watching her out for the count, he was reminded of mornings in a past life when they'd woken together slowly. When they'd had plenty to say to each other, and when she'd looked him in the eye and smiled.

It was for some reason very hard to roll out of bed quietly and leave her without rediscovering that. To put what he knew was right for her ahead of what he suddenly found himself missing badly.

He packed it all away again as he got dressed in the spare room. Work. There was work to do. A killer to find. His team to help.

And there was Milly too. Who so often made him smile, even while she sometimes also reduced him to helpless frustration.

He'd wolfed down coffee and two slices of toast by the time his daughter announced that she was awake a short while later, which was a luxury. He grinned to himself as he went up to fetch her. She'd pulled herself up to a standing position in the cot again, balancing against the bars, and she gave a shout of happiness as he appeared. An undeniably lovely vision that was in no way marred by the fact that she clearly needed a nappy change.

'Hey, Millsybobs,' he said, and lifted her out of the cot. He'd never considered himself the sort of person who would use cute nicknames with a baby, but there was no question that it had happened to him. She was *Millsybobs*, *Dodo*, *Boonut* and pretty much anything else that came to mind.

For some reason, the nicknames made him think, in a dark lurch, of the Bonfire Killer name, and he felt irritated with himself. It wasn't just that it was intruding on his time with his daughter. He had always resisted, strongly, the temptation to make any of these killers legendary. So many serial killers were looking for the kind of validation the press had given this guy. But it was impossible to avoid picking up the name. It was everywhere now, in every news report and on every news presenter's summary. And at least if people remembered it, they would remain on their guard. They might even be looking out for each other.

By the time he made it to the station, he'd cleaned two lots of milk off his shirt and changed three nappies, thanks to Milly having a productive morning. He'd managed to enjoy almost all of it.

'Update me on last night,' he said to his team the moment they were assembled in the large meeting room. One of the few perks of working on a Sunday was having unlimited access to the biggest, most comfortable room, with a window to the outside world.

'Not a huge amount of progress so far,' Ben Lightman told him. 'We visited the pub, spoke to the barman, who didn't have anything to add, and a poll of other staff and patrons produced nobody who was sure they'd seen her. But another staff member agreed there had been a dark-haired woman in her forties at one of the tables early on. We've scouted for CCTV, and it's a bit sparse in that bit of town. But there's one at a cashpoint and another outside the pharmacy.'

Jonah could well imagine the problem. He knew Totton well. His drive from Ashurst to the station each day took him directly through it, and he often used the big Asda for supplies. Totton reached out from the edge of the River Test into the New Forest, its predominantly thirties and forties housing marked out in grids between the main roads. Most of Totton was residential, and the pub Lindsay had been sighted in was right towards the New Forest side. There were only a few scattered shops out there. The chance of picking Lindsay up on cameras was frustratingly slim. Though she'd walked some distance to get to the pub in the first place.

'It's a fair distance from the pub to Lindsay's house,' he said out loud.

'Just over half a mile, chief,' Lightman confirmed immediately.

Jonah grinned. Of course Ben had looked that up and remembered it. It didn't matter that he was only three days out from his father's funeral, Ben was still very much Ben.

'So she might have been given a lift by our perpetrator,' Jonah said.

'Dylan says she's a big walker, though,' Hanson put in. 'Half a mile isn't a lot for someone who likes to walk. Even to go to the pub.'

'True,' Jonah agreed. 'And if she'd arrived on foot and met someone, it might be an excuse for them to offer her a lift home.'

They suspected that Lindsay had got into a car with their perpetrator at some point that evening. The last message she had sent, to her son Dylan, had been at ten fifty-eight p.m. It had pinged the Southampton cellular mast, but from a subtly different direction to the earlier ping, indicating that Lindsay had been closer to where she had been found dead by then. More to the south, towards Lyndhurst. Possibly close to Jonah's own house, which lay just off the route out to Lyndhurst. It gave him a pang of frustration.

That location would not have been Lindsay's own route home, but the message had contained no hint of alarm. Which suggested that she'd been happy to go with the perpetrator somewhere other than her house. Something that Dylan had found very surprising.

'Mum barely socialised,' he'd told them, a few minutes after his arrival at the station yesterday. He had looked grey. Broken. The awful reality of a young man who had seen too little of his mother in recent years, had now lost both his parents, and was facing a world that looked hostile and lonely. 'I've been worried about her but she said she just liked her own company. All these walks on her own, and working on her own mostly too.' He'd given a very ragged breath in. 'Siobhan and I always meant to move back in a while. We said we'd be near her family for a few years, and then move to be near Mum.' He'd swallowed repeatedly, but there had still been tears oozing out of his eyes.

That, Jonah thought, was one of the worst things about what killers did. That guilt they landed on the people left behind. People who weren't ready to lose their loved ones and had so much unfinished business.

He would be seeing Dylan again this morning, to update him on where they stood. Which was, in reality, not much further on than where they'd been yesterday. Lindsay's phone records showed, like Jacqueline's, very few calls and messages back and forth over the past year. There was nothing in her movements to suggest that she'd been seeing a new boyfriend or friend in that time. She seemed, in fact, to spend her time either at home or walking – and although it wasn't possible to prove that this was all undertaken alone, a few selfies that she'd shared with Dylan suggested it had been.

'All right,' he said, once they'd established that there was little else to pass on right now. 'Sounds like I should leave you all to it and do a pastry run.'

Jonah was readying himself to talk to Dylan Kernow once again at just before eleven when Hanson tapped on his door.

'We've got Lindsay on CCTV,' she said with clear

satisfaction. 'At the cashpoint. It's not the best angle but she's there, and she's with someone.'

Jonah moved quickly to join the team at their desks. O'Malley was sitting back in his chair, his expression thoughtful, while Lightman had moved round behind Hanson and was sitting perched against an empty desk.

Hanson settled herself and played the black-and-white clip that was paused on her screen. It showed a very sharply angled view of the pavement in front of the cashpoint from above. The camera was clearly in one corner of a recess, and as Jonah watched, two people walked from right to left in the background. Thanks to the angle, their backs were largely to the camera, and only their heads, shoulders and hips were visible. But one of them had short, dark hair and the black trousers and top they'd found Lindsay Kernow wearing.

He barely had time to register the other figure, who was further from the camera. They were on and off the screen too quickly.

Hanson halted and then rewound the video. This time, as she played it, Jonah saved all his attention for that second figure.

It was definitely a man, he thought. Wearing what looked like a navy sweater and jeans. As well as the poor camera angle and the fact that he was beyond – and partially obscured by – Lindsay, his face was further masked by a cap.

Hanson paused the video, then rewound it frame by frame to the point where the man was on-screen and at his clearest. Which was to say that they could see a flash of the skin of his jaw and neck. Enough to be certain at least that he was white. It looked as though he might be bearded too, though it was hard to tell whether that was a shadow cast by the high collar of his sweater.

'Do we think we can tell hair colour?' Jonah asked. 'Lightish?'

'Maybe mid-brown?' Hanson said. 'There's not much visible under the cap.'

'Height?' Jonah said. 'He doesn't look tall compared to Lindsay.'

'We can do some calculation,' Lightman agreed. 'Though it's not clear from this angle whether he's walking on the pavement or the road at this point. The pavement is quite narrow there so it'll be hard to tell whether he's standing on the pavement or the road, and whether we need to account for the height of the kerb in there. He could be taller.'

Jonah gave a sigh. 'All right. Let's get a range of heights at least. And then get the constables asking folks who live around there if they saw anyone parked up outside, or close to them. See if anyone saw Lindsay and this man walking past. And check ANPR in the Co-op car park too. If we can get a complete list, that's something for them to be working through.'

It was seriously bad luck that there were no ANPR cameras on the Lyndhurst road. With even a rough window of when Lindsay was driven down there, they could have derived a list of suspect vehicles that had passed through it.

But all this was something. It was at least something.

9

Aisling had thought about claiming illness and skipping the meeting at VePlec. Just avoiding any chance of seeing Jack O'Keane, at least for now.

She'd thought, too, about abandoning her role on the board of this firm altogether. There were lots of reasons why that wasn't a bad idea. A paranoid CEO was a pretty terrible start, wasn't it? She didn't want to be involved with that, did she?

But every time she considered bottling it, a small part of her resisted. It pushed back with a feeling that she was being ridiculous. That this was her *job*, and she wasn't going to let any man get in the way of that.

And hidden away in that other part of her was a small, treacherous ache to see him. To see Jack O'Keane face to face for the first time in years and let all the past come crashing down on her.

Which was just as ridiculous as the part that yearned to hide. What did she want out of him? Absolution? For him to still care about her?

She'd promised herself that she'd leave well alone after that one time that she'd crumbled and looked him up on Facebook. The feeling she'd had seeing his wedding photos to a glorious-looking woman with blonde ringlets had made it clear that she needed to shut that whole train of curiosity down.

It was only late on Sunday night that she finally gave in to the temptation to hunt him down online once again. She'd had three full days of her thoughts bouncing between her father, her mother, Tullamore . . . and Jack. It had been too much in the end.

And so she'd gone on Facebook again, under her assumed name, knowing that she had access she shouldn't have had. She'd added a socialite friend from school years before, who'd accepted her with no idea who she actually was and had presumably forgotten about her. That had given her full access to Jack's profile as a friend of a friend.

She found herself staring at his profile picture this time, and realised that his profile had a lot more privacy controls these days. She sighed, guessing it was only natural, now that he was a private investigator. There were only a few photos: a profile picture, and a few previous profile and cover photo updates on display.

The images were all of Jack on his own, not that this told her much. She clicked on the most recent one, and it filled half the screen. She felt as though she'd been sucker-punched.

Jack had barely changed. True, he was more lined. His skin rougher-looking and his hairline a different shape. True, too, that he had more hollowed cheekbones now and a five o'clock shadow, plus a pair of Ray-Bans the old Jack would never have considered. But he was still Jack in spite of that. Still the dimpled, cheerful boy who had pursued her despite her dowdy dresses and her lack of experience of TV, alcohol and cigarettes. The boy who had first introduced her to gaming. The first boy she had ever loved, and the one it had broken her heart to leave behind on that terrible, urgent night.

She minimised it and scrolled down through the other photos again, looking for some suggestion of his wife.

Perhaps of kids. But there were so few images and they were largely of running events and nice scenery.

It doesn't matter, she thought. *His marital status is none of your business.*

The exercise had only made her anxiety worse. She'd barely slept, and felt ragged today. She didn't know what it was that had propelled her all the way here, to Holborn, with her smart black trousers and striped jacket. But whatever it was, it had deposited her here, now, at the offices of VePlec. And as one of the sales team buzzed her in she felt genuinely dizzy.

She didn't see Jack anywhere as she darted her eyes around the closest part of the open-plan office. She didn't see him as she was let into the boardroom either. He wasn't sitting in with them, and as the door was closed, she allowed herself to breathe.

She felt off her game and slow as the meeting went on, but having strong opinions about the market positioning of the game, Aisling made sure to voice them. And although the CEO looked affronted by her suggestions, she could see nods and consideration from the others, and even a warm smile from the young man who ran their marketing. And then, somehow, the meeting was over, and she was out and free. With just the gauntlet of the office to run again.

She could feel her adrenaline rising once more as the marketing director held the door for her. But a quick scan of all the faces at desks showed no sign of Jack. Everyone here was younger. Different.

She turned to say goodbye to the rest of the board with a feeling of relief strangely tinged with disappointment, and then heard, from just round the corner, an unmistakable Tullamore brogue.

'Hey, Nick, are we doing the plotting meeting at two still?'

Aisling turned away, panic coursing through her.

'Yeah, that's at two,' she heard the CEO replying. And then the words she was dreading, 'Have you met our external board member, Aisling?'

In a scramble, she pulled her phone out and jammed it to her ear, then half turned to flash an apologetic smile at the CEO. She pointed towards the door, as though an emergency had just struck, and then began to hurry away.

She had a momentary impression of Jack's form, his feet planted and his expression faintly surprised. *Please don't recognise me*, she thought.

It would only have been the briefest view of her face. There couldn't have been time for him to work out who she was.

'Ahhh . . .' she could hear him saying, as she pushed the green button on the door to escape. 'Aisling, you said?'

'Yeah, you might know her name? She created *Survive the Light* . . .'

The door swung open and Aisling all but ran out, her heart pounding.

She couldn't believe that, thirty years on, she was running out on Jack O'Keane without an explanation all over again. But despite a rush of guilt, she realised that there was no part of her that was strong enough to stay and face him.

IO

Jonah knew the moment Ben Lightman knocked on his door that the DNA results were through, and he'd rarely had a more welcome piece of news.

The investigation into Lindsay Kernow's murder felt like it was going the same way as their attempt to solve Jacqueline Clarke's. Lead after lead had proved to be false or unfruitful. Nobody had, it seemed, seen Lindsay or the man who'd probably killed her walking through Totton. They estimated that she'd left the pub between ten forty and ten fifty, and those who weren't still in bars or at parties at that point were at home watching the *Hootenanny* or the build-up to the fireworks. Only a handful were moving between venues, and most of those were seriously drunk. There was nothing to give them a lead on the vehicle and, infuriatingly, no other CCTV to help them.

Circulating the image from the cashpoint had provided a series of time-consuming tip-offs from the public. Every individual suggested to them had turned out to be either provably elsewhere that night or to lack obvious access to a vehicle. A few of them remained on their interesting persons list, but none of the team were convinced. In each case the tip-off had been anonymous, vague and based on very little.

But this, today, was a result. Some kind of a match for the blood. Actual evidence.

He found himself getting up to join his team with a feeling of real nervousness. This could be just what they needed.

Ben had set them up in one of the smaller meeting rooms with the Globalry website ready to view on O'Malley's laptop. He also had his own laptop to one side with Microsoft Teams open. Jonah was pleased to note that Cassie Logan was already on screen, looking efficient and capable in her thick black glasses.

Hanson and O'Malley came to stand alongside him, and Ben nodded for Cassie to start.

'OK,' Cassie said. 'The headline news is that we have what the site identifies as one fourth cousin and one third cousin once removed.'

Jonah nodded, feeling a fizz of disappointment that the results hadn't provided anyone closer.

'Are they on opposite sides of the family?' he asked, remembering what Cassie had said about the ease of finding someone if they could match a maternal and paternal relative.

'Unfortunately these are both maternal,' Cassie said. 'But that just means a little work to narrow down our person of interest.'

Jonah felt a further slump. That work would take time. Much longer than the few hours it might have taken if they'd been on opposite sides of the family.

'Are either of them local?' O'Malley asked. 'To here, I mean.'

'Actually,' Cassie said, 'one isn't that far from me. Syracuse, New York State. That's the third cousin once removed.'

Jonah nodded, not sure what to make of that.

'The other is in Limerick, Ireland,' she said, glancing at her own screen. 'But that doesn't mean they aren't in touch with a family member who lives near you. Let's see what they have to say.'

'OK,' Jonah said. 'Thanks.'

Once Cassie had rung off, Jonah turned to his team with a small smile. 'Even if she ends up with a very long list of names, it could be useful,' he said. 'And in the meantime let's push on with every other line of inquiry we have. Have the uniforms fielded any new calls today?'

'A couple,' Hanson said. 'One of them seems potentially non-crazy but also not necessarily that helpful. A woman who is pretty confident she saw Lindsay walking down Monkton Lane at around seven. She was heading east, so into town. She's confident Lindsay was alone. And, having looked into it, that means she either would have turned up Briarwood Road after that, or gone around the looping path that would eventually take her to Gradigge Way. We can check if anyone saw her along those specific routes. See if she met anyone while she was walking. But, as we've agreed, it seems more likely from the bartender's statement that she met someone at the pub.'

Jonah nodded. 'We'll take a statement from her anyway.'

It wasn't a lot, he thought, heavily. He hoped Cassie would come through somehow.

It was just after six when Lightman reappeared at his office door. During the interval, Jonah had talked with Dylan Kernow, relieved to note that even the smallest promise of some DNA progress had given him a little life back. Jonah had then looked over O'Malley's original report into crimes that might be related to Jacqueline Clarke's murder, wondering once again with a feeling of edgy anxiety whether there had been earlier victims. Victims from a time before their killer had perfected his methods. He had also managed to call home to speak to Michelle. He'd been able to make a few positive noises about being likely to be home before long.

'It's not a disaster if not,' Michelle had told him. 'Sabrina's free tonight. Rhona's got Milly so we'll get shit-faced if you can't make it and then hate ourselves tomorrow.'

There was a moment when he could have asked her to be careful. Without new leads, the story of the Bonfire Killer had inevitably slid from the headlines. There was only so much that could be rehashed. And with that slide Jonah could already see everyone beginning to relax. It was only natural, he thought. Without someone telling them to be afraid, people would find themselves distracted by other things.

It was hard for Jonah because he felt an ever-increasing anxiety. To him, the passage of time only made another killing more likely. He never wanted to lay too much on hunches, but it felt to him as though another attempt was an inevitability. He was braced to hear about a death, and to feel the terrible failure of not having done enough. But he was also weary, and as much afraid of pushing Michelle as he'd been when Lindsay's body had first been discovered. He wanted to go home and find a warm welcome waiting for him. And he knew his best chance was to let Michelle do the things that made her happy.

After a long pause, he told Michelle to have a good time, and then rang off. He returned to his work slowly.

Ben's tap on the door came as he was contemplating going home. His weariness evaporated in an instant as he caught, in Ben's usually unreadable face, a gleam of excitement.

'Cassie's called back,' he said. 'She's got a new development.'

Jonah followed him with a lurching feeling of hope, and his best deadpan expression in case this turned out not to mean anything. They all assembled once again in the small meeting room, with Cassie already poised. She was a little closer to the screen this time. Even more alert.

'Hi again,' she said with a wry grin. 'So I wasn't expecting to get back to you all so soon, but while I was starting work on our two cousins, I received a notification of a new match through the site.'

She looked between them all for a moment, checking that they'd all understood.

'So that's ... someone else's DNA that was recently uploaded?' Hanson asked.

'Exactly,' Cassie said. 'And it must have been uploaded within a few days of when we sent ours in, which is pretty staggering.'

'Is this person from the other side of the family? The paternal side?' Jonah asked, leaning forwards.

'No,' Cassie said. 'But that's not the headline. The big news is that it's a close relative. As in, extremely close. Whoever uploaded that DNA is our perp's mother or sister or daughter.'

11

17 January

'So we're looking at three people,' Jonah said, as Ben paused in his briefing.

They'd managed to bag the big meeting room again this morning, largely because it was a Saturday and most of the other officers working today were the DCs and constables co-opted onto their case. Four of their expanded team were in here with them, two of them studiously taking notes and the other two nodding along.

There was a palpable sense of excitement in the air. Three and a half months after Jacqueline Clarke's death they finally, finally had a list of suspects.

'Three people,' Ben agreed. 'Just her father and two sons, as far as we can make out. The two sons live with her, and we've got a pair of constables already in place watching each of them. We'll keep them under observation until I've been able to speak with the mother in person.'

Jonah nodded, somewhat taken aback by how quickly the team had managed to move on this. When he'd left the previous evening, they'd only just got the full name of the woman who'd uploaded the DNA. He felt, if he were honest with himself, both proud of his team and a little redundant.

'Interesting age profiles on the three,' O'Malley muttered. 'A man of sixty-two, a nineteen-year-old and a seventeen-year-old.'

'Not quite the kind of people you'd expect to go picking

up forty-something women from bars, are they?' Hanson asked. 'The sixty-two-year-old father is more likely, I think. Women do tend to date in an older age bracket in general. Particularly if they come across as well-moneyed or sophisticated.'

'What about the seventeen-year-old?' Jonah asked. 'Do we think he'd really be able to talk someone of forty-eight into leaving with him?'

'It seems less likely, but I guess it depends on confidence,' Hanson said with a shrug. 'And maybe on how it was done. He could have persuaded her that he needed help of some kind. Told her his mum was away and he was lonely . . .'

Jonah gave a thoughtful nod. 'OK. Some possibilities.'

'Just to clarify on the DNA,' O'Malley said, raising a hand, 'a half-sibling wouldn't be enough of a match, would they? So if this Aisling Cooley's father had some illegitimate son she doesn't know about, he's not of interest. It's just those three.'

'Exactly,' Ben agreed. 'The DNA matches too closely for a half-sibling. It can only be a full sibling. So a father, son or full brother of Aisling Cooley.'

'How are we getting on with tracking down the father?' Jonah asked.

'Slightly less well,' Ben admitted. 'She's registered him on the site as being called Dara Cooley, and her mother as Dymphna. We know that two people of that name lived in Hordle until 1989, when Dymphna died and the house was sold. The house was fully in her name. We haven't got any record of Dara buying anywhere nearby, and looking further afield we can't seem to find him at present. But there's no death certificate recorded for him either, so presumably he's around. We may have to wait to ask her any more.'

'We've asked Cassie Logan not to interrogate Aisling

Cooley at all prior to the in-person meeting,' Jonah interjected, glancing around at his expanded team. 'As far as Aisling is concerned at this point, Cassie has uploaded the DNA on behalf of someone called Ben, who wants to talk with her. Anything else risks her warning the three of them off.'

'I guess we can safely assume she doesn't know they were involved,' O'Malley commented. 'Or she'd not have risked uploading the DNA.'

'Unless she wants them caught,' Hanson replied, 'and had to find a way that didn't involve it being apparently deliberate. Fear of retribution.'

'Wouldn't want to assume either way,' Jonah said with a half-smile.

'Obviously,' Hanson said with a grin. 'Assumption being the father of all muck-ups.'

'That's the one,' Jonah agreed. 'What's the situation like at home?' he asked Ben. 'Between the mother and two sons.'

'Ben asked me to look into that,' O'Malley said. 'I've put a report up on the database, but, broad brushstrokes, it's a single-parent family after the dad ran off with someone else. Aisling is presumably well off. She created a video game called *Survive the Light*, which she sold to Sony back in 2002.'

'Seriously?' Hanson asked. 'Even I've heard of that.'

'I haven't,' O'Malley said cheerfully, 'but let's assume I should have. The father, Stephen Pagonis, seems to have moved abroad. He left when the older son would have been four and the younger one two. Divorce finalised three years later. Interestingly, looking him up provides a company address which is the same as an accountancy firm we know to have worked with some extremely nasty people, which could suggest that he's dodgy. But it could also be that he got recommended by someone dodgy.'

'Interesting. Any contact between them now?' Jonah asked.

'Hard to know,' O'Malley said. 'But their social media accounts would suggest not. No photos of them together, they're not connected, and the boys aren't connected with him either.'

'Any sign of another partner on the scene for Aisling?' Hanson asked.

'Nothing I could scout out,' O'Malley answered.

'How about the sons? Do we know much about them?'

'Both public-school educated nearby,' he said. 'Older one, Ethan, now working in a record shop. Plays in a band which seems to be his career of choice. Younger one is still at school. A prefect, but also a county tennis champion.'

'Hmm,' Hanson said. 'Privileged boys used to getting away with things, with a father who clearly no takes no responsibility for his actions as a role model.'

'Plenty to think about,' Jonah agreed. 'OK. Let's keep close tabs on them and see what else we can dig up.'

12

Hanson volunteered to help tail Finn Cooley home from tennis training. The points in the day where they were required to actively follow the two boys were being covered by detectives rather than uniformed officers. It was purely about practicality. Plain-clothes officers were a lot less noticeable.

The DCI had suggested that their co-opted DCs should cover the duties but Hanson had been keen to lay eyes on at least one of the boys. She wanted, quite fiercely, to know what they were like. Whether one of them really seemed capable of killing. And so she found herself sitting outside the tennis courts with one of the more likeable constables from DCI Acharya's team in a comfortable BMW with heated seats, wondering exactly why everyone seemed to have a nicer car than she had.

The drive over had produced a feeling of frustration in her. Two weeks after Lindsay's murder, people seemed to be forgetting about it. She'd seen woman after woman walking alone in the early dusk, two of them with headphones in.

In a few days they might be safe to behave like that once again, as far as the Bonfire Killer was concerned. He might even be under observation already. But even if they had eyes on the killer right now, there were others out there. There always were, something Hanson had only really understood since she'd joined the force. The current biggest threat might be the Bonfire Killer, and her goal might be to arrest him and get him off the streets, but nobody could ever really afford to be complacent. To assume that they were safe.

Though she wondered, as Casho parked up, whether that feeling of endless threat had partly been caused by her ex-boyfriend's actions over the past year. God knew she'd had reason to jump at shadows in that time.

She did her best to put the feeling aside and talk to her fellow DC. The two of them chatted for a while about the DNA, and then about the chief – who Casho had decided she wanted to work for in the long run, which Hanson understood but also felt a little jealous over – and then about whether the whole team should try to do some socialising together. And just after that Casho idly asked about Ben, and whether he was single.

Hanson found herself saying, before she'd really thought it out, 'Oh, he's involved in something a bit complicated, I think. Probably best to give him some space for a while.'

'Oh, cool,' Casho said. 'Yeah, I mean, I wasn't really asking for me.' Then, after a pause, she grinned at Hanson and said, 'He is fit, though, isn't he?'

Hanson laughed and changed the subject, wondering whether she'd done the right thing. Ben wasn't in the headspace to have anyone hitting on him just now, was he? Even nice, upbeat Casho. He'd had a huge amount to deal with. Not just with the death of his father, but in the longer term with what she now knew to have been trauma from sexual abuse as a child.

It was going to take a lot of work for Ben to feel comfortable in a relationship, she thought. A woman – his piano teacher, in fact – who he'd thought himself in love with had so profoundly abused his trust, and he'd felt utterly unable to tell anyone. He needed time to go through the therapy and get everything straight. Didn't he?

She was still spinning this over in her head when Finn Cooley emerged from the courts, illuminated by the floodlights around their perimeter. He'd put a tight-fitting red cycling jacket over his tennis shirt, and wore thermals under his tennis shorts, but he looked red-cheeked and warm. His breath turned to vapour in the air with each exhalation.

'He looks strong,' Casho murmured.

'He does,' Hanson agreed, looking over the wiry, athletic build of him.

But strong enough to carry a woman's body and dump it on a pyre? It was harder to carry a dead weight than anyone realised, and however that body had been carried, it had been done without any signs of dragging.

Finn paused on the grass between the courts and the pavement, and pulled out his phone. He spent a moment pressing buttons, and then held it up to his ear.

She watched him speak into the mouthpiece, wishing she could get close enough to hear what he said. She leaned forwards in the car – and then froze, as Finn turned his head, and looked straight towards her.

'Has he seen us?' Casho breathed.

Everything about Finn's body had gone still. He simply watched them, unmoving. And then, he suddenly turned and began walking across the grass, to join the road further up.

'Did he see us?' Casho asked.

'I don't know,' Hanson said. Surely it would be all but impossible. The lights had been reflecting off the windscreen. That and they had the advantage of the darkness inside the car.

And yet she'd felt pinned, like prey when a hunter has seen it. And the thought made her skin crawl.

Hanson had returned to the station by the time the call came in. It rang on the team's desk, and Lightman picked it up while she was still dumping her bag and scarf onto her chair.

She watched Ben's expression as he answered, and caught

the faint change that said that this was something important. The chief, emerging from his office for what was presumably an update, seemed to sense it too. He hovered alongside Lightman's desk until he was done.

'The desk sergeant passed through a call about a pyre,' he said. 'It doesn't sound like a time-waster to me. The guy says it was set not far from his stud farm, and it had burned itself almost out by the time he got there. He had the local police in and they agreed it was a well-laid fire with some kind of an accelerant used but they didn't link it to our case, because instead of burning a woman, they burned a horse.' He paused for a moment, and then added, 'A mare.'

13

The stud farm owners were clearly keen on security. Though whether that was a direct result of finding one of their horses burned on a pyre, Hanson had no way of knowing. Ben had to stop his Qashqai at a large metal gate across the road, and a hundred yards beyond it they could see a second, solid-steel gate across what must have been the entrance to the stable yard.

A big, bear-like figure in wellies, jeans and a fleece made his way over to them. He had his hand up to shield his face from the headlights until Ben dimmed them. When he lowered the hand, it was to reveal a dark head of hair and a cropped beard. More *Lord of the Rings* than hipster, Hanson thought.

'We're with Hampshire Constabulary,' he called. 'I think you have a crime scene for us to look at?'

The bear-like man nodded and reached out to press a button next to the gatepost. The gates swung inwards slowly, and Ben slid back in to drive through. The figure walked alongside them, gesturing for them to stop in the wide paved area in front of a second set of gates. These stood open, showing a stable yard beyond.

Hanson could make out a large farmhouse off to the right, and low stable blocks on the other side. The gates stood between a jutting-out part of the farmhouse and one set of stables. If those gates had been shut, it would have been challenging to get a horse in and out.

'DS Ben Lightman,' Ben said, the moment they'd climbed

out of the car. 'We spoke on the phone. This is DC Juliette Hanson.'

'Danny Murphy,' the big guy said, reaching out and shaking hands briefly without eye contact. 'Thanks for coming.' He cast a doubtful look at their shiny black shoes, and asked, 'Have you got better footwear?'

Hanson grinned at him. 'We brought boots. And torches and coats. Scene of crime should be here in a few minutes, and they'll set up lighting and collect evidence. But we'd like to talk through how they got in and then take a look.'

'All right,' Danny said.

'So were there signs of forced entry?'

'Ahhh, no,' Danny said, sounding reluctant. Hanson caught a swift glance towards the stable yard before he said, 'One of the team accidentally left the door to the stables unlocked at this end. It looks like someone climbed over the gate and walked in there, and then just unbolted the door at the far end onto the paddock.'

'Was it this closest block?' Hanson asked, nodding towards the stables to the left of the gate.

'Yeah,' Danny said. 'The foaling block. It's where we house the mares who are about to give birth.'

Hanson was about to ask about CCTV when there was the sound of a door opening. She could hear uneven footsteps echoing through the door to the yard.

'I thought we were done with you people,' a hoarse voice called, just before a shorter, slighter and much older version of Danny emerged through the door. He limped on what looked to Hanson like a frozen ankle, but he covered the distance between them rapidly enough in spite of it.

Ben took a step forwards, but before he could introduce himself, the older man drew to a stop and said loudly, 'It's late, and my staff need to sleep.'

Danny turned towards him. He looked, Hanson thought, more than a little anxious.

'Glad to meet you,' Ben said at that point, holding out his hand. 'Mr . . .'

'Murphy,' the older man said. 'I'm Michael Murphy, and last time I looked, I owned this bloody place. I didn't ask for more of you to come tramping over here.'

'It's OK, Dad,' Danny said, his voice soothing. 'They're just a different department. They think what happened might be related to some other crimes.'

'What other crimes?' His father's eyes were on Danny now, sharp and intense. He turned to Ben, and asked, 'Have there been other horse killings?'

'There have been murders,' Lightman said calmly. 'And if the murders and the killing of your horse have been committed by the same person, it's important that we look a lot more carefully at the scene.'

'Oh, I *see*,' Michael Murphy said with heavy irony. Even with the light behind him and the obscuring beard, Hanson could tell that he was smiling, and not humorously. 'So while it's just the theft and killing of my animals, it's not worth your time.'

'I'm afraid our team is only working this particular investigation at the moment,' Ben answered, unfazed as always. 'It was a different team that came to see you earlier. Either way, we're very keen to stop any more attacks on your animals.'

Mr Murphy gave Lightman a piercing look, but faced with total calm he seemed to deflate a little.

'You should be looking at the stalls,' he said. 'Work out how they got in.'

Hanson glanced towards Danny. He'd seemed to know exactly how it had happened. Had he not told his father?

Ben nodded. 'We will.'

There was a silence, while Mr Murphy shifted from foot to foot, and then without another word, he turned and walked away. Danny waited until he'd shut the farmhouse door before he nodded to them both in what looked like relief.

'Get your boots on, and let's go before he comes back out.'

A fine rain started not much later. It was, Hanson thought, impressively dark out here. Living in the city it was so easy to forget what real darkness, uninterrupted by street lights over the horizon, felt like. They were far enough from Minstead and the larger Lyndhurst to be free of light pollution, particularly given the woodlands that surrounded the stud farm. Even with flashlights, it was difficult to see whether their next steps would be onto flat ground or into a hole.

It was darker still under the trees. Between the three flashlights, Hanson felt as though she was only seeing snapshots of everything. They probably should have waited for scene of crime.

There wasn't much to see anyway. The fire had done its work. Though, somewhat heartbreakingly, the horse's hooves and shoes had largely made it through intact. The fire hadn't been quite large enough to encompass the creature's whole body.

They were big beasts, Hanson thought to herself. Bigger than she might have expected, and perhaps bigger than the person who'd made the fire had understood. 'How easy would it be for someone to lead a horse away?' she asked, her eyes on the charred remains. 'Would they go willingly with just anyone?'

'Some would,' Danny Murphy told her. There was a pause, while he looked like he was thinking. She got the impression that Danny Murphy thought quite carefully about everything. 'Some would make a fuss. Merivel was pretty easy-going. It's probably why she was the one they took.' He shook his head. 'From the CCTV it looks like she went willingly. They'd have had to drug her before burning her, though. She'd have fought her way off a bonfire harder than any man could do anything about.'

Hanson nodded, thinking of the ketamine in Lindsay Kernow's system. They needed to look at the farm's CCTV. And get everyone at the farm to look too. Danny had already told them on the way across the paddock that it was hard to see anything distinctive about the horse thief from the CCTV. They'd been well covered by nondescript clothing and a hat with a hood.

But it seemed such an unlikely piece of luck, their perpetrator just happening upon an unlocked door. Hanson felt it more likely that this had been done by someone who knew the stud farm. Maybe even the horses. Someone here might recognise them even if Danny hadn't.

'She wouldn't go with just anyone, though?' she pressed. 'You'd guess the person who took her knew how to handle a horse?'

Danny nodded, his dark eyes touched by anger. 'They had to halter her up to do it, and they led her out like they'd done it before. Hands in the right place, confident gait.' He shook his head.

'Would that take more than just lessons? Would they need to work with horses?'

'Not working with them, no. Not necessarily. But I'd say they must have ridden for a while at least.'

Hanson could see that this information bothered him. She guessed that it seemed like a betrayal. That someone could know animals and still do this. Or maybe he was thinking the same thing she was: that this had been done by someone who knew the stud farm well.

'Were they wearing gloves?' Lightman asked, from a little way away. 'Could you see on the video?'

'Oh . . . yeah, they were,' Danny said. 'Black ones. It was quite clear on the video. Are you thinking fingerprints?'

Ben gave a nod.

'OK, maybe not,' Danny said.

She pulled out her phone and tapped everything Danny had told them into some notes for the chief, and then another thought occurred to her. 'You didn't see any vehicles out here?' she asked. 'Earlier in the evening maybe?'

Danny shook his head, but then said, 'I – I told the police who came earlier . . . They didn't bring the wood for the pyre tonight. It's been here for a couple of weeks.'

Hanson had been poised ready to take a note, but she stopped at that. 'It was here before?'

'Yeah,' Danny said. 'It must have been early January it turned up. I saw someone out here with a torch late on and came out to have a look. By the time I got here, they'd gone, but they'd left the wood. I'm pretty sure it had just been put there. I kept an eye after that, but they didn't seem to come back for it and it isn't actually our land beyond the fence.'

She was aware of Ben treading carefully round the perimeter of the fire. His eyes were on the ground, following the light of his torch.

It wasn't opportunistic, Hanson thought. *This spot was planned.*

But would their killer really have gone to so much trouble to plan the death of a horse? It seemed more likely that the horse had been a replacement for the killing of a woman that hadn't gone to plan. And yet they'd known enough to get into the stables and take her.

'It'd be great to see the CCTV footage,' she told Danny. 'Let's take a look back at the farm, and then we can upload it to our system.'

'I – sure,' Danny said.

There was movement from somewhere outside their pools of light, and Hanson spun, her flashlight moving and then steadying. It lit up a young man with Danny's height and muscular build. He had a hand thrown over his face, protecting his eyes from the glare.

'Sorry, just me.'

Hanson lowered the flashlight, as Danny said, 'My brother. Antony.'

Hanson took a moment to look at the brother. Aside from his physique, he didn't bear a very strong resemblance to Danny. His light hair was in contrast to the absolute black of Danny's, and he was clean-shaven rather than neatly bearded.

'Everything OK?' Danny asked.

'Yeah,' Antony said. 'Fine. I just wanted to come and . . . see what was happening.'

'Is Henning still in the yard?'

'Yeah. He says he's waiting for the forensics guys?' He glanced over at the pyre and away. Hanson saw him shiver. 'Alison's going to stay in the yard to keep an eye while he brings them over.'

Danny nodded. He seemed to relax a little at this and Hanson wondered whether he'd been worried for his father or the horses.

'God, there's – there's not a lot left of her, is there?' Antony said, his face towards the pyre.

Hanson couldn't see much of his face now that she'd pointed her flashlight back at the ground, but Danny's brother sounded deeply upset by what he was seeing. As she shifted the torch, she caught a faint gleam from his eyes.

'You don't have to be here,' Danny said. It was gruff, but Hanson strongly suspected that it was meant kindly.

'No, I know. Sorry.' Antony took a slightly shaky breath. 'I just . . . I'm glad you're looking into it.'

'Was she a favourite of yours?' Hanson asked gently.

'Ah, you end up loving all of them,' Antony said. 'But – she'd had a hard time in labour. And . . . issues with her colt. It's pretty sad, knowing the foal won't get a chance at being mothered.'

'Except by Antony,' Danny said dryly.

'I'll do my best,' his brother said.

Ben came into Hanson's field of vision once again. He had moved inwards a little, working towards the edge of the fire. 'You said the horse was led away in harness but I can't see any sign of a halter. You'd expect some metal remaining. But there's nothing. Did they go back to the farm and leave it there?'

Danny shook his head. 'No, they didn't return after taking Merivel.'

'Why would they take it with them?' Lightman asked.

Hanson frowned. 'Did they bring it? The halter? Was there any sign of that in the footage?'

Danny was looking at the fire himself, his eyes searching it. 'He – he or she – had a string bag over a shoulder. It was bulky enough for a halter.'

Hanson let out a breath. This hadn't been a replacement for a human victim; it had been the plan. The horse had, for some reason, been his choice of victim.

Maybe killing Lindsay spooked him, she thought. *Maybe that pyre not burning has scared him.*

If you were someone with a constant itch to kill and to burn women, perhaps a brood mare offered a substitute. A way of keeping the desire in check while you worked out how to avoid making mistakes again.

Assuming, of course, that this *had* been done by the same killer. That this really was another Bonfire Killer pyre. But so much of it seemed the same. The care taken. The heat the fire must have achieved. The location.

Another pyre within a few miles of Aisling Cooley's house, she thought, with a sudden chill.

She wrote a swift addition to her notes, and then went over to Ben. 'Are the uniforms still watching the Cooley house?' she asked quietly.

Lightman nodded. 'They'll be watching the two sons right up until the samples are taken and analysed.'

'Good,' Hanson said. 'That's good.'

Though it was a shame they hadn't been watching them last night, when Merivel was taken and burned. They would have known for sure about two of their suspects, then. And despite Lightman's reassurance, she still felt on edge the whole time they were at the stud farm. The anxiety added to her discomfort as she grew wetter and colder, the rain even soaking through the proper outdoor clothing she was wearing this time.

It would have helped, she thought, if Michael Murphy had been a little more hospitable. Danny had attempted to make them all hot drinks, but had apparently been chased out of the farmhouse by his father.

By the time they finished up at almost one a.m., Hanson was about as cold and miserable as she'd ever been on a job.

'Where's the nearest services?' she asked Ben, as they made their way back towards the Qashqai. 'I could murder a bloody Starbucks.'

'We can go by the twenty-four-hour one on the motorway,' Ben offered.

It was only once they'd neared the stable block again and the security light flicked on that she saw something sitting on the bonnet of the Qashqai. A shiny, new-looking Star-bucks thermos flask.

The two of them drew closer, and somehow she wasn't surprised when she saw that there was a paper Starbucks sticker on it. It was sodden with rain. The word 'Juliette' was still clear, though, written in thick black marker pen. And underneath it, the slightly harder to read words 'from your guardian angel'.

14

19 January

Hanson arrived at CID at seven, having run the three miles from her home. Sleep had been almost impossible, even after a large glass of wine. Her mind had ricocheted from thoughts of the thermos and note, to Damian and whether it was really his style. In the few moments when she'd been able to stop going over it all, her brain had snapped her back to that damp, miserable pyre, and from there to Lindsay Kernow and Jacqueline Clarke.

It was impossible not to wonder whether the strange little acts of kindness had been done by someone other than Damian. As much as the rational side of her wanted to laugh at the idea, she had to acknowledge that there was someone else who might be interested in following her to a series of crime scenes: and that was the person who had set up those crime scenes.

She could see that this idea had occurred to Ben, too. He'd slid gloves on and bagged up the thermos flask and then insisted on escorting her into her house. He'd offered to sleep downstairs, too, but Hanson had immediately told him she'd be fine, and that he needed his sleep. She'd then turned away hot with embarrassment, but Ben had as usual seemed unworried. Before leaving, he'd checked the locks on all the doors and insisted that she add him to a speed-dial shortcut on her phone.

For the first time in her career, Hanson felt as though she

was doing more than simply protecting others with her work. It felt as though she was putting herself in harm's way.

She tried to imagine each of their three suspects choosing to do this to her. Would either of Aisling's sons want to? They could both drive, even if Finn's licence was provisional, and could potentially have evaded the constables watching them. Or was this the work of Aisling's father, the missing man who was still in the shadows?

Running to work this morning was, of course, riskier than driving. She was making her way down largely empty streets in pre-dawn darkness, her running light her only illumination. And it was highly likely that whoever her self-appointed guardian angel was, he knew where she lived. But Hanson had already endured months of stalking from her ex-boyfriend and had felt her life shrinking. She'd stopped running outside or even going out shopping alone, and begun jumping at every tiniest sound. Once she'd finally turned everything round on Damian, she'd vowed to stop being that person. She was done being cowed.

And if it is the Bonfire Killer, she thought, breathlessly, *then we might have him pinned down soon.*

And that, at least, was a consoling thought. Today was the day that Ben was to meet Aisling Cooley. It was also the day when Aisling's two sons, and hopefully her father, were to be arrested – in an amicable and discreet fashion – in order to obtain a DNA swab.

This arrest, swab and release-pending-results pattern was growing more and more common in modern-day policing. So much crime was now solved using forensic evidence rather than relying on witnesses and interviews. Where once every suspect would have been interviewed and evidence gathered long before making an arrest, to give them as much time as possible to build their case before they ran out of time to charge, it now often happened that someone was brought in under arrest based on their DNA or some other purely factual evidence.

The team would know, without doubt, which of Aisling's family was their likely perpetrator within a mere four hours. That meant it was a much safer course of action to arrest them before swabbing. They would then keep them under the tightest observation during the four hours they would be waiting for results. If any of the three ran, they would then do so as fugitives.

But before any of that, Hanson wanted to work at connecting one of the Cooleys with the stud farm out at Minstead. She had gone to sleep full of the certainty that the brood mare had been killed by the Bonfire Killer, and that it meant something.

She knew that they'd be pulled into a briefing the moment the DCI arrived at the station, and that they'd have to talk through the thermos flask and the coat and her car being dragged out of the mud, too. That meant she needed to get her head down and work first. So she went straight to change out of her running clothes once she'd made it to CID, not taking any time to be relieved at having got there in one piece, and refusing to glance out of the huge windows as she crossed back from the bathroom to check if anyone was watching her.

Ben gave her a piercing look once he'd arrived, and asked, 'No other weird events?'

'Nothing except me mysteriously having no clean socks,' she said with a wry smile.

Ben frowned at her wet hair. 'Did you run here?'

'I needed the cardio,' she said with a slight heat in her cheeks.

Ben hesitated before saying, 'Do you think it might be an idea to . . . avoid running alone? Just for now?'

Hanson let out a sigh. 'Maybe. But it's a bit shit, isn't it?'

'If you mean running is a bit shit, then yes,' Ben said. 'Yes, it is.'

Hanson laughed, and then gave him a more serious nod. 'I'll try the gym tomorrow. Unless we've caught him by then.'

'Good plan.'

Having made tea for both of them, Hanson loaded up her desktop machine and started looking into the stud farm where the pyre had been found. She kept coming back to the thought that the killer could be familiar with the stud farm itself. They had known where to go to find the horses, as well as how to lure one of them away, and had somehow arrived on the one night when the door to the stable block had been left unlocked. They'd managed to review the CCTV, too, and Hanson felt there had been a look of purpose to the way the figure had jumped over the fence and gone to the door of the stables.

Before doing anything else, she sent a quick email over to Danny Murphy, asking him if he had any of the CCTV from the past few weeks available to send over too, and also asking for a list of their current and former staff members. She thought about offering an explanation, and then decided that no explanation at all was probably the better option. It was a professional query that he might interpret how he liked.

After that, she scoured any online mentions of Finn and Ethan Cooley to see if either of them had any links with the stud farm. Nothing came up, and so she looked, next, to see if either of them had ever ridden horses. There was nothing in their social media about that, or any articles online, but absence of evidence didn't mean evidence of absence.

Hanson decided to move on to look at the folks at the farm, noting that she was feeling a lot less jittery already. Work was always the best distraction.

She already had the names of the owners of the stud farm:

Michael Murphy, and his sons Antony and Danny, plus one of the stable hands, Henning Andersen. Was there a chance that Michael Murphy or Henning Andersen was really Dara Cooley?

It wasn't hard to find out about either of them, luckily. Henning Andersen, the stable hand who'd left the door unlocked, had grown up in Denmark but had been born near Newbury, to a family with quite a bit of English blood in it. As a result, he was entitled to a British passport and had used it to move back over here some two years ago. He was also only thirty-three, not remotely old enough to be Dara Cooley, and his parentage proved fairly conclusively that he couldn't be some unknown child of Dara's who was helping him to steal horses.

She felt as though that probably put Henning well into the clear, though like the chief she wasn't going to absolutely rule anyone in or out. Moving on to Michael Murphy, however, she found her heart rate increasing slightly.

Michael Murphy was, it emerged, Irish. He'd gained British citizenship in 1981. The clue had been in his voice, she realised. The brogue had still been there as he'd barked at them. And Michael Murphy really hadn't wanted them there looking at the pyre. That much had been clear.

But as she looked into the man further, her excitement began to wane. Michael had moved to the UK in eighty-one with his wife, Celine. Not with Dymphna Cooley and Aisling, who had emigrated four years later.

Michael had bought the stud farm at that point and run it ever since. And the fact that he had a son born in eighty-six, a year before Dara vanished, plus a particularly time-intensive job that would have involved extremely early mornings and late nights, made it very unlikely that he could have got away with moonlighting as two people.

She sighed. It looked as though he wasn't Dara Cooley. But

that didn't mean that he hadn't employed Dara at some point. She'd wait to see what Danny Murphy's employee files said.

She didn't have to wait long to get them. Danny sent two emails, one with a list of named employees, their dates of birth, and their National Insurance numbers. The second one – a link to a WeTransfer upload – had a full two months' worth of CCTV.

She looked across CID towards the area occupied by DCI Acharya's team. Their three co-opted DCs all worked there, and she was pleased to see that the buoyant Casho was already at her desk. And, even better, Jason Walker, who Hanson had dated for a while before things had ended uncomfortably thanks to Damian's intrusion, was nowhere to be seen. It was still a source of slight stress to her having him working in close proximity, though at least he sat at Casho's end of the room now instead of at the next desk along from Hanson. She was pretty sure the chief had arranged that little move before she'd had to ask about it.

Hanson had come armed with Fox's biscuits the day before, and took the half-full packet over to Casho's desk. 'I have biscuits and a request for some CCTV help,' she said.

Casho laughed. 'Even I can't eat biscuits at seven thirty. But I suppose I can take some for later.'

'I can only admire your self-control,' Hanson said, taking one and demolishing it. She figured she'd run off at least five biscuits this morning, and if they really were in the home strait on this investigation, she'd be fitting in a lot more exercise once again soon.

Assuming my guardian angel really is the killer, she added silently to herself.

Back at her desk, she opened up the list of employees at the Murphy farm once again and sorted it by date of birth. She knew that she was looking, at least in the first instance, for either some sign that Ethan or Finn Cooley had worked there on summer jobs, or for someone who might turn out to be Dara Cooley.

'Damn it,' she said, after a few minutes. 'None of them is right.'

At Ben's polite, 'What gives?' Hanson explained that her hunch that one of the Cooleys was connected to the stud farm hadn't paid off so far.

'The farm doesn't give riding lessons, so none of them can have learned there,' she added. 'They just breed horses.'

She heard movement behind her, and turned to find Casho standing over her shoulder.

'Hey,' the detective constable said. 'I've got something. Looks like your horse killer tried before.'

Hanson rose quickly, and was pleased to note that Ben was coming with them to Casho's desk too.

'OK,' Casho said, settling herself and pressing the play button on a video clip.

It looked like the same CCTV footage that Hanson had watched through in the office at the stud farm. The view of the yard was the same, and an eerily similar figure emerged at a climb over the yard gate. Hanson was confident, as she had been on that other footage, that it was a male. But the time and date stamp was a week ago, on January the tenth.

And this time the figure landed elegantly and turned towards the gate. Instead of heading for the stable block, as he had the night before last, he moved to the small door that was set into the side of the larger gates and turned the handle. The door opened easily, as Hanson had known it would. Danny had explained that door was on a Yale lock, and although it was impossible to open from outside without a key, from inside it was simple.

The figure shut the door again without going through it

and then, looking around carefully, walked towards the stable block, where he tried the handle of that door. He seemed surprised to find it locked. He tried it several more times and then, with what looked like frustration, retraced his steps.

He let himself out of the smaller door, and disappeared from view as he shut it behind him.

'He was doing recon, wasn't he?' Casho said. 'Found the door locked and had to come back another night.'

Hanson frowned. 'But why risk it another night? There was every chance it would be locked again.'

'Unless he was loitering outside the gate the whole time on attempt number two,' Casho commented, 'and has been doing, so he knew that door hadn't been locked.'

'Or unless he came back with lock picks this time,' Lightman commented.

Hanson nodded slowly. 'He looks more athletic on this tape, doesn't he?' she said. 'On the one from the other night he tripped slightly on landing. But here he looks nimble. Could he really be Dara Cooley's age? Scaling that gate and landing like that?'

'Dara Cooley is, what, sixty-two?' Lightman said. 'I'd say it's unlikely.'

'You're forgetting Tom Cruise,' Casho said, grinning.

'Dara could have sent someone to get the horse for him,' Hanson said. 'This could be that person. Say a son.'

They all watched the tape through again, and Hanson found her skin crawling as she watched it. There was something in the cool patience with which the figure walked away that made her feel a thread of alarm. This wasn't the uncontrolled action of a man who made big mistakes and then suffered for them. He looked more like a careful predator.

'See if he's on any of the other tapes,' she said, before walking back to her desk.

A short while later, the central team of four was squashed into the big meeting room. The chief was, unsurprisingly, keen to hear about the thermos flask left on the bonnet of the Qashqai. Hanson felt a squirming humiliation that this was overshadowing the investigation, particularly when it might still be Damian.

'Has your ex-boyfriend done anything like this before?' the chief asked, his expression thoughtful. Non-judgemental.

Hanson grimaced. 'It's . . . he would sometimes do these weird little things for other people. I had an elderly neighbour who he suddenly decided to drive to Tesco's. And then he acted like Mother Teresa towards her for the next month, and expected to be constantly praised for it by me *and* the neighbour, until he got bored.' She shook her head.

'But nothing anonymous?' the chief pressed. 'Nothing that he wouldn't immediately get credit for?'

Hanson thought for a minute, and then shook her head. 'It did tend to be with an agenda,' she said. 'The few nice things he did for me were used as a weapon against any criticism next time we spoke, and god forbid you didn't thank him profusely for them.' She watched the chief nodding, and felt compelled to add, 'But that doesn't mean he hasn't changed tack. He hasn't harassed me at all in a while. This might be just his new way. I mean, it is quite unsettling, isn't it?'

'True,' the chief said. And then, after a moment, he added, 'But I'd like to be careful about this. I can arrange to have you put up in a hotel anonymously for a few days. I'd feel more comfortable if you did that. And until we're sure we know what we're dealing with, I think you need to make absolutely sure you aren't going anywhere alone.' He looked into the distance. 'If I can swing it, it might even be worth getting a couple of other DCs to tail you subtly and keep an eye on your vehicle and belongings. If this *is* our killer, then it would be an easy way of trapping him. And bloody useful if we could do a DNA match without having to rely on the Globalry stuff.'

Hanson gave Ben a sidelong grin. 'Don't say that in front of Ben! Pet project.'

'Yeah, he'll be crying in the toilets next,' O'Malley said.

'You know me so well,' Ben said, deadpan.

The meeting broke up shortly afterwards in a lighter mood, but Hanson caught the chief watching her as she left, and she could see that he felt as perturbed by all this as she did.

15

Aisling had barely managed to talk to her sons this morning. She'd answered on autopilot as Ethan had requested a lift, and as Finn had made comments about a news report on the Bonfire Killer, which still seemed disconnected from her reality, despite how close to home it all was.

'You are being careful, aren't you, Mummo?' he asked her at one point. 'I can come with you if you need to go anywhere. Like . . . London or wherever.'

'I'm not going to London,' she'd said, trying to sound reassuring. And then she'd almost fed Barks for the second time that morning before Finn said, 'He really doesn't need second breakfast, Mum.'

She'd barely been present, in fact, so lost had she been in thoughts of the profile she'd received back from Globalry. The matches it had found. In particular, the big match. With someone known only on the site as NewForester.

This person is either a father, brother or son to you.

She could remember the dizzy sensation as she'd read that. The rush of absolute joy, and then the drop of terror.

What could she say to him? This man who might be her father?

She'd still been trying to work that out when a message had arrived from his account. Only it hadn't been from him.

Hi, my name is Cassie. I wanted to get in touch to say that I
actually came on here on behalf of someone else, someone called

Ben. Would you be willing to meet him? He'd really like to talk to you and thinks you might be able to help him.

Was this not her father then? Was he a brother she'd never known she had? Or had he taken on a new identity when he'd walked out? Her dad had certainly eluded her efforts at finding him during her mother's illness. So perhaps this was the answer.

She'd spent so much of the time since yesterday morning trying to imagine who Cassie might be. For some reason she'd felt unable to ask.

She must be someone close to him, she'd thought over and over. *Close relative. Girlfriend. Wife. Who else would you trust to do that for you?*

She was standing frozen in the hall, thinking all of this over again, as Ethan crashed down the stairs with Barks jumping at his heels.

'Are you all right, *Maman?*'

He sounded touchingly concerned. And she smiled at him for a moment, realising that he was back to his normal self. No longer the grumpy teenager he'd been for a good couple of weeks.

'I'm great,' she said. And then, reaching to ruffle his hair, she added, 'Whereas you, my darling, are fifteen minutes late, and you're not even out of the door. I've genuinely seen glaciers move more quickly.'

He grinned at her, looped his second bag strap over his shoulder and then leaned in for a hug. 'They actually hired me for my glacier-like qualities,' he said into her hair. 'They told me at my review. I'm *icing* it. Ha!'

'Awful,' she said. 'Just awful.'

She sank into the hug, relieved for a moment to have her happy-go-lucky son back.

'Ethan, have you stolen my bloody sandwich?' Finn's voice rang out from the kitchen. It was, she thought suddenly, so much more focused than his brother's. The voice of someone who was going somewhere, and wanted you to know it. So much more his father's voice than hers.

Ethan released her, his expression now thoughtful.

'Uhhhh, I took *a* sandwich,' he called back.

'God's sake!' The fridge door slammed very audibly, and Finn emerged into the hall, his expression somewhere between amused and exasperated. 'Give it back! How do you think it got in there, bruh? Do you think it, like, grew in there?'

Ethan gave a sigh, swung his bag off again and rooted around in it. 'I just thought the mother ship might have taken pity on me for once and, you know, made me some food.'

'Aww, I guess I just don't love you enough,' Aisling said with a regretful shake of her head.

'You know she'd make *me* some lunch if I asked,' Finn said, taking the foil-wrapped sandwich triumphantly. 'She loves me more.'

'I dislike you both equally,' she said, and pulled Finn into a hug this time.

'You'll definitely love me more when you hear what Ethan's done to his carpet,' Finn said with a wide grin.

'Nooo, you traitor!' Ethan cried. But he was smiling as he opened the front door.

'God, I can't wait for you to both move out,' she said, and then added, 'Don't screw up at work!'

'You too, *Mutter*,' Ethan called.

'Are you not going to ask me about the carpet?' her younger son asked, sounding slightly disappointed. 'I mean, I don't care. I'm not the one who paid for it . . .'

'Snitches wear stitches,' she told him. And then, after a moment, she asked, 'Go on. What did he do?'

'A small, controlled fire that turned out to be not actually that controlled.'

Aisling put a hand up to her head reflexively. 'God. It's like he's wired to be destructive. Why does he always want to burn things? What was it this time?'

'Some old revision notes, plus a can of deodorant, as far as I know,' Finn said.

'Fantastic.'

It filled her with an immediate sense of stress, the thought of having to sort the carpet out. It wasn't just the money, which was enough of a problem; it was the thought of having to manage it all. Of having to choose a new carpet, and haul all Ethan's mess and furniture out in order to have it fitted. It felt like too much just now.

'Well, you can't have two perfect sons,' Finn said, with a grin. 'Anyway, he won't care about a burnt carpet. You can leave him to it.'

'I suppose so,' she said. But in her head, she added, *Until we have to sell*. And then she wondered whether they might just be able to cover it with a cheap rug.

Finn pulled his blazer on, straightened his already straight tie in the mirror, and then was gone. He left her alone with her fear, and with an hour to go before she'd need to leave.

Somehow, the time passed absurdly quickly, spinning past, picking her up, and spitting her out onto Lyndhurst Road at ten twenty.

She felt not quite present as she drew nearer to the coffee shop. A little unreal. She looked in the glass of each shopfront as she passed, not to check that she looked all right, but to confirm that she was actually there. That this was her, doing this.

At each one a wide-eyed woman would stare back at her, the sheen of her sweat visible even in a poor reflection. A strangely modified version of herself that wasn't quite the anchor she needed.

The one real thing in her body was the twisting ball of anxiety at the bottom of her ribcage. A nervous feeling that she hadn't felt since exam results day. And it seemed appropriate that she'd been taken right back to that age. To a time before everything had crumbled.

The coffee shop was suddenly right there, but the door seemed to jump around with her heartbeat. Then all at once, she was through it.

Her eyes went to the nearest tables, scanning for someone who looked like Dad. All strong brow and wide jaw. Though she knew she might be meeting someone who looked totally different.

And then a man was rising. A tall, movie-star handsome man with dark hair and pale eyes. And even though he was saying, 'Aisling?' she thought that this couldn't, *couldn't* be him.

'I – are you – Ben?'

He nodded, and showed her the latte he'd already ordered her, as Cassie had promised. She felt even less connected to herself as she drew out one of the padded stools and sat.

'I need to tell you, before I say anything else, that I'm not related to you,' he said, quietly. 'I'm very sorry to cause any disappointment, but it's incredibly important that I talk to you, and I hope you'll see why shortly.'

There was a moment of no feeling at all, in which she just looked over his beautiful face, and then it was as if someone had reached inside her and crushed her breath out of her.

'You aren't . . . ? But I thought . . .'

'Cassie, who you spoke to, uploaded the DNA onto the site in order to find someone related to the owner of it,' he said. 'I work for the police. And we're desperate to find help with a crime.'

She found herself staring at him, a heavy feeling in her stomach fighting with anxiety.

'What are you saying?' she asked him. 'That . . . that the DNA is from a crime scene?'

Ben – or whatever his name really was – nodded. 'Yes. It's a very significant scene. We've been unable to connect it to anyone we have a record of, so this seemed the only way.' He glanced down, and then said, 'I'm sorry. I know this isn't easy.'

She looked away from him, trying to get her scattered thoughts to gather. To coalesce into something meaningful.

'It must have been something serious,' she said, and then she looked at him again. 'This crime. What was it?'

'It was a murder,' he said quietly. 'The thing – the thing is that this sort of evidence isn't usually used by the police. At least not here. I've had to work hard to let this go ahead. We're going to need a lot of help from you to move forwards.'

She couldn't bring herself to say anything else. It was enough just to stay sitting on the stool. To keep breathing.

Ben paused again. 'All we know is that someone related to you was present at this crime, or after it. The degree of close-ness indicates it would be – either a sibling, a parent or a child of yours.' He focused on her, the blue gaze piercing. 'You've only listed on the site that you have two sons and a father living.'

She understood him then, even while she didn't want to. And she wasn't sure whether the crumbling feeling within her was because she might never find out the truth about her father, or because they thought one of her boys might have killed someone.

16

Jonah was impatient to be moving. It wasn't just the months without progress that were driving him. It was also his worry that Aisling Cooley would be loyal to her family, and would alert the three of them. The last thing they wanted was any or all of them bolting.

The fact that her two sons were under observation gave him some small comfort, but even with a watch on them, it was possible for them to slip away if they knew how. And Aisling's as-yet-unlocated father was a lot more of a worry. It was unusual for his team to make quite such heavy weather of locating someone who didn't have a common name, and this alone made him feel uneasy about Dara Cooley.

He'd also hoped that the attack on the brood mare might provide some obvious leads to make their case against one of the three watertight, even without the DNA, but nothing had so far come of it. It seemed much more like Jacqueline Clarke's death than like Lindsay Kernow's: a patiently executed, carefully staged affair with little to point them in anyone's direction.

That all made getting Aisling Cooley's information vital. The moment Ben arrived back at CID, Jonah called his core team of three into the meeting room with him. He was eager for the other, co-opted detectives to stay on the hunt for Dara Cooley right up until Ben could tell them more.

'OK,' he said, once they were inside with the door shut. 'What do we know about Aisling's father?'

'Unfortunately,' Lightman replied a little wryly, 'it's not a huge amount. Dara Cooley disappeared in 1987, some two years after the family moved to the New Forest. He walked out, leaving a note apologising and a signed deed transferring the house into his wife's name alone. It seems he'd already removed himself as signatory on their joint bank account. Aisling hasn't heard from him since.'

Jonah sighed. 'Of course she hasn't.'

'If he staged a vanishing act, that would tie in with what we've found so far,' Hanson said. 'We have a Dara Cooley on the HMRC database who was on the payroll of a specialist music publishing company based in Swindon. His PAYE runs from the beginning of 1985 until March eighty-seven. That syncs in with him moving to the New Forest and then walking out on his family two years later.'

'Where were the family living before 1985?' Jonah asked.

'Tullamore, in Ireland, Aisling says,' Lightman answered. 'But it was clear that she didn't want to talk about any of that period of her life. I'd say that suggests that there's some history with the father she's not keen to talk about.'

'Sounds like there's a good chance he went back home to Ireland after he vanished, at least initially,' Jonah said, trying to keep thinking and not give in to frustration that one of their three suspects probably wasn't in contact with his family. 'I'd like her to provide their old address. Photographs of him. Where he used to work.'

'I'll get in touch with her,' Ben said.

Jonah nodded. 'How about the sons? Their whereabouts on New Year's Eve?'

Ben had gone to speak with Aisling with two main aims: the first being to find out about her father, and the second to find out what her sons had been doing the night Lindsay Kernow had died. Ben hadn't asked her about October the third yet, the night when Jacqueline had been murdered. One possible murder scene was bad enough, but at least it would leave Aisling hoping that whichever one had been there had just got involved in some sort of a fight or a terrible accident. To suggest that one of her family might be a serial killer was too much.

'She says both Ethan and Finn were at New Year's parties,' Lightman replied. 'Ethan at one in Lyndhurst, and Finn at a pub in Totton.'

Jonah found his interest sharpening at that. Lindsay Kernow had lived in Totton. And Finn's way home from a pub on the New Forest side of the town would have been along the route they were certain Lindsay Kernow had taken before ending up dead on Lyndhurst Heath.

Facts like these would support their decision to arrest the two boys. They gave reasons beyond the Globalry matches.

'Let's try to confirm alibis, as subtly as possible,' Jonah said. 'And build a more thorough profile for each of them. Look at whether they have any knowledge of fire building, and where either of them might have purchased ketamine. It's not like everyone has it lying around.' He looked at each of them. 'I'd suggest that each of you takes charge of looking into one of the suspects, and works with the other DCs on it.'

'Ooh, give me the vanished dad,' O'Malley said immediately. 'Love me a disappearance to get my teeth into.'

'Guess I'd better take the school prefect, for obvious reasons,' Ben said, clearly getting in there before either of the other two could.

'Well, I'm happy with either of the two over-privileged boys,' Hanson said, with a grin. 'And I guess the one who's left school and not found the world falling at his oh-so-talented feet is a good bet.'

'Good,' Jonah said. 'Now I'm supposed to have a budget

meeting in forty-five minutes, so somebody make some progress before then for pity's sake.'

Jonah returned to his office, brooding on more than one
thing. Despite the pressing nature of this investigation, and
the inevitable backlog of other work, part of Jonah's mind
was on his home life.

The DCS had rung early this morning, and Jonah had
jogged out to his car to take the call, escaping the noise Milly
was making with her ever-patient nanny in the kitchen. Having
thought he'd be ready to go straight after the call, he'd realised
that he'd left his thermos behind and gone back in to get it.

Michelle, who often did some work before heading into
the city after rush hour, was on the phone in her study, and it
was clear that she hadn't heard him coming back in. She was
deeply engaged in conversation.

He hadn't really registered the first part of what she said,
but his hearing had tuned in at the point when Michelle had
said, 'It's just . . . I'm so irritable all the time. Just all the time.
I feel like I've developed some kind of a reaction to him. Like
I have antibodies or something. Any time he's here, I just feel
angry and sort of resentful. I'm – I'm really worried I'm going
to end up hating him. And if I do, what happens to Milly?'

It had been little short of crushing. Jonah had opened the
door in silence, and let himself back outside, doing without
the thermos and his previous sense of vague optimism about
the future of their relationship.

He had spent the drive battling a feeling of betrayal. He
had chosen Michelle in spite of everything. He had given up
a new relationship he had already invested himself in for her.
Not just that, but with Jojo Magos, a woman he had long
held a torch for. All because a single, drunken encounter
with Michelle just before that relationship had blossomed

had resulted in a pregnancy, one that had gone undetected until they'd had very few options.

He'd done the right thing, hadn't he? He'd chosen the hardest path, but the one he knew in his heart that he'd had to. He couldn't let Michelle bring up his child alone. And yet, somehow, that was being thrown back in his face. Less than a year into their newly forged relationship, she was finding him so irritating she thought it might turn into hatred.

Without meaning to, he started playing back their inter-actions with each other, looking for signs of her dislike. He'd known that she was unhappy in those early days of Milly's life. He'd tried to step in and do more, understanding that she'd ended up shouldering the hardest parts of parenting a newborn, and that the hormonal effects of all of it had been huge too. But had he been misreading some of her behav-iour too? Her distance from him? The way she'd resisted physical closeness and avoided sleeping in the same room? Was that more to do with her deeper feelings towards him?

He found himself remembering something his friend Sophie had said to him: that he had gone into this whole thing half-heartedly. That he had still wanted to be with Jojo Magos and not with Michelle, and that the mother of his child might understand that on some level. Might feel hurt and betrayed herself.

Was this his fault then? Had he made the wrong decision? Or just not managed to follow through on that decision well enough to make Michelle feel loved?

He hadn't managed to answer any of his own questions by the time he'd arrived at work. And Jonah, who was usually so adept at setting aside everything personal, now found him-self replaying Michelle's words over and over as he sat behind his desk.

He badly wanted to talk it all through with someone, but

there was nobody he could really do that with. His one close male friend, Roy, never gave an opinion on anything, preferring to agree with Jonah – as he did with his wife Sophie. Sophie, on the other hand, was bluntly opinionated, but had yet to meet Michelle and was inclined to judge Jonah harshly if his partner was unhappy. He didn't feel tough enough to withstand accusations of having brought this on himself right now.

It was a struggle to admit to himself that the one person he wanted to call was the one person he absolutely could not. Jojo would know exactly what Michelle had meant. She had an uncanny knack of seeing into the heart of people. And she would make him laugh while she did it. She'd still managed to make him laugh ten months ago, as he was breaking the two of them apart.

The urge to send a quick 'How are you doing?' message to start off a chat was almost overwhelming. But he couldn't do it.

It wasn't just that asking Jojo was deeply unfair on Michelle; it was deeply unfair on Jojo too. The last time he'd seen her, she'd told him that she'd started seeing someone new, and he needed to leave her to move on.

And he would not, *would not*, be that ex who slides into your messages when their new relationship is going sour, looking for a quick ego boost or a little nostalgia trip before cheering up and forgetting about it. He respected her far too much to behave that way.

It was always possible that this thing with Michelle was just a blip. Or him overreacting to a casual rant.

So he pushed the phone away, and instead started writing an email to the comms team about two arrests made. He'd be sending it out that evening, once they'd picked up the Cooley boys. He just hoped that, by then, he'd be able to add that they'd arrested a sixty-two-year-old man, too.

17

'That's right,' O'Malley said, giving the phone handset the benefit of his most cheerful brogue. 'Detective sergeant. My team and I are looking into whether Dara Cooley should be deemed a missing person after all this time. I'd love to find out a bit more about him. See if I should add him to my list or cross him off, like.'

O'Malley had been happy to note that Leatherwaites, the publishing company Aisling's father had worked for, still existed. It had survived despite being a tiny enterprise dedicated to the distribution of church music and pew books.

Their website was actually only a decade or so out of date stylistically, a lot more modern than he'd been anticipating, and the young lad who answered the phone had put him on to his boss, a man who sounded to be no more than fifty.

'Huh. Dara Cooley,' the boss said now, with a weight of what sounded like both disappointment and relish. O'Malley was satisfied to hear it. It meant that there was a story there. 'I've got a few things to say about him.'

'Ahh, that would be useful,' O'Malley said. 'Could I ask, are you the business owner, or . . . ?'

'I'm the MD,' the voice told him. 'I have been for thirty years. Dara was one of my hires, and I was proud of him at first.'

'Could I take a name?'

'What? Oh, I see. Terry Lyons,' he said a little impatiently. It seemed as though Terry was keener on telling the story than on getting the credit for it.

'So when did Dara start working for you?'

'January eighty-five,' he said at once. 'I hired him six months after I took charge.'

'And what was his job?'

'He was customer relations,' Terry said. 'A salesman really. But in our business it's a lot more . . . friendly than that. It's about building relationships with each individual church.'

'Ah, so he went to each church, and made sure they had what they needed?' O'Malley asked, trying to make sure that he sounded fascinated in this.

'Yes,' Terry agreed. 'He also started selling to churches we'd never sold to before. He would call up clergymen and arrange to meet them. Talk through what items they were missing, what music they might need. Discuss his own favourites, that sort of thing. And the thing that made him so good was that he could appeal to the Catholics as well as the Anglicans. He had such a passion for church music of all kinds that he could talk most of them into buying a new mass setting for special occasions, or a set of *Psalm 52*s. Even a batch of *Carols for Choirs*, at the less elaborate end of the spectrum.'

O'Malley made murmuring noises of assent without having a clue what any of this meant, as out of touch with everything church music related as he was with his protestant upbringing. As Terry spoke, he was thinking of two murders, and wondering how a man who sold sacred music might fit the mould of a serial killer. It would have been, he thought, the most wonderful front if he'd kept it up. A great way to meet vulnerable women, too.

He scribbled a note to check whether Jacqueline Clarke or Lindsay Kernow had been churchgoers, even occasional ones, and then asked, 'So he was well-liked? He charmed people?'

'Yes,' Terry said. '"Well-liked" is right. He wasn't charming exactly. He was too quiet to be overtly charming. But what I saw in him was a gentleness and a willingness to listen that was immediately appealing. It set people at ease and made them want to buy from him. Which meant from us.'

'But then things went awry,' O'Malley suggested.

'Yes, well,' Terry said tightly. O'Malley imagined him pursing his lips before he spoke again. 'Most people have their weaknesses, but I was surprised to realise that Dara's was women.'

'An affair?' O'Malley asked.

'Oh, it was painfully obvious,' Terry said with a sigh. 'When salesmen suddenly express a determined urge to target a particular area, there's always a personal reason, and it's usually a love interest. But they're usually unmarried, and that wasn't the case for Dara Cooley.'

This was extremely interesting news to O'Malley. Aisling Cooley hadn't mentioned an affair. Was it possible her father had simply moved out of his own home, into his new woman's?

'Which area was this?'

'Newbury, and all the tiny village churches around it,' Terry said wearily.

'Did you find out who he was having the affair with?'

'We had a pretty good idea,' Terry said. 'One of our binders saw him with a young woman there, and took it upon himself to follow him to her address.'

O'Malley couldn't help grinning to himself. God bless those who made other people's business their own. 'Do you have a name and address then?'

'I can probably dig it out,' Terry said. 'But I wouldn't rely on finding Dara there. I went round myself, not long after he disappeared, hoping to persuade him to carry on for at least a few more weeks. But he wasn't there, and the young woman in question was quite distressed that I'd come. She said she hadn't seen him in weeks, and didn't expect to see him again.'

'Ah, maybe a dead end, so,' O'Malley agreed. 'But if you could find that address for me all the same, I'd be able to tick it off, you know?'

Inwardly he was thinking that a young woman might well cover for her lover if he was in trouble. And even if Dara Cooley was no longer at the mistress's house, it was possible they could trace him onwards from there.

'If you hold on, I can probably look at the notes we kept on Dara,' Terry said. 'We were encouraged by our solicitors to annotate everything. I'll be right back.'

O'Malley occupied himself with looking up the distances between Swindon, Newbury and Hordle – where Dara Cooley had settled with his wife and Aisling – on Google Maps. They were all within fairly easy driving distance of each other. All between one- and two-hour drives. It was clear that Dara Cooley would have been able to see a mistress without even needing to stay overnight, particularly if he had an excuse for driving around.

There was a scuffling sound as Terry picked up the phone once again, and then he said, 'I have it. The address is Manor Stud Farm, in West Gradley.'

O'Malley felt an immediate chime of recognition, something he had not expected. Where had that address come to his attention recently?

'Thank you,' he said, writing it down. 'That's incredibly helpful of you.'

He was already typing the address into their database as the call ended, and he felt a strange kick of adrenaline as his search brought back a single result.

Anneka Foley, Manor Farm Cottage, West Gradley

Of course it was familiar. He had looked at this suspicious death more than once, questioning, repeatedly, whether there might be some link between her death and the murder of Jacqueline Clarke. It seemed that he now had his answer.

18

Ethan Cooley had been at the house party of his friend Matthew Downing on New Year's Eve, according to Aisling Cooley. Hanson called Matthew to check up on that alibi, but his number rung out. She'd left a message, trying not to let it sound as impatient as she felt, and had gone on to look at who Ethan actually was.

By mid-afternoon she'd found out only the bare bones of Ethan Cooley's life, and none of it told her whether he might have killed two lonely forty-something women. Though most of it suggested that he'd had easy access to quite a number of women.

Ethan was in a band called the Great Unsaid, an all-male four-piece that had pages up on Facebook and Bandcamp and a channel on YouTube. Their Facebook page listed a series of gigs around Southampton, Portsmouth and Bournemouth – as well as in London, Dublin and even a few abroad. Every post or photograph had responses from enthusiastic female fans. Sometimes hundreds of them.

Looked at objectively, she could see why Ethan was popular with these women. He was a tall, handsome, alternative-looking nineteen-year-old who could easily have passed as being in his mid-twenties. And in every image or video clip of him performing, he looked immersed. Otherworldly.

She navigated to the band's own website, wondering now whether there was a chance that Lindsay Kernow and Jacqueline Clarke had gone to some of Ethan's gigs. Could they have been fans? Had they been drawn in by his musical persona, and allowed themselves to be lured to their deaths?

But why would Ethan single them out, if so? Out of all the armies of female admirers? They were his mother's age, she thought.

That, in fact, might have something in it. Hanson knew from her psychology degree that a lot of unhealthy feelings towards women were either modelled on how young men saw their fathers treating women, or on their own relationship with their mother. Maternal relationships could be influenced by a father figure but could also be toxic in their own right.

Was the relationship between Ethan and his mother deeply dysfunctional? Had Aisling Cooley made him feel inadequate, or mistreated him in some way, driving him to seek out women of a similar type in order to punish them?

She found herself eager to watch the two of them together. To observe the dynamic and assess what was going on. Insights like that were never the way a case was proved, but they were, as the chief often said, the weathervanes that pointed the way. Follow them, and the evidence usually emerged.

Hanson scrolled through the Great Unsaid's website. Along with a summary of their vision as artists, and a series of photographs of Ethan and the others performing, there was a SoundCloud insert which would let her listen to several of their songs.

Plugging her headphones into her desktop and putting them on, she pressed the play button on the first track, 'The One Bright'.

She was braced for loud guitar or edgy electronic pulp. What she got instead, however, was a wash of uplifting sound with a single, mournful guitar line over the top. It was surprisingly emotional, and she felt a little awkward experiencing it in the middle of CID.

And then Ethan's voice came in, mid-pitched and soft with a tiny hoarse edge at times. He sang about the loss of the only person who had mattered to him, and she shivered. She could see this appealing to Lindsay Kernow and Jacqueline Clarke all too well.

She remembered, then, something Pippa Clarke had said about her mother. That she had been happiest alone with her dog and music nobody had ever heard of.

Hanson opened her Outlook up and sent a quick email to each of the Clarke daughters, asking if they knew if their mother had been to any live gigs. Though she strongly suspected that they would have mentioned it if they'd known.

Squinting at the Great Unsaid's webpage, she decided to look up some of the other band members. Two of the three had private social media and no website, but Dan Olwe, the keyboard player, had his own site where he offered music lessons.

Hanson sent him a quick message asking if he could come into the station to look at some photos, and then removed her headphones. Ben, opposite her, was sitting back in his chair thoughtfully.

'Anything giving?' she asked.

'Not a lot,' Lightman replied. 'Finn's friends can vaguely confirm that he was at the pub with them in Totton on New Year's Eve. Some of them think he was there until late, others aren't sure. Profile-wise, he's quite interesting.'

'Tell me,' Hanson said, immediately.

'OK,' Ben answered, and then glanced over at O'Malley's chaotic desk. 'Though I genuinely can't handle looking at Domnall's desk any longer. It's got to a critical stage. I'm going to tidy it while I talk.'

'Ooh, I'll help,' Hanson said happily. 'He'll freak out, and it'll serve him right for the mouse-switching prank.'

The two of them went to work quietly, sorting O'Malley's pens and paperwork, and putting empty takeaway cups and wrappers into an old Sainsbury's bag. Hanson made a separate pile for the four reusable cups that were in various stages of moulding over. Though a little disgusting, it was strangely soothing work.

'Finn is a pretty model citizen,' Ben told her. 'He pops up in numerous articles about sporting achievements, particularly in tennis, where he's an under-seventeens champion. He also does a lot of running and represents the school at debating.'

'OK, so smart and athletic,' Hanson said. 'Strong.'

'Capable of planning the murder of a grown woman and moving her body?' Ben asked mildly, piling up a load of old newspapers and then sliding them into the waste bin, 'I'd say yes.'

'Over-privileged too,' Hanson added. 'A prefect at a public school. Handsome and athletic. He'll be used to talking his way out of anything. He'd think he could get away with this.'

'Possibly,' Lightman agreed equably. 'Though we haven't actually met him yet.'

'But if he comes across nicely, that just makes it more likely he'd get away with stuff,' Hanson shot back with a grin. 'Any online spats or questionable misogynistic opinions?'

'No, and that's actually what I was just wondering about,' Ben admitted. 'His social media presence is perfect. Respectful towards women, minority groups and people of other faiths.' He paused and lifted a plastic tray. 'Wow. This might actually be alive.' Hanson saw something sitting on it that had an inch-thick fur of mould. 'I'm going to take that to the kitchen and destroy it.' He set it temporarily on his own desk and then continued, 'Finn gets involved in debates, but only in a quiet, polite, "let's try to empathise" kind of way. No rabble-rousing. No inappropriate jokes. No harsh banter.'

'So . . . you think he might just be a really nice kid who's been brought up to respect people?' Hanson asked, hefting the plastic bag of takeaway cups. Ben followed her towards the kitchen, picking up the furry-food object on the way. 'Where's the fun in that?'

'I know,' he said with a small smile. 'Not exactly the profile of a serial killer, is it?'

'But then, as the chief says,' Hanson countered, 'profiling is . . .'

'Complete bollocks, yes,' Ben agreed.

The comment surprised a laugh out of her. 'I think he normally says "unproven to have any statistical significance", but yes. Basically.' She came to a halt in the kitchen, thinking, and then moved over to the sink. The takeaway cups were all recyclable once she'd washed the muck out of them. 'He would have easy access to ketamine, though. Posh schools like that are definite targets for drug pushers.'

'If he was willing to risk it,' Ben said. 'School prefect and all that. He had a lot to lose.'

'But pretending for a minute that profiling isn't bollocks, there is a classic type of perfectionist under a lot of pressure who cracks.' She gave a crooked grin. 'Or he could be an out-and-out psychopath who's playing a part the whole time.'

'There's a lot of it about,' Ben agreed, throwing the final lid into the recycling.

They returned to O'Malley's desk, and rearranged his remaining items, including his Irish Rugby scarf which she folded over the back of his chair. Looking at it, Hanson found herself thinking suddenly of how many people involved in all this had links to Ireland. Aisling's family had emigrated from there, as had Michael Murphy who owned the stud farm – a place that might or might not be involved. Dylan Kernow had also moved to Dublin.

'Where is the place Aisling's parents are from?' she asked Ben, as they were settling back behind their desks.

'Tullamore? It's almost bang in the middle of the country,' he answered. 'Small, historically very Catholic. Lots of industry, including whiskey distilleries.' He gave her a small smile. 'Wikipedia is my friend.'

'I was just wondering, while O'Malley isn't here to take the piss out of me for it, whether there might be some link between Aisling Cooley's father and Dylan Kernow,' she said. 'Or maybe between them and the Murphy family. And I know. It's like meeting an American and asking if they know someone else you know from America.'

'Yeah, it is,' Ben agreed. 'Though did I tell you about when I was in California, and someone did exactly that to me?' He shook his head slightly. 'This guy who was driving us to a tourist spot said, "Oh, I know someone British. He's called Harris Cornwallis." And I bloody DID know him. He used to work with my dad. And it was so annoying having to admit that I did.'

Hanson sat back and laughed. 'Nooo! That is so strange!'

'Random, meaningless coincidences are everywhere,' Ben said with a nod.

'You should write birthday cards,' Hanson said with a grin.

19

Aisling was exhausted. Emotion had run through her like a river today, and the worst was still to come. Later today, she was still going to have to tell her sons that the police were there. That they thought one of them might be a killer.

Of course, that wasn't how she was going to say it at first. And she refused – flatly refused – to accept that she had a murderer for a son. They were her kids. They were two wonderful, empathetic human beings. She didn't believe that they'd hurt anyone. But the awful truth was that she either had to believe that one of her sons had done this – or that her father had. That her wonderful, beloved daddy had killed a woman her age, only miles from her doorstep.

There was still part of her that wanted to believe the DNA had got there in some other way. And although she knew what Ben had really meant when he'd said they 'wanted to talk' to the three of them – Ben, who she was now trying to think of as DS Ben Lightman instead of as someone who might have been part of her family – she'd been heartened that he'd gone on to say more.

'All we know is that one of them was there,' he'd told her. 'And that means they probably know what happened and can point us to the killer.'

It had made her feel fractionally less like her world had shattered. Not because of what he'd said so much as because he was so clearly taking care. She could tell that he was conscientious, and logical, and wouldn't rush to conclusions or assume guilt. And that was exactly what she badly needed him to be.

That incremental improvement had lessened her adrenaline and allowed her brain to start crunching this properly.

'Was it blood?' she had asked him. 'Was that the DNA you found? Or hair? It wasn't . . .' She almost finished the sentence, but somehow couldn't quite say it to him. Which was more because it seemed a terrible thing to ask the handsome DS than because of the implications.

But she knew it was possible. She knew how often women were raped before being murdered. She knew that most crimes against women were sexually motivated. She'd spent too many hours in self-employed procrastination on news sites not to understand this.

'I'm really sorry,' DS Lightman had said after a beat, 'but I can't give any details of the crime scene without risking the integrity of the investigation.' He gave her what looked like a genuinely sympathetic look. She realised he must be practised at feigning sympathy in his line of work, but he at least bothered to do it. 'I know that must be frustrating,' he added.

So it might have been anything, that DNA. She felt cold run up her spine, and it had seemed necessary to defend her two sons.

'I don't believe, for a moment, that either of them would ever hurt anyone.' She had shaken her head. Gripped her left hand hard with her right. 'They're . . . you'll understand it when you meet them. Neither of them has a violent bone in their bodies. And I know all mothers probably have warped views of their children, but I know them. I've brought them up on my own for most of their lives. They're good. Kind. Empathetic. *Happy*.' She met his eye. 'They didn't do this.'

He'd nodded, seeming to think over her certainty. To take it on board.

But as firmly as she'd said it, Aisling had felt a trickle of doubt. For a second she had been back in the past, when things had been . . . not good. Not happy. Not based on empathy. For the first time in years she'd found herself remembering her child's hysterical crying. Her desperate, furious need to escape it. And then, with an awful drop, she remembered Ethan's terrible mood after New Year's Eve. And Finn's phone call. And she'd felt as though it was written all over her face.

'I'm sure it will be all right,' DS Lightman was saying, and Aisling had felt herself wheeling back to the present as if she'd travelled miles in a moment.

She'd focused on him. On the quiet professionalism. And she'd nodded, as if everything was going to be fine. As if there weren't going to be officers on standby until Ben returned. She knew what those officers would be for. They thought one of the boys might run. She supposed she understood it from the police point of view. Logically there was a two-thirds chance of the murderer being one of her sons.

Logic means nothing. A new and almost frightening thought. Aisling had always believed in logic. In solving the puzzle, and making it through. It was possibly what had drawn her to gaming early on, and she had always clung to this belief in hard times. But how could you apply logic to this? To the knowledge that someone you loved had probably committed murder?

She had returned home defeated and heartbroken. She'd seen herself once again in the shop windows, and it was as if she had been replaced with another person all over again. The Aisling of this morning, so blissfully unaware of what was going to happen, was gone. It had been a version of her that had only existed briefly. One that had thought she might have found her dad at long last, only to be crushed beneath the boot heel of this hollow-eyed zombie.

She'd shut the house door behind her and moved without

143

any conscious thought up to the boxes in the spare room. She had pulled them out all over again and pored over each and every photograph of her father. And for the first time she'd let herself really, truly miss him.

Mammy had been sick with anger and humiliation when he'd first gone, her skin white and sheeny for a full month. Her appetite shrunk to nothing. Her voice shaking with rage and grief.

Talking about Aisling's father had been forbidden, at least in any affectionate terms. Aisling had been told that she must stop calling him *Daddy*. That if she mentioned him, it must be only as *Dara*. His newly minted first name. As though he were no longer a member of their family. And, of course, this name must only be said in tones of anger. Of righteous condemnation.

Even with these rules in place, hearing about him had sometimes been too much for her mother. In the middle of an impassioned speech by Aisling, Mammy would suddenly snap 'Enough!', eyes ablaze and watery, her lean hands rigid on whatever task she was doing and a shake all through her body.

It had been sad to realise how little Mammy's faith could help her. It neither comforted her, nor offered her any ability to forgive. She had remained angry right up until the day she had died, the fury lasting even through her first two strokes, to be smoothed away only by the third and final one. Aisling had been seven months pregnant when she'd died.

The grief Aisling had felt at her mother's passing had been a terrible thing. She knew, in her heart, that it had been made up of unexpressed mourning over her father's absence, and for the loss of her life back in Ireland. She knew too that the complex relationship she'd had with her mother had made her passing harder. Guilt at never being closer had warred with anger at a lifetime of being kept at arm's length. At all her memories of being told to be quiet or to stop bothering her mother. Or, worse still, memories of being told that she was *a disgrace in god's eyes*. Sometimes *a wicked child*.

She knew, too, that there had been other features to her grief. Elements of trauma that she had carried with her from her previous life. They had been a complex, spiky part of it. And alongside them she'd cradled a bone-deep feeling of loss that her own child would never get to meet her family. Her blood, and his.

Now, faced with the shattering loss of her father all over again, she thought back to how she'd been in those awful early weeks after her son's birth. And she wondered how different it might have been if she'd had not Stephen's empty platitudes but her father's bear hugs. His open, sympathetic gaze, and his quiet tuts of empathy.

The ache to hug him once again was terrible, and now she was faced with the reality that if she ever saw him again, she might witness the real man. Not the kind, patient father, but the callous man who had abandoned them.

The killer.

Overwhelmed by that thought, she rose, quickly, and made for the safe haven of her study. She sat back in the black-and-red gaming chair, letting it cushion her shoulders, and she swung herself from side to side until she could breathe properly. And then she found herself waking the computer, her usual form of distraction. Her inbox was open on the screen – the last thing she'd been looking at.

A few new emails had come in this morning. The third one down was about the new fridges installed in the kitchen at VePlec. It came from one Jack O'Keane.

Aisling opened it, feeling strangely voyeuristic. The irony of Jack being in this company as an undercover PI only the executive board knew about, while she was the one who was reading his emails without him knowing, was not lost on her.

It wasn't a long email. Or, in fact, a particularly work-related one.

> Just to say to whoever took my chicken sandwich, there are only so many times you can get away with that before the swarm of angry chicken sandwiches arrives. You have been warned.
>
> J. O.'K.

And just like that, she was back in Tullamore. Not in her parents' quiet, still, china-filled house, but in Jack's den, where she had sneaked off to play *Mario Kart*. And Jack had been telling her all about the game his cousin had played in America.

'It's called *The Legend of Zelda*, and it's going to change gaming as we know it,' Jack had told her, as she'd wrestled her car back onto the track for the tenth time.

Jack had been quite unique in never making her feel stupid at not being able to play well. In fact, he'd complimented her far more than she'd ever deserved, constantly telling her that he practised this game all the time, and she was much more of a natural.

'What's so great about it?' she'd asked him.

'The story,' he'd said. 'Think *Prince of Persia* meets *Dungeons and Dragons*. It's going to be mind-blowing.'

By the time they'd finished talking she'd been burning with the desire to play it. She'd gone home to her diary and marked the *Legend of Zelda* release date with a star.

But of course she'd been gone from Tullamore long before that date, and it had no longer been a new release by the time she'd been able to play it. Months later, it had been Daddy who had persuaded her mother that she should have her own computer and a chance to play the things she wanted to.

'She needs something to lift her out of the pit she's in, Dymphna,' he'd said, and Aisling had heard the rumble of his voice from up the stairs. For once he hadn't sounded cowed or apologetic. He'd sounded firm. Immovable.

So they'd got her a computer and let her choose a game. And it had helped her, playing *Zelda*. Though she'd thought of Jack as she played, and had cried over and over again.

Jack's chicken-sandwich email was a direct reference to that very same game. He was joking about *cuccos*, little chicken-like creatures that were harmless until you killed too many of them, and then they would attack you in a swarm. The *cuccos* hadn't entered the games until years later. By that time Aisling had been trying not to think about Jack. And yet she'd still known that he would have loved them.

She found herself reading his email again, and laughing, her eyes bright. How could he be making her laugh like this? How, thirty years after she'd left him, and on a day like today?

She was gripped by a sudden feeling of significance. Aisling had never much believed in signs, but surely, surely this was one. Her private investigator ex-boyfriend had emailed her, without his knowledge, today. Right when she most needed someone to help find out what had happened to her boys, and to prove them innocent.

If anyone can help me, it's Jack, she thought.

She copied his address into a new email. And then she began to type, her fingers shaking on the keys.

20

It was lucky, O'Malley thought, that the cottage was too out-of-the-way and tiny to have been bothered with. If it had stood within the tidy, well-tended village of West Gradley itself, it would probably have been entirely demolished. Or at least rebuilt and sold on.

But Manor Farm Cottage was tucked away down a farm track a good quarter of a mile from the village proper, shielded by pine, birch and maple trees. The farm itself was off a fork to the left, which had its own, tarmacked road, while the cottage driveway forked right, an old paved path. The weeds growing through it were over a foot high in some places. They made crunching sounds as O'Malley drove over them.

O'Malley hadn't come here in person last year, when they'd first identified this case, though Juliette and Ben had. He'd reviewed their findings and agreed with their hesitant conclusion that Anneka Foley's death probably, on balance, wasn't connected to Jacqueline Clarke's.

Anneka had died three years ago, in her house, rather than in woodland. The cottage was forty-five miles from where Jacqueline Clarke had died. And the coroner had, in the end, given a verdict of accidental death.

But there had been several factors that had pulled at their attention. Enough to make them hesitant to rule it out.

The first was that the origins of the fire were suspected to be a pile of wood doused in kerosene. The fire had been made up in a fireplace, in what had been the living room.

Anneka – or the sparse remains of her – had been found dead close to the hearth. The twisted remains of a can of kerosene had been intertwined with her body.

The second was that Anneka had been forty-seven when she had died, a very similar age to Jacqueline Clarke.

And the third was that she had been described as isolated. Her death might have gone unnoticed for days if the house hadn't gone up like a torch.

Had the kerosene and fire been elsewhere in the house, the verdict would probably have been that this was arson with intent. The fact that it was in the hearth made it considerably less clear. It was entirely possible, the coroner felt, that Anneka had set the fire herself, and had attempted to use kerosene to accelerate it, without realising the huge dangers. It wouldn't be the first such tragic accident the coroner had seen.

But the size of the fire still drew questions. It had clearly involved a very large amount of wood. The pattern of scorching and kerosene remains showed that it had over-spilled the hearth itself. It was impossible to tell whether Anneka had been dead before the fire, but Juliette and Ben had felt she might have been killed and then burned.

It was also possible that Anneka had decided to take her own life in a ball of fire. She might, as the coroner had noted three years ago, have been well aware of the dangers of kerosene.

The coroner had, sensibly, called an inquest into her death. His investigations had been thorough. He had attempted to link the purchase of the kerosene to Anneka, which he had been unable to do. He had approached those who knew Anneka – who had turned out to be only the residents of West Gradley, as she had no family – and questioned them over Anneka's state of mind.

At that point O'Malley could see why things had ended up leaning towards accidental death. Discussions had revealed that Anneka was well known in the village, despite having few friends. She was infamous for being what they would have called 'The Village Crazy Lady' back where O'Malley had grown up.

Anneka had increasingly liked to stride around the town predicting doom and death for its residents. She had almost always been dressed bizarrely, sometimes barely dressed at all, and seemed to be absolutely unaware of the weather on any occasion. She generally talked a lot to herself when she wasn't haranguing someone, and would sometimes jump at nothing, or turn to look at things that weren't there.

The clincher for the coroner had been that she had often been seen with burn marks. It had looked as though she liked to press a poker against her skin at times, for long enough to leave a blister that would turn into a scar.

It made O'Malley deeply sad to read about her life all over again. Here was a woman who had so clearly been in need of serious mental health support. O'Malley would have looked at that behaviour as a non-medic and guessed she might be suffering from schizophrenia, but nobody in the reports mentioned her getting any help or support except from her neighbours, who would take her food parcels and unwanted clothing. It was unclear how she supported herself aside from that.

The big question for him now, however, was whether Dara Cooley had been involved in her death. Although no boyfriend had been mentioned in the coroner's report, that wasn't to say that nobody knew of one. And if Dara Cooley had lived with, and killed, Anneka Foley, then there was every chance that he had also killed Jacqueline Clarke and Lindsay Kernow.

O'Malley knew there wasn't likely to be much for him to see in the sparse remains of Anneka's house, which amounted to little more than two blackened walls, some heaps of brick, a twisted boiler and stove, and the vaguest outline of where the rooms had once been. Juliette and Ben had come here previously and found barely anything to comment on. Though they hadn't called in scene of crime once again. It had seemed, they agreed, a slightly hopeless case.

Off to one side, there sat a bathtub, which had presumably been moved outside the house by the original crime scene team rather than falling there. It had been cast iron, and was now blackened, but largely whole. A strange and almost comic-looking remainder.

As pointless as the lengthy expedition might seem, O'Malley was determined to pick through the scene. If he could link Dara Cooley to Anneka Foley's murder, they had ample reason to arrest him, without relying on the difficult Globalry DNA match. Even more significantly, he might find out where Dara had gone to next and be able to arrest the guy.

And, of course, aside from any of that, O'Malley wanted to know that they had discovered the full extent of his crimes. That if Dara Cooley *had* killed Anneka Foley, he was brought to justice for that too.

O'Malley stepped over a thistle so large it looked ornamental and then crossed what had once been the threshold of Anneka's home. It was a large enough space, but with the surrounding trees it must have been gloomy inside. He guessed it would have been a depressing place to live.

He wondered whether Anneka had noticed the gloom, or whether she'd been too greatly removed from reality to take it in. The dimness certainly wouldn't have helped his own mental state.

In three years of sitting unsold, the house had been invaded by plant life as much as the driveway. There were saplings shooting up through the floor, and several areas of thick moss. The greenery softened the edges of the destruction but didn't quite hide it. Much of the floor was a bed of ash, and there were scorch marks on the remaining walls and on the bricks, each one finishing in a singed, jagged edge.

He trod through it all for a while, using his feet to lift a few fallen bits of metal carefully. There were fragments of Anneka's life buried here, many of them charred or melted. A metal cup that looked as though it had been ornamental, and which he bagged up and sealed. A molten kettle. A collection of distorted cutlery which looked as though it might have been antique.

It was clear that these items hadn't been deemed relevant to the inquest, and so had been left where they were. O'Malley had the heavy feeling that the investigators had been on the money about relevance, but he took extensive photographs anyway.

Twenty minutes later, having delved under bricks and burnt sections of kitchen worktop, he thought to shove the stove aside, and discovered what was unquestionably a metal picture frame wedged between the back of it and the largest remaining piece of wall.

He lifted it, gingerly. He could feel ash and grit against his fingers, even through the gloves, but the shape of it was still solid. It had been shielded, he supposed, by the stove, and saved from melting in the end by the fire engines that had eventually arrived to douse the place.

Pulled out into the light, it was revealed as a photograph in a frame that must have hung on the wall. A photograph of a strikingly beautiful dark-haired young woman in a very eighties blouse, alongside a short but obviously handsome man in a tweed jacket. The two of them looked fresh, hopeful. Their arms were round each other, her head a few inches higher than his. The difference in height didn't seem to bother either of them.

He felt both satisfied and disconcerted by it. If this had been taken in the eighties, then the young woman was the right age to be Anneka Foley. Had she really been this clear-eyed beauty? Or was this a sibling? Perhaps a sister and her husband?

But she'd had no siblings, he remembered. It had been just Anneka and her parents living in this house, until they'd died in quick succession during the late seventies. She'd lived here alone for thirty-five years.

So if this photograph proved to be Anneka, then the man might be Dara Cooley. A man they had no photograph of as yet, thanks to his lack of criminal record and online presence.

Well, they'd have one soon enough from Aisling once they went to the house to arrest the boys. He sent a quick message to Hanson reminding her to pick at least one up, and then as an afterthought added a request to check whether there were any men of a similar name living in West Gradley.

He spent a little longer digging around after that, and then took the photo with him and went back to the car. He'd show it to some of the locals, he decided. It might jog their memories about seeing Dara Cooley, and if any of them knew where he was now, then their search would be over.

He manoeuvred the car over the weeds once again and back down the drive. He'd never been easily spooked, but he found himself quite glad to be driving away from the burnt husk of Anneka Foley's life.

Jonah brought Hanson and Lightman back into one of the smaller meeting rooms for an update at four thirty.

'We're still waiting for a return call from this Matthew Downing to confirm Ethan Cooley's alibi,' Hanson said. 'I'll try him again shortly. I've also been looking into Dara Cooley for Domnall. He was keen to find out whether he'd settled around West Gradley, but the interesting thing is that he wasn't born Dara Cooley.'

Jonah sat back from the table, genuinely surprised. 'He changed his name?'

Hanson nodded. 'I checked the general registry, and he was actually born Patrick Horan. He changed his name on his arrival in England. His wife and daughter also changed their names. Aisling was born Martha Horan.'

Jonah looked away as he mulled this over. 'Aisling Cooley didn't mention any former identity,' he said thoughtfully. 'And she put her new name on the Globalry site.'

'She didn't seem to want to talk about her family at all,' Ben agreed. 'She's still delaying on even providing a photograph of her father.'

'Interesting,' Jonah muttered. 'You wouldn't change your name to Dara Cooley to try to fit in more, would you? You'd be just as identifiably Irish.'

'That's what I figured,' Hanson agreed. 'To me it sounds more like they were trying to hide something. Or from something.'

2 1

The reply from Jack had taken forty-five minutes to arrive. Forty-five minutes in which Aisling had paced shakily around the house with her phone in her hand, unsure whether to be more frightened of his response or of what the police would say later. Which was ridiculous. Frankly ridiculous.

She'd reread her message ten or twelve times, regretting every phrase of it by the time she'd finished. Even though really there had been little else she could have said.

> Jack, you may not remember me, but this is Martha Horan from Tullamore. I'm on the board of the firm you're working for. It's a strange, small world, isn't it?
>
> As you can see, I'm no longer known as Martha, and haven't been since we left Ireland. I'm having some big trouble, and would really value your help (professional, of course).
>
> Might we meet tomorrow? I can come to London if needed.
>
> I really hope you're doing well.
>
> Regards,
> Aisling (Martha)

Her phone eventually chimed two minutes after she'd given up carrying it and gone to wipe down the already-clean kitchen table.

She picked it up with immediate terror. Her initial thought that Jack had replied was replaced by awful imaginings that this was the police. That they were on their way to arrest one of the boys, and that her three-person family was out of time.

But this was an email, not a message, and the sender was Jack O'Keane. He'd replied from what looked to be a private Gmail address rather than the one he'd been set up with at VePlec.

Aisling's hands shook as she opened it. It was absurd to be so nervous about what a man she hadn't seen for thirty years might say.

His very first line made her eyes prick with tears.

Martha/Aisling,

It's only a good thing to hear from you. I'm really glad to be in touch, and it's even better if I can help you somehow.

Are you London-based or elsewhere? I can come to meet you somewhere this evening after work and a meeting with the CEO. Happy to jump on a train (I'll just charge it to your expenses).

Let me know and looking forward to catching up,

Jack

PS I was joking about the expenses ☺

Her vision was a little watery as she replied, telling him that she was in Lyndhurst. That she might not be able to go anywhere today. Which she would explain too, but it involved the police and she'd rather do it in person. But she didn't want to drag him all the way here, so should they just Skype or something?

Having sent it, she realised that she would need to go into the police station with the boys for their DNA test. How long would that take? Should she allow an hour? Two?

She sent a quick extra email to say that she'd probably

have to be out of the house until eight p.m., judging by what she'd been told by the police.

Jack's reply came a minute later.

I can be there by nine thirty this evening. Absolutely no bother. Just tell me the address. Police sounds stressful but let's see what we can do.

It was strange to find herself, on today of all days, smiling in a way she hadn't for years.

22

At a quarter past five, as Hanson was getting ready to head to the Cooley house, Matthew Downing finally chose to return her call.

'Sorry for the wait,' he said airily.

'Ah, that's OK,' Hanson said brightly. 'It's hard to catch people when they're at work.'

'Oh, I'm not office-based,' Matthew replied. 'I was recording. Really in the zone. I didn't want to get my head into this really negative space while I was in the middle of it by calling back, you know?'

Hanson blinked, and then said, 'I just wanted to check up about this party of yours on New Year's Eve.'

'Look, there wasn't any trouble,' Matthew said immediately. A little scathingly. 'If anyone's complained . . .'

'I'm just checking up on who was there at this stage,' Hanson said breezily. 'We were looking at a couple of comings-and-goings around the party, which weren't directly connected with it.'

'Oh.' Matthew let out a breath. 'All right.'

She began with easy questions about the start time and format. Matthew responded with a strange mixture of bad grace and slight bragging. Comments like, 'We had Bly Palmer here. The actress?' contrasted with disgruntled complaints that it was hard to remember a list of twenty or thirty people and when they'd arrived.

About Ethan Cooley, he was at least fairly clear. He'd definitely been there.

'And he was late to the point of rudeness,' Matthew said.

'Oh, really? What time was that then?' she asked.

'Eleven fifty-five.'

'Right . . .' Hanson could feel her heart thumping in her neck. 'Definitely not earlier?'

'Definitely,' Matthew said just as flatly, and it sounded like he wasn't going to help any further. But then the slightly superior side to him seemed to take over and he added, 'Literally five minutes before midnight. He apologised for being late, and I told him he'd missed the chance to play a set for us all. He looked pretty pissed off, but he brought it on himself.'

'So that would be a singing set?'

'Yes.'

Matthew volunteered nothing more, so Hanson asked, 'Did he explain why he was late?'

'He messaged an excuse earlier on,' Matthew said. And of course that was all he said. Nothing volunteered.

'What did he say?'

'Just that he'd had to help his brother with something.' And she wasn't sure, but she suddenly thought that Matthew might actually be enjoying telling her this. As if he knew exactly why she was asking these questions.

23

O'Malley pulled up in what looked to be the centre of West Gradley. It wasn't by any means a large place. It had a single building that served as post office and local shop combined, plus a church and a pub.

The shop had its shutters down, despite it not yet having hit five. There was a sheet of paper taped to the door announcing new, reduced opening hours.

But the pub was evidently open, and had two cars parked outside. Open but quiet was his favourite situation for a pub. It was the easiest scenario to get staff chatting.

He let himself in through the door, experiencing a welcome blast of heat as he crossed the threshold. Though unseasonably warm for January, it was still cold now that the sun had set. He glanced at the horizon, thinking that it was a little lighter than at this time a week ago. He felt as though he were hanging on for spring this year. Not least because he badly needed to sort his health out and warmer weather really helped.

He glanced at the two customers currently sitting at the bar, one elderly gent in a flat cap and a woman of forty or so further down. He'd lay money on it that they'd both lived here for some years, which could prove useful.

As O'Malley approached the bar, a fifty-something man appeared, rising from where he'd clearly been crouched to restock the shelves. He had the easy authority of the landlord about him. He gave O'Malley a good-natured grin.

'What can I get for you?'

'Ahh, an orange juice is all I'm good for,' O'Malley said. 'If I could trouble you for one. On duty.'

Although true, this was an excuse O'Malley had used many times before to avoid drinking alcohol. He was fifteen years sober, the only choice he'd been able to make in order to regain his life and find himself a job.

It was a lot easier for him than it had been in those early days, but the thrill of anticipation still hit him when he crossed the threshold of a pub. This, his subconscious had already told him, would be a great place to try a few new ales and read the paper, spreading it out over one of the big oak tables.

'Orange juice it is.' The landlord picked up a glass, gave O'Malley an assessing glance, and said, 'Police, is it?'

''Fraid so.' O'Malley placed the framed photograph face down onto the bar and leaned his elbows on the counter as the landlord turned to pull a bottle of Luscombe orange juice out of the fridge. A much more upmarket brand than O'Malley usually got in the pubs around Southampton. 'I'm just here finding out about a past resident. I wanted to ask you about her, actually.'

The landlord put the orange juice down in front of him, and O'Malley held out his card to pay.

'Sure, ask away,' the landlord said, as he took payment. 'I'll help if I knew her.'

'Her name was Anneka Foley,' O'Malley said.

It was clear from the way the landlord sighed, and glanced towards the elderly patron, that he knew her well. O'Malley guessed that the old man knew her too.

'Yeah, I can help.' He gave O'Malley a sharp look. 'You know she died a few years back?'

'I found that out,' O'Malley agreed. 'What I was interested in was her life. A little more about her.'

The landlord nodded. 'It's not a cheerful story that. She'd lived here since she was born.' He nodded towards the door. 'Her parents used to own a stud farm out here. The one the cottage sits near. It's just a dairy farm and a few cramped houses now. A shame. The place was a great employer for the youngsters here, me included. They had good money, those two, and they treated people well.'

The landlord picked up a cloth and started to wipe the bar down. O'Malley had the distinct impression from the way he'd spoken that he'd told this story before. It had the air of a practised routine. 'And the other draw to work there was Anneka. She was – well, she was a beauty. No other way to describe her. And also different from everyone else I'd ever met. Wild and brave and exciting. She wasn't afraid of any horse, or to climb anything, run anywhere at any time of night. We were all half in love with her. But she wasn't interested in any of us.'

'Did she never have a boyfriend?' O'Malley asked.

'Well, she did later,' the landlord admitted. 'After I'd stopped working there, I saw her around with this good-looking guy. God, it drove me spare, seeing her. She was so obviously crazy about him. But then it turned out he had a wife and was stringing her along.' He gave a shrug. 'I think that might have been the start of things slipping for her. And then her parents died, first one, then the other. And we stopped seeing her often, but when we did, she seemed . . . not right, any more. Like she'd say things that made no sense. Or would turn up in the village wearing just a slip. Or once a ballgown.' He shook his head.

'You think her mental health was suffering?'

'It was, it was,' the landlord agreed. 'I tried to get the local GP and then the mental health crisis team to step in, but they kept asking her to call them or make appointments herself, and of course she didn't or couldn't. We got as far as driving her to A & E once when she'd burned herself badly and then run out into a storm, but they just patched her up, and then when we tried to say she was a danger to herself, told us she had to ring the mental health team.' He sighed. 'It was no good at all.'

O'Malley nodded, feeling a familiar heavy sadness at the terrible state of social care. The support offered had diminished, and it had affected his own job. There were times when they were passed non-investigative cases simply because the uniformed police were overwhelmed. And as well as cuts to uniformed numbers, a lot of that was the result of the closure of mental health facilities, and a lack of help when people desperately needed it. Where there was nobody else to step in, it was increasingly becoming the role of the police to persuade troubled folks not to commit violence or take their own lives.

'It sounds as though she was let down quite badly.'

'She was,' the landlord agreed. 'A lot of us were very angry when she died. Angry, but not surprised. That's what happens when you put budgets ahead of people who need help.'

'So what happened to this boyfriend of hers?' O'Malley asked. 'Did he stick around?'

'No, he stopped coming,' the landlord said.

'Do you know when that might have been?'

The landlord let out a short laugh. 'Well, this is all decades ago, you know? I mean . . . a while after I worked at the stables.' He paused. 'Mid-eighties? Maybe eighty-four or -five when he disappeared off the scene? I don't think . . . I can't really say any more than that.'

O'Malley nodded, thinking that the maths on that wasn't quite right. Aisling Cooley said her father had vanished in eighty-seven. Perhaps this was the landlord's faulty memory.

Or perhaps Dara Cooley had been visiting West Gradley long before he'd moved to England.

O'Malley turned the photograph from the cottage over. 'Is this him?'

The landlord twisted his head slightly. 'Yup. That's the one.' He shook his head.

'You know his name?'

'Mikey, she called him.' The landlord sniffed. It was strange how carefully people could carry old hurts like this. Old resentments. Here it was in this gentle-seeming man, a vein of anger towards Anneka's lover, even after thirty years.

O'Malley wondered at the name. Had Dara Cooley had a whole new identity here? A different cover? Was Mikey the name they should be looking into, or had he walked into a new identity somewhere else?

'And you definitely didn't see him after he left?' O'Malley pressed. 'Not recently, like? Before she died?'

The landlord shook his head. 'No. I reckon him leaving was a lot of why she became so sad. Her parents dying and then him proving a cheat . . . I felt angry that the world handed that to her. Though angrier at him.'

O'Malley felt a heavy drop of disappointment. It would, he supposed, have been too easy to have immediately found Dara Cooley. But he'd hoped for some sort of a lead. Something to point him onwards.

'You should tell him about the kid,' the elderly man said suddenly, his voice gravelly. 'That's family.'

'A kid?'

'Ahh, that's another sad side of it,' the landlord said. He paused for a moment, and then said, 'Back when she first retreated from everyone, a visiting neighbour saw this little boy, and it turned out he was Anneka's. Boyfriend must have been the father.'

'Tell him about the state of the lad,' the elderly patron said.

'Ah, I only saw him the once,' the landlord replied. 'I'd brought her some smoked ham, and saw the mite in the garden. He looked filthy, and too thin, and that was the first time I tried calling her doctor. I was worried about him.' He turned to grab a glass, and O'Malley realised he was pouring himself a drink. 'You know, the only thing they did was take the kid away? Out of everything? They never lifted a finger to help her. And I feel – I feel responsible for that, because as much as I cared about the kid, it must have been fearful hard on her, losing him too.'

He filled himself a full pint glass of lager, and began to sink it.

It was natural that O'Malley's mind went to those DNA results. He knew Cassie had said the DNA had come from a full brother, but was that absolutely set in stone? Could a child of Aisling's father, one he'd had with a woman other than her mother, be a close enough relative to have matched the profile? Maybe if Anneka Foley was related to the Cooleys some way back?

'What year do you think the boy was born then?' he asked.

'Ahh, hard to say,' the landlord said, pausing in his drinking.

'Must have been eighty-five or eighty-six, I think,' the elderly gent said, surprising both of them. 'Few years after the sale of the stud farm, you'll remember. It was eighty-seven when I bought the pasture land off Anneka. I remember thinking, when I found out about the kid, as it made sense of it. That she'd want to have the money to support him, and not a farm to run.'

O'Malley nodded. 'And do you know anything about who picked him up?'

'Social services, I think it must have been,' the landlord replied. 'In eighty-nine. The kid would have been three or four. She told me about it, as much as she told me anything. She was screaming about some treacherous bastard with his suit come to get him.'

O'Malley thanked them and walked thoughtfully back to the car, wondering about that child, and whether they now had a fourth suspect to find.

24

Hanson and Lightman arrived at Aisling Cooley's house at just before six. Having failed to prove definitive alibis for either of the Cooley brothers – and knowing that Ethan hadn't been at the party all evening like he'd told his mum – they were moving on to do what they had planned: to arrest and take a cheek swab.

Hanson tried not to show her embarrassment as two uniformed DCs got ready to become their invisible tail. It was somehow made more humiliating by the fact that one of them was Casho.

Could be worse, she thought, as she glanced across CID at the hunched form of her most recent ex-boyfriend. *They could have sent Jason.*

But even that small relief was crushed when one of the other DCs who'd been co-opted leaned over to talk to her ex. Jason lifted his head, and turned to stare at the departing DCs and then back at her. He looked slightly concerned.

She felt like walking over and saying a breezy, 'Oh, don't worry. I'm probably just being stalked by the psychotic ex-boyfriend you believed instead of me. Nothing to worry about.' But she was aware that this was both petty and unfair. She hadn't broken up with Jason solely because he'd been willing to believe Damian's terrible stories about her; she'd also realised that Jason had represented safety and normality but not love.

She followed Ben out to the car park, and was relieved to see that Casho and her colleague had already vanished. They were presumably now in a car, ready to follow Hanson at a distance and see if they could catch whoever was stalking her.

Twenty minutes later, Aisling Cooley opened the door to them. She was unmistakably tense, a marked contrast with her overenthusiastic terrier. The dog followed them into the sitting room and then launched himself at Hanson's lap.

'God, sorry,' Aisling said, as she dragged him off by his collar.

'What's his name?' Hanson asked, grinning. She was, luckily, very much a dog person, even if she was slightly worried by the enthusiastic claws coming into contact with one of her nicest suits.

'Barks,' Aisling told her. And then added, sharply, 'Barks!' as the terrier managed to wriggle free and make a bolt for Ben's legs.

Ben was, of course, unfazed. He put a hand down and rubbed at the terrier's head, which caused the dog to wag so hard that his entire back end rotated.

'Good name,' Ben commented.

'It's short for Count Barku Barku of Barkchester,' Aisling said, before manhandling him to the door and booting him out. 'Which is what happens when you allow teenage boys to name a dog.'

'That's excellent,' Ben said. 'My sister and I called our childhood Labrador Secret Spaniel, which my parents were seriously unimpressed by.'

Hanson snorted, not having heard this particular gem before. And then, for a strange moment, felt unaccountably sad as she imagined how much sillier and more light-hearted Ben might have been if he had never met his piano teacher. Never been subjected to abuse and the guilt that went with it.

'That is . . . quite something,' Aisling said, half laughing.

'She just got called Span all the time, to be honest,' Ben admitted.

Aisling Cooley gave another laugh, this one slightly manic, and Hanson wondered whether she had any reason for being particularly nervous. It was clearly a stressful situation, but it might be that she had specific doubts about her sons.

'Do you need a drink?' Aisling asked. 'Tea? Coffee?'

'I'm all right for now,' Hanson replied.

'Yeah, I can wait a bit,' Ben agreed.

'OK,' Aisling said. And then she added, 'It'll be Ethan home first. It's a twenty-minute drive back from Beat and Press and he finishes at five thirty. He's usually home by ten past six. Which I guess tells you how much cleaning those guys do at the end of a shift.'

She paused, looking slightly stricken, and Hanson gave her a sympathetic look. She could guess the thoughts running through Aisling's head just then: the second-guessing about whether anything she said might make her sons seem more likely to have murdered a woman.

Once Aisling had let herself back out into the kitchen, Hanson wandered through the sitting room. She'd already taken the time to have a good stroll round the outside of the house, and had gone from professional curiosity to envy pretty quickly. It wasn't a particularly big place, except for the hefty kitchen extension, but from its sandstone exterior to its very natural-feeling garden, it was absolutely her cup of tea.

It was the same story inside. It was surprisingly spacious, beautifully lit and attractive in spite of being lived-in. Jackets were flung onto hooks and rugs over sofas. There had been large numbers of shoes in the hall, and there were photographs everywhere, particularly here in the sitting room.

Hanson moved to one wall and focused in on the pictures. There were repeated images of the two boys, sizing up through school, grinning and then frowning and then grinning again as they aged. There were shots of Aisling and the two of them on a raft. At what looked like Comic Con. On a beach.

The trio invariably looked like they were mid-joke, laughing in a way that was infectious. Scattered through these photos were older pictures. They showed a large-framed, sandy-haired man with a beard, and a small, slight woman, who shared Aisling's rounded cheeks and lips but whose whole expression was tighter. In one or two of the photos, they were joined by a girl who must have been Aisling when young.

Hanson clocked these with interest. The man must be Aisling's father, Dara Cooley – or Patrick Horan – and the woman her mother, Dymphna. She pulled her phone out and took a close-up of Dara's face, then messaged it to O'Malley.

She knew that she shouldn't lose sight of Dara Cooley as a suspect. He was, as they'd established, a believable age to prey on women in their mid-forties. To this, she could add that there was clearly something murky in the way he'd left Ireland and changed names. The fact that he had later abandoned his family showed impulsive tendencies. He'd presumably set up a new life for himself in secret too, which made Hanson think that impulsivity and secrecy were habitual modes of behaviour for him.

She carried on her stroll around the room, realising belatedly that there were no photos of the boys' father. The banker might as well not have existed. Which possibly gave a little insight into the boys' psychology. Their mother must be very central to their lives. Was that relationship a healthy one?

She moved away from the pictures, letting her eyes fall on the very modern, good-quality furniture. She decided that she liked the way the exposed, light-coloured beams contrasted with slightly fantasy-orientated artwork and film posters in frames.

She murmured to Ben, 'Keep.'

Ben grinned at her. 'I'm definitely going for keep. But it needs a tennis court. I'm surprised they haven't done it already, considering Finn's career.'

'Er . . . maybe because they're not millionaires?' Hanson hazarded.

It was rare for them to visit a house that made it onto their 'keep' list. Their long-running game of keep-sell-demolish had thrown up a lot of places they would demolish and a number they would sell for profit, but she and Ben were both too picky to like many of them enough for keeping.

It was particularly unusual to find somewhere they'd both go for, even though they tended to agree on what to demolish. The clash always came over Hanson's liking for big spaces versus Lightman's love of cute little cottages. Which Hanson always found inexplicable considering the height of him.

'I even like the decor,' she added, coming to sit next to him. 'And this sofa's actual bliss.'

'You'd never make it to work, though,' Ben countered. 'I keep my sofa hard and unwelcoming just so I'm not tempted to sit on it too long.'

'Ahh, I always thought that was just to match your soul,' Hanson said, turning to grin at him.

'That too.'

They sat in amicable silence, checking their iPads and phones now and then, until the distinctive sound of someone failing to get the key into a lock brought them to attention.

Hanson caught Lightman's eye in amusement as, after what must have been the fifth go, the door was finally unlocked. Aisling had said it would be Ethan first. The musician. Was he drunk?

But his voice sounded normal enough as he called out, 'Hey, *Maman.*'

Hanson heard Aisling's immediate response: 'Hey, villain.' And she raised an eyebrow at Ben. Presumably a joke name between them rather than an indication of anything else. But a weird thing to say with the police listening in.

'I picked up the car,' Ethan said. 'Only cost a bit more than buying a new one.'

His voice quietened as he headed down into the kitchen, and Aisling's reply was lost. She would presumably now explain why there were police officers in the living room.

It was strangely tense sitting and waiting for Aisling to tell him everything. Even though that glimpse of their relationship had seemed healthy, Hanson knew almost nothing about the real Ethan. There was a reasonable chance he was the Bonfire Killer, and this could be the moment he realised that he was trapped.

They heard a few murmurs, and then a long pause. Hanson found herself bolt upright on the soft sofa now, her heart a very palpable thump in her chest. Would Ethan try to run?

And then the door opened quietly, and she and Lightman rose.

It was interesting to see the full development of Ethan's hair now that he was nineteen. It had graduated from short curls into a shaggy but somehow innately stylish mass.

He looked anxious. Undeniably so. But what nineteen-year-old boy who'd never been in trouble with the law wouldn't be? And there was no suggestion that he was drunk. So his inability with a key must be simple ineptitude. Which wasn't an immediately obvious fit with their careful killer.

'This is Ethan,' Aisling said, from over his shoulder.

'Detective Sergeant Ben Lightman,' Ben said, holding out a hand. 'And this is Detective Constable Juliette Hanson.'

Hanson gave Ethan as warm and supportive a smile as she could. Ethan's fingers were cold to the point where it was unsettling as she shook his hand. From the cool weather or a surge of anxiety, she wasn't sure.

'Mum said – you need us to come to the station? Me and Finn?'

'That's right,' Ben said, gently. 'We found DNA at a crime scene that is a match for someone related to your mother. That means we need to swab each of you to rule you out.' He gave both Ethan and his mother a sympathetic look. 'That has to be under arrest. But the kind of unintrusive arrest that just means escorting you to the station, asking you a few questions and bailing you until we get the results. If you're cleared, you won't have a criminal record. Nothing to carry with you. You can go on as normal.'

It was well put: reassuring and designed to make Ethan come quietly. But Hanson could hear the unspoken other half to this: *If you aren't cleared . . .*

Ethan looked pinched. White. 'How accurate is the test going to be?' he asked. 'Could they . . . make a mistake, and think it was me?'

'It's very reliable,' Hanson told him, with a smile. 'This was DNA gathered soon after it was left, and prepared perfectly for modern testing. The lab analyses it thoroughly, using enough markers to be sure whether it's a match, and we'll have results quickly. Maybe even tonight.'

She could see Ethan thinking over what she had said. Trying to process it. For some reason he didn't seem all that reassured.

25

Jonah had failed to dodge the last meeting of the day, their monthly cross-divisional heads-together with local services to look at tackling youth crime.

It was something that Jonah believed wholeheartedly in trying to combat. He had started out, two years ago, enthusiastic about contributing to the scheme. But somewhere along the way, he'd begun to feel a creeping sense of futility. They might meet once a month, but meanwhile there were cuts to every single service that might have helped tackle the problem. Youth outreach programmes were going. PCSOs were desperately thin on the ground and no longer able to spend time getting to know the kids who might be steered away from gangs.

Today, with his own concerns and a major investigation under way, he found it impossible to engage with any of the tabled discussions. It was too hard to hear, once again, from youth workers who knew they were losing kids to a life none of them wanted to lead. All of them driven by fear of the alternative – or fear of what was happening back at home.

He found himself thinking, inescapably, of Milly. He'd always assumed that she'd grow up just fine, because he loved her and was determined to do right by her. But what if Michelle did end up hating him? What if Milly found herself caught between two bitter, unhappy parents? Would she be the sunny-tempered child he saw now? Or would she turn out damaged? Disaffected?

He left the meeting at five in a state of unusual depression, to find a message waiting from Michelle. It was a brief line telling him she was going to head out with Kathryn that evening, a colleague from work, but that she'd made sure Rhona was OK to hold the fort.

Jonah would usually have messaged back something warm and supportive about it being good for her to see her friends. But today, he found himself unable to summon up the energy. He messaged back a quick, OK. See you later. And then he shut himself into his office and tried to find something good to think about.

O'Malley was back at his desk when Hanson's photo message arrived. It was a single image, which she'd captioned with the words 'Dara Cooley'.

O'Malley sat up, feeling a hit of surprise. This was not the fairly short, handsome man in the picture with Anneka Foley. This man looked nothing like him. He had a much broader forehead, lighter hair and features that were much less classically good-looking. Dara's eyes were even the wrong colour: a mid-brown that contrasted with his light hair. The only point of similarity was, in fact, that both had sported beards.

O'Malley found himself looking between the two of them in consternation, before realising that the simplest answer was the clearest: Anneka had been seeing another man before Dara Cooley. It made sense of what the guys in the pub had said about the handsome fellow disappearing in eighty-five.

Assuming that the guy who worked in Leatherwaites had been right about Dara seeing Anneka, she'd had two boyfriends who had led her on, only to abandon her, O'Malley thought. And the death of her parents to deal with too. All of that, and nobody to talk to, would have been devastating for her mental health.

What this meant, practically, was that it was going to be

even harder to find Dara Cooley through the West Gradley link than he'd anticipated. Dara had been, presumably, subtler about his affair than this man. Though not subtle enough that someone from his company hadn't at last sniffed it out.

With a sigh, he went to make himself another coffee as he tried once again to think of ways to find a man who'd been missing for twenty-eight years.

26

By the time Hanson and Lightman had gone through the process of arresting Ethan – the least formal, kindest sort of arrest possible – the older Cooley brother was visibly shaking. Hanson knew that they couldn't read much into that. Most kids found arrest stressful. Unreal. Scary. But so did the guilty.

Hanson was itching to ask him about where he'd been on New Year's Eve, but all questions would have to wait until the formal interview at the station with the chief present. They'd agreed on that.

Ethan descended into silence as they waited for his brother. He sat himself down on an armchair, his head lowered and his left leg jigging up and down rhythmically.

Hanson was relieved when there were sounds in the hallway. It took only a few minutes for Aisling to talk with her younger son outside, and then she was opening the door to admit Finn.

The younger Cooley brother looked a little more collected, Hanson thought. Despite the evident dampness of both his pale blue tennis shirt and his dark hair, he still exuded well-groomed vigour.

Hanson briefly remembered the way he'd looked towards her car the day before, and searched for signs of recognition. But there was no visible reaction.

Finn shook hands with both of them firmly, and before either Hanson or Lightman could say any more, he said, 'I'm really sorry to hear there's been a murder. If I can help, I will.'

'Thank you,' Ben said. 'The biggest help will be taking a cheek swab from each of you, so we can include or exclude you both. I'm sorry that that has to be under arrest.'

Finn frowned. 'Will that be made public?'

'No, we want to keep everything as low-profile as possible,' Ben answered. 'And, as I was telling your brother, this won't mean a criminal record if you're cleared straight afterwards.'

'OK,' Finn said, letting out a breath. 'When was it? The . . . crime? Because you might be able to rule us out straight away if we weren't around.'

Hanson saw Ben glance sideways at her, before saying steadily, 'New Year's Eve.'

Finn nodded. And then, just afterwards, his gaze slid over to his brother.

Hanson saw Ethan's expression change. His chest moved slightly, and he opened his mouth.

But then, out of the corner of her eye, she saw Finn shake his head. It was the slightest of gestures, but she saw it. And she knew that there was more here than met the eye.

Hanson found herself so caught up in analysing that exchange that she barely registered returning to Lightman's Qashqai. It was only when Ben said, 'No treats waiting for us this time,' that she remembered that she was supposed to be on the lookout. That whoever was stalking her was out there.

'Unless you count a car with working heating,' she said after she'd dragged herself back to the present.

It might just be a good thing that those DCs were watching her.

27

Hanson appeared in Jonah's doorway and announced that they had the Cooley boys – and Aisling – here with them. It was seven twenty p.m., and CID was quieter now. A handful of detectives remained on the floor, working late shifts or their own time-sensitive cases. Or perhaps, Jonah suddenly thought, avoiding going home.

'Aisling's in reception, and the two boys are being swabbed,' Hanson told him. 'We've taken their devices. I can call down to the cyber team to get data downloaded.' She gave him a slightly significant look. 'Along with Ethan not being where he told his mother, I think both the brothers know something about New Year's Eve. There was some silent communication going on that would be worth digging into.'

'Interesting,' Jonah said. 'I'll have a word with the mother first. We still need to ask her about the name change, and I'll press her on the boys. Can you show her into Room Three if it's still free, and ask Ben to be ready? I'm going to make coffee on the way.'

'Sure thing, chief,' Hanson said brightly.

Jonah had to smile. Hanson was a lot newer to the job than he was, having only been a detective for some eighteen months. But she'd had to do a lot of grinding casework over that time, including hours of headache-inducing CCTV review. Yet her enthusiasm seemed to have stayed throughout, even during the last few exhausting months. A particularly impressive feat while she was waiting for her abusive ex-boyfriend to stand trial.

'Juliette,' he said, just as she was about to leave, 'I – wanted to apologise for you having to talk very publicly about your, um, ex earlier. And to say that I know it's an even further invasion of your privacy having a couple of DCs following you, but I think it's probably worth it. We have to bear in mind the small possibility that the DNA we have was from a witness to the killing, and not from the killer, apart from anything else.' He gave a slight smile. 'And if it does just turn out to be Damian doing this guardian-angel stuff, then it's more to throw into the court case.'

'Oh.' Hanson gave a short, clearly embarrassed laugh. 'Thank you, that's – I agree.' She grinned. 'And I'm pretty used to being followed around now, so it's no biggie.'

Jonah nodded. Smiled. 'All right. Just . . . keep me posted about anything beyond that. Emails, phone calls . . . you know. I want to help.'

Juliette gave him a small smile in return. 'Will do. If you promise to kneecap Damian on the quiet.'

She left with a wider smile, and Jonah sat back feeling like a better boss. And a better friend, too, which was also important.

Once Hanson had gone, he headed to the kitchen, mulling over everything he wanted to discuss with Aisling while he made coffee. Digging into Finn and Ethan's whereabouts on both New Year's Eve and October the third were key to that.

O'Malley had also reported all his findings, many of which were interesting. Jonah had already sent a message to Cassie in the US, asking whether their DNA match could possibly include a half-brother if there was some additional family relationship between Anneka Foley and the Cooleys. They didn't yet know whether Anneka Foley really had borne Dara Cooley a child, but the troubled upbringing of that boy sounded as though it could chime with a man who had later committed violence against women.

Then there was the fact that Dara Cooley had left his home town in a hurry. Jonah wanted to ask Aisling about the events leading to that. And whether she had any doubts about where her sons had been on New Year's Eve.

This would be a difficult interview. Aisling had vested interests in every direction, though he suspected her loyalties would lie more with her sons than her estranged father. At least they would have some firm answers soon. That was something to hold onto. It shouldn't take long for Cassie to let them know about this possible half-brother, and with the boys now swabbed, they'd have lab results back before eleven. That meant Finn and Ethan could be happily ruled out in a few short hours – or one of them firmly ruled in.

He drank a first sip of coffee, relieved to find his thoughts back on work once again. As long as he could do his job, everything else would be OK. He had to trust in that.

Aisling was pacing as Jonah and Ben walked into the interview room. Although her jeans, slouch sweater and messy bun were casual, her posture was anything but. She swung to face them with what looked to be frustration and fear.

'I'm DCI Jonah Sheens.' He held a hand out to her, and she flinched slightly, before stepping forwards quickly to take it. 'I'm the senior investigating officer for the case you've discussed with DS Lightman here. There are a few things I think it's time we shared with you.'

Jonah drew out one of the chairs and settled himself in it. Ben quietly did the same. Aisling looked as though the idea of sitting was beyond her. But then she said, 'I . . . right. OK,' and took her seat opposite Ben.

Jonah watched the way she perched on the very edge of the chair, sitting well back from the table and coiled as if to rise at any moment. She looked, he thought, very much unlike someone who spent their working hours in front of a computer.

'So,' he began, once the preamble was done for the sake of the videotape, 'I know DS Lightman has explained that the location we recovered DNA from was a murder scene. But there's more to it. I don't know if you've been keeping up with the news on the subject, but the case we're investigating is actually two murders. Both women in their mid-forties, and both placed on home-made pyres.'

He saw the colour leave Aisling's face. The way she looked suddenly nauseous. This was news to her, he was sure. She'd had no idea that they were looking at the Bonfire Killer's crimes.

'That's . . . I've seen about them . . .' She shook her head. Gave a brief, tight laugh. 'There's no way on earth that – that my sons were involved with those. And I don't think . . .' She swallowed. 'My dad wasn't a psychopath.'

Jonah nodded. 'It's very difficult to discuss this, I know. You feel like you know your own family, which I'm sure is true. But you'd be surprised, for example, how often kids turn out to have hidden a whole side of themselves from their family. It might be that they were being bullied viciously at school, or had been struggling with their mental health.'

'But they talk to me,' Aisling protested. 'They're not monosyllabic grunters. When something bothers them, they come and talk about it. It's the way they are. The way we've always been. So, you know, I've got to hear about their troubles, the whole way through. Like when Ethan was having trouble at his first school.' She looked over at Lightman. 'I knew all about it because he told me how unhappy he was, and we – I – did something about it. First through the school and then, when they didn't help, by moving him to one where that kind of thing didn't happen.'

'Of course,' Jonah said soothingly. 'But your father did have secrets, didn't he?'

Aisling's brow creased. 'I don't . . . well, yes, perhaps. But we don't know what those were. It could have been that he'd got in trouble with money, or at work, or . . .'

'The firm he worked for believed he was having an affair,' Jonah said, quietly. 'With a woman who lived near Newbury.'

Aisling said nothing for a few seconds, and then Jonah was surprised to see her turn away, her throat moving. She was trying to hold back tears.

'I'm sorry if that's difficult news,' he said.

'Ah, it was always the most likely explanation,' she said thickly. She rubbed at her eyes with the sleeve of the sweater. 'It's just – hearing it's true . . .' She shook her head. 'Do you know where he is then?'

'We haven't tracked him down yet,' Jonah admitted. 'We found out the address of the woman concerned, but she's since deceased. Her name was Anneka Foley.' He paused. 'Is that name familiar to you?'

Aisling shook her head, her eyes still oozing tears. 'No. Was she – did she work with him?'

Jonah shook his head. 'It's possible he met her through work, though.' He left a pause of a few seconds, and then he asked, 'Aisling, your family changed names when they came over here. Can you explain to me why?'

It was clear that this question had an effect on Aisling, one almost as marked as the effect of his revelation about the affair. Her whole body stiffened, and she folded her arms over herself.

'That – it has nothing to do with any of this.'

'It would still be useful for us to know why,' Lightman said gently, voicing his first remark since the interview had started.

'If your father did something that was – well, that might indicate a certain state of mind . . .'

Aisling looked across at him, and there was a slight easing of the tension in her. 'It wasn't that. It was because – it was because we needed to hide from someone, that's all. From a cousin, who was threatening to bring his whole extended family down on us.' She sighed. 'It was because of Donagh.'

Jonah frowned. 'Had your father done something to anger him?'

'No, it – not really.' Aisling looked uncomfortable once again. 'He wanted to marry me. That was all. He wanted to marry me, and I didn't want him. So it was my fault.'

Jonah watched her, in silence. He was unsure of whether to push her further on this. He didn't get the impression she was out-and-out lying to him, but it was quite possible that she was hiding something about her family in this truth.

His mind returned, however, to the two boys waiting to be interviewed, so he asked, 'All right. Can you tell me instead about Finn and Ethan's relationship with their dad?'

Aisling's face flushed with what looked at first to be embarrassment, until she said, 'They *have* no relationship with him.' She sat up further, her head lifting and her eyes very slightly bright. 'He walked out on all of us, because he found being a father boring. He wasn't even in love with the woman he left us for. She was just a convenient excuse.' She shook her head, less angry, he thought, than resigned.

'So they're not in touch with him?' Lightman asked.

'No, they're not. They think he's an arsehole, even though I never told them that myself. But that doesn't mean they've turned into bitter young men. It means they've got good judgement and know how to treat women and children.'

Jonah couldn't help smiling slightly. 'OK. That's useful to know, thank you. Finally, I just need to ask whether either of your sons has ever donated bone marrow or stem cells to anyone. This would be through a donor selection process, and an operation within a hospital setting that they would have undergone. This is just to rule out the possibility that their DNA would be showing up erroneously in someone else's blood.'

Aisling gave him a very wide-eyed look, and then shook her head. 'I . . . No. They haven't. I think Ethan was going to sign up for bone marrow, but then Barks chewed the sample packet, and the sample would have been contaminated.' Her mouth twitched. 'We had visions of him being asked in to donate and it being for an Alsatian or something.'

Jonah actually laughed at that. 'OK. And your father? Do you know if he did so while you were living with him?'

Aisling shook her head. 'It's not something he ever mentioned. I can't answer for later on.'

'OK, that's very useful, thank you. I'd like a quick chat with Finn and Ethan, maybe after everyone's had a coffee. Finn should have you with him, as a minor, even if it's just an informal interview.'

'Oh . . . yeah, OK. I'd like to be there with him.' She paused, and then said, 'I can come in with Ethan too. It might help.'

'I don't think it's necessary for Ethan to be accompanied just now,' Jonah replied. 'But we can get you if he feels in any way uncomfortable.' He smiled at her. 'This really is just an initial chat. If there's anything either of them wants to tell us, we'll be happy to bring a solicitor in.'

He could see the effect that his words had on Aisling. She moved slightly sideways, and then put a hand out to the table as if dizzy.

28

Aisling's body sagged the moment the two officers had left. The simple act of holding it all together while her anxiety and sense of grief had mounted was exhausting.

It was both reassuring and worrying to meet the detective chief inspector. Like his sergeant, Ben, he was evidently someone who took great care. But she'd also seen a hard edge to him. And it was clear that he was extremely smart too, which might be a very good thing, or a very bad one.

It was impossible to avoid overanalysing everything she said in the face of his all-seeing expression. To overthink all the things she wasn't saying, too, and to wonder whether she should be telling him every last thing about herself and her family so that he might help somehow.

She'd felt genuinely ill when he'd mentioned a solicitor. And having him ask about Tullamore, and why they'd left, had been profoundly unsettling. There was so much there that she simply did not want to think about. That awful night. Her mother's tight-lipped fury, and the way Aisling had pleaded with her father.

Without wanting to, she found herself remembering, almost in slow motion, Donagh arriving home. His handsome face and form appearing out of his car with such confidence. Before everything had turned to blood.

No, she thought. She almost said it aloud. *You can't afford to think about that now.*

But what else could she think about? About whether or

not her sons might have been lying to her? About whether one of them might have been involved in all this?

She'd been pushing tiny fragments of doubt away all day. They'd been kept at bay by the thought that one of her boys might have got tangled up in something, might possibly have done something infinitely stupid *by accident* and then scrambled to cover it up. That little island of carefully managed doubt could not withstand a sudden tsunami of knowledge. The wall of water that was the Bonfire Killer.

She pulled her iPhone out of her pocket and opened up Safari. For a moment she hung there, not wanting to go down this route. But then she typed 'Bonfire Killer Murders' into the search bar.

Second victim found in New Forest killings – police suspect serial killer

It was the most relevant article the BBC had to offer. The link was purple, she saw. This was an article she'd already read.

Rereading it now, the article reminded her of a lot of details she'd forgotten. That Lindsay Kernow had lived alone, like Jacqueline Clarke. That she hadn't been seen since her adult son had visited from Ireland over Christmas. That she'd lived in Totton, where she worked freelance as a book editor.

Aisling read that, and felt coldness crawl up her back and into her neck as she remembered Finn bounding over to his brother on New Year's Eve.

Fancy giving me a lift into Totton in your mad-wagon, brother mine? There's shubz going down at the Beekeepers.

Aisling remembered the way Ethan had shaken his head at

his brother and told him he was way too middle-class to get away with saying 'shubz' and that it didn't even count as 'shubz' if it was in a pub. He'd also grumbled about giving Finn a lift, but had done it. She remembered, too, waving them off to enjoy their New Year's Eve out before she'd settled onto the sofa with a bottle of Chablis.

Both her boys had been in Lindsay Kernow's home town. Finn might even have gone to the same pub. Ethan might have driven past her on his way home . . .

But neither of them would have spoken to her at length, surely. Her picture showed a woman who was obviously well into her forties. A woman with dark, wavy hair dyed with a hint of artificial red. She was pretty, but she wasn't beautiful, like Ethan's various girlfriends, or Finn's long-distance partner. Nor like the young women who flocked around Ethan at the end of every gig.

Though, Aisling thought, there were sometimes older women at those gigs. A few who became fixated on her son's talent and beauty and seemed to forget who they were. What they had to offer. Ethan had told her about some of them.

She suddenly imagined Lindsay trying to seduce Ethan. Trying to force him to go somewhere private with her after the end of a set. And Ethan being too gentle and well mannered to say no. Ending up following her, until it had all gone way, way too far.

She shoved her chair back quickly and stood, moving to get away from the image.

Nothing like that happened, she thought. *You've brought them up to treat all women with respect. They're feminists. And they dote on you. They'd never do this to another woman. Never.*

And yet the sick sense of doubt remained.

29

Jonah went to stand in the viewing gallery outside Room Four. He watched Ethan Cooley steadily for a while, taking in the slouched, unconcerned posture that was belied by the constant jigging of his leg. The hair that partially covered his eyes. The way his hands tapped the table in front of him.

In Room Three Finn was a very different picture. He sat with his back straight and his head tilted to one side. He looked around at times, but largely just seemed to be thinking about something relatively pleasant.

Did either of them look like the kind of man who could drug and then strangle two women, and then place them on a pyre?

Yes, Jonah thought. *Because killers look like anyone. Anyone at all.*

'Thank you for agreeing to the swab,' Jonah said to Finn, once he, Aisling and Lightman had all taken their seats round the table. Finn had jumped up to shake his hand, and then immediately sat down tidily.

Finn's handshake had been firm and his gaze direct, and Jonah had got the impression that the boy was looking at this as if it were a practice university interview. A situation where he could impress his way to the outcome he wanted.

'We should have the results in a few hours,' Jonah went on. 'I'd like to know whether you think the DNA will turn out to be yours.'

'I'm sure it won't,' Finn said immediately. 'I haven't been involved in anything like that.'

189

'I think my sergeant has explained to you that the body and the DNA were found on New Year's Day.' Jonah watched Finn's expression. 'Could you tell us what you were doing the night before?'

'Sure.' Finn gave a willing smile. 'I met up with some friends at a pub, but it was completely rammed. After we'd waited an hour and a half trying to find somewhere to sit, we gave up. Well, some of us did. I think a few of them stayed on.'

'What time did you leave?'

'Ten thirty, I think? Something like that?'

'Where was the pub?' Lightman asked. He had his iPad open and was taking his usual meticulous notes.

'The near side of Totton. The Beekeepers.'

'Did you use public transport to get there?'

'No, my brother gave me a lift.'

So, Jonah thought, both brothers were in Totton that evening.

'Ethan didn't stay at the pub?' Jonah asked.

'No, he had some party of his own to go to,' Finn replied without apparent worry.

'How did you get home?' Lightman was not one to be drawn away from pinning the details down. It was a way of working that Jonah, who was inclined to pursue a sudden new line of inquiry, found useful, even while it felt as though it slowed him down at times.

'I jogged it, I think,' Finn said. And then, 'Yeah, I looked and there were no cabs for an hour or something, so I just jogged back along the A35.'

'You ran?' Jonah asked, not sure whether or not to be sceptical. It was less disbelief that Finn would run that distance, and more that it seemed an unlikely thing to do on New Year's Eve after a few drinks. He could see Aisling staring at her son, too, and thought he detected a trace of horror in her expression.

'Yeah, I do it quite a lot.' Finn gave a shrug, somewhere between self-deprecating and self-satisfied. He seemed un-aware of his mother's reaction. 'It's, you know, only four miles back home, and it's good training. I generally just make sure I take a running backpack out with me so I'm free to pound the pavements afterwards.'

'But this was late at night,' Jonah said. 'Is your mother happy with you doing that?'

He glanced over at Aisling, who looked caught out.

'I . . .' She cleared her throat. 'No, I . . . I wouldn't have been happy if I'd known.'

'I was fine, though,' Finn said with a hint of irritation.

'How long would that take you?' he asked. 'To run four miles.'

'Having a gentle jog like that? Probably thirty-two minutes or so.'

Jonah had to laugh. 'That's quite a lot faster than me, even when I'm sober.'

'Ahh, you probably just need all the training I've been through,' Finn said with a proper smile. 'I was a lot slower before I got taught how to do it right.'

'I'll bear it in mind,' Jonah answered. 'So the A35 . . . that takes you straight back past Lyndhurst Heath, doesn't it?'

'Along one edge, yes,' Finn agreed, smiling a little less.

'You didn't stop off at all?' Lightman chipped in. 'Go onto the heath to relieve yourself or to look at the early fireworks?'

'No, I just ran.' Finn glanced at Aisling. 'Headphones in, running light on and go. That's the general plan.'

Aisling shook her head quickly, as though at the stupidity of doing this at ten thirty at night.

'Do you remember passing anyone?' Jonah tried. 'Or see-ing anyone who looked like they were in trouble, or were making trouble?'

Finn seemed to think about this, but then shook his head more slowly. 'Sorry. I don't think I saw many people. I can imagine seeing someone walking their dog, because that happens quite a lot, you know? But no idea if that was actually New Year's. Could be from a different night. I run that road quite a lot.'

'Was your mum still up and about when you got home?' he asked.

Finn shook his head. Glanced at his mother. 'I don't think so. The lights were off, weren't they? You must have crashed. Or dozed off on the sofa.'

'I don't remember you getting back,' Aisling said slowly. 'I passed out kind of early. Too much wine. So I guess I'd have been in bed by the time you let yourself in. What would that be? Eleven?'

'Or a bit later, yeah,' Finn said. 'If I stretched outside.'

Jonah could see Aisling thinking this over, before nodding. He wondered whether her reaction was frustration at his careless behaviour, or whether she wasn't convinced he'd been back by then.

Jonah nodded. 'All right. Do you know, or have you met, a woman called Lindsay Kernow?'

Jonah passed a photograph of Lindsay, taken a year before her death, over the table. It was, her son had said, still a good likeness. It showed dark, wavy hair cut into the same short style she'd had when they'd found her on the heath. Her expression was a little uncertain, which Dylan had said was normal for her too.

Finn looked down, seeming to at least take the question seriously as he studied the photo for a moment.

'No, I don't think so.' He shook his head. 'I don't recognise her and, to be honest, aside from a few teachers, I don't know many people of that kind of age.' He gave his mother a brief, flickering smile. 'Ma is the only ancient person I can put up with.'

Jonah gave a nod, thinking that Finn could have had time to prepare his lack of reaction, but having at least ensured that the question had been asked. 'OK, thank you. Let's talk about the bigger picture.' He glanced at Aisling, who gave a brief, telling shudder. 'We aren't looking at just one murder,' he told Finn as gently as possible, 'but two of them, as I've explained to your mum. We're fairly certain that they were both committed by the same individual. So if there's anything you can tell us . . .'

Jonah was very conscious of the way Aisling's eyes moved between her son and himself, searching for a reaction as clearly as he was.

Finn's expression seemed to be one of surprise. His mouth opened very slightly, and he looked blankly at Jonah for several seconds. And then his strong-jawed face tightened, and Jonah wondered whether he was seeing anxiety or a touch of anger.

'God, that's awful,' Finn said, his public-school drawl sounding exaggerated. Jonah wondered whether he was playing up the posh-boy act in an effort to seem more innocent, or whether it was an unconscious reaction to authority when feeling threatened. 'I really do want to help. The trouble is, I didn't, you know, see anything while I was running. Not that I remember anyway. I mean, I can try and think back, but there really isn't a lot I can bring to mind. I wouldn't even remember my times if I didn't have them recorded on Strava.'

Finn gave an open, self-deprecating smile.

'Would we be able to see the run?' Jonah asked. 'On Strava?'

Finn looked taken aback. 'I . . . guess so.' He glanced at Aisling. 'When you give my phone back. Assuming I remembered to record it.'

Jonah watched him again, for a moment, and then passed another photograph across the table.

'Do you recognise this woman?' Jonah stayed sitting forwards, his hand out to the photograph. 'Her name's Jacqueline Clarke. She lived in Brockenhurst.'

Finn's expression tightened slightly. Again, however, he looked carefully at the photograph. Jonah could see him taking in Jacqueline's very pretty, almost elfin face. Her strikingly blue eyes. The bright, slightly hard expression. 'Sorry. I don't think I've ever seen her either.' He shook his head and looked up. 'We don't go to Brockenhurst that often.'

Jonah nodded, and then, after a brief pause, he asked, 'Can you tell me if you remember what you were doing on the third of October?'

'Umm, well . . . Not sure, to be honest.' He gave a half-smile. 'What day of the week was it?'

'A Friday,' Lightman said.

'OK . . .' He could see Finn remembering. Or at least making a good show of it. 'Oh.' He brightened suddenly. 'That was the first weekend I went to see Marian.'

'Marian is . . . ?' Lightman asked.

'My girlfriend,' he said with a touch of pride.

'So that's long-distance?' Jonah queried.

'Yeah, she lives in Harrogate. We met at the Nat. Champs over the summer,' Finn said. 'She's a really good tennis player. She's actually the number one ranked under-seventeen player nationally.'

It interested Jonah that Finn hadn't felt the need to assert his own ability as he said this. He hadn't added that she was the top-ranking *girls'* player. Or suggested that the men's competition was harder, which a depressingly large number of sportsmen Jonah's age did at every opportunity.

'So you're quite a distance apart,' he said.

194

'Yeah. It's a bit tricky, to be honest.'

'So this visit to her,' Jonah went on. 'When did you leave?'

'It was . . . so I left the Friday. At lunchtime.'

The younger Cooley brother suddenly looked tense. A muscle next to his mouth had begun rhythmically tightening and then loosening.

'What time did you travel?'

'In the afternoon,' Finn said. 'I had some free study periods, so I left then. I went on the train.'

'And you arrived at hers when?'

'Oh, umm . . .' He cleared his throat. 'I actually split the journey. I stayed in a hostel overnight on the way. In London.'

Jonah saw Aisling's eyes dart over to her son, an expression of obvious surprise on her face.

'Right . . .' Jonah glanced at Lightman. 'It's, what? A five-hour journey to Harrogate?'

'Depends which trains,' Finn said a little defensively. 'Sometimes five and a half.'

'But you could easily have done it in an afternoon,' Jonah pressed.

'Yes, but I didn't really want to.' Finn cleared his throat again. 'I'm not a massive fan of long journeys, and I didn't want to make her parents wait to eat dinner or anything.'

'But you only had the weekend to spend with her,' Jonah pointed out. 'Did you not want to get there quickly?'

'We had plenty of time,' Finn said firmly.

Alongside him, his mother looked as though she wanted to say something. Her forehead was creased. Her expression more than concerned.

'What time did you eventually arrive on the Saturday?'

'Late morning.' Finn's head was now down, his eyes on his own hands.

'What did you do while you were in London?' Lightman asked.

'Not much.' Finn gave another shrug. 'Went to an Italian restaurant. Got an early night.'

'Your girlfriend didn't meet you there,' Lightman said. It was more a statement than a question.

'No.' Finn's voice was slightly hoarse.

'And you missed training to do that? To travel on the Friday?' Jonah asked.

There was a brief silence, and then Finn said quietly, 'Sometimes it's nice to have an excuse not to do it. I train six days a week, and get just one rest day. It's – sometimes it's nice just to be a teenager instead of a sports star. You know?'

Which sounded almost believable. But for some reason Jonah wasn't convinced.

30

The silence that Aisling and Finn were left in was deep, taut and suffocating. Aisling felt it stretching over her like a plasticky film. Any words were caught and held before they'd become audible.

She was looking at her son as if for the first time. As if she had no knowledge of his humour, his wonderful manners on the tennis court and his obsessive tidiness. No memory of his howling emergence into the world, or of the night terrors he had experienced right up until he turned fifteen. Without remembering his struggles with dyslexia, or how he'd cried for days at the death of their first dog, Charlton.

And she wondered whether those things were necessary to see him as he really was, or whether they clouded her judgement. Whether seventeen years of experience was stopping her from seeing the young man he had become.

She found herself thinking of a documentary she'd watched about Ted Bundy. About how Ted's mother had been adamant for years that her son was not a killer. It had taken a series of her son's confessions to convince her that she'd been wrong about him. And watching it, Aisling had felt furious with the woman. Surely she'd been able to see this side of her son.

Was Aisling no better?

For god's sake, she thought. *He's not Ted Bundy. He's Finn. You would know. You know everything about him.*

And yet it now appeared that she didn't. She hadn't known about that trip to London. She had checked in with him that evening, and he'd never mentioned that he wasn't in Harrogate. He must have lied to her, by omission if nothing else.

Because she'd asked him how Marian was, and what her house was like. She knew she had.

And he'd lied to the police too. She was certain of it. He didn't resent all the training.

And there was something else troubling her.

I train six days a week . . .

But it was seven days a week now, wasn't it? He'd put in an extra session, which his coach had said he'd do for free. That was what Finn had said, wasn't it?

She felt a shiver run through her.

What if that wasn't where he was going every Tuesday?

But surely, surely she would have noticed something wrong if he'd killed a woman? He couldn't have come and made eggs with her on New Year's Day after that, and chattered away about such reasonable things, could he?

And then, like a blow, she remembered that he'd had a cut on his leg. One she didn't think she'd seen before.

It felt like having the floor fall away from underneath her, that memory. She wanted, so desperately, to turn to him and ask him about it. To have him tell her, with a roll of his eyes, that he'd tripped over a stick while playing with Barks, or scratched himself on a bramble. To tell her that she remembered it. That he'd told her.

But something about that made her feel a little queasy too. Because Finn was always the competent one. The one who knew the answers. He was always, somehow, in control.

And it was dizzying and awful to suddenly think of every interaction between them differently. To wonder whether Finn had been playing her and Ethan all along.

She turned sharply away from him at that point.

Don't be ridiculous. You know your son!

There would be a reason why he'd lied. Some other reason.

So what isn't he telling me? she thought. And then, angrily,

Why didn't he just tell me the fecking truth, back when it happened? I'd have been able to help him. I'd be able to help him now.

Her anger boiled in her for minute after minute. She was furious with him for lying when she had worked so hard to create an atmosphere without criticism. One in which they could always be truthful.

And then, in a strangely subtle slide, she found herself remembering how she'd lied and lied to her parents in order to see Jack O'Keane.

Can I stay with Siobhan this evening, Daddy? She's been given the film of Far From the Madding Crowd *and it'd be really useful to watch for English . . .*

Can I go to youth group tonight?

Would you mind if I stayed late at school to hear this lecture on chemistry?

She looked again at Finn, and suddenly saw herself in him. She saw that, despite everything she'd done to give them the freedom to admit anything, there were still things he hadn't been able to tell her. And that, she realised, wasn't his fault any more than it was hers.

She wanted to tell him that it was all right if he'd been doing something he was ashamed of. Even something illegal. She wanted to say that if he was cheating on his girlfriend with someone from London, they could sort it out.

Anything was better than murder. Anything.

For just a moment she wondered if she could come to terms with that, even. If it would be possible to love Finn – or Ethan – if either of them really had killed two women.

She found herself reaching out to take her son's hand. Squeezing it.

And when, after a fraction of a second, he squeezed hers in return, she felt a fierce rush of love for him.

Whatever you've done, you're my son, she thought. *You're my son.*

31

Cassie Logan's call came in as O'Malley was searching for variations on the name 'Michael' and 'Mikey' in the area around Newbury. It was gruelling work, and he knew it was possibly fruitless too. Dara Cooley seemed only too happy to change names at will, and would probably have moved on to a different one by now.

'So sorry for making you wait,' Cassie said. 'I was at a meeting with the FBI, believe it or not.'

'I do believe it,' O'Malley told her. 'And it's no bother. We're hugely grateful for the help.'

'So you wanted to know about a possible love child of Dara Cooley's,' she said, all business. 'I wanted to explain it properly, because it's a little complex.'

'OK,' O'Malley said.

'The percentage of DNA shared by Aisling Cooley and your perp is in the range that could fall under a half-brother's,' she said. 'It's two thousand two hundred centimorgans, which is in the range for both a sibling and a half-sibling.'

'So you're saying he *could* possibly be a half-sibling?' O'Malley asked. 'Was that report over-simplifying it, like?'

'No, I actually agree in full with the conclusions of the Globalry report,' Cassie answered. 'Because it's not as simple as the percentage of overlap. It's about how many regions are fully identical instead of half identical. And Aisling Cooley shares several fully identical regions with your perp.' She lifted her eyebrows. 'That can't happen through any additional consanguinity. It means she has to be a full sibling. Or, as we've established, a mother or a daughter.'

'OK,' O'Malley said. 'I think I understand. Anneka's child is definitely ruled out. Which means our perp is still her father or one of her sons.'

Though, in fact, O'Malley felt it increasingly likely that it could only be Aisling's father. Only Dara Cooley had been connected to Anneka Foley, the first woman to die on a pyre.

32

The accident of being born sixteen months before his brother had left Ethan to face an interview alone, without his mother. And although Jonah wasn't out to press him hard this evening, he was certainly out to let him trip himself up.

'I don't remember, like . . . how late I stayed out.' Ethan said, a sheen of sweat on his upper lip, when they asked him about New Year's Eve. He cleared his throat. 'I was a bit drunk, so . . . it's not all clear, you know? I definitely stayed until after midnight but then I got kind of bored after that. I maybe stayed an hour after. Could have been two. Then I went home.'

'So there was a lot of drinking at this party?' Jonah asked.

Ethan shrugged. 'It was New Year's Eve. There was some.'

'So you didn't drive home.'

'No, I dropped Finn and then I left the car at the party,' Ethan said. 'Matt's got this massive driveway, so . . .'

'And you picked it up the next morning?'

'Er, afternoon,' Ethan said, and Jonah saw him smile for the first time. 'I was, like, intensely hungover. I didn't get out of bed until, you know, late. In time for brunch.'

'So quite a big night,' Jonah said, returning to his earlier comment. 'Any drug-taking?'

'It was just a house party, you know? Not a rave,' Ethan replied with obvious defensiveness.

Jonah nodded. 'But you didn't go straight to the party, did you?'

Ethan's eyes widened slightly. 'Sorry?'

'After you dropped your brother in Totton,' Jonah said. 'You didn't go straight to the party at Matthew Downing's house.'

Ethan frowned. Gave a short laugh. 'I'm pretty sure I did.'

'Matthew Downing tells us that you didn't arrive until eleven fifty-five,' Jonah said.

He watched Ethan swallow, and then say, 'Seriously, Matthew's got that, like, massively wrong. He was drunk and he'd been off outside shooting one of his videos . . . I think he forgot I'd already been there before.'

'Right.' Jonah glanced down at his notes. 'But he tells us that he specifically asked you where you'd been. And you said you'd been helping your brother with something.'

Ethan gave a huff of air outwards. 'I really don't think I had that conversation with him.'

'So you think other people at the party will confirm that you were there earlier?'

There was a momentary pause, and then Ethan said, 'Yeah. Yeah, I think they will.'

'And you and your brother didn't do anything together in Totton,' Lightman chipped in.

Ethan gave a shrug. 'I just drove him in, you know?'

'OK,' Jonah said, giving him a smile. 'That's helpful.'

He slid the photographs of Lindsay Kernow and Jacqueline Clarke over the table, and Ethan suddenly seemed to lose patience.

'I don't know them,' Ethan said angrily. 'I've honestly got nothing to do with this. I don't understand why there was DNA from me or Finn or our grandfather at the last one, but I did not know these people.'

'Do you think there's a chance the DNA might be yours?' Jonah asked.

'No. I mean, not unless someone's planted it there. I don't

know . . . why anyone would want to. Or how they got it or anything. But I haven't been anywhere near these women, and I didn't go to that heath, OK?'

Jonah nodded, attempting to look supportive. Understanding. There were times to press a suspect hard, and times to play their best and most trusted friend, and Jonah knew instinctively that this was the latter.

'We have to ask these questions. I'm sorry if they're uncomfortable. It's important to have your statements about the DNA before the results come back. So can you help me out here?'

'Then why are you throwing these pictures at me like I killed them?' Ethan asked, his voice rising in pitch.

'We're just interested in whether the photos jog any memories,' Jonah said quietly. 'If you saw something you've since forgotten, something you didn't think was important, then it's vital that we know about it. We need to find out what happened to these two women.'

Ethan looked down, letting his hair fall over his eyes. There was a brief silence, and then he nodded. 'OK. Fair enough.'

Though he sounded calmer, Jonah could still see the vibration running through him caused by that twitching left leg. It was evident that the situation was upsetting Ethan a lot.

Jonah watched his hands for a few moments, where they picked at the table. Like his brother, he was clearly strong, though in Ethan's case it was a sinewy sort of strength. The sort of strength that probably came from spending hours playing guitar every day.

It was debatable whether either of them would be strong enough to lift and carry a body alone into the wilderness, of course. That was inevitably a great deal harder than anyone imagined. And even if the women had been drugged to the point of unconsciousness rather than death, they would have been just as difficult to carry.

There was a two out of three chance that one of them had put Lindsay Kernow on that pyre, or at least been directly involved. But just because one of them had been there didn't mean the other brother hadn't been there too.

'What are your thoughts on the DNA being your brother's?' he asked abruptly.

'What?' Ethan looked up through his hair, and then at Lightman. 'It's not . . . I thought you didn't have the results yet.'

Jonah gave him a smile. 'It's a hypothetical question. But if you're saying it isn't yours, then the trace could still be Finn's. If we rule you out, there's a fifty per cent chance.' He looked expectantly at Ethan. 'So how do you think it would have got there, if so? Do you think your brother might have got into an argument on his way home?'

'For fuck's sake.' Ethan looked away, clearly both angry and upset. 'No, I don't think he did. And I don't think he killed anyone else either. He's a good guy. Ask fucking anyone.'

Jonah watched him for a long while, but nothing in Ethan's face shifted from his expression of anger.

'All right,' Jonah said. 'We'll just need the contact details of anyone else at Matthew Downing's party, and then we'll get you bailed and sent home.'

'OK,' Ethan said. Though Jonah thought he could see his mind working, as if he were trying to think of a way to get out of it.

Jonah and Lightman came to a stop alongside Hanson's desk. She turned her chair to face them.

'Interviews done,' Jonah told her. 'We'll need bail

arranging if you can call downstairs to sort it. And then we need to notify the uniforms who'll be on observation this evening.'

The two Cooley boys might be going home, but they would be doing so under full observation. They still represented two thirds of their suspect pool, and that meant he needed to know where they were – and what they were doing – until those DNA results came through. The last thing they wanted was another killing on their hands just as they were closing in on their murderer.

Though with Dara Cooley still out there, Jonah wished he had enough officers to flood the streets. Enough of them to keep every woman in the New Forest safe.

'I can sort the stake-out teams,' Hanson offered.

'Cassie Logan replied about the love child,' O'Malley called over. 'It's a no-go. Even if the kid at West Gradley was Dara Cooley's, and Anneka was related to him, he wouldn't have had as much identical DNA with Aisling Cooley as our perp.'

'I guess that keeps things simple,' Jonah said. 'We just need to find Dara Cooley.' He hesitated for a moment. 'I'd also like to ask local taxi firms if they took Finn anywhere on the night of October third last year. He claims to have stayed in London that night, when Jacqueline Clarke died, having left Southampton in the afternoon, but it's more than a bit suspicious. CCTV from the train station here could confirm for us whether he travelled by train at all that night. He claims he left in the afternoon.'

He could see Hanson scribbling a note onto the huge desktop pad she'd positioned under her keyboard. It was covered in her slanting scrawl, the notes she made comprehensible only to her.

O'Malley was now, in contrast, leaning back in his chair with a thoughtful expression. Jonah was amused to note that the desk that Hanson and Lightman had tidied for him – much to his outrage – was already littered with scraps of paper.

'We should request ANPR data for Ethan Cooley's car for October,' O'Malley commented. 'He could have driven Jacqueline, or even Jacqueline and his brother, to Longbeech Campsite.'

'Good shout,' Jonah said.

'I sent a request in for Aisling and Ethan Cooley's reg plates on New Year's Eve earlier on,' Lightman told O'Malley. 'I can add to that.'

'Thanks,' Jonah said. 'We also have contact details for a few others at the New Year's Eve party Ethan Cooley went to.'

'I'll follow them up,' Hanson offered.

'Let's use one of the other DCs,' Jonah said. 'They should be the ones digging into the burning of the horse too. Trying to look for links there. I think one of you ought to be with Domnall on trying to find Dara Cooley. We at least know where Finn and Ethan are right now, and will have them under observation.' He paused for a moment, and then added, 'And let's keep our ears to the ground for anything else that's happening. I'll brief the other DCs on actively looking into live reports coming in. Whether it's women or animals.'

He didn't need to add what they all felt: that six co-opted DCs and a handful of constables weren't going to stop anyone else dying if Dara Cooley was their killer and they couldn't find him.

33

O'Malley sat back in his chair a little wearily, trying to think of other ways to track down Dara Cooley. Following his ideas on the Cooley boys, he found himself thinking, again, of cars – but this time in relation to Dara Cooley.

ANPR data was typically stored for three years if it wasn't related to a high-profile inquiry. At that point, data protection laws required it to be deleted, which at first glance sounded like a dead end. It was profoundly unlikely that Dara Cooley was still driving the same car he'd had when he'd left his family and vanished twenty-eight years ago.

A quick check showed him that Dara had driven a Ford Orion, and though he had never sold it or declared it scrapped, he'd presumably just run it into the ground and never notified anyone. Perhaps because keeping it off-record made it – and him – harder to trace.

But that meant he'd probably driven it for a few years after he disappeared, assuming he hadn't simply taken the plates off. If they could somehow track it to a new location, they might have an idea of where to look for him. And that's what O'Malley was now thinking about.

ANPR data would have been deleted, but individual reports compiled for statistical analysis wouldn't have been. These would have been reports into cars pulled over. Some assistant chief constable might ask the intelligence team to compile data into, for example, cars pulled over with illegal tyre treads or faulty brake lights and see if it was a rising trend. All those reports still existed, but although O'Malley could download them, open them up and search them, none of their findings would appear as entries on the database. They were just statistical data rather than deliberately held records of crimes associated with a person or licence plate. So what it came down to was asking himself whether he was willing to waste potentially hours of his time opening up and searching hundreds of records for the chance that Dara Cooley had been pulled over at some point.

With a sigh, he searched for all compiled reports run anywhere in the country from 2 February 1987, the day that Dara Cooley had disappeared, until the same date in 1992. He'd limit himself to five years of arduous searching for now.

The search came back with six hundred and eighteen reports.

He resisted the urge to close the search down again, and opened the first one up, which had been compiled just four days after Dara Cooley had vanished.

'Just do the first fifty,' he told himself, 'and you can have a coffee and a Hobnob.'

It wouldn't take too long to do each one, he told himself. Just open it, put the licence plate into the search box, hit enter and then close it again.

That first one, a report into tail lights, took him about thirty seconds to search. No result.

He had the second one opened up and searched within a minute. He barely looked at the title of this – something to do with suspected drug dealing that had been compiled a week after Dara's disappearance. He pasted the registration number in again, hit return – and felt his jaw go slack as he came up with a result.

'Jesus,' he said, as the screen arrived at a highlighted row with the same registration number filled in.

Scrolling sideways, he read the summary of the pull-over. Which hadn't, in fact, been so much a pulling-over as a check. At one a.m. on 3 February 1987, an IC1 male had been pulled up at the point of Glenridding Beck, Cumbria, a site identified as being currently used by drug dealers for exchanges. Officers on patrol had approached and questioned the car's occupant, who had seemed disorientated. He'd explained that he had nothing to do with any drugs, and had just been having some troubles at home. He'd been sitting watching the water, thinking about what to do. Officers had politely asked him to move on, which he had done.

O'Malley reread it, and then sat back in his chair with a feeling he couldn't quite identify. After a moment, he opened up Google Maps and searched for Glenridding Beck. It was, he found, a village on the edge of Ullswater in the Lake District. It was a six-hour drive from Dara Cooley's home. The officers had found him there on the very night he had disappeared.

With a cold feeling in the pit of his stomach, O'Malley lifted his phone, beginning to think he might know what had happened to Dara Cooley.

34

Aisling barely managed to force a word out of each of her sons for most of the drive home. She was burning to know about so much: including why Finn had lied, and whether Ethan had also lied about New Year's Eve.

Finding herself unable to ask about any of that, she tried to find out at least how Ethan's interview had gone, but he seemed incapable of satisfying her curiosity. Her usually sunny-tempered and talkative son would only tell her that the interview had been 'fine'.

She tried asking him whether he'd told them about New Year's Eve, and about his movements in early October. 'And did you say you didn't recognise any of the photos?'

'Yes, obviously,' he said, with a trace of truculence that was so unlike him that she almost felt tempted to drop her questions. But there was too much that she needed to know, and she found herself pushing on.

'So you can't think of anything, any reason why it might be your DNA?'

'Of course I can't!' Ethan had snapped. 'Jesus, Mother. It's not like I spend my nights stalking middle-aged women.' He turned his head towards the back of the car, where Finn was scrolling on his phone again. 'Why aren't you asking Finn?'

'What?' His younger brother clearly hadn't been listening. Though Aisling couldn't see much of him when she glanced in the mirror, he seemed distracted. Like he'd been dragged out of some deep thought.

'The DNA could have been either of ours, or flipping

neither, so why am I the only one getting the third degree?' Ethan said, his voice more plaintive now.

'For god's sake,' Aisling said, giving in momentarily to her frustration. 'I'm trying to help, Ethan. And I can't do that if you don't tell me what's going on!'

Ethan turned away, and Aisling had to resist the urge to keep shouting until he told her something. She breathed, and then said, 'I was there when your brother was interviewed. He's not my favourite. I detest you both equally, remember.' She put a hand out to pat Ethan's arm, before returning it to the steering wheel.

'I *should* be your favourite,' Finn commented.

'Nope,' Aisling said, flashing him a grin. 'You're a brat.'

'Harsh.'

There was a brief pause, and then Ethan said, 'You can be *my* favourite if you like, Finny,' his voice full of patronising humour.

The banter made Aisling feel immediately better. This was how they should be. Teasing each other. Laughing about it. And quietly loving each other to bits.

Ethan grinned, and then stretched mightily. For a few minutes they drove on in a much more comfortable almost-silence. Aisling decided to let everything drop, even though none of her questions had actually been answered.

It was only as they were entering Lyndhurst that Ethan asked, 'What if someone's planted our DNA there? Mine or Finn's?'

Aisling felt another squeeze of fear. This was something she had tried not to think about: a situation that might leave them powerless. However unlikely it might be, it gave her the cold sweats to think of it. Because there might be nothing they could do to stop a trial if one of her boys' DNA had been planted. It was the biggest reason she'd contacted Jack, in fact. He might know what to do.

But what mattered right now wasn't that slim possibility. What mattered was comforting Ethan.

'Then we'll make sure they work out who did it,' she said firmly. 'They're not stupid, and I won't let them make any assumptions.'

'But what if it's actually the police who've planted it?' Ethan pressed. 'I mean, like in *Making a Murderer*. If that happens, you're screwed. Even if you have really expensive lawyers, which we can't afford.'

Aisling sighed. 'It's less likely over here, I think. We don't have such an ingrained attitude that the police can do no wrong. And – and the officers seem like decent people. I don't think they'd have any reason to want to frame anyone, least of all you.' She reached out again, to rub his shoulder this time. 'Annoying as you are, you aren't actually a criminal, or trying to sue them, or anything.'

'True,' Ethan said after a moment. 'I suppose so.'

'We should be talking about Grandad,' Finn said suddenly from the back of the car. 'You said it's one of the three of us. So tell us what you think.'

Aisling glanced at him in the rear-view mirror, taking advantage of a red traffic light. Her younger son's expression was fixed. Determined.

'Are you asking me if I think he killed someone?'

'Yeah. You said he was gentle,' Finn said, leaning forwards. 'But was he always? You never saw him do anything violent or aggressive? Not to you maybe, but to someone else?'

With that Aisling found herself thinking back to that one, awful night. And to that part of her life she didn't want to remember – *she didn't want to remember* – and she said tightly, 'Only once. And it was – it wasn't his fault. He was provoked.'

There was a brief silence, and then Finn said, 'But he was capable of it, wasn't he? If he could do it that once.'

Aisling couldn't find the energy to argue. She pulled the car into the driveway at eight forty-five feeling as though the day had lasted weeks, and aware that there were still hours of it to go. She was wrung out. Drained. And yet still fizzing with anxiety.

For a moment she resisted getting out of the car. It all felt like too much. Way, way too much. The DNA swabs, which would be turned round within the next two hours. Jack O'Keane's imminent arrival. The questions about her family that were ripping into her carefully built-up defences. And, almost worst of all, the way all of it was making her finally think about Donagh. The one person she couldn't bear to think about at all.

How had it been possible for him to arrive in their lives with such smiling brilliance? With such a feeling of excitement?

She could still feel it, even now. Still hear it in her daddy's voice when he'd first told her that Donagh would come.

One of your mam's cousins . . . He's turned himself round. Followed a godly path. He'll be coming to stay in a few weeks . . .

It had been dizzying. Brilliant. The idea of her solitary, closed-off mammy having a young cousin only ten years older than Aisling. A man who was *family*, at last, after a lifetime of estrangement from the only other relatives Aisling had.

They aren't good people, her mammy had always said before that. *People of worldliness and sin. There are only so many times you can extend the hand of friendship and forgiveness to people of their kind.*

But now one of them had changed, it seemed. He'd become a good man. Which meant he was finally worthy.

Such heavy irony in that. She wished she could somehow warn the Aisling of back then. Though perhaps she would still have been powerless, even if she'd known. Her parents had been seduced by Donagh too.

Her daddy had been lost the moment he'd heard about

him. He'd told Aisling, one evening when it had just been the two of them, that he'd longed fiercely for a family of his own for much of his life. With no brothers or sisters and both parents lost young, he'd felt alone in the world for a long time.

Not that I ever thought you and your mammy weren't enough, he'd added with a gentle smile. *But that big, warm, boisterous family . . . I'd love that. Here's my chance now, I suppose. He's part of my blood by marriage. My cousin, as much as he is yours or your mammy's. And if he's been brought round to a good way of life, then he can bring some of the others too, I'm sure.*

They had both been so ready to accept him, from that first meeting in the china-stuffed sitting room, right up until the truth about Donagh had emerged, too raw and wet for even the two of them to ignore it.

In an awful slide, Aisling found herself inhabiting the worst memory of them all. She was no longer slumped in their car on the driveway, but sitting on the wall outside school, her clarinet case in one hand and her feet kicking at the brickwork. And a lithe, handsome form had slid its way onto the wall beside her.

'Hey.'

She jumped as she felt a hand on her shoulder. It was Finn. Just Finn, leaning in at the driver's door. She was home. Safe.

'Are you coming in, or should I bring you a pillow out?' he asked with an ironic lift of his eyebrow.

'Ugh,' Aisling said, trying to smile at him. 'Do I really have to move?'

She started to climb out of the car, not sure whether she was a fifteen-year-old girl in uniform or a mother of forty-five wearing jeans.

'Should we make some food?' Finn asked her, as she moved clumsily into the hall. Ethan was already homing in on the kitchen, presumably to raid the cupboard for snacks.

'I think it's a takeaway night, if there ever was one,' Aisling answered.

She let the two boys drift upstairs while she pulled her phone out. They usually ordered together, and made the process almost the best part. The three of them had discovered, some years ago, that the website of the local pizza restaurant, Milo's, would let you design every single ingredient of your pizza, including a bizarre range of sauces, unlimited extra cheese or toppings, and dictating which half of the pizza everything went on. They'd seen it as their mission to create the weirdest pizzas, and so far Finn's pickles, banana and pesto base with six extra cheeses and a totally naked right-hand side had won.

They sometimes, admittedly, struggled to eat the insanity that would arrive, but it was worth it for the few gems – like learning how delicious strawberries were on a savoury pizza – and the way the regular delivery guys would shake their heads at them and ask what in the name of all that was holy they'd ordered this time.

Tonight, she decided to play it safe with some actual flavours that worked, but still found the process almost impossible to complete. She was caught between the past and present, and somehow took ten minutes over adding three pizzas to her cart.

It was only as she was about to pay that she wondered whether she should order something for Jack. He would be arriving at roughly the same time the pizzas did.

After dithering for a moment, she put an extra stuffed crust Hawaiian into the basket and clicked the order button. She'd just have to trust that, however much Jack might have changed, he still liked ham and pineapple enough to roll with it.

It was at that point that the fact of Jack being only half an hour off arriving collided, in her head, with the fact that she hadn't mentioned him to Ethan and Finn. And she wondered what on earth she'd been thinking.

Probably, she acknowledged, about imminent DNA results, serial killers and her estranged father. But it was still a huge failure of communication.

She looked up the stairs towards their rooms. Should she go and explain now, in case he was early? She'd been hoping to jump in the shower and put something a little tidier on, and she'd need to be ready for the pizza to arrive in twenty minutes. It was going to be tight.

But she knew her sons had had enough stress for one day without an unexpected stranger showing up. She kicked off her boots, and trod quickly up the stairs.

Ethan's door, the closest to the stairs, stood open, giving her a clear view of the chaos of technology and litter inside. Ethan himself was absent.

She caught a low, murmured voice from further down the landing. And for some reason, instead of announcing her presence as she normally would have done, she kept quiet. There was something in the tone of those voices that raised wariness in her. A sense of something secret.

She padded onwards, avoiding the few noisy floorboards with practised ease. These were the same boards she'd dodged when her boys had been tiny, erratic sleepers. The same floorboards she'd crept over when she'd begun to realise that something was very wrong with Stephen's late-night phone calls. Boards she'd never expected to be dodging in order to eavesdrop on her sons.

They were in Finn's room. That much was obvious. Ethan had presumably sought his younger brother out.

'. . . not what I'm saying,' she heard, a little louder.

Her hammering heart gave a lurch, and she almost

overbalanced. It was only with an effort of will that she steadied herself without stumbling.

It had been Finn speaking, and her youngest son had sounded angry. Forceful. He was still audible as he continued, though he was more controlled.

'You know it's about more than the two of us, and this – stuff.'

'How can anything be more than this?' Ethan asked, his voice harsh in a way that sounded unlike him.

She imagined Finn gesturing to him, telling him to keep his voice down, before he replied more quietly, 'I'm not saying it's nothing, but it's a *chance* of big trouble versus *definite* trouble. You know what would happen if you tell them. We both do.'

There was a long silence, in which Finn's closed wooden door seemed to pulse with Aisling's heartbeat. And then Ethan said, 'It's a fucking mess.'

After a beat, Finn replied, 'It'll be all right. I promise.'

And then one of them shifted enough for the floorboards to creak, and Aisling was hurrying away from them, away from everything she'd heard.

35

Jonah called home at nine thirty, in an effort to catch Michelle before she turned in. With the guarantee of at least two wake-ups during the night, his partner would generally crawl into bed by nine forty-five on her nights in. She'd generally been in the habit of coming back from her evenings out at a similar time, though he'd noticed a tendency to stay out longer recently.

He had to admit that he felt a lot like dodging his customary check-in this evening. Now that he'd heard how irritated he made her, he wondered whether calling was actually a source of annoyance rather than support.

He picked up his mobile, breathed out a very long sigh, and then pressed the call button on their landline number. He tried to think of upbeat things to say as he waited for her to pick up. But, in fact, it was the nanny who answered.

'Is Michelle back?' he asked her, once Rhona had assured him that Milly was sound asleep.

'No, she's still out,' Rhona told him. 'She called half an hour ago, and I told her I've got things covered and am happy to do the first night feed. So hopefully she won't rush back.'

'That's incredibly kind, thank you,' Jonah said. He'd once felt guilty, asking Rhona to do extra duties, but she seemed genuinely delighted to be allowed to step in and feel useful. She was a godsend.

Hanging up, he felt torn all over again. So much of him wanted Michelle to be out, rediscovering herself. But aside from the danger he knew still existed, he felt a new thrill of worry.

Was she out with her friends, telling them how fed up she was with him? Would they be encouraging her to leave him? Or suggesting ways of making things work? Or was she, in fact, out meeting other men, and wondering why she was wasting her time with Jonah? Reminding herself that she was attractive and interesting, and didn't need to settle for second best?

He wished, wholeheartedly, that he hadn't overheard what he had. He would have been so pleased for her if he'd known nothing about it.

He briefly considered messaging Michelle. He thought about telling her how glad he was that she was having a proper night out. It was what he would have done before, but to do it when he knew she was unhappy seemed manipulative somehow. So instead, he put his phone back into his pocket and woke his desktop up once again.

There was a lot of waiting going on this evening, which wasn't helpful for his current mood. The DNA results were still probably an hour off, and O'Malley's lead on Dara Cooley was also taking time to action. Hanson and Lightman were now pushing to find out where Finn and Ethan Cooley had been on New Year's Eve, but it being late, he didn't expect their friends to reply until tomorrow, in reality.

But, loading up his emails, he was happy to note that the cyber team had the reports for the Cooley brothers' phones back. Trawling through the data was absolutely not his job, and was the kind of work he would never admit to his DCS that he sometimes did. But right now he wanted unthinking grunt work, and with the rest of his team occupied he had the perfect excuse.

36

Aisling had retreated to the safe haven of the shower after overhearing her sons' conversation. She knew it was a cowardly decision, but felt unable to face anything else right now.

At least let me have hot water, and clean clothes, and some make-up on for when Jack gets here, she thought. *At least give me that, and I'll maybe keep it all hanging together.*

In fact, she felt dangerously close to unravelling. Or to just climbing into bed and refusing to deal with the crushing mixture of emotions she was experiencing.

The cut on Finn's leg on New Year's Day. The look that had passed between them. Ethan's fear of her talking to Matthew, and the terrible mood he'd been in for days. They knew something about Lindsay Kernow's murder. God, what had they got wrapped up in?

But whatever they'd done, they still needed her. They were terrified of what might happen. She knew that. As terrified of their little trio being ripped apart as she was. She had to keep it together. For them.

And so she'd pulled on her nicest jeans and sweater, blasted her hair dry and relined her eyes. And then she rooted a bottle of white wine out of the understairs cupboard and drank a third of it straight down, at room temperature, thankful that it was good enough to do that without wincing.

Even before it had time to act, she felt less like she was drifting away. Less like she was fragmenting into the past. As she shoved the cork back in and crammed it into the freezer for later, she was able to tell herself that she could do this, and almost believe it.

When the doorbell rang for the first time, she padded over without hurry, assuming it was the pizza. But even through the frosted glass side panel, she could see the shape of Jack.

The hallway suddenly stretched out, making it seem half a mile to the door. Her hand shook as she opened it.

But the air that washed into the front hall was damp and cool, and seemed to bring with it the scent of the peat bogs around Tullamore.

'Martha.'

The word had the sound of a long-anticipated arrival. The answer to a riddle maybe. And she knew that her answering 'Jack' was imbued with the same.

And, of course, Ethan called down the stairs asking if it was the pizza, and she had to call up, 'No, not yet!' before she could say anything more, or even take in the rest of him.

He both was and wasn't the Jack she remembered. The dark Kurt-Cobain fringe had been shortened. It had part greyed too. The effect had somehow lightened his eyes, making them seem backlit. Luminous.

There were creases to him too. And he was no longer lanky, but a little stocky, as if the food had finally stuck to him after all these years of trying.

She'd seen some of these changes in the photos online, but the sense of him – of the unstoppably cheerful, absolutely dependable nature of him – was so absolutely the boy she'd known that she found herself beaming at him in spite of everything.

Barks chose that moment to make his presence known, launching himself at Jack with abandon. She saw Jack grin as he ducked down to stroke him, sliding his backpack off his shoulder.

'Come in now,' she said, hearing herself talking in the accent she'd had as a child for the first time in decades. 'There's pizza on the way. And I'll get you a glass of something. Wine? Beer?'

'Beer'd be grand.'

And there it was, his voice. Jack O'Keane's voice. As fully a Tullamore boy's as you'd ever heard.

He stepped inside, and she saw that he had a small overnight bag with him as well as the backpack.

'Am I OK to leave this here?' he asked. 'I've not been to the hotel yet.'

'Sure,' she said. 'It's so – you're so kind to come so quickly.'

She was aware of him physically as he followed her to the kitchen, in a way that might have had something to do with the wine. She was aware, too, of her own body. But not worried about it, and its changes. It felt comfortable.

She waited until she'd poured the beer and set it in front of him, and then until he'd taken the first mouthful, before she started talking.

The first sentence was the hardest, the one where she said, 'My sons might be in trouble . . .' But after that, she was talking with terrible urgency. She knew she might only have a short time to tell him all this, before the mundanity of pizza and having to explain everything to her sons.

So she told him, the words rattling out, about her daddy leaving them after two years, and her mammy's death. The fact of Stephen abandoning her just like her father had, and of her life with her sons now. The DNA and how she'd gone to meet someone called Ben. What had happened since.

And then about what she'd overheard them saying to each other, and how she was afraid she hadn't been a good enough parent to them. About how she'd gone to pieces after Ethan's birth.

223

'It's – awful, having to admit it now,' she told him. 'The way I loved them, it was distant. A little bit resentful maybe. But I was never really close to them until Stephen walked out.' She rose and went to find herself another drink. Something to keep the feeling of haziness going. And with her back to him, while she rooted in the freezer for the bottle she'd started, she said, 'I wasn't a good mother to them until he'd gone, and I realised I had to do this. That they only had me. And I made a decision to step forwards instead of retreating.' She found the bottle. Pulled it out and turned to him again. 'They'd lived a lot of years by then. Four of them, in Ethan's case. Some things . . . some things must have been fixed in them already, mustn't they?'

'I don't think there's a parent in the world who isn't afraid they've messed their kids up,' Jack said gently.

He had listened to everything she'd said, his eyes alight with sympathy. With interest. With a calm expression that said this was *his* problem now too. Which was inexplicable. How could he be so willing, after everything?

She faltered, at that thought. She came to sit in front of him again, and then said, 'God, Jack, I'm saying this all in the wrong order. Because there's something I need to tell you. That – that – that I should have told you thirty years ago. It's the reason my parents took me away and why – why I never contacted you. I'm so sorry, Jack.'

Her throat closed down on her, just when she needed most to talk to him. She felt her eyes fill and spill over. Fill and spill over.

Jack reached out and took her hand, a touch that should have been a shock, or a source of anxiety. Possibly even something that should have felt like a liberty. But it felt immediately familiar, and safe.

'It's OK,' he said. 'I knew . . . something wasn't right before.'

He gave a brief sigh. 'It was to do with your cousin Donagh, wasn't it?'

It was like a shock from a faulty switch, hearing him say the name.

Donagh . . . The young, charismatic and undeniably handsome cousin her parents had let into their home; and who they'd trusted to teach their fifteen-year-old daughter her Bible lessons.

She found herself back on that wall again. Feeling Donagh's hand move up her thigh. Feeling the urge to run.

I thought you were such a good little girl. But now I understand. You're not good at all, are you? You're a whore.

She didn't let that awful memory go further. She instead remembered what had happened much later on that night.

She'd run from her own house, all the way to Jack's. She'd tapped on his window, rousing him from sleep, intending to tell him everything.

And then, after she'd somehow clambered inside, she'd looked at this boy, this bedraggled, sleepy, wonderful, good young man, and she'd kissed him, furiously. She'd buried herself and the memory of Donagh's touch in Jack, and in the touch of their two bodies together, and hadn't been afraid of any of it at all.

The snap back to the present was strange. Electric. She was looking at Jack with an echo of that feeling. As the heat rose in her cheeks, she realised that there was something of the same expression on his face too.

But before she could gather herself to say anything – anything at all – Finn had suddenly appeared. He looked between them with confusion.

'Er, is the pizza really not here yet?'

'Oh.' Aisling swallowed twice, the heat growing in her cheeks. 'It's probably – I haven't been checking the app . . . This is Jack.'

And then down the stairs thundered Ethan, just as Finn was asking Jack, 'Are you with the police?'

'No,' Aisling said, quickly. 'Sorry. I didn't have a chance . . . Jack is someone from back in Tullamore. And he's a private investigator. I thought he might be able to help us, maybe. Even though it really isn't his problem.' She looked over at him, and there was such wry humour in Jack's expression that she started to laugh. 'God, that was the world's worst introduction.'

'I mean, I'll be honest, I've had better drum rolls,' Jack said.

Finn looked between the two of them, his face creased with thought, and Ethan came to a stop behind him.

'Wait,' Finn said. 'When you say someone from back home . . .'

'Did you say "private investigator"?' Ethan asked.

And almost at the same time, Finn said, 'Do you mean *boyfriend*?'

And, of course, at exactly that moment, the pizza delivery arrived with a loud rap at the door.

37

O'Malley was once again waiting for a call-back from an Inspector at Cumbria Constabulary. He'd been in touch with her twice in the last two and a half hours, and was aware that this particular wait might be lengthy.

O'Malley didn't know anyone in particular on the force in Cumbria, so his first call had been with a desk sergeant, who had kept him on hold for some while. O'Malley had used the time to look in more detail at a map of Glenridding Beck and the surrounding area.

He'd eventually been put through to an Inspector Karen Douglas, who had started out wary.

'I hear you're looking for help with a historic stop and search,' she'd said, her voice reluctant.

'Ah, not really help with that,' O'Malley said, trying not to sound irritated at the desk sergeant's apparent inability to understand his request. 'What I want is your help locating a missing person, and I think a historic stop and search may have provided a strong pointer to where he went.'

'Ah,' Inspector Douglas said. 'OK. I'm listening.'

'We have a missing male, forty years old at the time, named Dara Cooley,' O'Malley told her. 'He walked out on his family, leaving a note saying he couldn't lead a duplicitous life any more. Nobody's heard anything from him since, but when I checked through a compiled report from your constabulary, I found that he'd been approached by a squad car at Glenridding Beck at one a.m. This was some hours after he left his family. He was parked up in his Ford Orion. They thought he might have been involved in drug dealing, for which there had been complaints, but it turned out he was sitting in his car, looking at the lake, and said he'd been having family troubles. No drugs found.'

'OK . . .' the Inspector said, clearly following.

'We're confirming now whether there was any other traffic stop involving that car over the next years, but so far we have nothing, and it was never sold or SORNED.'

'Right.'

'Over the last few days, we've found out that Dara Cooley was almost certainly conducting an affair with a young woman who it seems he also abandoned,' O'Malley went on. 'So what I'm thinking, is that Ullswater is a deep enough lake for a man – say a man who was religious, and felt a great deal of guilt at what he'd done – to drive his car into it, and for that car to remain undiscovered for twenty-eight years.'

There had been a brief silence, and then Karen Douglas had said, 'Not there, he wouldn't. Not at Glenridding Beck. The water isn't deep enough, and there's a sailing club right there. He'd have been seen.'

'Sure,' O'Malley agreed. 'But he drove away from there when the police asked him to. I think he drove in somewhere else.'

The inspector had given a short laugh. 'Are you asking us to search the whole damn lake?'

'No, of course not,' O'Malley soothed. 'I've had some thoughts myself. Looking at the map, there's a point not much further north on the A592 where there's a track up to-wards a farm. This is on Glencoyne Bridge. By my reckoning a person would be able to drive a car at speed down the track and end up in the lake.'

There was a pause, and O'Malley could tell from faint noises in the background that Inspector Karen Douglas was checking this on her own computer.

'I mean . . . it's possible, but I'm questioning how likely it is.'

'What I was thinking,' O'Malley said, 'is that you could check your microfiche files. See if there were any reports of tyre marks or cars going off the road at that point. Any concerns. And if there are, then I think it's worth getting a dive team down to the lake. In part, because the missing man's DNA may have turned up at a serial murder scene here.'

There was another pause. 'All right.' Karen sounded a little more enthusiastic now. 'I have someone who can check the microfiche files. Should be possible within the hour.'

'Thank you,' O'Malley had said with relief.

'What if there isn't any record of that, though?' Karen had asked. 'I mean, if nothing was called in?'

'Well,' O'Malley had said, as warmly as he could, 'I'd still like you to get a dive team down and drag the lake.'

Though O'Malley's strange luck that night had held. He hadn't needed to push, because there, on the microfiche records held by the station from the years before everything had gone digital, was a report from a concerned member of the public about a car going into the water north of Norfolk Island. Cumbria Constabulary had checked tyre marks, which they had felt were slightly inconclusive, and sent out a police boat to take a look. But no car had been sighted, and it was believed that the marks were from someone who had driven right up to the edge and then reversed sharply.

Karen Douglas's voice had been wryly amused as she'd called him back with the news.

'It's not going to make anyone happy, but we'll get out there and search,' she said. 'I take it this is time-pressured.'

'Yes,' O'Malley said, thinking that it all hung on whether or not Dara Cooley was down there with that car. 'It's the

Bonfire Killer investigation, and we need to know whether this suspect is still alive.'

'We're on it,' Inspector Douglas had said.

That second call had been just over two hours ago, and O'Malley was well aware he could be waiting many more hours for an answer. To get a dive team mobilised and out to the site could easily take hours alone. And then the search itself could take serious time, not helped by the darkness. It would depend on the conditions in the lake. The exact depth at that point. How far out they had to search. How good their equipment was. It was quite possible that they'd have to come back again in daylight.

So he was, in the meantime, checking every other historic report stored from 1987 to 1992, cringing at the thought that he might come across a much later mention of the car, disproving his entire theory.

And, of course, even finding no evidence of the car in these reports wasn't proof that Dara Cooley hadn't been alive and driving it around after 1987. It proved only that it hadn't been picked up in a random search that had later been recorded and stored.

O'Malley had ground his way up until the middle of 1990 with no results by the time Inspector Karen Douglas rang again. He had the phone up and at his ear before the first ring had stopped.

'Divers have pulled up a car,' the inspector said. 'It's in a pretty bad state, so we won't be able to confirm the licence plate or other details for some while, but it looks a good match for a 1980s Ford Orion according to my sergeant who, god bless him, is down there now.'

'That's incredible work,' O'Malley said with feeling. 'Thank you.'

'There are remains in the driver's seat,' Karen Douglas

went on. 'They're belted into the car. Obviously no possibility of any ID for a good while. The pathologist is on his way and we'll see what we can do about getting the PM booked in for tomorrow.'

'You're an actual legend.'

'I still can't quite believe your inspired guesswork paid off,' Karen said wryly. 'But well done, OK? That's some good work there.'

O'Malley hung up with that rare mood that struck every officer at times: a feeling of having done something genuinely brilliant. They couldn't make any absolute assumptions, of course. There was still a chance that the car didn't contain Dara Cooley's remains. But on the balance of probability, it looked incredibly likely that his disappearance twenty-eight years ago had ended in suicide, and that they had their killer under observation at Aisling Cooley's house right now.

The DCI appeared at that point, timing it perfectly for O'Malley to announce to them all. 'Cumbria have pulled up a car with remains in from Ullswater. It looks highly likely to be Dara Cooley, and it looks like he's been there since 1987.'

He saw Hanson's excited grin, and Lightman's nod of approval. Only the chief looked disconcerted.

'Right. Well, that's . . . thrown everything in the air a bit.'

'I consider throwing things in the air to be my only real talent,' O'Malley said with a grin.

'Not to steal your thunder or anything, but I have my own news,' the chief said. 'The lab just called through with the DNA results for the Cooley brothers. Neither of them is a match.'

38

Lightman called through to Aisling Cooley minutes after they received the news, and established that she and her sons were still up and about, with no intention of going to bed in the immediate future.

'We've just a few more questions,' he said, soothingly, to what Hanson strongly suspected was a fairly stressed woman on the other end of the line. It seemed cruel to leave her hanging about the DNA results until they got there, but the chief wanted Hanson and Lightman there to break the news and ask some difficult questions.

O'Malley was keen to stay while he pinned down whether or not Dara Cooley had died in that car, as aside from there being a totally unknown family member Aisling had failed to mention, their only – admittedly flimsy – theory to explain the DNA results was that Dara Cooley had faked his own death. None of them found it particularly convincing, however. There seemed little point in pretending to be dead if nobody actually thought that you were.

Hanson offered to drive this time, but was relieved when Ben said he'd take them in his Qashqai instead. It was a lot larger and warmer than her Nissan, and she had a growing headache from too many cups of coffee that evening. It was already eleven and they were all of them running on caffeine, gearing themselves up for an even later night.

It was only once they were in the car, being tailed by two DCs for the second time that day, that she realised she had no idea how Ben was holding up. He'd been quietly supporting her with all this stalker stuff, as he had while Damian had been at his most obnoxious. But he had so much of his own to deal with, too, and she was conscious that she should be checking in.

The car was sometimes the best place to get him talking a bit, so a few minutes in, she asked, 'How's the therapy going?'

Ben considered this for a moment. 'Quite well, I think.' He glanced away from her, slightly, his eyes following a sign to Lyndhurst. 'It's . . . weird. Breaking the habit of a lifetime. But I think talking about stuff is – maybe it's not the worst thing that could happen.'

Hanson smiled. Nodded. And left him room to continue. She knew that she needed to both encourage him to talk, and accept that he often wouldn't be able to.

'I would . . . she thinks it would be a good idea to tell you,' Ben went on, after a minute. 'About all the shit when I was growing up.' He paused, and then added, 'If that's OK.'

'Definitely OK,' Hanson said immediately. 'You know I'm a nosy bastard.' And then, with a feeling of heat in her cheeks, she asked, 'Did she say me specifically, or just – someone?'

'You,' Ben said simply. 'I told her, you know, how we actually talk about stuff occasionally.' He paused, and then added, 'I obviously also explained that you're a massive pain in the arse.'

Hanson grinned at him. 'Good to know.'

There was a pause, and then Ben said, 'I'm really looking forward to wrapping this one up. Not just because it'd be good to track down a serial killer, but so we can do normal things again. You know. Go to the pub. Talk crap.'

'I've talked quite a lot of crap anyway,' Hanson said.

'True,' Ben said. 'But you know what I mean.'

'Yeah, I do,' she agreed, even though she wasn't absolutely sure she did. 'We just need to hang in there, don't we?'

Ben nodded. 'And then get unbelievably fucking pissed.'

Hanson laughed properly. 'Yeah, and that too.'

They drove on in companionable silence, with Hanson mentally trying to fit together Finn and Ethan not being where they said they'd been, Dara Cooley's possible death and DNA that didn't match what they knew from the report. She kept coming back to that last question: how could the blood have been from Aisling's son, brother or father if it didn't match any of them who were alive?

She was also curious to see what was going on at Aisling's house now. The DCs staking the place out had passed on that a man of early middle age had arrived in a taxi at Aisling's house an hour ago. They'd been fairly confident that it hadn't been Aisling's ex-husband, but, beyond that, they couldn't confirm anything.

The Cooley house was still well lit by the time they drew up on the gravel driveway. Hanson could hear Barks going mad in the house as soon as she opened the door. 'Eesh. Terriers,' she muttered.

She stood behind Ben's shoulder as he rapped on the door using the unique style of the police. It was a take-no-prisoners, unrelenting hammer that didn't allow anyone to say they hadn't heard or were just in the shower.

Aisling appeared in the opening, her face absolutely bleached of colour, and for a moment, in spite of all the hard questions they needed to ask, Hanson felt nothing but sympathy.

Five minutes later, they were all in the sitting room; Ben had gently suggested moving away from the kitchen. The general rule was to interview in a room that wasn't full of domestic weaponry.

They'd been introduced to the mysterious late-night

visitor simply as 'Jack, a very old friend,' and Hanson had spent the next few minutes giving him a thorough checking over while pretending she wasn't looking at him.

He looked around Aisling's age or older, she thought. And his dark colouring could have made him a relative. But aside from them knowing that Aisling had very few family members living, something in the way the two of them interacted immediately made her think that these two weren't related. They looked more like a couple or a couple in the making.

Jack seemed totally unfazed by their sudden arrival too, something Hanson found a little suspicious. Finn, Ethan and Aisling were clearly all nervous as they piled into the living room – which they had every right to be, with the DNA results looming over them. But even if Jack wasn't aware of that particular worry, he seemed to be reacting with none of the stress the ordinary man generally showed when a pair of detectives showed up.

At one point, as they were settling themselves into various sofas and armchairs, Jack caught her looking at him and gave her a small, knowing smile. And Hanson felt caught out for a moment before she said impulsively, 'Are you job?'

He didn't seem to mind the question.

'I was,' he said with that same small smile. 'Met detective. But I promise it's not as bad as it sounds. I left to try and save my marriage.'

Hanson was aware of both Ben and Aisling looking at him sharply. It seemed as though this was new information to everyone. But she nodded, glad her guess had been right. She'd learned that there were certain tells in coppers and ex-coppers. Particularly when they were suddenly confronted with their colleagues.

They were all sitting now. The two Cooley brothers were lined up alongside Aisling on the large sofa, with Ethan closest to her. He had his arm looped round his mother, and Hanson suspected this was more for his own comfort than for hers.

Jack had perched himself on the arm next to Aisling, not touching her, but still close by. It was a close-knit set-up, and a slightly defensive one. Hanson felt very definitely outside it from her position in an armchair opposite and was glad she had Ben on her team in case anything got heated.

'So we've got some updates for you, and they've led to further questions,' Ben said, as calmly as ever. 'If you're sure you're happy for everyone present to hear them, Ms Cooley?'

'Yes,' Aisling Cooley said, her voice hoarse. 'We need to hear.'

Ben nodded. 'So the good news is that the DNA is not a match for either Ethan or Finn.'

Hanson saw the reaction that came after half a second. The way Aisling's body collapsed in the middle. Ethan's sudden removal of his arm from her to rub at his head. The way Finn looked away from them all. It was clearly a huge relief to all of them.

'See, *Maman*?' Ethan said, a moment later. 'Not quite the vicious killers you thought.'

Aisling gave a tense laugh. 'They said that was the good news . . .'

Ben gave a nod. 'I'm sorry to be bringing you sadder news too. In searching for your father, we found evidence pointing to him having driven up to the Lake District the night he disappeared. Within the last hour, divers found what looks to be his car submerged in lake Ullswater. There are remains within the car. We'll try to find out as quickly as we can who they belong to, but it looks extremely likely that they're your father's. I'm very sorry, Ms Cooley.'

No officer in the world likes breaking bad news, or watching it break, and Hanson felt the familiar dangerous surge of sadness for Aisling Cooley. Hanson's own dad had walked out on her and her mother, and she knew that underneath all the anger and the furious determination to do without him, part of her would always want him to come back and say he was sorry. That he'd been wrong and he loved them. So Hanson did her best to detach herself as tears began running from Aisling's eyes. She saw Ethan's arm go back round her, and squeeze her tightly, and then, after a few moments, she saw Jack squeeze her shoulder too.

'Please take a few minutes if you need to. This isn't easy,' Ben said. 'I know having us ask questions is the last thing you want. It's just that this changes things for us.'

Hanson saw the way Finn was looking at Ben. His gaze was sharp, full of understanding.

'It means the DNA was someone else's, doesn't it?' he said. 'If Daideo Cooley died when he vanished, and it's not me or Ethan, which we could have told you . . . So it's, like, gotta be someone still related.' He turned his head sharply. 'Like a cousin or something? But it has to be Mum's relation, right? And a male?'

'It has to be a close male relation,' Hanson agreed, sitting forwards. 'And that means it can't be a cousin. It can only be a father, or a brother, or a son.' She looked over at Aisling. 'So what we need to know, when you're ready, is if there's any chance you could have a brother who wasn't brought up with you.'

Aisling looked up at them both, her eyes wide, and confused. 'What? No, I didn't. My parents only met two years before they had me. There was never.'

'And you don't have any children from a previous relationship?' she pressed.

'No.' Aisling shook her head.

'No previous pregnancies at all?'

Aisling jolted then. Something in her body seemed to flinch away. 'I did – but I lost . . . I don't want to . . .' She looked towards Jack, her eyes pleading. 'If I could have done anything, I would have done.'

'You lost a child?' Hanson asked.

Aisling looked over at her briefly, her expression imploring. 'Maybe if I'd been in hospital, he would have made it, but . . .' And then her eyes went glassy, and her hand went to her mouth. 'Oh my god.'

Hanson looked over at Ben, recognising in him the same feeling she had. The feeling of being on the edge of an answer finally.

'Can you explain, Aisling?' she asked, as quietly as she could.

Aisling shook her head, and then shook it again. 'They said he'd died. They said he'd died. I cried over his grave for months.' She leaned forwards, and her voice was suddenly a wail. 'How could they do that to me?'

'Who had died, Aisling?' Ben asked.

'My – my – my son.' She turned and looked up at Jack. 'Our son, Jack. Our son.'

PART TWO

39

A strange sense of numbness had descended over Aisling. She supposed there was only so much it was possible to feel in one day.

It was a blessing, that loss of feeling. If she hadn't shut down, then the way that Jack had stared at her coldly before walking out of the house . . . it might have torn her apart. After every terrible thing she'd learned tonight, it could have crushed her. But instead she'd been able to watch him go from within what felt like a cocoon of nothingness.

DS Ben Lightman and his colleague Juliette had been incredibly kind to her as they'd talked it all through afterwards. They'd asked if she wanted some time just with her sons, but somehow it had seemed easier for them to hear this together for the first time: the truth about her life, and the awful shame she'd been made to feel.

'My parents were Catholics,' she began. 'Fierce, zealous Catholics of the kind you'd think had died out but truly haven't. Or at least, my mammy was.' She glanced at her sons. 'Daideo Cooley loved her, and had a strong faith of his own, but it didn't define him in the same way. It wasn't the core of his being, I think. So he was much easier on me. He'd let me get away with seeing friends from time to time, and he'd argue my case when Mammy was on the warpath about something. But there was no TV, no books with heathen messages, no parties. And definitely, definitely no boys.'

Aisling paused, and took a deep breath, thinking of how it had happened with Jack. How little by little, the time they'd spent working together as lab partners at school and then doing homework together had opened up something so clear and shining in them both that she'd realised she no longer cared about her mammy's warnings. She'd just wanted to be with him.

'Jack and I started seeing each other in secret. I had to lie, constantly, to see him. I knew I couldn't even let my dad know the truth. He'd have felt compelled to tell her, I think. Or at least he would have felt torn apart. And worried for me too. I think part of him really did believe that my immortal soul would be in danger if I touched a boy. You know.'

Aisling swallowed, and found herself being handed a cup of tea by Juliette. She hadn't even noticed that she'd left the room.

'So we'd been doing this – this covert relationship for over a year when it was suddenly announced to me that my mother's cousin, Donagh, would be visiting. And I was fascinated. Mammy had broken with her family entirely because they were, she said, a lot of sinners. They'd fallen into awful vices, including real crime. Gangster stuff. She couldn't bear to see them, so she'd left them the moment she married my daddy, moved with him to Tullamore and refused to see them again.'

'Where were they from?' Ben asked her. 'Your mother's family?'

'Limerick,' she said. 'Around Limerick.' She drank some of the tea, and was surprised to find that it tasted just the same as it usually did. For some reason she'd expected it to be as empty of flavour as the way she felt.

And she told them, then, about how Donagh had arrived. About how she had been bowled over by him. She had been a slim, awkward fifteen-year-old who it turned out was thought beautiful by some. Donagh had made it clear that he thought her so, and at first she had been flattered.

'We were all putty in his hands,' she said. 'This twenty-five-year-old, deadly handsome, Bible-quoting charmer. He flirted with all of us, my daddy included, and we every one of us fell for it. The only person who saw him for what he really was, was Jack, and that was because he wasn't subjected to the charm. Jack obviously never came to our house or spent time with me in public. He was just seeing the effects of Donagh on me. The way my head was turned when he called me clever, or insightful, or a truly beautiful soul.'

The thought of this made her feel nauseous. When Donagh had offered her Bible lessons, she'd jumped at the chance, delighted at the idea of sitting and worshipping at his fount of knowledge. Worse still was the thought of how she'd told Jack his suspicions were ridiculous. That it was just misplaced jealousy. All the while knowing that her feelings for her cousin were hot and confused and complex.

'And then,' she said, surprised to find that her steady voice was suddenly shaking, 'Donagh found out about Jack. He saw us sneaking back to school from the fields behind, where we'd gone to do no more than hold hands and talk. And he – he told me I was a whore. And he used it – this knowledge – to force me to . . .'

Aisling had to pause then. This wasn't something she should be saying in front of her sons. It was a terrible thing that she was doing.

'I'm sorry,' she said, turning, to Finn. To Ethan. They looked so disgusted. 'You don't need to hear all this. You should – you can go upstairs. This is awful.'

'No way,' Ethan said, his face full of fury. 'The guy was clearly a total prick. I want to know about it. And I think the police should know about it too.'

'Yeah,' Finn agreed. 'There are so many men out there

who get away with this shit, and we're going to support you in making sure he doesn't.'

Aisling felt her eyes stinging. How had she managed to bring up two such wonderful young men? When so often she'd just been flinging any solutions she could find at problems? She didn't deserve them.

She picked up each of their hands, and squeezed them.

'That's definitely something that can be looked into,' Juliette said. 'I would encourage some consideration of whether you'd like to make a formal statement against him to the Gardai.'

'Thank you,' Aisling said.

'Can I ask then, whether you're sure that the child you mentioned . . . wasn't your cousin's?' Juliette asked, next.

Aisling shook her head. 'He didn't – he was careful . . . And anyway . . . that wasn't his thing. He liked to humiliate.' She was surprised to find that she could think of even that without panic, just now. 'It was because of him, though, that I – that Jack and I . . . I think I just needed to feel like I was in control of myself. And so we . . .'

She remembered, then, that she was telling this to her sons.

'Sorry,' she said. 'Jesus. It's . . . Anyway, three months down the line, when I had only just realised that I was pregnant, my mammy figured it out too. And she went . . . she went mad. Just, mad. She accused me of whoring myself out. And, god, I was so angry then that their precious Donagh was doing all that stuff to me and *I* was the one being called a whore. So I told her – them both – what he'd been doing. I had nothing to lose. I let them believe the child was his. I didn't mention Jack just then.'

Aisling took a deep breath. This was the first time she'd really let herself remember that night for decades.

'My mammy wouldn't have it,' she went on. 'She said I was

244

a liar and I'd go to hell. She was half in love with Donagh herself. But Daddy just went very quiet. And then, when Donagh arrived back home a few minutes later, Daddy walked out to him in the driveway, and he hit him. And he hit him. The sound was awful. Like a butcher cleaving meat.'

'Did he kill him?' Ethan asked.

She looked at Ethan, and could see that some part of him was hoping that her father might have killed Donagh. And that fact made her ache.

'Oh, god, no. No,' she said. 'But he made a mess of his face, and – and by the time he was done, Donagh was wheezing something terrible. And then Daddy roared at him to leave, which Donagh did. But as he went, he told him that we were all of us dead. That his family would rain down pain on us. How he'd kill the two of them and force me to marry him, and bear his children, because there would be nobody to protect me.'

There was quiet for a few moments. Aisling, looking up properly, realised that Finn had vanished at some point. He reappeared a minute later carrying Barks. Someone must have let the dog out earlier, as he was mud-covered and damp. Finn himself looked wet through. Thank god her younger son had the wherewithal to remember the dog at a time like this.

'He'd got stuck in the fence,' Finn said, shaking his head. 'Some dog walker had seen him and was freeing him.'

'A dog walker?' Ben Lightman asked.

'Yeah,' Finn agreed. 'Just some guy walking on the track behind the house.'

'Someone you know?'

Finn shook his head, and shrugged. 'I couldn't really see. He left as soon as he'd freed him. Kept walking.'

Aisling half registered the way Ben glanced over at Juliette, and then rose smoothly.

'I'll check in with the station and be back,' he said.

Aisling felt sudden worry. Was there something wrong with this dog walker being there?

Juliette gave Aisling a warm, reassuring smile, and Aisling's surge of worry faded.

'So all that . . .' Ethan said, after a pause, 'it's why you left Ireland. And came here.'

Aisling gave him a wry grin. 'It's one reason. The other was my mother's shame. And, god, she was ashamed. How could she look anyone in church in the eye again? With me pregnant at fifteen, and her own cousin the father?'

'Did you ever tell your parents the baby wasn't his?' Ethan asked.

'I told Daideo Cooley,' Aisling said. 'Once we'd come here, with our new names and the terrible threats to never contact anyone from home . . . I told him, because I wanted him to understand that I loved this child and wanted to keep him. I was afraid they'd take him away.'

She tried not to think of Jack just then. Of the anger in his expression as he'd left.

'I told him,' she went on. 'And I begged him not to tell Mammy.' She shook her head. 'I could see what it did to him, holding onto that secret. It was so painful to him. But he did. He agreed that we could keep the child and raise it as my sibling, and he convinced Mammy. Or at least, I thought he had. I was so grateful to him. But then . . . then when the time came for him to be born . . . it had to be done in private, they said. So we could pretend to everyone that he was my little brother. They had a friend come to the house who was a midwife. And after the birth, after I'd held my baby for a few minutes, she gave me an injection to help expel the placenta. It made me dizzy and tired.'

To Aisling's distress, the numbness seemed to be sliding

away from her. She was feeling this all again, and she didn't want to be. She didn't want to be. But she had to tell them somehow.

'And when I woke up, they looked at me with – the way they looked, I just, I just thought, no . . . no . . .' She rubbed at her eyes again. 'They said the baby had stopped breathing. That they'd tried to resuscitate him. But that he'd gone. And they'd had to bury him.'

And she remembered, then, what her mother had said – her own mother – after she'd told her. The sentence that had broken the remains of their relationship in two.

Maybe it was for the best, Martha . . .

She looked up at Juliette and asked, 'How could they do that? How could they?'

40

Hanson gave a heartfelt sigh as she climbed back into the Qashqai.

'Jesus,' she said. 'That poor woman.'

Ben nodded. 'You go in expecting to find out some hard stories, don't you? But I hadn't been braced for anything quite so . . .' He shook his head.

'I hope the chief has some thoughts on how we go about finding the kid,' Hanson said. 'Because I don't feel like we're on the home stretch any more.'

She'd run over any possible leads with Aisling before Ben had let himself back into the room. Those leads were unsurprisingly few, given that Aisling had spent twenty-nine years believing her son to be dead. But she had promised to get out all the paperwork her mother had left behind on her death. They would pick it up from her in the morning, once they had all hopefully had a little sleep.

'What if I got rid of something important without even realising?' Aisling had asked Hanson, suddenly stricken. 'There were things I told them to just throw away. I can't even remember what . . .'

'There's a good chance we'll be able to find him anyway,' Hanson had told her, as reassuringly as possible. It had been the right thing to say, but she'd felt a rush of frustration. So many missing children stayed that way thanks to lack of records. This was urgent. Vital. How were they going to find him before he took another victim?

'What happened with the dog walker?' she asked Ben, pulling her seat belt on. 'Did they find him?'

Lightman shook his head. 'The field out at the back is pitch dark. We didn't catch anybody going down the nearest cut-through, but it looks like there are a lot of different routes back into the town. Lots of little lanes and tracks between houses.' He gave a small shrug. 'It could have been just a dog walker . . .'

Hanson looked out once again at the filthy, cold rain that was falling. She'd been half soaked just walking to the car. And at that time of night, why would you choose such a dark, muddy path to walk on? 'Pretty committed to their pets.'

'You're not wrong,' Ben agreed. After a moment, he added, 'I'm not going to assume anything, but if it was Aisling's son, and he is your helpful guardian angel, he could have followed us here the first time. And, once here, he might be well aware of who Aisling is. The helpful behaviour – rescuing her dog – could mean a number of things, including that he's thinking of her as his next target.'

'I guess we'd better update the chief,' Hanson said.

41

It was almost twelve, and O'Malley had told the chief to sod off home. It wasn't usually his role to order his senior officer around, but the man had looked haggard, and O'Malley didn't want to think about him being woken up by a five-month-old on top of that.

'The grunt work is for the grunts,' Domnall said. 'Juliette and Ben are on their way back, and I'll be here.'

The chief had given him wry thanks and departed. At which point O'Malley had set about trying to trace a child who might never have officially existed.

He had inevitably found himself thinking once again of the child taken from Anneka Foley. It occurred to him that Dara Cooley's firm might have got his interest in Anneka Foley entirely wrong. Was it possible that he had, in fact, been going to see her frequently because he wanted to visit his grandson? A child she had agreed to raise for him?

The note Dara had left suggested some level of guilt at his duplicity. An affair made sense, but perhaps guilt over concealing his daughter's child from her did too.

Or, he thought, *perhaps it was both. A woman he'd asked to raise this child, who he then fell in love with during his visits.*

The pub landlord's report that the child had been mistreated was another note that strongly supported their theory Anneka's child was really Aisling's son. A child whose apparent mother had abused him was that much more likely to go on to harm women as an adult.

They often had talks from criminal psychologists to inform

their policing, and one of those, a few years ago, had been from a psychologist who worked with category-A offenders. Almost all his patients had been men who had raped or murdered women. A hideous job, O'Malley thought. The psychologist had told them that the vast majority of their inmates had suffered some form of abuse as children, some parental, and almost all of the abusers unconvicted. The abused went on to abuse, and sometimes to kill, and so the cycle continued.

It had been eye-opening and awful at once, and it had had the effect of confirming in O'Malley a belief in salvation. So much suffering could be helped, he had often thought, if people could be saved when they were young enough. Sure, there would still be born narcissists and psychopaths. The entitled assholes who thought they could have any woman they wanted, or get away with anything. But for the most part, if society as a whole could find some way of caring for each and every person, O'Malley was pretty confident that most policing would become redundant.

He sighed to himself, trying to think rationally. They had a child who had suddenly appeared in Anneka Foley's house – a child who officially did not exist, given that Anneka had died with no legal heirs. That lack of record made O'Malley's life enormously difficult. He needed to find out if social services really had come to take the kid, as the landlord in West Gradley had suggested. He had no name to give them, and no date for when the child was seized. He had only the address, and the identity of the mother.

He called social services for West Berkshire, nonetheless, and detailed for them exactly who he was looking for.

'OK,' the guy on the other end, a young-sounding lad, said. 'We can try to have a look, but it's after hours so realistically you're looking at tomorrow morning before we're likely to have anything. None of the admin staff are in. It's just urgent support.'

O'Malley sighed. 'Are you mad busy?' he asked. 'I'm not trying to make life difficult for you, but if there's any downtime for you or a colleague between now and then, I'd really appreciate it. It's a serial murder inquiry, and the offender looks to have made another attempt last night. We need to find out what happened to this kid.'

There was a pause, and the young lad said, 'Well, I can try. I'm not really . . . I mean, there are people who'd be a lot better at it. But . . . sure. I'll give it a go.'

'Thank you,' O'Malley said. 'I really appreciate it.'

'Do you have a date of birth or anything?'

'So, assuming he's the kid I think he is, he was born on the twentieth of January 1986,' O'Malley said. 'But I wouldn't assume that exact date on any records. I'd try any date around then. He was given into the care of an Anneka Foley, living in West Gradley, and he was ultimately taken away from her. The locals claim it was your guys who came to get the kid because he was being mistreated. The mother had severe mental health issues and was demonstrably incapable of care.'

'OK,' the lad said. And then he added, 'With her name and address, that might not actually be too hard. Give me a bit, and I'll see what I can do.'

'Seriously appreciate it,' O'Malley said warmly. He left his direct dial and mobile, and then sat staring at the screensaver of his desktop.

Anneka Foley was the only real lead they had so far. If that proved to be a dead end, then they were waiting on information from Aisling Cooley. Or, he thought, doing this the slow and painful way: trawling through all registered births of the right age, and primary-school registrations the right year, within a very wide radius. He really hoped that it wouldn't come to that.

He spent a while looking up methods of tracing kids in the care system, and then ran out of steam. He'd gone to make himself a cup of tea when his mobile buzzed. His social services guy had only taken twenty-five minutes to call back.

'It actually wasn't too difficult to do the search,' he said, sounding pleased with himself. 'I just used keywords, and I tried every one of them. I only took a while because I wanted to be thorough.'

'Ahh, is that to say you didn't find anything?' O'Malley asked, with a feeling of resignation.

'No, I'm afraid not,' he said. 'We definitely didn't pick up any child from that address or from that individual at any time since the fifties, and actually there are very few children who were taken from parents during that time period anyway. It doesn't happen as often as you'd think. The records were all digitised in 2003, so they'd be there. I hope that helps.'

'Thanks, it does,' O'Malley said graciously. Though, in fact, he felt as though his luck had ended for the night.

The landlord and his regulars had been certain that the child had been taken away from her. So if not by social services, then who by? And how the hell was he going to track him down?

42

It was well after midnight by the time Jonah made it in through his front door. The downstairs of the house was quiet, but it was slightly surprising – and perhaps a little worrying – to find that Michelle was not tucked up in bed. She was clearly still out.

He felt a sudden rush of doubt. Their killer was undeniably still out there.

He opened Find My Friends, checking on her location for the first time he could remember. The dot that represented her phone was showing up on the Totton bypass. It moved onwards as he watched, further south-west. It looked like she was on her way home.

With a squeeze of fear, he thought of Lindsay Kernow. Of how she'd been driven down that road. How she'd died somewhere between the outskirts of Ashurst and Lyndhurst Heath.

He found himself watching the dot with absolute focus. Was Michelle in a taxi? Was it a real taxi? Could it be someone posing as a driver?

The sweat was standing out on him as he saw the dot inch out along the A35 and onto Hunters Hill. What would he do if the vehicle went right on past the turning towards home? Should he do something before that? Call her? Or wait and call a squad car?

He watched it draw towards Ashurst, somehow certain that it wasn't going to take the turn.

And then suddenly the point was a short distance down Whartons Lane. It had turned.

He watched it most of the way up the road but minimised the app before it had turned the corner for the final approach. He felt weak with relief. And ridiculous.

He found himself going to the fridge and pulling out one of the bottles of Corona he'd stashed in the door. He'd drunk half of it by the time Michelle's key turned in the Yale lock of the front door, but it had done little to make him feel any less stupid.

He heard Michelle stumble slightly as she walked in. He could hear her heading for the kitchen, where he was waiting like a lemming. He turned away, towards the sofa and chairs at the back. He suddenly wasn't sure how to greet her.

Her footsteps halted, and she said, 'Good evening.'

Her voice sounded arch. And merry. And possibly confrontational.

Jonah turned towards her as he sat on the sofa, trying to smile. It was somehow harder to look at her when she was so much more her old self once again. When she was as drunk as she'd often got in their previous life, looking at him with a hint of challenge.

She'd curled her hair tonight, and though the curls had loosened now and her eyeshadow was smudged, she looked beautiful, he thought. Gleaming.

'Hi,' he said. 'Did you have a good time?'

'You've been ignoring me,' Michelle said, swaying towards him. 'Where have all the loving little texts been?'

Jonah grimaced without meaning to. 'Ahh, they're probably kind of annoying, aren't they? Figured I'd leave you to have some time to yourself.'

Michelle's eyes narrowed. 'Don't believe you. You've been up to something.'

'Sadly, just work,' he said.

But Michelle had swayed the rest of the way over, and suddenly was kneeling over him, her legs either side of his thighs and her dress riding up. It was overwhelmingly sexual, and so different from everything that had gone on between them for the last six or more months.

'Don't believe you,' Michelle said, looking down at him. She was half smiling, and half challenging still. 'Work couldn't possibly be more interesting than messaging me.'

'Of course it wasn't,' Jonah said.

He felt indescribably relieved, and somehow also deeply sad as they began to kiss, and then Michelle started to pull at her dress. He attempted to tug his shirt off and laughed as he got stuck with it half over his arms. She had to help him pull it off the rest of the way.

'We should probably go upstairs,' he said quietly, as she began to work at the hooks on her bra. He could imagine Rhona walking in on them, and the thought was anything but sexy.

Michelle hesitated, and then climbed off him with a nod. She bent to pick up her dress, and turned to watch him as he rose and grabbed his shirt.

'After you,' he said.

But he saw how she was looking at him now, her expression confused. And somehow sad.

'God, sorry,' she said. 'I'm a bit too drunk. I probably . . .'

And then she turned and walked away from him, pulling her dress back on with what looked a little like shame, and Jonah watched her go, and then sat back down to finish his beer.

43

Aisling knew she wouldn't sleep. Not for hours. In spite of the tiredness, she couldn't tuck herself up in bed when the answer to her son's whereabouts might be hidden in the boxes in her spare room.

She'd started carrying them all down to the kitchen table. She'd passed Ethan on the way, and he'd silently gone to pick up the last few.

'Shall I help you look?' he'd asked, as he'd dumped them on the table, though his eyes had been heavy with sleep.

'Ahh, don't,' she said. 'I'll be an emotional wreck and it's embarrassing enough dealing with that by myself. You sod off to bed, and make me pancakes in the morning.'

Ethan snorted. 'You're definitely asking the wrong child there, *Madre*.'

'No, I'm just an eternal optimist.' She'd reached up to him for a hug, and then as he retreated, she wondered briefly but powerfully whether her two sons would keep on being good men. Men who were there for their loved ones.

Somehow, all the other men in Aisling's life seemed to be the other kind. The kind who left. Her father. Stephen.

Even Jack, she thought.

Perhaps it had been unreasonable of her to expect more. To expect him to stay and do this with her. She had run out on him too. It must have hurt him terribly.

But that had never been her choice. And now, here she was, her life shredded by grief, and by terrible revelation after terrible revelation. But instead of staying to support her, he had left. He'd left her to deal with it alone.

She put a hand down onto the table, steadying herself.

You're strong enough to do it, she thought. *Screw the lot of them.*

And it was somehow the most rejuvenating thought she'd had in days.

She'd told Ben and Juliette she needed time to dig out her father's paperwork, and they'd accepted that and said they'd come back tomorrow. They presumably wouldn't be doing much work on it this late anyway. So she had until morning to look through them.

She pulled out the stack of papers from her dad's old filing cabinet again. Within it was a series of foolscap files, divided by year, each one labelled with Daddy's very rounded writing. *Council Tax. Business Receipts. Travel. Utilities. Credit Card. Car.*

She'd looked through these on Sunday, skipping through most of it. Many of the contents were nothing more than bank statements or bills, but there had been the odd memento hidden away. Certificates of his qualifications. Some of hers too. A few letters from significant people in the church or from his firm back in Ireland. Notifications of awards for excellence.

But there was also a lot that was less personal. More mundane. And yet it might tell her more than she'd ever known. Because if her daddy had hidden her child somewhere, then there surely must be some trace. Some sign.

He'd had so much opportunity to hide the baby, she realised. His job had given him huge freedom to travel and to meet people. It had made him free to live a double life.

But it might also mean records. His journeys existed now in the form of expenses. Receipts that would help her to map where he had been.

She pulled out the folder for 1986, the year when Daddy had taken her son away on a bitterly cold January night. And then she paused, her heart squeezing, as she realised that the twentieth of January had already dawned. It was the early hours of her son's birthday.

Her child was twenty-nine years old, and she hadn't seen him once in all that time.

And then it occurred to her that she might have seen him in passing somewhere. Twenty-five years ago, she might have seen a child out for a walk in the forest. A child who was terribly unhappy. One being mistreated by his family. Hurt. Damaged by them. One of the children she had caught sight of out in public, and worried about, and then – because she was trained to do it – had left behind her as she walked on past.

He might have been one of the troubled teens she'd seen out in Lyndhurst or Southampton and moved to avoid. Or one of the unhappy-looking twenty-somethings drinking themselves into a stupor in bars, with nobody to tell them it was time to go home and gently take the glass off them.

It was amazing that the thought only really came to her now: that he could have been any one of them, and she might have saved him without even knowing it was him, if only she'd done something. She could have saved him, and those women.

It was almost impossible to see the receipts she began dragging out of their folders. In her mind she was seeing only desperate faces.

A gentle knock at the front door cut through the feeling. She was disconcerted for a moment. It was almost one. Who could be knocking now?

But then she realised that it must be Jack. Of course it must.

She felt a surge of anger towards him all over again. How could he have just walked out like that?

And then the thought occurred to her, as she pushed back her chair and trod down the hall, that he didn't know everything yet. He'd left before she could really explain.

Her anger ebbed, and she knew that some of this was on her. She owed him the whole truth.

His figure through the glass was just the same, but the smile she gave him as she opened the door was much sadder. And he looked sadder too. Sad and beaten, but here anyway.

'I'm sorry,' he said, just as she said the same words. And they both ducked their heads wryly.

'Will you come in?' she asked him.

They returned to the kitchen again, Jack bringing his backpack with him and sliding it onto the seat beside him. No overnight bag, she saw. He must have gone to his hotel in the interval.

She kept the lights dim this time. Just the downlight over the kitchen table and the papers spread over one end. A late-night mood suffused the place and it felt only right.

Jack looked over the papers, and nodded in understanding.

She turned and pulled the remainder of the wine out of the fridge.

'I shouldn't have naffed off,' Jack said, as he sat at the clear end of table and let her pour him a large glass. 'It was just that ... the break-up of my marriage wasn't really about work. It was because we couldn't have kids. That was it really. Though maybe that just exposed the cracks that were already there and chiselled them wide open. I don't know.'

Aisling felt a rush of hurt for him. 'Oh, Jack. I'm so sorry.'

'I came to be all right about it,' he said. 'Really, I did. It was thought initially that stress had a lot to do with our failure to conceive, and after a lot of discussion with Stella, I gave up my job with the Met and started doing this PI stuff. Only that turned out not to help.' He gave a short laugh and drank a

large gulp of the wine. 'Having vowed to love each other forever, it took five years to never want to see each other again.
Quick work. And, on a side note, that wine is amazing.'

Aisling gave a short laugh. 'You can blame my ex-husband
for the expensive taste,' she said. 'He was always an aspir-
ational drinker.' And then, sitting in front of him, she said,
'So tonight you found out that you do have a son, one you
never knew about. And the first you get to hear of it is that
he's wanted for murdering two women . . .'

'Yeah,' Jack said, his mouth twisting in dark humour, 'that
about sums it up. Bit of a head-fuck, no?'

'God, Jack,' she said, reaching out and squeezing his hand.
'I should have told you a long, long time ago.'

'Aisling,' he said intently, 'if there's one word I would be
happy to remove from human language, it's that bloody word
"should". We only ever use it to control other people, or to
beat ourselves up about things we haven't done.' He let out a
long sigh. 'There is no "should" about the actions you took.
Like all of us who are just trying to work life out one step at
a time, you did what you did because you only knew what
you knew then, not what you do now. And what good would
telling me have done? When you thought he'd died?' He
returned the pressure on her hand. 'I understand so well why
you felt you couldn't. I only regret it because I could have
supported you.' He shook his head at her. 'What a thing to
go through on your own. My god.'

She returned her hand to her glass, but was glad that they'd
had that moment of touch. 'My dad was . . . kind,' she said.
'I mean, I think, after I told him that the baby was yours, it
did change his opinion of me. When he thought it was Donagh's and that everything had been his fault, at least I was still
his little girl. Innocent and abused. But then, when I told him
the truth . . .'

'Everything that church made him believe was toxic,' Jack said, quietly and with venom. 'It isn't faith, that. I've known so many people since who have faith stronger than anything and are forgiving. Kind. Understanding. Who would have supported you.'

Aisling nodded. 'I don't know how to feel about him now, though. What he did to me was terrible. But it must have been what Mammy wanted. Otherwise, she would have told me the truth after he left. And he had all these secrets we were making him swear to keep. Mammy making him swear not to tell me where our son was. Me making him swear not to tell her he was your child. And perhaps an affair of his own too.' She shook her head. 'I'm so angry with him for doing it, and for leaving us, but I also wonder whether between us we broke him.'

They descended into silence for a few moments, until the wine in each glass was gone. And then Jack said, 'Are you going to help the police to find him?'

Aisling knew that he meant their lost child, and saw that he was thinking as she had. That this was their son. A man who had grown up without the chance of being loved by them, as he had deserved.

'I'm going to do everything I can to find him,' she said, 'before they can.'

And Jack smiled at her. 'I'm right with you,' he said.

44

It was hard to define the mood as the team met that morning. They'd agreed to assemble at seven thirty, and it felt brutally early with so many late nights coming before it.

Hanson's own feelings had been knocked sideways when she had received, at six forty-one, another email from Damian. It had come, of course, looking as though it were from someone else. All his emails had been disguised in order to make her read them, and many had been sent by setting up new mailboxes.

This one was apparently from someone called Daniel Conlon. It was titled 'Witness statement 03/01'. But the contents made it immediately clear what was going on, and she'd felt a sick drop to her stomach.

Juliette,

I'm sorry for the subterfuge to get you to read this. I just wanted to say that I've had lots of time to think in recent months and I can see that I've been acting like an utter idiot. I don't know why I thought any of my behaviour was reasonable.

I think I just wanted your attention or some kind of a reaction, but looking back on it now gives me the cold sweats. It's like waking up from a bad dream. I'm really, really sorry.

I know it'll be hard to forgive me, but I really hope we can end up on the same side again. I really do wish you well.

If there's any way we can put all that shit behind us and just start over, I would be so grateful. It's become really clear to me that you're just trying to get on with your life and I should let you. I don't want to drag you through this court case either.

If you ever want to meet for a genuinely friendly coffee, let me know. I totally understand if you don't want to, but the offer is there and meant.

Wishing you well,
Damian

Juliette let out a long, very tired sigh. How very like Damian to have suddenly decided that none of this was in his interest. And how very classic to try to persuade her that she didn't want to go through with a court case.

What he was clearly unaware of was that the court case was going to proceed anyway, regardless of how Juliette felt about it. It was the Crown against Damian Sawyer, not Juliette Hanson against him.

She knew the drill now, as instructed by her lawyer anyway. She wrote a swift reply, that read simply:

Damian,

Thanks for emailing, but I'm afraid I can't communicate further until the trial is over.

Thanks for your understanding,
Juliette

She'd sent it, blocked this new address and then carried on making herself breakfast.

She'd tried not to think about Damian any further as she got ready for what she knew might be a significant day in the Bonfire Killer case. By agreement Ben came to pick her up at seven. She knew that there had been two DCs on watch since before she got up, and winced at the thought that they were losing sleep just for her. None of the detectives following her had seen anything suspicious, and it was beginning to make her feel her guardian angel had somehow been in her head.

She was at least able to thank Ben for the lift through the universal currency of baked goods. She'd defrosted some of her mum's cookie dough the night before and whacked it into the oven when she got up. It had been worth the extra-early wake-up to hear Ben tell her it might be the best thing anyone had ever done.

They'd arrived at CID at seven fifteen and had to walk past a reasonable press presence outside, one that had swelled since the comms team had announced the arrests last night. The journalists' questions, reasonable though they were, didn't help Hanson's mood. There was implicit pressure in them.

'What's happening with the two young men arrested?'

'Have there been any major break-throughs?'

'Should the public still be on guard?'

'When is the Bonfire Killer going to be caught?'

Hanson felt like telling them their guess was as good as hers. But it had been consoling to huddle in the kitchen with Ben and Domnall and share that feeling of intense pressure.

'Let's just hope we don't screw it all up,' O'Malley had said cheerfully.

Now, all clustered together in the big meeting room, it was clear that the pressure was being felt by everyone. As the chief settled himself at the front of the room, there was a moment when he looked like a man with the weight of the world on his shoulders.

Hanson felt a pang of sympathy. It was easy to forget that this all landed on him, and that he was managing a small child and what sounded like a complex home dynamic.

'So, a quick sitrep,' the chief said, still managing to sound together. 'We've had confirmation from Cumbria that the car in Ullswater was Dara Cooley's. There are personal effects that belong to Aisling's father, and the remains – which will be PMed this morning – are a match for a man of his age.' He glanced up at all of them. 'We won't completely close down that avenue, but I'm not going to pursue it any further right now. I think we're probably all in agreement that the Bonfire Killer is most likely to be Aisling Cooley's missing son.'

Hanson saw the other two nodding along with her.

'Plan for today. You've got the paperwork to collect from Aisling Cooley, haven't you?' he asked Hanson and Lightman.

'We said nine thirty,' Hanson agreed.

'On top of picking up paperwork,' the chief said, 'I think we need to discuss with her the possibility that she's at risk.'

'I think that'd be good,' Hanson said. 'As well as the strange dog walker last night, she's in the target age range and lives in the right area. And, you know, this might all be about her.'

The chief nodded. 'I've arranged for a uniformed patrol to do regular drive-bys of her house. I think we should also be asking her not to go anywhere alone.' He paused, and then said, 'I'd like O'Malley to take one of the DCs and head to the Murphy Stud Farm again.'

'Sure,' he agreed. 'Am I looking at the scene of crime, or . . . ?'

'I'm more interested in the people who work there,' the chief told him. 'Looking over that footage, and what we know about the stables, it just seems unlikely to me that someone would break in there with no prior knowledge.'

'Do we have anything back from forensics about the scene?' O'Malley asked.

'Not a lot,' the chief said with a slight sigh. 'Some Hunter wellington boot prints in an eleven that don't match anyone who approached the scene. Possibly relevant, possibly not.'

That interested Hanson. Hunters were reasonably pricey, and more often worn by would-be country folk than by people who actually lived and worked on the land. Damian had owned a pair during what she'd liked to term his Country Gent phase. Did this mean that their killer was actually a middle-class occasional rider rather than someone who spent a lot of time in stables?

It was funny how she'd immediately assumed Aisling's son had grown up poor. Something about the idea of a child who had suffered enough to become a killer had led her to that conclusion. And yet she knew, from very recent case experience, that some of the worst abuse could come from middle-class families.

'Judging by the CCTV, the guy who took the horse could have been wearing Hunters,' Lightman commented. 'Where were the prints?'

'Found twenty metres from the pyre, and then further off,' the chief replied. 'An isolated print further towards the farm. Could have happened while leaving coffee on the Qashqai,' he added, nodding to Hanson. 'The report's on the database now, so any other thoughts are welcome. Tyre marks from surrounding woodland car parks are more difficult, as many look to have been driven over in the twenty-four hours or so after the fire was set. It's possible that our culprit drove out there, parked at a distance and walked. But it's also possible that he lives somewhere on that farm. Or that he used to.'

'I have a list of all the staff who've worked there,' Hanson volunteered. 'I was trying to look for Dara Cooley but there's a chance that Aisling's son is one of them.'

The briefing broke up soon after that, and Hanson headed out to the car park with Ben, who had once again turned down her offer of a lift.

'You can drive us in your mini-fridge once it's warmer,' he said with a grin.

45

It was a strange morning for Aisling. She was hit by a wash of yesterday's emotions, half tempered by sleep, the moment she opened her eyes. They were like the smaller waves that come just after the big one that knocked you over. The tumbling drag and draw of every revelation.

My father is dead.

My first-born son is alive. But he may be a killer.

Finn and Ethan are innocent.

Jack O'Keane is here, in my house.

That last fact seemed somehow the strangest of them all, and one she felt compelled to check.

She rose, realising that it was still only seven forty and barely light. She crept out onto the landing and saw that the door to the spare room stood open.

For a second she felt as though she was falling.

He wasn't here. It didn't happen.

But then she saw that the bed had been slept in, and that Jack's coat was still slung over a chair. Everything seemed right again.

Aisling trod carefully downstairs, hopeful that Finn and Ethan might still be asleep. But then she caught the murmur of voices from the kitchen. She emerged to find Finn and Jack standing at the counter, one buttering toast and the other making coffee, engaged in a deep conversation about different strategies for playing *The Sims 4*.

Jack was wearing one of Ethan's smaller Basement Jaxx

T-shirts, and she was struck by the strength and capability of him all over again. By how much she liked him being here.

'Morning,' Jack said, interrupting Finn's diatribe about how easy it was to earn money as an artist in the game. 'Coffee?'

'Ahhh ... yeah, I'd love one.' Aisling shook her head slightly. How could Jack be making coffee in her kitchen as if it were normal? When they'd seen each other for the first time in thirty years only twelve hours ago, and were now trying to hunt down their child – a child who had murdered two women?

They had, in fairness, caught up on a lot of the last thirty years last night. And in the hours they'd spent poring over receipts, invoices, and letters, the remaining gap had closed a long way too. It had been the two of them, together, in the dim light of the kitchen, with their son's past and future in their hands.

They'd used the paperwork to trace her father around half the country. They'd latched onto possibilities, and written notes to follow up on.

Over and over again, Jack had asked whether she remembered anything further.

'It's possible that he talked about some of it without really meaning to,' he'd said. 'Or that somewhere in your memories of the everyday you know something that's key to unravelling it.'

At some crazy hour of the night she'd thought that they ought to try to find the midwife who had delivered their son.

'She must have been registered somewhere, mustn't she?' she asked.

Jack had nodded slowly. 'Assuming she really was a midwife,' he said. 'It sounds like she knew something about childbirth so hopefully she was. We can probably look and see anyway. I'll get someone in the office on it. Do you remember a name at all?'

Aisling had shaken her head, trying to draw the memory of those hours back around her. 'I don't. I just . . . she was just the midwife, you know? Someone my dad had arranged to come.'

'He'd have to have paid her,' Jack said thoughtfully. 'But there's nothing in his bank statements that looks like that. Maybe we should look at paperwork for the end of the year before. He might have paid her in advance. Though it's also possible he paid cash.'

They'd spent a while looking at October to December 1985, but had found nothing there either.

'You don't remember your parents having any friends at that time?' Jack asked, after that. 'People who they saw in the run-up to the birth? They wouldn't have handed the child to just anyone, I think. It would have had to have been arranged. Maybe even before they left Ireland.'

'I don't know,' Aisling had said. 'We left pretty quickly. The day after everything kicked off.'

Jack had nodded, considering this. 'OK. So maybe your dad found some way of getting in touch with people. Some kind of a contact. There must be networks of people who've lost children, or who are struggling to have them.' He frowned for a moment, thinking. 'If they hadn't come here, I'd have thought of the church itself. It's not like there isn't a history of vanishing illegitimate children.'

Aisling nodded, knowing that he was thinking of the Magdalene Laundries. Those institutions designed around young women's shame. 'But they wouldn't have come here and sent him back to Ireland, would they?' she asked. 'And if he really is doing these things, in the New Forest, then surely he must have been adopted by someone who lived near here.'

Jack gave this some consideration, and then nodded again. 'So maybe they moved to the New Forest specifically to meet someone. Someone who was going to take the child. Do you remember them meeting any friends before you had him?'

Aisling felt as though she *must* be able to remember something about this, but there was nothing. 'I don't remember them having any friends at all after they came here,' she said. 'It was just the three of us for so many months. Me locked away, pretending to be sick so nobody would realise I'd been tainted. The two of them playing the parents of an invalid daughter to the neighbours.'

'But they said the midwife was a friend?' Jack asked.

'Yes,' Aisling said slowly. 'Yes, they told me that specifically. That she was a friend who'd keep our secret.'

Jack nodded. 'I'll check any midwives we can find living nearby. I should talk to the neighbours too. If they weren't seeing many other people, it might have been one of them who put them in touch with both the midwife and the family they gave him to. And I'll see if there were support groups for bereaved parents and those with fertility issues in the area. You lived in Hordle, you said? That's not too far.'

They'd carried on looking for another hour after that, but eventually had exhausted her father's supply of paperwork for 1986. It had made Aisling feel sad to come to the end of it. There were only another two months of papers to come in her dad's life. Only January and a few short days of February in 1987 before he had driven his car into Ullswater.

'I guess we should get some sleep,' she'd said in the end. It was almost four a.m., and she'd barely slept the night before. She was going to be no use to anybody. 'I've got the spare bed made up if you want it,' she added a little awkwardly.

'Thanks,' Jack said with a tired smile. 'That'd be grand. After I stormed out, I checked into a hotel in Southampton. I left my overnight bag there, but if you don't mind lending me a toothbrush . . .'

'Of course,' Aisling said. And then she grinned. 'And you can raid the clothes Ethan keeps in the drawers in the spare room. Overspill from his own chaos. Take what you need.'

'Great,' he said, standing and stretching. 'I'll try not to sleep in. There's a lot to get on with here.'

'Do you not have to work tomorrow?' she'd asked. 'At VePlec, I mean?'

Jack shook his head. 'Your firm has a solid flexible working policy. And the CEO can't complain about me working from home without it looking suspicious. Anyway, I'll just hint I'm following up a lead with another developer. It's fine.'

He'd followed her to the spare room, and waited while she fetched him a towel and showed him where the guest bathroom was.

'It's Finn's bathroom too,' she said. 'Which is lucky, as he isn't quite such a disgusting human being as his brother.'

'I'm not judging,' Jack had said with a grin. 'I was a teenage boy once too.'

She'd stood in front of him, feeling a weight of sadness for the son she'd never known descend on her. And Jack had stepped forwards and wrapped his arms round her.

'We'll find him,' he'd said. And Aisling had stayed where she was, held by him and holding him, for a good long while before she'd retreated down the hall to her own room.

She thought of that hug again as she watched Jack brew coffee, and she suspected that it showed in her eyes as he eventually deposited a cappuccino in front of her, complete with froth from the Aeroccino. He gave her a slow, tentative sort of a smile in return, and she was glad that Finn was watching the toaster.

'Are you going to school today?' she asked her younger son after a moment. He'd be pushing it, she thought, to get there on time.

273

'I thought I might be ill today,' Finn said airily. And Aisling couldn't help grinning at him. It was such an un-Finn thing to do, to pull a sickie. She couldn't remember the last time he'd had a day off school. It had been years, she thought.

'I might be able to support you in that untruth,' she said.

To her surprise Ethan rolled in at that point, accompanied by an exuberant Barks. He was up a good two hours before his usual habit on a non-work day. He looked a little less bleary than usual too, though he still had the aura of someone who wasn't quite sure what was happening.

'Who woke the Balrog?' she asked.

'Barks, mostly,' he said. 'Either I didn't shut my door fully or Barks is secretly a door-opening raptor, because I woke to a small, huffing hound on my chest. Unnecessary.'

'Can you open doors, lil Barks?' Finn asked, abandoning the toast to stroke him. 'Well done. Well done, Barku.'

The terrier did the rounds while they got breakfast onto the table, eventually settling on Jack's lap.

'I'd love to say he's a good judge of character,' Aisling told him, as Jack attempted to eat toast and jam over the top of him, 'but he'll honestly be friends with anyone who has food. Shittest guard dog you ever met.'

'Don't listen to her, Barks,' Finn told the dog.

Ethan, who had finished wolfing down his toast and cereal, put his knife down and said, 'Can we – tell you about something?'

Finn paused with a piece of toast halfway to his mouth, and then carried on eating it, slowly, his eyes on his brother.

'Sure,' Aisling said. 'What sort of thing?'

'Can I just check,' Ethan said, looking at Jack. 'As a PI, if we tell you something, and it'd get someone in trouble if you, like, told the police, would you feel like you had to tell them?'

Jack blinked at him, and then grinned. 'One of the nicest

things about having left the police is that I don't have to tell anyone anything. In fact, most of my work involves keeping my mouth shut.' He glanced at Finn. 'I might try and persuade you to talk to the police if there's been a serious crime committed, but I wouldn't go and do it for you.'

'Ethan!' Finn said urgently. 'You know it could wreck everything!'

'We need to let Mummo make up her own mind what she wants to do about it,' Ethan said back, a lot more firmly than usual. 'We made her sit and tell us everything about everything last night. And it's not flipping fair if we, you know, don't do the same.'

Aisling looked between the two of them, feeling more than a little sick. She wasn't sure she wanted to know any more.

Finn looked far from convinced. 'Bruh, come on, that's putting her in –'

But Ethan said loudly, across him, 'When we lied to the police, about what we were doing on New Year's Eve, we were seeing Dad.' Despite his defiant voice, he said it to a point on the table, not meeting Aisling's eye.

Aisling felt kicked. A rush of hurt. Of betrayal. And a feeling of dizzying anxiety.

'How . . . ?'

'He got in touch eighteen months ago,' Ethan went on. 'He told us we had to keep it quiet because he's – well, as he put it, he got himself involved with some employers who turned out not to be quite legit and who he decided to run off from. He's been hiding in Latvia for most of the last while, building himself a new business.' He watched her face, his expression anxious. 'He's actually here now, which is why we were freaking out about telling anyone, including the police.'

Aisling looked between him and Finn, both of them clearly embarrassed. She was stunned that they could have kept this from her for that long. And also mortified that they'd felt they had to.

'I'm – you could have told me you wanted to see him.'

'How could we do that?' Finn asked, suddenly sitting up and looking directly at her. 'If we'd said anything, you'd have felt like you had to tell the police. You would have been, you know, like, complicit in it. And I don't think he's bullshitting when he says he's in big trouble with them. I think he might have run off with their money if I'm honest.'

'We didn't even *want* to see him, actually,' Ethan cut in. 'It wasn't about missing him or anything. He's still a massive tool.' He let out a huff of air. 'But Finn saw that you were, you know, almost out of money. We worked out that you're going to have to give up the house, so we figured . . . Dad actually owes you money, and us too. Maintenance and stuff. And he said originally that he's been smashing it over in Latvia. So we pretended we wanted to chat, and encouraged him to like us.'

There was a pause, and then Aisling asked, 'So he's been giving you . . . money?'

Ethan winced, and then nodded. 'Driving lessons for Finn – which he's been doing on Tuesdays when he said he has extra training – and a synth for me . . . And quite a bit of cash. We may have . . . massaged the truth a bit.' He glanced at his brother, his cheeks slightly reddening. 'We said how you clearly still really miss him and respect him, and how you don't blame him at all for following his heart. How it's been really hard on you – that kind of thing.'

Aisling could only stare at him, not knowing which of many emotions to give into.

'I've got three grand in a bank account so far,' Finn muttered. 'Made up of birthday and Christmas presents for each of us, and something, umm, for you for Christmas.'

'But the big thing is . . .' Ethan said, shifting, 'he's loaded now. Totally loaded. And he said he didn't want us losing the house. He'd been trying to find a way of getting some big money to you, which is why we were meeting on New Year's Eve. For him to hand it over. But the total dickhead turned up without it.' Ethan looked furious. Hurt. 'He said he'd had to prioritise an investment, because it was a limited-time opportunity. But that he'd have the cash in a few weeks. And, to be honest, I know Finn thinks we can hang on in there and get it, but I think he's full of shit and letting us down all over again.'

At that Aisling reached a point of overwhelm. She leaned forwards onto the table and put her head in her hands. She wasn't sure if she was laughing or crying as she said, 'Oh, god.'

46

Hanson was pleased to note that Aisling Cooley seemed ready for them, despite being still dressed in pyjamas and a dressing gown. There were four boxes stacked up in the hallway, and Aisling explained to them what was in each of them.

Hanson was interested to note that Jack O'Keane was in the hallway just behind her, and bore the unmistakable signs of someone who had slept there. She wondered whether they should be concerned about Jack's involvement in all this. An ex-Met officer who was now a PI could really get in the way if he wanted to.

'Thank you for these,' Hanson said, her face a mask of politeness, as she took hold of the last of the boxes. 'We'll log them all. I know they must mean a lot to you.' She hesitated. 'Are you sure we've got everything that might be relevant? There isn't anything else . . . ?'

'Yes, that's all,' Aisling said quickly. 'You know that, whatever happened to him, it's not – his fault?' She looked meaningfully at Hanson, and then at Ben. 'The way my two boys are now – happy and responsible and kind – they're how he could have been if he'd been given the chance. It's our fault, if it's anyone's, that those women died. Not his.'

Hanson gave an involuntary sigh. She could understand wholly where Aisling was coming from. The guilt. The love. The feeling of still wanting to reach out for that lost baby. But he wasn't a baby any more. He was a man, who had needlessly taken the lives of two women, if not a greater number. Aisling hadn't had to sit with Lindsay or Jacqueline's children and witness their grief. She hadn't got to know heartbreaking little details about them. And however much Aisling's son had suffered, Hanson believed that he'd still had a choice. What he'd done hadn't been forced on him.

All she could do was to nod, and to say, 'I don't think you can blame yourself for what happened.'

'While we're looking into this,' Lightman said, over her shoulder, 'we'd like you to take care over your safety. As well as being in the right age range for the Bonfire Killer's victims, it's possible that your son was told who his parents are at some point.'

Aisling blinked at him. 'But wouldn't he have tried to get in touch?'

'That depends what he was told, I would imagine,' Ben said quietly. 'Can you think of anyone new who's entered your life recently? Anyone you've encountered more than once?'

There was a pause as Aisling clearly thought about this, and then shook her head. 'No,' she said. 'Jack's the only one, and he doesn't count. I'm pretty antisocial, really.'

Ben nodded. 'We'd be happier if you didn't go anywhere alone. And when here, make sure you keep someone else in the house with you.'

Aisling nodded slowly. 'The lads are both around today.'

'That's good,' Lightman said. 'If you're worried by anything, call us. And 999 too, if it's urgent.'

And then they left, carrying the remnants of Dara Cooley's life.

47

O'Malley made his way into the stable yard, glad to be out in the cold air and away from paperwork. Despite the fact that some of his best work had been done at his desk, he was forever chafing at it. Getting out on his feet, looking for evidence and talking to people – this was what felt like real policing to him.

The yard was empty, but a sign over one of the doors informed him that it was the Stud Office. He ambled over, and was in the process of opening the door when someone called from behind him, 'Can I help?'

He turned, to see a large, bear-like man with dark hair and a beard approaching across the yard. He walked surprisingly quietly for a big man in sturdy boots.

'DS Domnall O'Malley,' he said, holding his hand out with a smile. 'I'm just following up on what happened to your horse.'

He watched the big man's eyes flick towards the stable block.

'I'm Danny Murphy. Is there – much more you need? Dad's on the warpath about things getting in the way of work.'

'Hopefully not too much,' O'Malley said reassuringly. 'A few short questions.'

Danny gestured towards the office, but O'Malley said, 'Ah, probably better to have a stroll around. Good to get an idea of the place.'

He could see that this disconcerted Danny for a moment, but then he nodded. 'All right.'

'Can you tell me, first of all,' O'Malley tried, as they started walking towards the stable block next to the gate, 'whether there is ketamine kept on the property?'

Danny faltered, and turned to stare at him. 'It's a controlled substance. We can't keep it here.'

'Ah, I know,' O'Malley said, waving a hand. 'I understand that officially it's not done – and I wouldn't be asking to try to catch you out. I also understand that there might be times when a vet might leave extra doses with you after surgery or the like, and that you might have ended up with leftovers.'

Danny frowned, shook his head, and said, 'It's never happened on my watch.'

O'Malley nodded. 'How about kerosene?' he asked. 'Could the horse thief have taken that from the property?'

'I – there was no sign of that on the CCTV,' Danny said.

'But you have some here?'

Danny paused outside the door to the stables before he said, 'Yes. The boiler runs off kerosene. We have a few drums of it in the shed outside.' He nodded towards the open steel gates.

'Why don't we take a look?' O'Malley suggested. 'See if it's still there?'

Danny didn't protest, but he was silent as he led O'Malley out of the gate and over to a sloping shed that had been built onto the exterior farmhouse wall. O'Malley watched him use a big set of keys from his gilet pocket to unlock a very large padlock, and swing open the wooden door. It was inches thick. Not easy to break into.

It was dark within the shed until Danny flicked on a very fluorescent overhead light that must have been a relic from the nineties. O'Malley's eyes travelled over the shapes of a sit-on mower, and – at the back of the shed – piles of timber. He couldn't immediately see any kerosene.

He had to follow Danny's gaze to work out where to look. To the left-hand side of the shed were three circular marks on the floor, free of dust and grime. It was at these that Danny was staring.

'Is that where the kerosene is supposed to be?' O'Malley asked quietly.

Danny continued to stare, and then said, 'I need to talk to Dad.'

48

Hanson and Lightman did their best to divide the files from Aisling Cooley's house up systematically between the various team members and themselves. They piled the paperwork up on their desks, noting that all of it came from Dara Cooley's time in the UK. There were no records earlier than June 1985. But, even then, there would be a good few hours of work just in sorting what they had and working out whether any of it might give them a lead.

'At least it's pretty organised,' Hanson said, opening the first folder and beginning to flick through. 'It's nothing like my filing system. By which I mean the pile of paper on my kitchen table that I eventually start to do something with when it threatens to fall over.'

Ben grinned and shook his head at her. 'Incomprehensible.'

They'd barely started digging through when the desk sergeant called through to say that someone had arrived to see Hanson.

'A Daniel Olwe?' she queried.

Hanson remembered, with a jolt, the requests she'd made the night before to Ethan's band members, in what seemed like another age. She'd been trying to establish whether Jacqueline Clarke or Lindsay Kernow had been at one of Ethan's gigs.

But that had been before the DNA results, and before they'd realised that Aisling Cooley had a third, older son. In all the rapid changes, she'd forgotten to message again and put them off.

That said, good police work often meant ticking every box, and they still didn't know how their culprit had met their two victims. If Dan Olwe had seen either victim at some point, it was possible they'd be able to find people who'd seen their killer.

'Ahh, thanks,' she said to the desk sergeant, after a beat, trying to pretend that she'd been expecting this. 'Can you show him up?'

Ben raised an eyebrow at her as she hung up, and she gave him a wry smile. 'Slight screw-up. Forgot to cancel someone Ethan Cooley knows. But there's a chance he might still know something about the victims, so . . .'

Ben gave her a thoughtful nod. 'Do you want me to start bringing in some of the other seven billion people on the planet to question too? Alphabetically suit you?'

'Sod off,' she said cheerfully.

Dan Olwe was tall and strong-looking but seemed awkward in his frame. He looked as though he also disliked eye contact, which seemed a little strange for someone who was pursuing a career onstage. But then Hanson imagined him hunching over a keyboard or synth set-up, never having to look at the crowds, and she supposed it made a sort of sense.

'This shouldn't take more than a few minutes,' she told him, as she settled into a chair across from him. They were in the interview suite to record Dan's reaction to photos of the victims. As purposeless as this exercise might turn out to be, she was going to do it right.

'Thanks,' Dan said, ducking his head.

She pulled out her folder of photographs. She'd decided to begin with Lindsay Kernow's photo.

'Can you tell me whether you recognise the woman in the photograph?'

Dan took a moment looking it over, and then shrugged. 'I don't think so.'

'You don't recall seeing her at one of your concerts?'

Dan breathed, and said, 'No, sorry. I mean . . . It's not easy to see people from the stage. She could've . . . You should probably ask the other guys, like.'

'OK, thanks. What about this woman?'

She passed over the image of striking, sandy-haired Jacqueline Clarke, and Dan sat up.

'Ohh, I think . . . Yeah, I've seen her.' Dan gave a short laugh. 'Easier to remember. Yeah. She was definitely at a gig.'

Hanson could feel her pulse kicking up a few gears. 'Can you remember which gig that was?'

Dan pulled at his lip, his eyes on the photo as he thought. 'It was a while ago. I think . . . maybe one of the ones we did at the Porterhouse.'

'Would you be able to check the dates?'

'Yeah,' Dan said. 'Sure. Gimme a second.'

He opened up his phone and started to scroll through what she guessed was Google Calendar. He paused, scrolled onwards. Paused, scrolled, and then stopped. He looked into the distance for a moment, and then nodded.

'Yeah, OK. I think it must've been the Porterhouse gig in October. Cos Nick was ill for that one.'

'Do you have the date?'

'Friday October the third,' Dan said.

Hanson wrote it down, feeling a bubble of adrenaline-fuelled joy.

The night Jacqueline died, she thought. *He saw her the night she died. How has he missed all the news about her at the time? All the press?*

And then another thought hit her. *And how did Ethan Cooley?*

'So did you talk to her?' she asked, trying to organise her thoughts. To think of the questions she should be asking in an interview she'd never expected to be conducting.

'Nawww, not me,' Dan said, laughing. 'Matt did. I mean, she talked to him, you know? He was trying to get away without being rude when she'd just bought three albums and a T-shirt. She was – she was one of them who gets a bit obsessed.'

'Sorry . . . Matt is . . . ?'

'Oh yeah,' Dan said with a grin. 'Sorry. He's not actually in the band. He was standing in for Nick because he had full-on flu. Matthew Downing. He's a friend of Ethan's.'

49

'Not that it's any business of yours,' Michael Murphy said starkly, 'but I moved them.'

'You moved them?' Danny asked, clearly not following. 'Why?'

'Because someone has to be concerned about fire safety around here,' Danny's father said in what was almost a shout. O'Malley wondered whether he was feeling attacked, or whether angry retorts were part of his usual repertoire.

They were in the smaller paddock behind the foaling barn, where Michael Murphy had apparently been training one of the older foals. Though to O'Malley, it largely looked like the foal was running in circles while the man stood there and watched.

'Where did you put them?' Danny tried.

'In the cellar,' Michael said.

'When?'

Michael gave a noise of impatience, his eyes on the horse. 'Some time after that fire last summer.'

'Had any of them gone missing?' O'Malley chipped in. 'Was that why you were worried?'

Michael's brow set lower. 'I thought maybe one had.'

'And this was last summer?' O'Malley asked.

Michael turned towards him, profound irritation clear in his expression. 'It was.'

'Who might have got into that shed?'

Danny replied before he could. 'There are keys hanging in the office, and Dad and I carry a set around.'

'So anyone on the farm?' O'Malley persisted.

'Along with any Tom, Dick or Harry who happened by when Danny's idiot brother left the thing unlocked,' Michael snapped.

'Ah,' O'Malley said. 'It was left open at some point?'

'More than once,' Michael said darkly. 'That boy has cost me countless lost materials. And now a brood mare.'

'Dad . . .' Danny said quietly. Placatingly.

But Michael rounded on his son. 'Don't cover for him,' he said. 'There's only one here stupid enough to leave that door unlocked, and I am the man unfortunate enough to have to call him my son.'

He stalked off into the field, leaving O'Malley watching him with interest. Danny Murphy stood looking too for a moment, his expression profoundly embarrassed, and then began to walk back towards the door to the barn wordlessly.

O'Malley decided he'd better follow him, despite the silence.

'It wasn't Antony,' Danny said suddenly, once they were inside the barn and among the quiet sounds of moving horses. 'The one who left the barn door unlocked the other night. It was one of the stable hands. Antony won't let me tell Dad.'

O'Malley raised his eyebrows. 'Doesn't sound like it's improved their relationship any.'

Danny gave a tired smile. 'It'd be hard to make it worse. And Dad's not going to throw him off the farm.'

'He might not throw me out, either,' a voice said from further down the barn.

O'Malley actually started, something he rarely did. He'd been certain they were alone with the animals. But out of the second stall from the end came a short, slightly stocky man with piercing blue eyes. He wore a fleece, gilet and jeans – an almost identical outfit to Danny's except that he wore wellingtons instead of hiking boots, and a beanie covering what looked like a close-cropped head of hair.

He gave O'Malley a very worldly smile and held out his hand.

'I'm Henning Andersen,' he said. 'The one these brothers have been covering for.'

Danny nodded, and O'Malley saw the big man smiling properly for the first time. 'Only because the farm would fall apart without him.'

'Good to meet you,' O'Malley said. 'So what's your job here?'

'General dogsbody,' Henning said, slipping his hands into his gilet pockets.

'Henning heads up the foaling team,' Danny told him. 'That means he gets no sleep at this time of year.'

'So that's . . . delivering the baby horses, like?' O'Malley asked.

'That's right,' Henning agreed with a laugh.

'He also feeds them, trains them and knows them inside out,' Danny commented.

'Are you involved much in the running of the farm too?' O'Malley asked, finding himself looking at Henning's navy blue boots.

Henning gave a short laugh. 'I'm at least ten years off being trusted to do that.'

'Sorry,' O'Malley said after a moment. 'Just distracted by your boots. Those are much better than anything I've ever owned. Where did you get them?'

'Oh, the Hunters?' Henning made a slightly embarrassed noise. 'Present from my wonderful mother. Be warned: you wear them somewhere like this, and everyone will take the piss.'

'Only a little,' Danny said.

O'Malley nodded. They were Hunters, just like the footprints they'd found by the pyre. He was working out how to find out what size he took when a shadow fell across the doorway to the yard.

'Are you . . . with the police?'

O'Malley couldn't really see the face of the tall, strong-looking young man until he stepped inside. There was a hint of similarity with Danny, he thought, though the hair was blond and the face longer and clean-shaven.

'Antony . . .' Danny said, stepping forwards uncertainly.

'There's something I need to tell you,' the other Murphy brother said, his face stricken. 'It's important.'

50

The news that Jacqueline Clarke had been at the Porterhouse, flirting with Matthew Downing, had driven the entire team into a frenzy of activity. They immediately set about creating a full profile for Matthew, and requesting CCTV footage from the pub.

It seemed strange and unfair that they'd only managed to pin down Jacqueline's movements now, two weeks after Lindsay Kernow had lost her life. Though when the CCTV came through from the Porterhouse doorway, in what might have been record time, it became clear why Jacqueline had not been remembered. After twenty minutes with three officers scrolling through it, it was only Ben who managed to spot her.

He turned his screen to show them all a figure wearing jeans, Converse, an off-the-shoulder T-shirt and a fake-leather jacket. Her sandy hair had even been gathered up under a baseball cap.

'I've got to hand it to you, Ben,' Jonah said to Lightman. 'I can see you're right, but I would have looked at her and carried right on. She looks nothing like she does in any of the photos we have.'

'It's the face shape that gives her away,' Ben said neutrally. 'I realised she has particularly pronounced flares to the cheekbones and looked out for those.'

It was clear from the tape, which had been shot looking out towards the street, that Jacqueline had arrived alone.

'But she became fixated on Matthew Downing during the

performance,' Jonah said, quietly. 'And presumably didn't leave alone.'

Though as he watched the tape over again, he wondered whether Jacqueline had arranged to meet Matthew or another individual there. She was scanning the crowds as if looking for someone.

Though it seemed unlikely from what Dan Olwe had said that she'd been meeting Matthew Downing. She'd apparently been pushing to talk to him after the performance, handing him a very plain business card and telling him that she worked in music production and could help his career along.

It was strange, surprising news. Nothing they'd heard so far about Jacqueline had suggested that this was normal behaviour for her. Though when Hanson had called her daughter Rosie to ask, tentatively, whether she might have attended any live music events and perhaps been interested in getting to know band members, she'd said, 'Oh. Well, Mum loved music. I mean, she always had something on in the background. I never thought of her as going to gigs, but . . . well, she was lonely, wasn't she? Maybe she did.'

It looked from Jacqueline's bank statements as though she'd bought the outfit she'd been wearing some months before. And a scour of her internet history on the desktop they'd picked up showed a depressing reality. She had, it seemed, been obsessed with the Great Unsaid. Video after video of theirs was cued up on her playlist. None of this had featured in their initial investigation because none of it had been part of what they'd been looking for. They'd wanted to know about messages. Assignations. Dating apps. Not about private obsessions.

Two of their co-opted constables had also searched through the photographs and evidence from Jacqueline's house and found a whole pile of the business cards. They were black and had Jacqueline's name in white, and looked in fairness like the stylish kind of minimalist card that a music producer might carry.

It was just possible that Jacqueline had gone to the gig that night with the intention of tricking one of them into going for a drink with her. It was duplicitous behaviour, and it jarred with everything they'd previously thought about her. But that, he knew, was the thing about victims. They weren't always straightforward innocents. They were complex, multi-layered people. Sometimes they were even driven to do strange or immoral things. But that didn't mean they deserved to die.

He wondered how Matthew Downing had ended up being the focus of Jacqueline's attention. Had he perhaps been the only one to respond? Was it also possible that he'd been convinced enough by her producer story to go with her, and then become angry when it turned out to be a lie?

'I'll see if I can find her again later,' Ben said, scrolling forwards through the CCTV feed.

Hanson and Lightman had gone to pick Matthew Downing up and bring him in for questioning. The first thing Jonah wanted to know was whether Matthew could be Aisling Cooley's son. The second was what had happened after Jacqueline Clarke pushed that business card on him.

51

O'Malley was sitting with the two Murphy brothers in the chaotic space of Antony's flat. The living area was covered in dozens of books, unopened letters, eclectic torches, clips and unidentifiable pieces of hardware. Beyond was a kitchenette that was scattered with empty plates and unwashed pans. It made O'Malley feel quite at home.

Danny had already made them all a cuppa from Antony's supply of Twinings tea bags, a slightly unexpected note in a farm kitchen. Though various objects suggested Antony was probably not the average stable hand. Books on astronomy vied with classics and French philosophical titles. He was clearly a big reader and not, it seemed from several broken objects, the most practical of people.

O'Malley was now waiting for him to start talking, but Antony seemed to have hit a road block of some kind.

'So,' O'Malley tried gently, 'whenever you're ready.'

'Right.' Antony looked away from him for a moment, opened his mouth and then closed it again.

'Was there something about Merivel's death?' O'Malley offered.

Antony looked at him blankly, and then said, 'No, I . . . shit.' He shifted. 'I should've said when you came before.'

'It's OK,' Danny said, before O'Malley could reply. 'Nobody's judging you.'

'You will,' Antony said to his brother, and gave a tight laugh. 'I . . . On New Year's Eve, I snuck out onto the heath to watch the Quadrantids. The meteors, you know. I drove the Land Rover down there and I was parked up, watching, when there was this – this blaze.' He rubbed his right eye with the heel of his hand. 'I caught it out of the corner of my eye. It wasn't like a bonfire. It was really *burning*, you know? And it was so close to the woods and the dry gorse. I just thought of how close that gorse fire got to us last year. And I grabbed the extinguisher and ran over and – I put it out.'

O'Malley could see a pulse in Danny's temple. It was out of rhythm with his own very noticeable heartbeat.

'Was it just a fire?' O'Malley asked quietly.

Antony shook his head, his expression wretched. 'There was . . . there was a woman.' He looked up at O'Malley. His eyes large. Staring. And then he turned with a sort of appeal to his brother, as though he might help somehow. 'She – when I shone my phone light on her, I could see she was – dead.'

There were shivers running through Antony's arms and torso now. He clenched his fists, but it did nothing to stop the convulsions. O'Malley, watching, was at a loss to know whether this was guilt or trauma at work.

'I'm really sorry,' Antony said after a moment. 'I should have . . . I just thought . . . everyone would think it was me. Dad would . . .' He took a breath. 'And it was fucking horrible. Seeing her like that. I couldn't seem to think afterwards.'

O'Malley nodded, keeping his expression sympathetic, though Antony wasn't looking at him. 'Did you see anyone? Anyone who might have set the fire?'

Antony's eyes locked onto him. His mouth opened and closed a few times, and then he said, 'I didn't even . . . I didn't think. I didn't even look around.'

O'Malley let out a long breath, trying not to show all the various things he was thinking. And then he said, 'I'd like you to come to the station and explain all that to my chief.'

52

Hanson and Lightman climbed out of the Qashqai outside Matthew Downing's large, well-maintained house on the edge of Lyndhurst. Hanson nodded towards a small attached paddock, in which two horses had lifted their heads from grazing to watch them.

'Looks like he might know how to handle horses, after all,' she murmured to Lightman.

They both looked up at the house itself, a very square, nineties build that had a lot of space and little character.

'Demolish,' Hanson said, at exactly the same time as Ben, and it was difficult to recover a straight face in time to knock on the door.

It was Matthew who eventually answered the knock, after leaving them waiting a good couple of minutes. The expression in his heavily lined eyes shifted from curious to irritated as they introduced themselves.

'I'm in the middle of recording,' he said. 'It'll have to be later.'

'I'm afraid this can't wait until later,' Hanson said firmly. 'But we'll try and be quick.'

Matthew sighed, and led them into a very large sitting room that was dominated by a long, bare brick wall on one side. Hung across it were several acoustic guitars and one signed electric one.

On the other, painted wall there were photographs, and Hanson gravitated towards these with interest. Many of them were of Matthew playing at gigs, but a whole series at one side were family portraits.

Hanson moved closer to a very formal photo of a toddler who must have been Matthew standing in front of the man and woman who appeared elsewhere. The father was short, stocky and fair-haired. The mother, curvy and with nonde-script, honey-blonde hair. Her face was rounded and her expression warm.

Matthew, despite his young age, already looked as though he would outgrow both of them. His form was slimmer and taller, and his dark colouring far more dramatic.

He looked, in fact, nothing like either of them.

Hanson turned, and asked, 'Were you adopted?'

Matthew had just flung himself into an armchair, and turned to stare at her, his expression startled and then quickly affronted. 'What's that got to do with you?'

'It could be important, strangely enough,' Hanson replied, with a slightly earnest expression. 'You don't look much like either of your parents.'

Matthew's jaw worked slightly, and then he said, 'It doesn't matter. My mum and dad loved me way more than the pair of arseholes who gave me up.'

53

'So you panicked?'

Antony Murphy nodded, his expression wretched. 'Yeah.' He cleared his throat. 'I don't know what I was thinking. I was just really scared you'd think it was me who'd done it.'

His mouth twisted as he continued to stare at Jonah, who looked coolly back.

'So, to recap,' Jonah said, sitting up slightly, 'you were on Lyndhurst Heath to watch . . .'

'The Quadrantids.' Antony nodded. And then, when Jonah raised his eyebrows, he went on, 'Sorry. They're meteors. You only get to see them right at the start of January each year, and only on clear nights after the moon's set. The peak is on the first or second of January generally. It was supposed to be particularly good this year, because it was an almost completely new moon. Not much to block them out. So I thought, sod it, that's more fun than a crap pub, and I went to watch.'

Jonah nodded slowly. Antony clearly seemed to know his stuff. But then he'd had plenty of time to look all of it up. 'So you parked up where?'

'On the north side of the heath, just beyond the woods. I wanted to make sure the light pollution from Lyndhurst was still beyond the hill. I'd worked the spot out kind of carefully.' Antony gave a crooked smile.

'And what time did you get there?'

'Nine thirty,' he said immediately.

'And you watched from inside your car?'

'No, I sat on the bonnet. I'd brought lots of warm layers and some coffee and stuff.'

'Any alcohol?'

Antony smiled slightly. 'Like, two shots in the coffee which I drank half of. I don't drink and drive.'

Jonah kept watching him. Although his voice was quiet, Antony didn't seem to be stumbling over any of this.

'What do they look like?' Jonah tried.

'Sorry?'

'The Quadrantids,' he said with his best disarming smile. 'Are they bright?'

'No, most of them are really faint,' Antony said, and shifted slightly. 'That's why they're not so famous. They're easy to miss. But in a good year you get some amazing effects. Like fireballs travelling across the sky. And with no moon they were pretty spectacular.'

'You didn't photograph them?'

Antony shook his head. 'I tried before, but I didn't even pick them up. You need a much better camera than I have. And you'd want to video them really. It's the way they move that's the good bit.'

'What time did you see this fire?' Jonah asked, coming back to the pyre.

Antony shook his head slightly. 'I don't know exactly. If I had to guess . . . maybe after a couple of hours? I'd definitely seen quite a few clusters and the coffee had gone tepid by then. I was thinking about going home.'

'So you thought it might be an out-of-control fire?' Jonah asked him.

'It looked intense,' Antony agreed.

'When did you realise there was a body on it?'

'Only when I got closer,' he said. 'And then I – I thought

I'd saved her.' He gave a shaky breath outwards. 'But when I switched my phone light on, I could see – she was dead.'

Jonah gave a slow nod. 'When you said you thought you'd saved her, what do you mean?'

'I sprayed the – the foam on everything,' he said. 'Before I turned the flashlight on.'

'And it worked?'

'Yeah. It was – weirdly effective.' He frowned. 'The fire went out in no time.'

'No mishaps?' Jonah tried.

Antony gave him a slightly confused look, and shook his head.

Jonah glanced down at his notes, interested in that. He'd expected Antony to say that he'd cut himself doing it. But it didn't seem as though he was here to explain away his blood at the scene.

Which made Jonah wonder whether he might actually be telling the truth, and the blood might not be his. And yet O'Malley had said that Michael Murphy seemed to dislike Antony. That he favoured Danny over him. It was still possible that Antony was Aisling Cooley's missing child. Adopted, and then replaced in their affections.

The good side to that was that they could swab him now and have the results in a matter of hours.

With the thought that if Antony *was* telling the truth, he'd been perfectly placed to see their killer, he asked, 'And you're sure you didn't see anyone nearby?'

'I'm sure,' Antony said. 'I think . . . maybe if I'd seen someone, I wouldn't have been so keen to run in there? I don't know.'

'What about earlier?' Jonah tried. 'When you drove over there or when you were parked up. Anyone on the heath?'

Antony's gaze grew distant. He started to shake his head,

and then said, 'Actually I did drive past a group of lads on my way over. I think they were just walking out there to drink, but they would have been a few hundred yards away. Maybe you can ask if they saw anything.' He sat up straighter. 'I knew at least one of them. Matthew Downing. I was at school with him.'

Jonah tried to hide any reaction from his face. He wondered whether Antony Murphy somehow knew they were looking at Matthew Downing as a suspect. If he really had seen him, this could be enough to cross the threshold of prosecution against Matthew.

'Matthew Downing – he lives in Lyndhurst, doesn't he?' Jonah asked, as casually as he could.

'Yeah,' Antony agreed. 'I see him around sometimes.'

'Do you ever go and watch him play?'

'In his band?' Antony asked with a small smile. 'No. Not really my thing. And Matthew's bands are always . . . Well, they're a disaster. I heard enough of them at school.'

Jonah gave him a good-natured smile. 'So who do you prefer?'

'Honestly, I'd prefer to listen to something classical,' Antony said, and then grimaced slightly. 'You can tell I'm popular at parties.'

'OK,' Jonah said, nodding. 'We'll just take a DNA swab to exclude you from anything found at the scene. And then you'll be free to go.'

'Sure,' Antony said, nodding repeatedly with what looked to be a mixture of nervousness and relief. 'That'd be great, thanks.'

'I've found Jacqueline Clarke leaving the pub,' Ben said, his voice low. He'd come to catch Jonah on his way out of the interview. 'But the footage doesn't give us much. The nearest man to her may or may not actually have been leaving with her. He's walking a bit behind and she doesn't turn to look at him. If he *is* our killer, there's very little to distinguish him. He has a very ordinary dark jacket on with the collar up, and a cap pulled a long way down. The camera's high up so there's not much we can get from it apart from his build, which is muscular. There's nothing to say it's *not* the same man Lindsay Kernow was with passing that cashpoint, but nothing to prove it is, either.'

Jonah gave a short sigh. 'See if you can take a punt at guessing his height. And look for other cameras elsewhere that might have caught them.'

Lightman nodded and left.

Jonah dropped in to see Danny Murphy before he was done in the interview suite. He was interested in the younger brother's thoughts.

He was a quiet man, Danny Murphy. That much had been clear from Jonah's efforts at conversation with him when the two had arrived. But there was a presence about him, nonetheless. Something that made Jonah instinctively want to ask for his thoughts. Which was an unusual thing in someone who must have been at most in his early thirties.

'This . . . meteor watching,' Jonah began. 'Would you say it was in character for your brother?'

Danny gave a small smile. 'Yeah, it is. He's big into astronomy, biology, weather patterns, history, the classics, all that stuff. Always has been.'

'He mentioned that he was at school with Matthew Downing,' Jonah said. 'Is he someone you know too?'

Danny Murphy's face showed sudden amusement. 'Everyone round Lyndhurst knows Matthew,' he said. 'His dad pays thousands to get him and his band venues around the place, and then he plasters the place with posters to get punters in.

But the gigs are only ever about half full. Matthew's at most a local celebrity, and, at worst, a bit of a joke.'

'You say his dad,' Jonah said. 'Is his mum not on the scene?'

'No, he's like us,' Danny replied. 'Lost her quite young. I don't know if it was cancer or something. One of the teachers asked Antony to be there as a friend and support him, but Matthew didn't want to know obviously.'

'Why obviously?'

Danny gave a shrug. 'Who wants the nerdy kid who smells of horses as a friend when they're destined for greatness?'

'Do you think it's possible that he had something to do with your horse killing?' Jonah asked, deciding to ask the blunt question.

Danny looked surprised. 'Matthew? I wouldn't have thought he could. I mean, I don't know if he's ever ridden or not. He didn't ride at school that I knew of.' He gave a considering breath outwards. 'I suppose his parents had the money, though. It could be something he did on the side. We only really knew him as that guy who says he'll be famous, you know?'

Jonah nodded, and then said, as though it was irrelevant, 'You said Matthew was like you and Antony. Are you full brothers?'

Danny winced slightly. 'Ahhh . . . No, we aren't.'

Jonah found himself watching very intently as he asked, 'Is one of you adopted or . . . ?'

'No, we're – we're half-brothers,' Danny said.

'Ah,' Jonah said, nodding. 'Different fathers?'

Danny gave a short laugh. 'No. The same father. Different mothers.'

Jonah found himself struggling to compute that. Everything O'Malley had passed on about Michael Murphy's attitude towards Antony suggested that he wasn't his own flesh and blood.

'I know,' Danny said, quietly. 'You'd think Dad'd be a bit kinder, wouldn't you? But Antony is – he represents our father's immorality.'

Jonah nodded slowly. 'So he had an affair.'

Danny nodded. 'And then Antony's mother died, so he had to own up to his past sins and take him in.'

'How old was he when he took him in?'

'Six,' Danny said.

Which ruled out him having been given to the Murphys by Dara Cooley, Jonah realised. Though it might be worth getting the team to check that.

'Thanks,' he said, rising. 'That's everything for now. I'll let you know if we think of anything else.'

Danny got to his feet, and then paused. 'And is ... is everything all right with my brother?' He looked piercingly between Jonah and Hanson. 'You do know he's not some psycho, don't you?'

Jonah gave a half-smile. 'Everything he's said seems to add up so far. But I'd like to wait on a DNA result before we make any definite decisions. He's free to go in the meantime. Make sure he doesn't go anywhere though. We may need to see him again.'

Danny nodded, slowly. 'OK,' he said. 'Thank you.'

54

Matthew Downing arrived at the station at three fifteen. It turned out that the process of bringing him there hadn't gone smoothly. Jonah felt huge sympathy for Hanson and Lightman as they explained how they'd ended up having to arrest him and escort him forcibly to the car.

'He just refused to come, and kept repeating that we were idiots and he had an alibi,' Hanson said. 'He shoved a laptop at me, which apparently has proof of his innocence, then he stalked off out to his recording studio and shut himself in. Luckily it turns out not to have a lock, so I opened the door to try and have a quiet word. I warned him that if he didn't come with us voluntarily, we'd have to use powers of arrest.'

'And then he swung a punch at her,' Lightman said, with a raised eyebrow. 'So at that point we both had to get a bit hands-on.'

They'd actually ended up making the decision to arrest him for aggravated assault rather than on suspicion of murder. There were full and reasonable grounds for doing so, when he had tried to assault an officer attempting to carry out her duties.

But on arrival at the station they'd had to endure Matthew telling all the waiting press that he had been wrongfully arrested for murder, all because he was the kind of person the police didn't like.

'He told them we think artists are scum,' Hanson said, her face still hot with rage. 'And he actually used the line, "I'm

Matthew Downing and I'm only guilty of the crime of trying to make music when they want us to sit in silence." '

Jonah snorted. 'Enterprising of him.' And then he added, 'It sounds like you did everything you could to stop it escalating. Whatever he said to the press is his own lookout. You haven't arrested him for murder, you've arrested him for assault on an officer. And it sounds like we have a lot to ask him about.'

'Just as long as you tear him to pieces,' Hanson said darkly.

Ten minutes into the interview, Jonah was beginning to feel doubtful. He wasn't touched by Matthew Downing's withering scorn, or the arrival of his solicitor, the expensive and competent Kathleen Maddox who Jonah had come up against once or twice in the past. He wasn't even too worried about what the press would report. His team had good grounds for asking to talk to him, and for arresting him too.

What concerned him more was Matthew's insistence that he'd been with his bandmates from the moment he set foot on Lyndhurst Heath until the moment he'd arrived back at his party. And that they had video footage of most of it.

'Go and check it,' Matthew said, leaning well forwards in his chair and looking between him and Lightman. 'I've got all the raw files on my laptop. Try looking and stop wasting my time.'

In the range of reactions from people who'd sat across an interview table from him, Jonah had witnessed anxiety, smugness and rage. But this frustrated sort of declaration usually, *usually* went with someone who knew they were in the right.

Occasionally, though, it went with someone who was very good at faking it.

'My team's busy checking it,' Jonah said with a small smile.

'And we should have your swab result back in a few hours. But let's talk about another evening for now. The third of October, when you played for the Great Unsaid.'

'Why?' Matthew asked with a sudden smirk. 'Did you want an autograph?'

Jonah slid a photo of Jacqueline Clarke towards him. 'You were approached by this woman on October third, weren't you?'

Matthew's expression grew disbelieving. 'Of course I wasn't! Don't think I don't know who that is.'

His solicitor leaned to murmur something, and Matthew closed his mouth, looking as though he badly wanted to say more. At this stage there was no question that it would be in Matthew's best interest to give a no-comment response to everything Jonah said. They hadn't checked the videos yet, after all, or had the DNA swab back. But it didn't seem as though Matthew was capable of keeping his thoughts to himself.

'We have at least one witness who can confirm that she came to talk to you after you finished your pieces,' Jonah said, quietly and deliberately.

'After the *set,*' Matthew said immediately.

'Ah, I see,' Jonah said. 'Sorry. So she did come to talk to you. After the *set.*'

'For god's sake.' Matthew clenched his fists. 'No, she did not come to talk to me. I haven't met her.'

Jonah glanced at his notes. 'See, our witness says she not only approached you, but gave you a business card. She told you she was a music producer.'

Matthew blinked. Opened and closed his mouth. 'That was *her?*'

'We've been able to confidently identify her since from CCTV footage,' Lightman confirmed.

'Well, I had – I had no idea that was the dead woman.'

His solicitor whispered something again, this time more urgently.

Jonah watched a change in Matthew's expression. It was like witnessing someone pull on a change of clothes, and it was disconcerting. He was suddenly giving a disarming smile. Holding up his hands.

'I'm sorry. I shouldn't be getting angry with you guys. You're just doing your job.' He put his hands to the table, flattening them. A calming, easing gesture. 'I hadn't realised that was . . . I'm really sorry, I've forgotten her name.'

'Jacqueline Clarke,' Lightman provided.

'Jacqueline. I didn't know that, or I'd have come forward earlier. She did approach me.'

'It must happen a lot,' Jonah said more conversationally. 'After you've performed.'

Matthew gave a self-deprecating shrug. 'It's part of the business, I think. People fixate on you a bit because they're watching you and enjoying your art. It isn't really about you.'

'Do you think Jacqueline was fixated?'

'She was just a bit . . . keen.'

Jonah could see the solicitor actually rolling her eyes. He almost felt sorry for her. What could you do when your client waded in and said everything you didn't want them to?

'And how did you respond?' Jonah asked.

'The usual way,' Matthew told him. 'I took her card. And I said I'd be in touch, without having any intention of being.'

Nothing from the solicitor.

Jonah nodded. Considered. 'You didn't meet up with her later? Go home with her?'

'Of course I didn't,' Matthew said with a flash of irritation. 'She was old enough to be my bloody mum!'

55

Aisling was killing time while Jack got ready to leave for Hordle. He was headed there to speak with her parents' old neighbours. She felt despondent that he was about to leave, and annoyed with herself about it. Though in part her despondency was about fear of having time to think. All the revelations of the last twenty-four hours still seemed to hang in the air, like a cloud of anxiety or absurdity that she kept walking into.

Her sons' determination to squeeze money out of their father was at least, she thought, ridiculous enough to be amusing. Though she felt a rush of furious embarrassment when she thought of what they'd said about her fond feelings for him.

'We're going to do without him,' she'd told them both firmly. 'Relying on someone unreliable is no good at all.' And then she paused, and said, 'Though if you fancy splitting that three grand three ways, I wouldn't say no . . .'

Jack, meanwhile, had taken it all in his stride remarkably well. He had ended up laughing with both her sons about all of it and then, shortly after that, discussing the upcoming release of the next *Fallout* instalment in some depth.

But that light-hearted interval had been an escape, and reality was waiting for them once the boys had headed upstairs and the police had left with the boxes of paperwork. She and Jack still had a child together: one who had probably murdered two women.

Jack re-emerged from the shower, looking tousled but refreshed.

'Keep thinking,' he said, seeing her hovering at the table. 'I think there will be memories buried somewhere that might help us.'

Aisling looked up at him. 'I keep wondering about the church, and what you said about the networks. The laundries . . . I know Mammy was terribly ashamed in front of everyone, but what if the priest did actually help them, on the quiet? What if he put them in touch with someone here? He seemed like the type to decide it was the right thing to do.'

Jack nodded, slowly. 'The old fire and brimstone guy . . .'

'Father McGrane, I think he was,' she said. 'He came to see us, just before we left and . . . maybe he knew the truth.' She frowned, remembering the way he'd pressed a hand to her forehead in blessing, and told her that this was her chance to walk a new path in life. 'Maybe he did . . .'

Jack was typing on his phone, clearly looking this Father McGrane up. But then Aisling found herself remembering Father McGrane wishing another family a fond farewell. This had been a much less hurried affair. A whole tea had been laid on, in a send-off for two of the most loyal members of their congregation. It must have been a few years before she and her parents had left.

'There was a couple that left the church a few years before,' she said slowly. 'They went to England. I remember that, as it made me feel like I could get away one day too.' She looked up at Jack. 'They went to take over the business left to her by her family, over here. She'd been born in England. But I remember my mammy saying it was all an excuse for her to come over and get fertility treatment for free. Mammy was angry about it for some reason, as she was about a lot of things. I had to ask my daddy what fertility treatment was, as she wouldn't tell me.

I suppose I was ten? Eleven? But – that would be the sort of family who would want a child, wouldn't it?'

Jack was looking straight back at her, his hands frozen. 'Do you remember the name of this family?'

'I . . . she was called Celine, like Celine Dion. I thought it was exotic at the time. Celine and her husband Michael.' She pressed at her forehead. 'I know their surname must be in there somewhere, but can we start with that?'

56

Hanson had succeeded, at last, in finding the videos Matthew Downing had recorded in the clutter of files on his laptop. There were five files from 31 December, all saved with a date and time as the title. They'd all been recorded between 10:56 and 11:25. Right across the earliest window of time in which Lindsay Kernow might have died.

She opened them up with a feeling neatly balanced between acceptance and scepticism. If these videos were legitimate, and Matthew Downing appeared in all of them, they effectively exonerated him. But it was also easy to save a file with a different time stamp. They couldn't rule him out until the cyber team checked when they were recorded.

She was glad that they'd swabbed Matthew anyway. Any remaining doubts about him could be pretty neatly squashed by the rapid DNA test.

The first two videos proved to be slightly dull recordings of Matthew playing his guitar and singing, all with a gorse bush in the background. He was highly lit, so there was little to make out beyond him. Little to prove when or where this had been filmed. His unremarkable voice was also rendered slightly ridiculous by the over-dramatic absorption in his facial expression.

The next two were variations on the original, with different backgrounds and subtly different mistakes.

The final video was time-stamped eleven twenty-five and was the shortest, just two minutes of footage. This time Matthew was standing on a small hill. The vista behind him was slightly easier to make out, as Matthew was lit less aggressively. She could see the rolling heath, with darker patches of gorse, and then a low line of trees. And she frowned, thinking this looked a lot like the view she'd had of the pyre from where she'd parked her car.

A minute and a half in, as Hanson was scanning the landscape, she caught a sudden, flickering light, a light that appeared right against the treeline.

Hanson leaned forwards, heart hammering. This was the pyre, she thought. They'd captured the lighting of the pyre.

It wasn't Matthew . . .

There was no way he could have been down there trying to burn Lindsay and up here filming. He couldn't be their killer. Unless there had been a whole group of them involved, which didn't tally with him leaving his blood at the scene.

Only a few seconds later, she caught a rhythmic noise, and then red and white flashing lights appeared over the horizon. The lights had only been present for a few seconds when that little flickering fire vanished. This was the moment when Antony Murphy had doused it.

Hanson glanced at the clock. There were only seconds left. She wanted to swear. If this clip had gone on longer, it might have caught the killer fleeing the scene.

It became obvious why the recording ended early, however. The rhythmic thumping became the loud, overbearing sound of a helicopter travelling low overhead.

Matthew stopped playing, looked up, and said, 'For fuck's sake! How often do you get a fucking rescue helicopter over here?' And then the film ended.

Hanson sighed and pulled out her earphones. 'It doesn't look like he did it,' she told O'Malley.

'Same finding here,' Domnall said, his expression wry.

'Matthew was adopted as a baby, a good two years after Aisling's son was born. All of it done legitimately, with plenty of paperwork. I'll keep digging, but . . .'

'So he's probably just a regular arsehole,' Hanson said glumly. 'And our killer is still somewhere else.'

'That about sums it up.'

57

They released Matthew Downing with a caution for assault four hours after he'd arrived at the station, at the point when the DNA results definitively proved him not to be a match. Jonah had put the DNA test through as an urgent priority and the lab had turned it round as quickly as was physically possible. Though McCullough had been at pains to point out that this was at the expense of a number of other urgent lab tests, including Jonah's own requests.

The team had also corroborated Matthew's presence on the heath and then at the party. The time he'd been there ran right across when they knew Lindsay Kernow must have been driven out to the heath and murdered. Together with the videos and proof of his parentage, there was no conceivable way he was the man they were looking for.

A four-hour arrest was the sort of sharp about-turn that might raise the DCS's eyebrows, particularly with the press waiting outside and Matthew only too willing to tell them how he'd been wrongfully imprisoned. But having fired off a statement that made it clear they had only arrested Matthew when he had attempted to assault an officer, Jonah felt ready to move on.

He told his team to do the same. Their priority was to push on to identify who Jacqueline Clarke had left the Porterhouse with on October the third, and to keep trying to work out what the Cooleys had done with Aisling's child.

'Did we get any further with CCTV after Jacqueline left the Porterhouse?' Jonah asked them.

'We've come up blank so far,' O'Malley said. 'Except that the Porterhouse is right on the edge of the city, in prime residential land. We might start calling neighbours about doorbell cams and private cameras.'

'That sounds . . . lengthy,' Jonah said with a sigh.

'I'll stick with it, sure,' O'Malley said good-naturedly. 'There's a chance the two of them went further into town, too. I'm looking out for Antony Murphy as well, just in case,' he said, nodding towards a printed photograph of Antony standing alongside his father, his body language tense despite their smiles for the camera. 'Just until we can rule him out on his cheek swab.'

'Thanks,' Jonah said, glancing at his watch. They'd put through Antony's swab as a normal priority, but he'd been assuming they'd have the results not long after the four-hour rapid window as usual, despite her team being occupied with getting Matthew Downing's test done. He thought about calling McCullough to chase it, and wondered whether there was any point. 'Anything from the paper trail on Dara Cooley?'

'Nothing that's jumping out at us so far,' Hanson told him. 'Except that he went to Newbury a lot. I'm sort of worrying that Domnall's original hunch was right, and he did give the kid to Anneka Foley. God knows how we go about tracking down a "man in a suit" who then took the child. It could have been a straight-up abduction.'

'Let's hope not,' Jonah said heavily. 'But if we find nothing from the paperwork, it may be worth getting back to West Gradley and questioning more people.'

O'Malley found himself losing focus after the catch-up with the DCI. For some reason it was Anneka Foley and the kid who were nagging at his attention and not the CCTV he was supposed to be absorbed in.

After several efforts at focusing, he found himself staring, blankly, at the printed photo of Antony Murphy. And as he blinked awake, he found himself looking for the first time not at Antony, but at his father.

In a sudden rush, he pushed an empty sandwich wrapper off his desk to reveal the framed photograph he'd brought home from Anneka Foley's house. Lifting it up, he looked from it to the photograph of the Murphy family. And then he held them both up towards Ben.

'Ben. Are these photographs of the same man?'

He watched Lightman's eyes shift between them, and then he said without any doubt at all, 'Yes, they are. That's the same man aged by around thirty years.'

58

Today was the first time Aisling had ever shared a car with Jack O'Keane, and despite the sombre reason for the drive, she genuinely enjoyed all ten minutes of it. Jack managed to set aside everything to do with their son, and spent the short journey regaling her with anecdotes about their childhood acquaintances. It was as if they were about to go and meet all these people, and had to catch up on all of it before they got there.

It was amazing how relaxed he could sound. And how much like the old Jack. The more he talked about the past, the more he slipped from his London-tinged accent into a pure Tullamore brogue.

'Barbara is now, honest to god, selling jewellery on a shopping channel,' he said. 'So I suppose she was right that she'd be a model one day. It's good to have ambition.'

'Seriously?' Aisling gasped. 'Barbara DeMaure, who probably spoke to me twice in our school career because I wasn't cool enough? I shouldn't mock, but what happened to "My mam's going to get me on the cover of *Vogue*?"'

'Well, Barb probably realised the shallowness of celebrity,' Jack said, deadpan, 'and chose a nobler path. She's doing great work, there, making sure those imitation diamonds go to a good home.'

It had been beyond strange to find herself laughing about it all. For thirty years she hadn't been able to think about her childhood without pain, and now here she was, cackling about it with him. Just revelling in it.

'What about that guy she used to date?' she'd asked next. 'Was it Noah . . . Noah Lehane?'

'Ohhh, I've such good stories on him,' Jack said. 'He played rugby for the Ireland under-eighteens, based on him having a head made entirely out of rock. But then it started going downhill as they realised that rock isn't great at taking account of strategy. So then he retrained at the Lyon Hotel and Restaurant. I'm told they stand him in the hall and guests hang coats on him.'

Aisling had laughed so hard it had been difficult to breathe. 'Stop it! I'm trying to fecking drive,' she'd said. And then, before she'd really stopped laughing, the sign for Murphy's Stud Farm had loomed up along the road, and she'd felt all the banished anxiety rush back into her stomach.

The gates to the farm stood open. There was nothing to hold them up or delay this.

She sensed Jack's own tension rising as she drove the Prius slowly down the concrete driveway. The buildings ahead of them were old-fashioned stone, and clustered around a large yard. There was a second, solid metal gate across the entrance to it, but it stood open, like the first, allowing people to come and go.

As they drew up on the paved area in front of the gate, two young men who seemed to be involved in mending a fence along the drive paused to watch them. One was tall, dark-haired and bear-like; the other was almost as tall, with a blond mop of hair that reminded her of Ethan's.

She pulled up not far from them, and took a deep breath. 'OK.'

Her legs were shaking slightly as she climbed out of the car. She took a few steps towards the two young men, and asked, 'Is Michael Murphy here?'

The blond one nodded, his eyes full of curiosity. 'He's around. Not quite sure where.'

'Do you think . . . ? We just need to talk to him.' She tried to smile. 'Trying to pick his brains.'

The other one, the dark-haired one, murmured, 'I'll find him,' and carefully spooled the wire he'd been using round the fence post before trudging towards the yard.

The light-haired one watched him go, and then went back to what he had been doing. He was hefting an oversized staple gun and using it to fasten the wire in place along the post.

Aisling found herself watching him, aware that Jack had moved towards the yard. Her eyes were on the wide shoulders – shoulders that looked as powerful as Finn's – and on that mop of blond hair.

Though as she watched, she felt a peculiar sense of slipping through time. Because something about him, about his face, reminded her less of Ethan, who'd inherited many of the lines of Stephen's classically handsome face, and more of her father.

He must be around thirty, she thought. A tanned, outdoorsy thirty.

'Are you a stable hand?' she asked, her voice too tight. Not the casual remark she'd intended.

He paused again, and rubbed the sleeve of his fleece over his forehead. 'Yeah, I am.' He gave a half-smile. 'I mean, I'm – it's my dad's farm, and I'm the oldest, so I guess I'm also sort of – the heir to the place, only that'll never happen.'

'Why not?'

He looked as though he wanted to go on working, but Aisling waited, her expression urging him on. Telling him, silently, that she wanted to hear what he had to say.

'Ahh, I'm not good at farm stuff really,' he said, grinning

slightly. But she could see hurt underneath it too. 'I think he feels a bit short-changed. Didn't get the son he wanted.' And then he shook his head, as though irritated with himself. 'I shouldn't be . . .'

But Aisling said immediately, 'That was like me and my mammy. I think she wondered how she'd managed to produce me. Her all godly and self-controlled and with this *plan* for her life, and me all scattered and impulsive.' She paused, and then said, 'Sorry. Giving my whole life story. And we've not even been introduced. Aisling.'

The young man looked at her, uncertainly, and then took her hand. His grip was surprisingly warm for someone who had been standing out in the cold. 'Antony.' He nodded towards the yard. 'That was my brother. Danny. Are you looking to buy, or . . . ?'

'Oh, just in need of some info for now,' she said, as lightly as she could. She let go of his hand, with a strange feeling of regret.

'Aisling?' It was Jack, saying her name quietly over her right shoulder. It was strange that she'd almost forgotten him, when only a few minutes ago she'd been so intensely aware of his presence in the passenger seat.

She turned and saw the other stable hand waiting for them next to an open door. She nodded. Smiled. But she turned to look back at Antony before she followed Jack through the door.

59

'Michael and Celine Murphy arrived in the New Forest four and a half years before the Cooleys did,' O'Malley was explaining to the chief, Hanson and Lightman. Hanson was aware of a fizzing excitement that made it almost impossible to sit still. 'Guess which Irish town they emigrated from?'

'I'm guessing Tullamore,' Hanson said immediately.

'Full marks, Detective Constable Hanson,' O'Malley said with a grin. 'Now a very interesting fact I learned about Celine Murphy is that she was a midwife, but also ran a support group for women who couldn't conceive. They certainly had no children themselves until suddenly, according to the dates the kids were registered with schools, they had *two* children born between December eighty-five and January eighty-six. They were basically born a month apart.'

'Not . . . really possible,' Lightman said.

'Well done on the biology there, Ben,' O'Malley said. 'So when I looked a little deeper, it became apparent that only Danny's birth was officially registered. Whatever documentation they've been using to get Antony Murphy into schools and the like is fake.'

Hanson found herself grinning at him. 'Antony is Aisling's son.'

'It looks pretty likely,' O'Malley said. 'My guess is, the Cooleys – or the Horans, as they were back then – moved to the New Forest purposely to be close to the Murphy family. I think it was in Dara and Dymphna Cooley's minds

322

that their childless friends might be willing to take the baby, and to keep quiet about it. It might even all have been arranged.'

'But then, presumably,' the chief said, 'Celine realised she was actually pregnant with Danny.'

'I think so,' O'Malley said. 'I think they went back on their agreement. They didn't want to be bringing up someone else's child along with their own. And it would have been obvious what they'd done, too. Two children only a month or so apart? It was medically impossible, and they were a little *too* different in age for them to claim they were twins.'

'So Michael arranged to give Antony to his mistress,' Hanson said, her expression rapt.

'It must have seemed the obvious solution,' O'Malley said. 'At that point she presumably seemed like she had it together. Perhaps she'd even told him she wanted a child. It's hard to know.'

'And then,' the DCI said slowly, 'later, he realised that she was mistreating the boy. And so he took him away and raised him as his older son.'

'How does Dara Cooley fit in with this?' Lightman asked. 'Do we think he knew about the arrangement, and went to visit his grandson?'

'And then fell for Anneka, yes,' O'Malley replied. 'That's what I think. And the combined guilt of keeping the child from his daughter, and then beginning an affair with Anneka, was too much.' He paused for a moment. 'He wouldn't have realised that in killing himself he was abandoning Anneka to growing madness, or Antony to torture.'

Hanson glanced at the chief, 'We don't even need to wait for that swab, do we? Antony Murphy was there on the heath when Lindsay Kernow died. Everything he said about putting out that fire must have been covering up what he really did.'

'I should have pushed him harder on it,' the DCI said, with a shake of his head. His expression was troubled. 'All of these murders have been circling Aisling Cooley's house, and it's entirely possible that Michael Murphy told him the truth of his parentage at some point. If he blames his mother for everything he suffered at Anneka's hands, then all of these women might represent Aisling.'

60

Michael Murphy limped ahead of Jack and Aisling into the big farmhouse kitchen. 'Coffee?' he said, as though it cost him.

'I – that's OK,' Aisling said, glancing at Jack. He looked as tense as she felt. 'We had one back at home.'

Michael moved over to the kettle. He clearly had some sort of injury to his leg, a change from the athletic man she half remembered from church. Though other things had changed too. Where he had once been roguishly handsome, the favourite of all the church ladies, Michael was now lined and dour. A man who looked as though he rarely smiled.

Aisling moved towards the table, and felt a jolt as she saw a boxed Marks and Spencer birthday cake on the table, several slices already cut out of it.

It's his birthday today . . .

She felt the need to see more of the life her son might have lived, and drifted over to a corkboard attached to the wall, on which a series of receipts and notes had been pinned. There were also, here and there, photographs of two boys growing up together. She found herself putting her hand out to them, tracing her fingers over them. Was one of these two boys really hers?

She could see that light hair of Antony's again in many of them, so very like her father's. And she paused as she saw two photographs of him without hair. One of them in a hospital bed, and one of them standing with his arm slung round his brother's shoulders. He looked to be only fourteen or fifteen in those photographs, but drawn and pale like an old man.

So Antony had been ill. Really, terribly ill. Was that the final answer to everything? Had he suffered some form of childhood cancer, without the love and support of parents who really cared for him? Had it undone him, and turned him into a man who killed women?

Her gaze drifted over the corkboard, finding a larger, more formal photograph to the top right. It showed the two boys with a woman, her dark hair styled into a wave. And Aisling felt a gut punch of shock.

She knew this woman. Knew the gentle, reassuring voice she'd used as she'd urged Aisling to wait until each contraction to push. To squeeze her hand when she needed to.

This had been the midwife who had helped steal her son.

'Is your wife – a midwife?' she asked, turning to Michael.

Michael paused in the act of getting mugs out, and then said in a voice of unmistakable finality, 'She was.'

Aisling put this fact into the wall of difficult things she had learned, wondering how she would process it later. That she wouldn't get to face the woman who had stolen her son.

And then she said, 'I really am sorry for intruding. I just need to ask . . .' She let him spoon instant coffee into a mug, swallowed, and said, 'Is Antony really your son?'

Michael froze in the act of putting the jar of coffee away. He looked at her with a flat sort of despair, and then he began to move towards the kettle. As he got there, he said, 'That's none of your business.'

'Please,' she said. 'I'm asking because I think . . . that he might be mine.'

Michael turned with what looked like anger. 'What?'

Aisling stepped forwards. 'I'm Martha Horan. You knew me – and my parents – from church in Tullamore. Jack and I –' she gestured to him – 'we had a child. Something my parents were deeply ashamed of. They brought me over here, and promised to bring him up, only they didn't. They gave him away. And they told me he'd died.' She could feel the tears she'd shed over and over in the last twenty-four hours threatening once again. She'd expected to feel anger at these people who had taken her child, not this profound sadness. 'I think your wife came and helped deliver the baby, and then kept him.'

She saw Michael's mouth lose its shape. He took a staggering step forwards, and then put his hand out to one of the dining chairs to brace himself.

Aisling found herself moving towards him, afraid that he would fall. She could feel Jack moving alongside her, and it was a relief to know that he was there.

'Sorry to give you a shock, Mr Murphy,' Jack said. He took the man's arm, but Michael Murphy snatched it away.

'I'm – I'm fine.' He pulled the chair towards himself and then manoeuvred round until he could sit in it, heavily. The kettle, on the stove, began to whistle.

Jack hesitated, and then went to the Aga and picked the kettle up, lowering the lid over the hot plate as he did. He carried it to the counter and poured hot water into the mug Michael had got ready.

'Do you take milk?' Jack asked.

It was madness, Aisling thought, feeling disconnected from everything. Here they were, confronting the man who had stolen their son, and they were making him coffee. Jack so calm and capable and kind, even with *him*. Even with him.

'A good lot of milk,' Michael agreed, his eyes on the table in front of him. 'And two sugars.'

Aisling waited until Jack had fetched both, and had finally handed Michael the coffee, before she took a seat herself.

'He is ours, isn't he?' She leaned towards him, her arms out on the table in appeal. 'My parents arranged for you to take him.'

Michael took a long slug of coffee, wiped his moustache and then finally looked at her. 'It's – they told us you never wanted to see him again.' He squinted at her, and then at Jack, and a look of anger passed over his face. 'Either of you. What right have you to suddenly change your minds now?'

Aisling could feel her own face twisting in sadness 'It was never true. They were the ones . . . I wanted to keep him.' She nodded at Jack. 'Jack never even knew about him. He didn't have the chance to choose. But I would have kept him. No matter what it cost me. They told me he'd died, Mr Murphy. I thought . . . I thought he'd died. And that maybe it was my fault, for him being born out of hospital, because of the shame I caused.'

Michael cleared his throat. 'I . . . I didn't know any of this. I did the best I could.'

'He said you thought him a failure,' Aisling said, her eyes stinging. 'Is that because you ended up with your own son to compare him with? Or is it just that he wasn't yours?'

Michael gave a frown. 'I've never thought him that. He's the strong one. The – he's better than anything I could have ever produced.' He gave a bitter laugh. 'Danny is the only one around here I can rely on.'

Aisling couldn't quite work out what was wrong with this, until she'd said it through to herself again.

'Danny . . . ?' She looked over at Jack, blank with confusion. 'Our son is – Danny?'

Michael nodded, and started to pull out his wallet. 'Your father said your one request had been to call him Daniel. So that's what we chose.' He opened the wallet with shaking hands. 'Here he is with Celine, the day she brought him home.'

Daniel, she thought, and wondered whether she'd said that in the haze of drugs. She could almost imagine looking down on him, and saying, *He looks like a Daniel.*

Michael held a dog-eared picture out to Aisling, and she took it with that same feeling of strange detachment. It showed a child who was clearly newborn. A child with dark hair, like Jack's, and eyes as big and brown as hers.

Their son. Unquestionably their son.

61

Jonah was driving as part of a convoy now. He'd refused to remain behind in the office, but had taken the lead, with Hanson in the passenger seat next to him. Lightman was in his Qashqai behind with O'Malley. Following the procession was a squad car driven by two constables. A convoy with the purpose of arresting their killer after three and a half months of frustration.

Even now, he found himself resisting the urge to make any assumptions. They still might be wrong about this. Until their swab came back from the lab, there was nothing definitive to prove that Antony Murphy was Aisling's son. But Jonah had to admit that his team's theory made a great deal of sense. Antony was within days of being the right age, and it would have been logical for Michael and Celine to take in and raise Aisling's child. It also made sense that they would have chosen to give him away when they realised they were having their own son.

And the landlord at West Gradley had said that Anneka was incapable of looking after the child. He felt a complex knot of pain, too, at the thought of Antony being starved and quite possibly hurt by her. Antony had probably done horrific things as an adult, but he'd been a helpless child back then.

Halfway through this thinking, and with ten minutes to go on the satnav until they arrived at the stud farm, the dashboard display lit up with a call from Linda McCullough's mobile. He saw Hanson shift in her seat as he answered it, and he felt just the same sense of excitement.

'Linda,' he said. 'Just who I wanted to talk to.'

'I did appreciate your string of "hurry the hell up" messages,' Linda said drily. 'Strangely they did little to change the speed of either the dogsbodies in the lab, or of chemical reactions and analysis.'

'Noted,' Jonah said, grinning. 'Have those chemical reactions now taken place?'

'They have,' Linda said. 'And I'm afraid you don't have a match. It's a close familial one again, though, as you'll be aware, the rapid test won't tell us exactly how close. But definitely not the same DNA.'

Jonah had to concentrate in order to keep his foot on the accelerator pedal. He felt not only startled by this revelation, but also intensely frustrated by it.

'Wow, OK,' he said. 'Thank you. Back to the drawing board, I guess.'

'Let me know when you have another no-hoper to try,' McCullough said, though he thought he detected a trace of sympathy underneath the sarcasm.

He ended the call, trying to get his head around this.

'So somehow Aisling Cooley is related to our suspect,' he muttered, as much to himself as to Hanson next to him. 'But so is Antony Murphy. And yet it isn't him.'

'It feels like it should fit,' Hanson said, next to him, with frustration. 'Michael Murphy and his wife are still the most likely people for Aisling's son to have been passed to.'

Jonah glanced at her, and then found himself remembering Danny Murphy, with his quiet kindness. His air of self-control.

'What if –' Hanson began, just as Jonah said, 'Did O'Malley say Danny Murphy was born in early eighty-six?'

'I'm looking,' Hanson said, pulling the cover off her iPad. After a moment, she said, 'He is. And his date of birth is down as January twentieth 1986. He's the right age.'

Jonah nodded, twice, and then said, 'Call Domnall and Ben, and tell them we we're going to be talking to the other brother.'

62

'We're not here to make any demands,' Jack said quietly.

Michael Murphy was shaking his head, as if he could make them – and all of this – go away. Aisling could see anger fighting with a great deal of other emotion in his expression. It was clear that Jack could see it too.

'We just want to talk to him,' Jack went on soothingly. 'He's – we think he's in trouble.'

'Trouble?' Michael asked, sounding genuinely startled. 'What kind of trouble could he be in?'

'His blood was found at a crime scene,' Aisling said. 'And if he was involved, then he might be involved in other crimes too.' There was a pause, and she said, 'We wanted to find him before the police did. Whatever he's done, we still love him. We want to help him.'

'*Danny?*' Michael asked. He looked at her like she was mad. 'Danny was never involved in any crime. You've got it wrong.'

'I know it must be hard to believe,' Jack said. 'And it's possible he didn't commit the crime himself. But his blood was there. And it'll only be a matter of time before the police realise that too.'

Something seemed to snap in Michael Murphy. He pushed his chair back and said explosively, 'Danny didn't do a damn thing! He's not – he's never been involved in anything bad. Not in anything. He – look. Look at this.' His took several uneven steps across the floor and unpinned a photograph from the corkboard. 'This is Danny, the day after he gave his marrow to save his brother. He knew how much it would hurt,

333

and how serious the operation was. But he did it because he was a good, kind boy. And he's a good, kind man now.'

'I believe he is,' Aisling said, hoping he could hear how much she meant it. 'I don't think he's bad, or evil. If it's anyone's fault, it's mine. Maybe my parents' fault, too. I think we harmed him, and this is what's come out of it.' She looked towards the board, where Celine only existed in photographs now. 'And maybe the loss of the woman he thought was his mother hurt him too. Maybe that's why he . . . hurt those women.'

Michael stared at her for several long seconds in silence, and then there was a crack in his voice as he asked, 'What women? What are you . . . Oh my god. You think . . .'

There was a sudden sound of movement in the doorway, and Aisling and Jack turned together to see Danny there, his expression dark. Pained. Haunted.

He never went back outside, Aisling thought. *He heard everything. All of it.*

She should have been afraid of him. Of this big, powerful man. But instead she felt an urge to comfort him.

She stood, to go to him – and then the sound of an engine – several engines – cut through the movement. She saw Danny's head turn towards the door.

'Danny,' she said, uncertain whether she was pleading with him to stay, or to run.

He looked back at her, as if her words might be trapping him there. But the car engines were louder now. They would be at the yard in seconds. And they all knew that these were the police, come to find him.

Danny shook his head, turned from her, and ran out into the yard.

63

The Mondeo's way into the farm was blocked, at least in part, by Antony Murphy. He stood in the middle of the gateway to the paved yard, his expression defiant. Beyond him, Jonah could see a young stable hand, her posture slack and surprised as she paused in the act of carrying a bucket of water across the yard.

Jonah pulled the Mondeo up a little way in front of Antony, and climbed out.

'We're looking for your brother,' he said, as quietly as possible. 'Where is he?'

Antony stared at him in absolute silence for a moment, some emotion working in his face, and then he said, 'I don't know. And you should leave him alone. He's a good man.'

Jonah tried not to let his frustration show. 'All we want to do right now is ask him a few questions.' He glanced over at Hanson, who took the lead and walked into the yard. O'Malley and Lightman followed, and the two constables came to stand behind Jonah to each side, a subtle blockading manoeuvre to make sure there was no easy way out of the yard gate. 'Do you know who Danny really is?'

Jonah was half watching Antony, and half watching his team disappear into three different doorways, their batons at the ready. He saw Antony's expression become slack. Confused. 'What do you mean?'

There was the sound of a door banging open, and a shout from Lightman. Jonah left Antony where he was, and ran through the open door to the stable, where Lightman had just disappeared.

He arrived to see Lightman already sprinting out of the far door. He could hear a horse's rapid gallop, and knew before he had run through the building and out onto the pasture that Danny was riding away from them.

Jonah was vaguely aware of another figure in the stable as he passed, but he didn't pause. It was Danny they needed.

He pulled his phone out as he pursued, some way behind Lightman. He recognised that it was futile but ran on anyway. The chestnut horse was already halfway across the field and showing no signs of slowing. Lightman, who was faster than he was, was already losing ground.

'This is DCI Jonah Sheens,' he panted at the switchboard as he ran. 'I have a suspect fleeing on horseback north of Minstead. I need ground and aerial pursuit.'

He slowed as Danny approached the fence at the far side of the paddock. The horse, which looked a little heavy around the middle for jumping, gathered herself and leaped. She cleared the fence easily, and within moments was lost into the trees on the far side.

'Shit,' Jonah said forcefully. And then he turned to yell towards a pursuing constable, 'Get back to the car, and head to the far side of those woods!'

Lightman kept going, and Jonah hesitated, and then followed, pulling his phone out as he went. There was a chance that Danny was headed to a bolthole nearby. They needed to be ready for it if it happened.

O'Malley doubled back out of the stables, where he'd seen the chief and Lightman in pursuit. He started to run for Lightman's car, thanking all the saints that the team had thought to insure themselves on each other's vehicles.

Hanson was standing in the doorway of the farmhouse, and O'Malley yelled as coherent a version of events as he could.

'Can you round everyone up?' he added. He was in the Qashqai seconds later.

Before he began to manoeuvre it back round to face the road, he saw a young, stocky figure in a beanie emerge from the other stable block. The figure stopped in the yard with his hands in his pockets, an expression of evident satisfaction on his face.

O'Malley took a moment to wind down the window, and yell to Hanson, 'Make sure you get him!'

Pursuing the horse through the forest was heavy-going. The ground was uneven, root-strewn and littered with fallen leaves that made obstacles difficult to see. Jonah was wearing his fairly practical black work shoes, but they were neither running shoes nor hiking boots. He half turned his ankle twice before he'd emerged onto a path that ran diagonally onwards from his current heading.

He could see Lightman jogging along it ahead of him. He'd chosen a direction, and it was obvious why. There were fresh hoof marks in the packed mud, deeply gouged ones that showed a horse going at a gallop.

'Just – work out – where the path – goes!' he called, and came to a halt with his chest heaving, and pulled out his phone.

O'Malley was trying to look at a satellite image on his phone while driving Lightman's unfamiliar Qashqai, an attempt he knew to be neither entirely safe nor strictly legal, even if he had shoved the phone into the holder Ben had installed on the dashboard.

The chief had reported that Danny was on a track ahead. It should converge with the road after about half a mile. From what O'Malley could see, it also ran alongside the road for a while before splitting off again. It was hard to know whether Danny had already passed him by along it or was still coming towards the road.

The one thing he really hoped was that he hadn't crossed over. The heathland to O'Malley's left was scrubby and open. It would be an awful lot easier to traverse on horseback than in a car.

The constable in his marked car was some way ahead of him, sirens going. He'd already told O'Malley over the radio that he was aiming to turn off at the next right, to end up at the far side of the wood.

O'Malley realised that the track was just up ahead. He was slowing to peer down it when a horse and rider emerged from the woods and careered straight across the road in front of his car. O'Malley braked sharply, but they were already across, galloping onto the heathland.

O'Malley slewed his car to a stop and turned it onto the heathland side of the track with a fervent swear word. The path ahead was rutted, with pools of water standing in many of the dips. The Qashqai might have been four-wheel-drive, but he doubted Ben would thank him for testing the suspension out for him.

The chief's number flashed up on his phone, and O'Malley took one hand off the wheel for long enough to answer it.

'I'm in pursuit,' O'Malley called, over the sound of the engine. 'Across the heath.'

He accelerated, feeling the first few jolts as Danny Murphy, up ahead, disappeared over the edge of a rise.

'I've called for aerial support,' the chief said. 'But they'll be some minutes away. Can you keep him in sight?'

'I'll do my best,' he said.

The speedo read thirty miles per hour, which was the fastest O'Malley felt he could go without concussing himself on the car roof as it jolted. It should, he thought, be enough to close in on a horse, given time.

He crested the rise, and saw that time was not on his side. Danny had broken off from the track to gallop across the heathland, and was heading for a large wooded area at the far side.

O'Malley swore. 'We need that air support now. I'm about to lose him.'

64

'I want to know where Danny is,' the detective constable – Juliette Hanson – said sharply.

Aisling had been relieved, at first, that they'd all been invited into the big dining room instead of being dragged to the station. She'd assumed it meant they were being treated as witnesses rather than anything else.

But as they'd been invited to move from the kitchen along with Michael, Antony and a stable hand, Jack had murmured, 'Getting us away from the sharp objects,' which had given her a little thrill of worry.

By the time Juliette had stationed a uniformed officer at the door, and marched to the head of the table, her face set, Aisling had felt slightly sick. Juliette had seemed warm and supportive the last time they'd spoken, but there wasn't a trace of sympathy on her face now.

'Where is he?' Juliette repeated. 'If this turns into a large-scale manhunt, a process that's already begun, then there's a high chance he'll end up injured or worse.'

They can't shoot him, she thought now in anguish. *They need to give him a chance to explain.*

'There's no justification for use of force at this point,' Jack said sharply next to her. 'You haven't yet definitively proved that the DNA is his. At present he's no more than a suspect, one you frightened off with the big arrival. And if he is guilty in some way, he doesn't necessarily represent a danger to life. He's not taken a hostage.'

Aisling watched Juliette sigh, and then give a slow nod.

There was a shift in her expression. 'We have no intention of letting any harm coming to Danny,' she said. 'But we need your help to find him before anything can escalate.'

She looked over at the stable hand, who had taken his hat off to reveal a closely shaven head. He was kneading the beanie in his hands now, but for some reason the gesture looked bored rather than anxious.

'You. Henning, isn't it?' Juliette asked. 'You helped him to saddle up, didn't you? Did he tell you where he was going?'

'No,' the stable hand said, and then went back to kneading his hat.

'He didn't give you any idea?' Juliette asked sceptically.

'He just said he needed the horse,' Henning replied with a hint of defiance. 'All the horses belong to him and the family, so I wasn't going to argue.'

Aisling felt a rush of warmth for this man: an employee who had been instinctively loyal to Danny, and who was now clearly protecting him.

Juliette seemed to sense the same. She shifted her focus to Antony. Danny's half-brother was pale and silent, as he had been since they all sat down. 'Where would your brother go, Antony?'

Antony looked up at her with a slightly surprised expression, as though his thoughts had been somewhere else. He shook his head, slowly. 'I have no idea. But you can trust him not to hurt anyone.'

'Perhaps his mother knows,' Juliette said, turning to Aisling at last. There was steel in her eyes. Aisling wondered how she'd thought this woman unthreatening in the past. 'You seemed to arrive just in time to warn him.'

'I don't know where he is,' Aisling said a little helplessly. 'I didn't warn him, and I didn't know he was here until this morning. Jack had the thought that they would have picked someone from church, and I realised that Michael and Celine had come over here a few years before we did.'

'So why didn't you let us know about this?' Juliette asked, her gaze still hard.

Aisling felt a sudden flicker of defiance. She wasn't the suspect here. 'I didn't tell you because I wasn't sure,' she said, meeting Juliette's eye. 'I wanted to come and talk to Michael and find out the truth. I know finding your killer means a lot to you, but finding my son means a lot to me too. I was desperate to know the truth, and to see him if I could.'

'Finding the killer should mean a lot to all of us,' Juliette said, her voice steely. 'Do you want to see another family lose their mother? Kids like Ethan and Finn?'

Aisling shook her head, her cheeks hot. She knew what they'd done had been selfish. But it had still been the right thing to do.

Juliette turned her gaze towards Michael. 'Did you have advance warning from Aisling that we would be on our way to arrest Danny?'

'I – no,' Michael said, his voice hoarse. 'I didn't even know *she* was coming. I was knocked back by it, tell the truth. I haven't had to think of Danny as anyone's but mine in a long time.'

Aisling could see Antony turning to stare at his father.

'You weren't aware that Danny was not your brother?' Juliette asked.

Antony's expression was mystified. Perhaps a little horrified. 'What . . . Dad, what is this?'

Michael Murphy's brow was creased. He kept his gaze on the table, and firmly away from his son. 'Danny was . . . adopted. Not officially.' He tutted. 'Not through an agency or anything.' He somehow managed to make it sound as though Antony should have known this. 'This is Danny's mother, and she came here to find him. The . . . friends . . . who gave him to me told me she didn't want him. Which wasn't true.' He caught Antony's eye, and snapped, 'For god's sake, boy, stop looking at me like it was a betrayal. I made a promise not to tell anyone. Danny never knew either. He grew up thinking he was ours.'

Antony stared at him, his face still that washed-out white. Aisling felt a rush of sadness for him. She'd thought, for a few brief minutes, that Antony was hers. That she could have offered him the love and respect he'd never had from his father. She wondered why Michael seemed so unable to love his own child. Surely that bond of blood should be enough?

But then she remembered Ethan's first months, when loving him had felt impossible. Perhaps the death of Michael's wife had hit him as hard as the death of Aisling's parents had hit her. Perhaps he'd never had proper psychiatric help, like she'd had, and had been stuck with that bitterness all these years.

She found herself glancing at Henning, and saw to her surprise that he looked furious. Absolutely furious. As though he wanted to throw a punch at Michael Murphy. Was it for Antony's sake that he felt this? Or for Danny's?

After half a minute of absolute silence, Juliette asked, 'Can you tell me about your connection with Anneka Foley?'

The two of them, father and son, looked round in confusion, and for the first time they looked as though they might be the same, underneath it all. As though there were something to link them after all.

'I don't . . .' Michael put a very unsteady hand up to his head. 'You shouldn't be asking me.'

Aisling could see Antony shaking his head, a little anger beginning to creep into his expression. 'Is there more to tell about her, too, Dad?' he asked. 'You've lied to us about Danny for decades . . . Have you been lying about everything else, too?'

'I did what I had to!' Michael said, his voice suddenly a bellow. 'Don't you dare criticise me for a situation that – that was impossible. Impossible.' With the last word, he slapped a hand down onto his leg. Aisling found herself wondering what it must have been like to have Michael Murphy as a father. Had her boy been frightened of him?

'I'm afraid I need to ask you about Anneka Foley, Mr Murphy,' Juliette said.

Michael gave an aggravated sigh. 'Anneka is Antony's mother, which he knows,' he said.

Juliette asked, 'Did you meet her while taking mares to her parents' stud farm?'

'I did,' Michael said flatly. And then, after a moment, as though he couldn't help justifying himself, he added, 'Celine and I were having trouble at that time. The lack of a child, and – she didn't make my life easy. Anneka would just smile at me and soothe me. She talked to me as though I had value.' He cleared his throat and shifted so that he was facing away from his son. 'But then we agreed to adopt Danny, and it was as though Celine had rediscovered herself. She began to plan a nursery and buy him clothes. It felt – like I had the love of my life back. I had to end to things with Anneka, and be a proper father and husband.' He coughed uncomfortably. 'She changed the moment I did. She became savage. It almost seemed like madness. So I stayed away, of course. I found excuses never to visit the farm.'

'Did you realise that Anneka had had your child?' Juliette asked.

'I didn't know anything about Antony until five years later,' he said gruffly. 'I avoided returning because I was trying to do the right thing. But – well, I found myself driving past her house after a race meeting and felt I should check on her. And it turned out that she had this boy . . .'

There was a momentary pause, and then Antony said, angrily, 'So you took me from her? Is that the truth? You took me like you took Danny from them?'

'For god's sake, boy,' Michael said. 'You were starving and injured. I rescued you and it would be reasonable to expect a little gratitude for that given what it cost me.'

Antony got quickly to his feet and walked to the door. He came face to face with the uniformed officer.

'Don't you walk out like I've let you down somehow,' Michael yelled after him. 'I've given you more than many men would.'

Antony was staring at the uniformed constable, his whole body vibrating.

'It's OK,' Juliette said, waving at the officer. 'He can go for now.' The constable stepped aside. 'Just don't leave the farm,' she called after him.

In the silence after he'd gone, Juliette turned towards Michael Murphy once again, her expression less hard. 'Can you think of any reason why Danny might have felt . . . anger towards Anneka Foley?'

'Why?' Michael asked, and then a little something in him seemed to collapse. 'Oh, my god.' And there were quite suddenly tears coursing down his weathered cheeks. 'I heard that she'd died. Danny can't have . . .'

'Did he know about her?' Juliette pressed.

'Not . . . I never told him. But there are things in the house which would have . . . I kept some of her letters.' For a moment he was no longer the angry disciplinarian who expected his sons to do as he said. He looked lost. 'Celine left a note, telling us that she'd lost all of us to that woman. To Anneka.'

65

An hour later, Jonah was attempting to interview Henning Andersen. They'd brought him to the farm office while the constables bagged up much of Danny Murphy's room and looked for samples of his hair. They needed evidence like this to build their case firmly, without reliance on the Globalry site. Danny's DNA could be checked without reference to the match Cassie Logan had made.

Instead of answering Jonah's questions, Henning was mulishly insistent both that he had no idea where Danny would go, and that he couldn't have murdered either of the two women.

'He was really ill in early October,' he said, at one point. 'There's no way he could have killed the first victim. I remember showing him the articles about it while he was recovering, and he was as horrified as I was.'

'We can check all that with him when we find him,' Jonah replied patiently. 'If he's innocent, as you say, there's nothing to be gained by him staying at large.'

'Except avoiding having some serious crimes he didn't do pinned on him,' Henning had answered sternly.

Jonah got the impression that Henning had taken an almost personal dislike to him, though perhaps that was just his manner. Either way, the interview had progressed nowhere by the time Lightman opened the door and asked to have a word.

'Danny Murphy has called in,' he said, quietly, once they'd reached the freezing air of the yard. 'He called through to the switchboard and they put it through to me. I thought I'd better talk to him rather than wait to find you.'

Jonah watched his illuminated breath chasing up in front of the security light like smoke, trying to take this in.

'What did he have to say?'

'He wants to give himself up,' Lightman said. 'We have to meet him in a Travelodge car park. He said he'll come quietly if his family are all there. He wants to talk to them before he's arrested. His whole family, he said. Michael, Aisling, Jack, and his brother.'

Jonah sighed. 'If he's managed to arm himself, there's a chance he could pick them all off as soon as they get out of a vehicle.'

'We could ask for Red Team help,' Lightman said. 'They could cover a lot of angles, and we could get the four family members vested up.'

Jonah considered this and then nodded. 'When does he want to do it?'

'In an hour,' Lightman told him. 'The Travelodge is the Stoney Cross one on the A31. Less than ten minutes by car, I'd say.'

'And how do we let him know we're coming?'

'He's given us a number to call,' Lightman said. 'Looks like he's found himself a burner phone somewhere.'

Jonah thought on this for a long minute, and then sighed. 'All right,' he said. 'Call back and tell him we'll be there, and that we'll be bringing an armed response team. But tell him we won't make any moves to fire if he does as he's promised.' He pulled out his mobile. 'I'll ring the Red Desk and see what they can come up with.'

66

It was ten minutes past seven when Aisling climbed out of the back of the squad car. She found it embarrassingly difficult to move with the bulky stab vest on, and had to lever herself out sideways.

'Are they supposed to be this tight?' she'd asked Jack, as she'd settled herself breathlessly into the back of the car.

'I guess they just had to bring the sizes they had handy,' Jack said. 'Mine is definitely digging into my gut.'

She'd looked at him with a surge of affection. 'Well, your gut still looks great to me, stab vest or no stab vest.'

Jack had reached out and taken her hand, in a gesture that was profoundly comforting. He hadn't let go of it until they'd pulled up at the Travelodge some minutes later.

It was icily cold out in the car park. There were clear skies above, and with an insistent north wind added into the mix, it wasn't the kind of weather to hang around in. Which was unfortunate, as she guessed there would be quite a bit of waiting.

There were two squad cars and two vans drawn up in a cluster at one end of the car park, which was either largely empty by coincidence or because the police had cleared out a lot of the cars. It all seemed ridiculously excessive to Aisling. This huge response for one man, and however tall and strong he was, Danny wouldn't be able to overpower a handful of officers and the four members of his disjointed family.

But he killed two women, she thought after that. *Perhaps it was rage that did it.*

She supposed it was guns they were worrying about. She found herself shivering as she glanced around at the empty space. At the blank windows of the Travelodge, and the trees that backed onto it. There were so many places for someone to hide at a distance.

The police hadn't given her any idea of why Danny had wanted them there. They'd said he wanted to talk to them, but that was it. If he'd passed on anything else, they hadn't let on.

She could think of a hundred things he might want to say to her. They were the same things she'd imagined asking her father if she'd ever seen him again.

How could you abandon me? Why didn't you love me more? Where were you when I needed you?

She felt a sob rising up in her at the terrible sadness of it all, but she swallowed it down. She had to be calm for him. Comforting. Whatever he needed her to be.

She could see the DCI, Juliette and Ben all watching them steadily. The team had handed over control of everything to another officer, one who seemed more like a soldier than a member of the police. But having those three here, still, was reassuring. Danny was not about to be arrested by these faceless men in black, but by the people who'd been working to find him. The team who had become familiar to her over the past day and a half.

She and Jack moved towards Antony and Michael Murphy. It occurred to her what a strange group they made: the two fathers, mother and brother who had known little or nothing of each other until today. Some part of her, though, felt as if she'd known the other two her whole life, and she tried to smile at Antony, whose eyes were bleak. Heartbroken.

'He's still your brother,' she said quietly. 'Isn't he? Whatever he's done. He'll be glad you're here.' And she managed a real smile then. 'I'm glad you're here too.'

And Antony nodded slowly. 'You know it's his birthday today?' he said. And then added, 'The day we celebrate it, anyway. As much as Dad celebrates anything.'

'It's the real date,' Aisling said, with a half-smile. Her throat was tight as she added, 'Some birthday.'

Antony's eyes slid past her, towards the trees, and she spun round.

It was unquestionably Danny who was approaching them. His big, bear-like form was unmistakable, even with his plaid shirt covered by a high-vis coat. To anyone else he might easily have passed for a Highways worker or builder, and she guessed that was why he'd dressed that way.

She could feel rather than see all the officers focusing on him now. Four of them had guns. So many for the one man.

She tried not to imagine them opening fire, and him falling onto the concrete of the car park.

Danny came to a stop a few yards from them, and lifted his hands slowly.

'I'm not armed or anything,' he said, loudly. 'I just want to say a few words to my family. And then I'll go. I'm happy to.'

It was Michael Murphy who he turned to first.

'Dad, I . . . I'm sorry.' Danny's deep voice sounded scratchy. 'I've let you down. This isn't your fault, it really isn't.'

'Look, I . . .' Michael said, his own voice anguished. 'I'm sorry, my boy.'

And although they'd been told, three times over, not to get close to Danny, he limped forwards and clutched his son in a fierce hug. It was a gesture so very much at odds with everything Aisling had seen of the man that it made her eyes sting.

'Shhh, it's all right,' Danny said. 'You've got Antony to look after. Don't worry about me. Just look after him, Dad.'

He held his father at arm's length, and looked at him

350

fiercely. And then he turned to his brother and held out an arm. Antony only hesitated for a moment before stepping into the hug, the three of them becoming a pile of family members together.

Antony let out a ragged sob, and said, 'Don't, Danny. You can't. Tell them you didn't do it. You can fight it. We can get a lawyer.'

But Danny muttered over the top of him, 'It's going to be all right now. I promise.'

It was a few seconds before he released them, and Aisling felt fiercely as though she shouldn't have been there. But then Danny turned towards her and Jack.

'I just wanted to . . . see you. Properly.' He nodded. 'And . . . I suppose to let you know that your son isn't just a killer. Before it turns into a court case, and evidence and – and people saying terrible things about me.' He gave a brief, strange laugh. 'I'm more than that. I really am.'

'Of course you are,' Aisling said, stepping towards him and then halting. She couldn't hug him. Not a man she'd never met. And yet this might be her only chance. This might be all she was going to get.

Two life sentences, she thought. *You could be dead by the time he's out.*

And so she stepped forwards, and let him envelop her in a hug that grew to encompass Jack too. A horse-smelling, terrifying and yet glorious hug. 'Whatever you've done, you're our son,' Aisling told him. 'And we'll be there for you. We'll be there for you.'

It was Jack, next to her, who asked, 'Are you sure about this, Danny? Are you sure?'

'I'm sure.'

A few seconds later, she found herself released into a night that felt suddenly even colder. Less certain. And Danny was holding his hands in the air as they came to arrest him.

67

For all his size and the terrible nature of his crimes, Danny Murphy looked anything but threatening as he waited for Jonah to begin. He was sitting back, a little hunched to fit into the interview-room chair, and his expression showed nothing but exhaustion.

Jonah had brought Hanson into the interview with him, deciding that her aura of sympathy would be likely to get the best response.

'Thank you for submitting to DNA testing,' Jonah began, after the introductions. 'While we wait for the results, we'd like to ask you about what happened on October the third and December the thirty-first last year.'

'You mean when Jacqueline Clarke and Lindsay Kernow died?' Danny asked, looking at him steadily. 'You should ask me about Merivel too.'

'Were you involved in their deaths?' Jonah asked.

'Yes,' Danny said.

Jonah found himself looking over at Hanson, wondering whether she had expected this flat, undemonstrative admission of guilt.

'How were you involved?'

There was a brief pause, and then Danny, who was still looking down at the table, said, 'I killed them. And Merivel. I killed her too.'

'Why did you kill Jacqueline and Lindsay?'

Danny hesitated, and then looked up at him, his expression thoughtful. Perhaps a little confused. 'I think . . . because they reminded me of my mum. But they weren't her. I just got – angry.'

'Why did you get angry?' Hanson asked. 'Did they treat you badly? Say harsh things to you?'

Another pause, and Danny said, 'Yes.'

'Or was it that they rejected you?' Jonah asked.

Danny sighed slightly. 'I don't know. Maybe.' He glanced between them. 'Does it really matter?'

'I think it will matter a great deal to their families,' Jonah said.

'And to the jury,' Hanson added.

Danny looked away, for a while, and then he said, 'It wasn't really about them. They didn't do anything wrong. I thought I could love them, but when it came to it . . . I wasn't good enough for them, and it made me angry. I've never been angry like that before.'

'Do you mean that you couldn't perform, sexually?'

Danny's expression was surprised. Perhaps even disgusted. And then he said, 'Yes, I suppose so.'

Jonah sat back, considering. 'Can you tell me how you met each of them?'

Danny paused again, and then said, 'In bars.' He shrugged. 'If you hang around long enough, you'll find someone who's lonely.'

Jonah had been waiting for a touch of disdain. For a little superiority, and the implication that these women were somehow pathetic. It was common in those who preyed upon women, that attempt to set themselves above their victims. That lack of fundamental respect for their lives. But Jonah hadn't picked up any of that disdain or self-aggrandisement. Danny spoke neutrally. Quietly.

'Which bar did you meet Jacqueline Clarke in?' Jonah asked.

Danny looked into the distance thoughtfully. 'You know, I can't even remember. I've been to so many, on the hunt.'

He could feel the switch of Hanson's gaze to him, and then back to Danny Murphy.

'You don't remember where you met one of the women you killed?' she asked.

Danny shrugged, and Jonah thought there was discomfort in it. 'I'm afraid not.'

'How about Lindsay Kernow?' Jonah asked. 'That was more recent.'

Danny breathed out. 'It was some place in Totton,' he said. 'I forget the name.'

Jonah watched him for a long moment, and then he asked, 'What about Anneka Foley?'

There was a long silence before Danny said, 'What about her?'

'Tell me about her.'

Danny sighed slightly. 'There's nothing much to tell.'

'Were you responsible for her death too?' Hanson asked.

Danny looked at Hanson for a little while, and then back at Jonah. 'No,' he said. 'I wasn't. Just the other two. And Merivel.'

Jonah left the interview room feeling profoundly troubled. He'd thought their capture of Danny Murphy had finally put an end to the killings. They knew that he was Aisling's son, and the only person whose DNA profile would fit the blood they'd found. He had run, and then confessed. It ought to be straightforward.

But Jonah had found out long ago that the truth could be anything but straightforward. And right now, he was convinced that Danny Murphy was lying to them.

'I'm picking up a lot of press calls,' Lightman said, as

Jonah came level with his desk. 'Do we have a statement for them?'

Jonah sighed, and then said, 'A man in his thirties has been placed under arrest and is helping us with our inquiries. To give any more information would endanger the investigation. That's all for now.'

Lightman simply nodded, and began to type. O'Malley, however, turned round in his chair and asked, 'So you're not convinced it was him.'

'I think the chance that he committed those murders alone is minimal,' Jonah replied. 'His blood was at the scene, so he must have been involved at least in Lindsay's death. But I think it more than likely he did it with someone – someone who actually picked these women up. Danny might have been no more than that person's accomplice.'

'He's being manipulated into covering for them?' Hanson asked.

'Or threatened,' Jonah agreed. 'Or he possibly just cares an awful lot about whoever it was who pushed him into this.'

'He didn't admit to killing Anneka Foley,' Hanson said thoughtfully. 'It looked like he didn't actually know about it. Could there be something there?'

'The coroner didn't make much headway with finding people who'd been at Anneka's house, or any possible witnesses,' O'Malley said, thoughtfully, 'but Michael Murphy knew about the place.'

Jonah glanced at him, and then nodded. 'Michael has a forceful personality, and all the apparent regret over taking Danny from the Cooleys could be a charade. Do we know what Michael Murphy was doing on October the third and on New Year's Eve?'

'Not so far,' O'Malley replied. 'But we can ask some questions.'

'I suppose the same goes for Antony Murphy,' Hanson said. 'Anneka Foley was his mother, and she abused him. Perhaps he remembered it.'

'I know he might not have a direct connection to Anneka Foley,' O'Malley offered, 'but what about the stable hand? The Scandinavian fella? He helped Danny saddle up in order to flee.'

Jonah remembered the trace of threat he'd felt from Henning Andersen as he'd stood in the stable block. His unwillingness to answer questions.

'He's been with the Murphy farm a couple of years, he said,' Jonah said slowly. 'But what about where he grew up? We know he lived near Newbury before his parents went home to Denmark . . . Could he have grown up on a stud farm in West Gradley, while Anneka Foley's parents ran it?'

68

Henning walked quietly over to the stud farm's crowded little office. He'd been worried that he'd missed his opportunity.

He'd waited patiently for Alison to head home, but Michael and Antony had arrived back from the Travelodge only a short while afterwards, their faces sombre. He'd guessed they would be taken to the station to give statements, but that clearly wasn't the plan. The father and son had been dropped off at the farm, and then the two constables stationed at the yard had taken themselves off.

Neither father nor son had volunteered any information about Danny when they'd passed Henning in the yard. Antony had merely squeezed Henning's shoulder and then gone to hide himself away with the foals on the pretence of checking them over.

It had been lucky for Henning that Michael, usually so careful to keep his property locked up, had walked slowly into the farmhouse and shut the kitchen door. He'd forgotten the farm office, and the fact that it had been open all afternoon.

Henning had waited until the two of them had been out of sight for a full minute, and then he'd gone quickly across the yard to the office door. The security lamp had come on, bathing him in light, but there had been no movement beyond the farmhouse curtains he'd closed earlier on, or from the foaling stable.

He let himself in through the door and closed it behind him. With the security light on, there was no need to turn on any of the office lamps for now. He had a good five minutes before it would switch off, and an idea of where he needed to look.

He approached the big calendar on the wall, and pulled this year's down so he could flick back through last year's. Michael Murphy would never get rid of it until the end of the year, in case he needed to check something.

Henning looked at December first, a month full of entries. Laying it down on the table, he turned back to November, then October. And then he used the perforations to very carefully tear all three pages out of the calendar.

The light flicked off outside as he was finishing, and he had to fold the stiff paper in darkness. With some effort, he managed to bend the sheets enough to make them A4 size, and almost flat.

He was stuffing them down into the rear waistband of his trousers when the security light flicked back on. He could see Antony out there, clearly illuminated and with his gaze fixed on the office. The older Murphy brother lifted a hand to shield his eyes, and began to walk towards the door.

Henning dragged his fleece down over the top of the folded pages, his heart pounding. It took him a moment to pick the calendars up, and hang both of them back on the hook. And then he was moving towards the desk.

He had the drawer out and was in the act of bending over it when Antony came in.

'Hey.' Antony's voice was tight. A little surprised.

Henning glanced up at him, and then back at the drawer. He took in the tension in the older Murphy brother. And the heavy baton torch he was carrying.

'What's up?' Antony tried. This sounded overly casual now. It was clear that he was distrustful.

'The door was unlocked,' Henning told him, closing the

drawer with a nod. 'I had this horrible thought that someone had made all this happen just to lure us away. I had to check that nothing had been taken, or burned, or . . .' He shook his head. 'I feel like I'm losing my mind.'

He straightened up and sighed, putting a hand to his head. He knew how to play this. How to be the heartbroken, slightly neurotic employee who wasn't used to feeling this way.

'That's – what I thought too,' Antony said with a more re-laxed laugh. 'I saw you in here, and I thought you were an intruder.'

'I'm glad you're arming yourself,' Henning said, nodding towards the torch. 'I regretted not bringing something with me the moment I stepped inside. I know it's paranoid, but . . . keep a weapon with you, will you? I want us all to be safe, until we're sure there's nobody else behind these deaths.'

'I will,' Antony said. He let out a long breath and perched on the table. 'I don't . . . believe it was him. I know him for fuck's sake.'

Henning focused on him, trying to read his expression. It was difficult, with all the light behind Antony's head.

'Do you think you know anything that could help defend him?' Henning asked. 'Anything definite that you could tell the police?'

Antony gazed back towards him, and then he shook his head. 'I don't think so.'

Henning gave a sigh. 'I guess it's hard to even remember last year. I can barely remember last week.'

He rubbed his head again. There was a sudden loud bang behind him, and they both jumped. Henning swung round and realised that it had been the calendar falling to the floor. In his rush he must have hung it back up badly.

'Jesus,' he said, trying to laugh. 'That's taken years off my life.' He bent down and, with his heart thumping, he lifted it to hang it up again, taking more care this time. 'I guess I must have knocked into it or something. Weird.'

He turned back to Antony and started to make his way back to the door. Antony was looking down at the torch in his hand thoughtfully. As Henning moved round the desk, he thought he might be able to detect a little of the older Murphy brother's expression. It looked like he was afraid.

'We should go for a drink,' Henning offered suddenly. 'However bad my day was, yours has been a lot worse. I'll drive you to the Queen's Head and we can dump the car there.'

Antony stood, as though pulling himself together. 'That's – OK. I think I just need tea and my own bed.' He paused for a moment. 'But thank you. And you should go. You haven't had a night off since bloody Christmas.'

Henning gave him a grin. 'I don't need telling twice.'

He headed out into the yard once again and was surprised to hear an engine approaching. The yard gate was still open, but Henning had expected Michael to have closed the gate onto the road. Everyone who had a key was here, so it must still be open.

Light flooded the yard, and Antony walked past him as he was still shielding his eyes. It was only as the engine shut off and the lights were extinguished that it became clear that this was Aisling, Danny's mother, and not the police returning.

Aisling climbed out of the car with a loud, 'I'm so sorry.' Henning trailed after Antony, and was close enough to hear Aisling saying more quietly, 'I know you probably want to go to bed. But I – really want to talk to you and your dad, about Danny. I still don't think he did it, and I know you think the same. So we need to work out why he's saying he did.'

Henning's eyes went to Antony, who was quiet for a moment, before saying, 'OK. Come and have a cup of tea and we'll talk about it.' He glanced round at Henning, and said, with a grin, 'It's OK. You can still head to the pub.'

'Well . . .' Henning faltered. 'I – I could stay. I might be able to help.'

'No, you should go.' Antony sighed slightly. 'You work too hard.'

Henning hesitated, looking for an excuse to end up in the kitchen too. But the two of them started to walk past him, Aisling's arm looped through Antony's in a way that made it clear that they were family, even if not by blood.

Henning went to his car, full of uncertainty. What would happen if he left? Was he safe to just walk away? Had Antony worked out what he was doing? And the biggest question: how much had Aisling figured out?

Even after he'd climbed behind the wheel, he still found himself hesitating for a good while, his hand on the ignition switch. But in the end he realised that they would be waiting for him to go, and he had to take those folded pieces of paper away from here.

And so he turned on the ignition, and began to bump his way along the track.

69

Aisling felt suddenly stupid and tactless. It was only as Michael Murphy came to the farmhouse door, his face haggard with grief, that the reality of his pain hit her.

Michael had raised Danny, and Antony had been a brother to him. They'd been his real, in-person family for twenty-nine years. Today's arrest meant more to them than it ever could to her, in spite of the blood she shared with him. In spite of the feeling of lost time.

What had happened to them was the equivalent of every nightmare scenario she'd imagined with Ethan and Finn. She had no business disturbing them just now, even if she wanted to save him somehow.

She wasn't even quite sure how she'd ended up here, in truth. She'd dropped Jack off at the Premier Inn in Southampton, where he needed to grab his suitcase before heading back to London. She'd been strangely broken-hearted at seeing him go, comforted only by his promise that he'd be back once he'd gone home to sort out a change of clothes and some unavoidable work.

'I think there's a lot more for us to talk about,' he'd said. 'A lot of years to catch up on. And the two of us are . . . we need to be there for him.'

And she'd been unable to do more than nod and kiss him on the cheek.

She'd planned on driving home after she'd waved him off. She'd left her sons alone for too long, particularly after an awful series of discoveries. They needed the sofa, and TV, and a pizza delivery with weird ingredients.

But when she'd called Finn from the Bluetooth system in the car, she'd found herself telling them that she needed to go back to the Murphy farm for an hour or so.

'I need answers to a few questions about your brother,' she said. 'So why don't you order pizza to arrive in an hour, and I'll come back and eat it with you then?'

'Pizza two nights in a row,' she could hear Ethan say in the background. 'Flipping win.'

But Finn, ever perceptive, had asked, 'Do you not think it was him?'

'I don't . . . know.' Aisling sighed. 'I thought it was, but there was something about the way he gave himself up. I just . . . I'd like to know what his family thinks.'

'OK, well, don't be too long,' Finn had said, as though he were the long-suffering adult. 'What do you want on it?'

'Ham, mushroom, strawberries . . . and seven extra cheese,' she said. 'It's been that kind of a day.'

'Wow, OK.' She could hear clicking sounds in the background, signs that Finn was already beginning the order. 'We may be about to blow Milo's mind.'

With that done, she'd gone straight to the Murphy Farm, her head full of questions about Danny's movements over the last few weeks, and whether there was someone in his life who might be threatening him or those he loved.

Now that she was here, in the big farmhouse kitchen again, most of those questions seemed ridiculous. As Antony drifted around making tea and Michael looked slumped and immovable in a chair, she felt as though she'd invaded their home and their peace.

She pulled a chair out from under the table, and found

herself sitting one place down from where she had earlier on. The photograph of Danny after he'd donated bone marrow to save Antony was still lying on the table, and it made her feel worse still.

You shouldn't be here, she told herself.

But as she was trying to find a way of leaving once again, Michael said, 'I want you to be right. I don't want him to have done it. But what he said . . .' He gave a long sigh. 'Even if he has, I'll still love him.' He gave a sudden, awful sob. 'With every apology to you for what I put you through, I'll still think of him as my son.'

'Why?' It was Antony who had asked it. He had paused in his tea-making, and turned towards his father. There was the same shaking anger running through him that Aisling had seen before he stormed out earlier today. 'Why do you still love him more than you love me, when he isn't even yours?'

Michael's mouth opened and shut twice, and then he said, 'It's not about loving him more . . . I . . . You aren't my son either, Antony. You aren't mine. And finding that out, I think it – it was almost as bad as losing Celine.'

Antony stared at him, his face childishly shocked. 'What do you mean?' He stood up straighter. 'Of course I'm yours! I'm the terrible mistake you made. I grew up with you feeling ashamed of me because you'd fathered me in sin. Don't fucking tell me I'm not yours!'

Aisling felt cold. Desperately cold. She wanted Michael Murphy to soothe Antony. To tell him that he cared about him. But Michael was shaking his head.

'I thought you were. Right up until you got sick, and they wanted to test to see who could be a donor for you.' Michael was red-faced. Furious, as if it was all happening right now. It was like her and the loss of her father, she thought. It was fresh because he'd never let himself talk about it. 'They told me I might not be able to donate marrow, even as your father. I didn't really think anything of it at first when it came back as not a match. Danny could do it for you, by luck, so it was all right. You were going to make it. But then this little – this little doubt started in the back of my mind. I'd thought when I came to get you that you were small for your age. Given that I knew when you must have been conceived.'

Aisling half rose, feeling like the worst intruder. 'I'm sorry,' she said. 'I should be leaving you two to talk.'

'No,' Antony said, his voice suddenly pleading. 'Please stay. You're ... honestly, you've been kinder to me today than this – this *old man* has in years, and ... I don't know if I can listen to any more of this shit on my own.'

Aisling saw the pain in him, and felt as deeply for him as if she'd known him for years. Perhaps as much for this over-looked, unhappy man as if he'd turned out to be her own son. She lowered herself back into the chair and nodded.

'Of course I'll stay, if you want me to,' she said gently.

'Tell me,' Antony said to Michael, his voice harder.

'Don't shout at me,' Michael snapped. 'I don't owe you this. I'm telling you because I want to.' He stared back at the man who was not his son, and Aisling saw in that stare how troubled their relationship was.

Antony looked away, and Michael nodded self-righteously, and then went on, 'I took a swab from you, when they were doing all the tests. I didn't tell you what it was for. I almost thought it would prove I was being ridiculous and be the end of it. I sent your sample and mine to a company that does paternity tests, and – and it came back conclusive. You weren't my son.'

Antony was silent for a moment. 'Then whose am I?'

'I haven't a clue,' Michael said scathingly. 'How could I?'

Antony turned away. For a second he was motionless, and

then he started to make the tea again. The only sound was the clinking of cups, and Aisling felt helpless to console either of them: the old man who must, underneath it all, feel riddled with guilt, or the younger one who had just lost the last member of his family to a DNA test taken years before.

'You should have told me,' Antony said after a while, his voice low and unsteady. 'I could have stopped wasting my time caring what you thought.'

'I brought you up as my own,' Michael said, the anger rising in him again. 'I did more than any man would have done.'

'You treated me like nothing,' Antony said, slamming the cutlery drawer shut. 'You made me feel worthless. Like the greatest disappointment you could have had as a son.'

He picked up two mugs of tea, and brought them to the table, his eyes anywhere but on his father. The larger mug, a huge thing with tractors all over it, he slammed down in front of his father. Aisling's he placed more gently on the table.

'What do you want me to say?' Michael asked, his voice full of mockery. 'That I'm sorry?'

'Well, are you sorry?' Antony asked, remaining standing. 'For making me grow into the pathetic failure you thought me?'

Aisling stood then. She moved round the table to Antony, and hugged him. This tall, blond boy who was so very like her father had once looked, even though there was none of her blood running in his veins.

'It's OK,' she said. 'It's all OK, I promise.'

She could feel Antony shaking, before he started to sob into her shoulder.

70

The team had begun to look at possible accomplices while the DCI prepared to interview Danny Murphy again. The chief was clear that he wanted more information before he walked in there. Something to challenge Danny with.

Hanson was focusing on who'd had the opportunity to commit each of the three murders and to kill the brood mare. It seemed as though Danny was an isolated man, who rarely left the farm. There were no particular friends he seemed likely to be under the spell of. And so she'd made herself a table which she was populating with what they knew of the Murphy family's movements, highlighting for herself where there were gaps, of which there were a daunting number.

They knew what Antony Murphy had been doing on New Year's Eve, by his own account at least. She filled in all the details she could glean from his interview, and found herself thinking again of how he'd caught sight of Matthew Downing.

Was there really nothing on those tapes Matthew had recorded? Matthew had been right there on the heath, a few hundred yards from the murder site.

She dug out her headphones, plugged them in, and started the first video up again.

Jonah called the DCS the moment he was back in his office. Wilkinson would be under pressure from the chief and deputy chief constables to provide a progress report, and Jonah sympathised. He felt grateful, for perhaps the hundredth time in his career, that the DCS was both smart and open-minded. He listened to Jonah's concerns and agreed that there were reasons for caution.

'If you have to apply for a custody extension, you'd have ample grounds,' Wilkinson said, his voice thoughtful. 'I think you're right to tread carefully. I'd want to be looking at your suspect's life in greater detail.'

'Thank you, sir.'

The call lasted less than ten minutes, and Jonah was then free to start planning his next interview with Danny Murphy.

It was hard to know what approach to take. Jonah's methodology with suspects who were lying to them varied, but often came down to either coaxing them into wanting to talk, or a brutal ripping apart of all the inconsistencies in their account.

He was certain the brutal approach wouldn't work with Danny Murphy. He was a man who seemed to have given up on himself, for whatever reason, and would likely only retreat further into admissions of his own guilt under attack. It would be unlikely to make him point the finger at his accomplice.

There were essentially two options, as Jonah saw it. The first was to appeal to his sense of guilt at the lives already lost. Which had a chance of failure, as it relied on Danny actually feeling remorse. It was hard to know whether he did.

The other was to appeal to his sense of what he was sacrificing, and who he was hurting by doing this. Which was, again, difficult. If his father, brother or the stable hand Henning were the unseen force behind this, then Danny might feel that he was betraying them more by telling the truth than by keeping quiet.

What Jonah really wanted was something concrete. Some

clear indication of who Danny was protecting, and how far they had been involved. He needed his team to produce something, and quickly.

The phone on his desk rang while he was immersed in these thoughts, and he took the call with a feeling of frustration. This was, presumably, either someone on the senior management team or a request from the press that had managed to sneak through.

'Jonah Sheens,' he said impatiently.

'I've got a call from a Henning Andersen, who says he needs to talk to you urgently,' the switchboard operator said. 'He believes you'd want to take his call. OK to put him through?'

'Yes,' Jonah said, his impatience evaporating. 'Put him on. Thanks.'

Hanson was almost all the way through the five videos, and felt frustrated. The close-up filming and bright foreground lighting in most of them rendered the background all but invisible, and there was no sign of anyone else on screen at any point. Nothing, either, in the chat at the end.

That fifth video where they'd caught the pyre lighting up had so much potential, but was at such a distance with such contrasting darkness that she doubted even the greatest enhancements could show them anything of their killer in the background.

She shivered as she saw the bonfire spring to life in the distance. And then the gradual thumping sound of the helicopter overhead, and Matthew's furious breaking off.

The camera view jolted, and then the film ended, leaving Hanson staring at her screen.

If you were setting a pyre to burn a murdered woman, she thought, *and a helicopter suddenly appeared, what would you do?*

And she knew the answer: you would douse the fire. You would douse it, and you would run.

'You need to come to the farm,' Henning said, his voice sounding anxious to Jonah, even over the line. 'I left to bring you evidence to help Danny, but now Aisling Cooley has arrived, and I think she's in danger.'

'Why would she be in danger?' Jonah asked, already getting to his feet.

'Because she's telling Antony and his father that she doesn't think Danny did it, and asking them to help her work out who the real killer is,' he said. 'And if she does work it out, I think she's going to end up dead.'

71

Antony had eventually stopped his hopeless sobbing but told them he needed some fresh air. He'd let himself out into the yard, leaving Aisling to sit in a truly awkward silence with Michael Murphy.

The stud owner had occupied himself with drinking his tea noisily, while Aisling had largely just stared at hers, thinking about the two brothers, and how their adoptive father's inability to love them had shaped them.

Danny must have badly wanted parental figures in his life, she thought. People who might have taken the place of the woman he'd thought was his mother, and the uncaring man he'd thought his father. He would have been easily manipulated by someone offering him praise. A very little of that would have gone a long way.

She looked up at Michael and found herself wondering. Was Danny's father not the man whose approval he most wanted? Wasn't Michael the one person who might have told Danny how to act, and been unthinkingly obeyed?

She imagined how it could be done. The moments of praise. The disdain if Danny didn't do as he was told. And quite suddenly she felt not as though she were intruding but as though she might be in danger. If Michael Murphy had that kind of power over Danny, how much power might he have over fragile Antony? A man who had already shown her how much his adoptive father's opinion meant to him?

She felt the hairs begin to stand up on her arms. She

needed to leave. And in case they tried to stop her she needed to make sure the police knew she was here too.

She dropped a hand to her jeans pocket, as if scratching an itch, reaching for her phone. And then, her heart sinking, she remembered flinging her phone onto the passenger seat of the car.

'It's gone nine thirty,' Michael said suddenly, his voice tired. 'I'll need my bed soon.'

'Me too,' Aisling said, relieved. She stood and stretched. 'I'm so sorry for coming here so late. Please apologise to Antony for me.'

But she'd no sooner said it than she heard the door to the yard opening. Antony stepped into the kitchen and stopped in the doorway, looking crestfallen. 'You're not going, are you?'

'I should really,' Aisling said. 'I'm pretty tired.'

'You can stay here,' Antony offered, his expression pleading. How much like a child he sometimes looked. 'Danny's room is free,' he offered.

'I couldn't do that.'

'You've not had your tea.'

'Sorry. I let it get cold.'

'Here.' Antony came to take it from the table, and hurried over to the microwave. He put it in and set it off, turned, smiled at her and then seemed unable to think what to say.

Aisling sat back down slowly, wondering how she could leave. She had to make herself seem unthreatening. But as the microwave hummed, she found herself unable to construct a sentence.

The silence was broken by Michael, who said in a quiet, slightly unclear voice, 'I was afraid . . . that you might leave.' He looked over at his son. 'And then . . . if you weren't my son, you could, couldn't you? Maybe it was that. Maybe that was why I couldn't tell you.'

She could see the effect these words had on Antony. He was frozen, unresponsive even as the microwave beeped to say that it was done.

Aisling found herself looking away from both of them and down at the photograph on the table. That picture of Danny, exhausted and clearly in pain after a major operation he'd submitted to. All in order to save the boy he thought was his brother.

And then she found herself thinking back to yesterday evening, when she and Ethan and Finn had been at the police station. When the DCI had asked her whether her sons had ever donated bone marrow to anyone.

This is just to rule out the possibility that their DNA would be showing up erroneously in someone else's blood . . .

And she felt cold spread across her chest. A real, profound cold that was almost paralysing.

'I'm – I'm sorry. I think I need to go to bed now,' Michael Murphy said, and when Aisling looked up at him, he was slumped in his chair, his eyelids heavy. 'This is all . . . I feel done in . . .'

'Let me help you,' Antony said, walking towards the table. He had Aisling's mug of tea in his hand now, reheated and ready for her to drink. 'I'll get him to bed,' he said to her with a smile. 'You drink up.'

Aisling tried to smile back at him. It felt unstable. Fake. But he seemed happy enough as she lifted the mug of tea and pretended to drink.

Ketamine, she thought. *Lindsay Kernow was drugged with ketamine . . .*

She kept on pretending to drink as Antony lifted his father's arm over his shoulder and began helping him towards the stairs. It seemed a long time before they were at the top, and beginning their slow progress along the landing.

Aisling didn't wait. She set the cup down, rose, and crept to the front door. It made almost no sound as she opened it and let herself out into the yard. The night air smelled cold and petrol-laced. Had it smelled like this before?

She winced as she closed the door behind her, but there was no sign of Antony through the frosted glass. The stairs remained empty.

She half ran to the car. The keys were still in there, she realised. She just had to get in, switch it on and drive away.

She put her hand to the driver's-side handle and pulled. But the door didn't open. The car she'd thought she'd left open was now firmly locked.

She put her hands to her jeans pockets again, pressing them desperately. What had she done? Had she put the key on the kitchen table? Had she really been that stupid?

And then she remembered how Antony had gone to get fresh air. How he'd been gone some minutes, and then returned looking much more collected.

And it was then that she realised she was in real trouble.

72

Jonah and his team were on the road, sirens and blue-and-whites in full use. There was no secrecy this time. He wanted Antony Murphy to know that they were coming.

Henning had been explaining how Antony had been away from the farm the nights of each murder when Hanson had burst into his office.

'Sir,' she'd said, before realising he was on the phone. 'Sorry.'

'No, it's OK,' Jonah said. 'Mr Andersen, can I give you another number to call me on? We're going to get moving.'

He'd reeled off his mobile number and then hung up, picking up his car keys.

'We're going to the Murphy farm,' he said.

'That's good,' Hanson had told him. 'Because I don't think Danny Murphy had anything to do with any of this. The blood we found was left by Antony. Danny donated bone marrow to him in ninety-nine. Danny's healthy bone marrow has taken over the production of blood, which means Antony's blood now has the DNA of Danny's. But, like with most donor recipients, his cheek swab has remained the same. I think the blood at the scene came from Antony, not Danny.'

'Shit,' Jonah had said, as he strode out into CID. 'Why didn't we pick up on the donation?'

'It's not on any of our records,' Hanson had said. 'I had to specifically search for news stories about bone marrow donation with their names in it. I also think,' she added, 'that Antony doused the fire on Lyndhurst Heath because a rescue helicopter flew over. He panicked, thinking it was police, and put it out, not realising he was bleeding and had left his DNA there.'

'And, boy, did he luck out on having blood that looked like Danny's,' Jonah had said, coming to a stop near Lightman and O'Malley.

'He really did,' Hanson said with feeling.

Jonah's two sergeants had looked up at him inquisitively, already grabbing their car keys. It was clear that Hanson had passed her findings on.

'We're going to the stud farm,' he told them. 'And hopefully getting there before Antony decides to do anything to Aisling Cooley. I want one of you to ring ahead now and explain that we're on our way to talk to Aisling since we know she's there. Make sure he thinks it's her we're interested in. I don't want him feeling desperate.'

'On it,' O'Malley said, pulling out his mobile.

Ten minutes later, they were roughly halfway to Lyndhurst. They'd notified a nearby squad car too, which might arrive a few minutes before they did.

Their calls to the house and Antony Murphy's mobile had remained unanswered, however, and Jonah felt a surge of worry.

Aisling was under threat in two ways, he thought. She shared numerous features with Antony's victims, each of whom Jonah was certain had represented a mother figure. But each of them had presumably later disappointed him or sparked a need for revenge. Worse still, Aisling was Danny's mother, and Jonah could guess how easily Antony might resent Danny having a mother of his own who had offered love and understanding.

He killed his own mother for rejecting him, Jonah thought, remembering how Anneka Foley had died. *How easily would he kill someone else's?*

Henning had called back a few minutes into the drive. He was a couple of miles from the farm and told them he was willing to return to it.

'I can't ask you to put yourself at risk,' Jonah said firmly.

'I'd rather that than let him hurt her,' Henning argued.

'We're only minutes away,' Jonah insisted. 'By all means phone him and tell him we're coming, but don't approach him, please. We have no idea if he's armed himself, and based on what you've said I think he's likely to consider you a threat.'

There was a pause before Henning agreed, and Jonah wasn't sure whether he was more worried at the idea of him charging in there anyway or of him obeying Jonah's instructions and leaving Aisling to fend for herself.

73

Aisling was still standing frozen next to her car by the time the door to the farmhouse opened.

'Are you all right?'

Antony's voice sounded politely concerned. There was nothing to let on that he'd done this. That he wished her harm.

'Yes,' she said after a moment. 'Well . . . I left my phone in the car and I need to message the boys again or they'll worry. I said I was coming out here for a quick chat. But now I can't find my car key.'

'It's probably somewhere inside,' Antony said. 'Why don't we go and have a hunt?'

'Thanks,' she said. And then she added, 'I hope they're not worrying about me. I said I wouldn't be long.'

Antony gave a laugh. 'They're teenagers, aren't they? They won't be worried unless they get left without food.'

Aisling made an effort to laugh too, and followed him towards the house slowly. The petrol scent increased, and she thought suddenly of all those fires.

Her eyes fell on a large metal drum alongside the door, and she felt her legs almost give up on her.

Then she realised that she could hear a phone ringing. Not her own mobile, but an old-fashioned landline. 'Is that your phone?' she asked, hoping that she could distract him for long enough to at least run. There would be places she could hide herself on the farm if he just turned his back for a while.

'Probably advertising,' Antony said, giving her a smile over his shoulder. She shivered at this glib response, but as his face turned towards the light, she saw that beneath the smile, he looked sad. Frightened. Not like a heartless psychopath at all.

And with the light above, throwing the lower half of his face into shadow, it was as if he had a beard. And he looked so very, very like her father that everything else dropped away. Even – momentarily – her fear.

'Antony,' she said. 'My dad . . . He was having an affair with your mum. With Anneka. Right when Michael, your dad, had stopped seeing her.'

Antony stopped, and he turned to her in what looked like genuine confusion. 'What? Your dad?'

She nodded, and put a hand out on to his arm. Her fingers were shaking.

'Michael asked my daddy to keep an eye on Anneka. But Daddy fell in love with her. It's one of the reasons he left us. He couldn't bear the double life he'd ended up leading.' She looked up at him, trying to impress the importance of this on him. 'He started seeing her in 1985, and he left us two years later when he couldn't bear it all any more. What year were you born?'

'I . . . eighty-five,' he said, slowly. 'December 1985. But actually . . . Dad said once that Mum had got it wrong, and I was months younger. He said I'm younger than Danny really, but it was too late to do anything about it. I didn't really get – why.'

Of course he said that, she thought. *It was the one thing he was willing to admit, when he realised you weren't his. That you were too young. He couldn't tell you that he'd been fooled into raising another man's son, but he could tell you he'd been fooled about your age.*

She squeezed his arm, and tried to smile at him.

'You aren't Michael's son; you're my dad's,' she said. 'I don't know why I didn't see it. He loved your mum, and you

379

look – you look so like him. So like him.' She found herself smiling up at him, for a moment. 'You're my brother. You're my family.'

Antony stared at her, his eyes full. 'So he didn't want me either,' he said flatly.

'I think he really did,' Aisling said. 'Just like he wanted me. But he was too ashamed of what he'd done. He took his own life, and it wasn't lack of love. It was despair and guilt and terrible shame.'

A wave of something seemed to move through Antony. And then he said, his voice low, 'You – you talk nicely to me now. But you won't. You aren't any different from any of them.' He drew an uneven breath in. 'You soothe me and then you'll – you'll turn on me, because that's what every single one of you did in the end. My mum. Jackie . . . Lindsay.'

The fear she'd felt descended on her again like a wave. He'd killed them. He really had. She'd been right. But she tried to keep smiling, and willed herself to keep holding his arm. To squeeze it.

You need to make him believe that you love him, she thought. *You would have still loved him if he was your son.*

'There's a lot of pain in you, but you're a good man, Antony.' And she did believe that. She did. She had to hang onto that.

Antony was staring at her uncertainly.

Aisling took a breath. 'I don't want you to do whatever it is you were going to do. I want you to live. And I'll be here, standing by you, through all of it.' She glanced towards the farmhouse, and said, 'And, you know, I think Michael might stand by you too.'

She saw his face twist, and her heart lurched. She'd said the wrong thing.

'He won't,' Antony said. 'He won't. He's – worse than all of them.'

He walked past the door suddenly, making for the large metal barrel.

'Antony,' she said urgently. 'Please, please be the brother I've always wanted.'

He had his hands on the barrel. And Aisling cried out and turned away, her arms over her head.

But there was no feeling of viscous kerosene. No wetness.

Aisling cringed and looked through her arms. He was frozen, with the barrel half lifted. It was dripping colourless liquid onto the lower half of his jeans. Some of it was bouncing up to splash her too, but she didn't step back.

She slowly, tentatively held a shaking hand out towards him. 'Will you come and have a cup of tea with me? Just sit with me, for a while?'

He looked so young right now. And so much like a man torn apart.

'If I – if I go to jail, I don't . . . I won't make it,' he said. 'I won't make it.'

'You're stronger than you think you are,' she said.

Still the kerosene was dripping out of the can, dousing his shoes, his jeans and the ground below him. The puddle was touching her feet.

Antony shook his head, very slowly, and suddenly let go of the barrel.

'I'm not,' he said. 'I'm not.'

He started to reach into his pocket. She knew he was going to pull out a lighter. That he was going to send everything up, and that her only chance was to run. Right now.

And yet she found herself frozen, unable to watch him burn his home, his father and himself.

Does he even know that he's covered in kerosene now? she thought, as he pulled a glinting metal object out of his pocket.

But then light washed over the yard. There was the roar of

an engine, and a little blue Ford raced into the yard and turned with a skid.

Out of it came Finn. He flew across the space between them and, seeming to understand what was happening, dragged her backwards.

'The lighter,' she told him urgently. 'We need to stop him.'

Antony had frozen. The barrel had rolled onto its side, and a thin stream of oily liquid was pouring over his foot.

Aisling could hear Ethan climbing out of the car too, and then she was released as first Finn and then Ethan charged towards Antony.

She saw him fumble with what must have been the lighter, as if trying to use it.

Oh, god, no, she thought, utterly cold. They were all so close to him. Too close. *Not all three of them. God, no.*

But before Antony could do any more, Finn took him in a flying tackle below the waist. Ethan grabbed at his arm the moment he was down, forcing it open.

And there in his palm, was not the lighter, but the key to her Prius, held out to her like an offering.

Aisling walked towards them, into the stink of the kerosene, and took it from him gently. Antony nodded, and then let his head fall back. He began to sob.

74

'It needs to be someone else,' Hanson said, her voice a little unsteady but her expression set.

Jonah had never known her shy away from an interview, let alone one with a confirmed criminal. She was usually the first to volunteer. She loved the interview room as much as he did.

'Sure,' he said, nodding. 'Is there . . . a particular reason?'

'I just can't go in there and pretend to be a sympathetic mate of his,' she said, her eyes slightly bright. 'Not after what he did to Jacqueline and Lindsay. However hard his life's been, he had choices. And I know it's part of the job sometimes, and I should be able to just get on with it,' she added. 'I know that. And I'm sure I will. I'm just . . . not there yet.'

Jonah nodded again. He understood only too well. It was going to be a very disingenuous sort of an interview. One where they would act as though Antony had done nothing wrong and that they sympathised with him, in order to draw out a full confession.

He could hardly blame Juliette for finding it profoundly distasteful. And, in fact, a good part of him was warmed by her moral strength. It took guts to say that to a superior officer.

'I can come in,' O'Malley offered. 'I don't disagree with anything Juliette's saying about what he's done, but I also think he's been dealt a terrible hand in life, and I wouldn't

want to assume I'd come out a good guy in those circum-
stances either. I'll be OK, thinking of that in there.'

'Thank you,' Jonah said, just as Juliette said the same.

Antony ignored the suggestions of his solicitor, and told
them everything he'd done. Or at least, his version of it. It
was a complete and quite heartbreaking account of the
deaths of three women and one horse.

'I didn't start by . . . wanting to hurt anyone,' he said, his
eyes on Jonah as he spoke. 'I need you to know that. I just . . .
something had broken between me and my dad. The man I
thought was my dad. And it drove me to find out more about
my mum and how she'd died. I had these scattered memories
of her being kind to me and then . . . being awful.' He shook
his head. 'All Dad had said was that she'd died in an accident,
so I went through his letters, and I found some from her. I
realised he'd lied to me. There were loads of them she'd sent
after he'd taken me, angry letters about how he'd stolen me
and she wanted me back.'

'That must have been a shock,' O'Malley said sympathet-
ically.

'It was . . . It made me feel like there was someone out
there who wanted me. By that time Dad clearly didn't . . .'
Antony gave a short, bitter laugh. 'So I went to see her in
secret. And at first, god, it was like . . . like having a real mum.'
His eyes gleamed in the bright lights of the interview room.
'She hugged me, and told me how much she'd missed me.
She was – a bit of a mess, but I thought I could help her
maybe. I told her she'd be in my life now. We sat together and
then, I don't know why . . . it was like some switch went in
her. She just . . . went for me. She grabbed a knife off the
counter and started to swing it at me while I stumbled away.
She told me I was the devil's child, and that I'd ruined her

384

life. That I was filth and she wished I'd died at birth.' His voice shook as he spoke, and it was clear to Jonah that this was the first time he'd described this scene. 'I don't really remember much of what happened, but there was no . . . intention to what I did. I just tried to stop her. And she ended up with the knife in her.' There were full tears in Antony's eyes now. 'I don't know if you . . . you might have seen someone die like that, I suppose but I . . . I had to watch her, while she carried on hating me even as she . . .' He gave a sob. 'I just . . . I didn't know what to do. I didn't know.'

Antony rubbed at his eyes with the back of his hand.

'So you concealed her death with the fire?' Jonah asked.

'Yes,' he said thickly. 'I've always been good with fires. It seemed like maybe I could make it seem like an accident. And then I – I don't know. I wanted to offer her some respect too. A funeral pyre. So I made it carefully, and doused it with kerosene. I set it alight, and I ran.' He grimaced. 'I burned my clothes too. I had to drive home with just a spare coat on. I waited until everyone was asleep and then let myself into the flat.'

He gave a long breath out. Jonah wondered whether he should pick away at this, more. Whether they should cast doubt on Anneka Foley as the original aggressor. But there was time for that, and he found himself – at least for now – believing Antony Murphy's account.

'Tell us about Jacqueline,' he said instead.

Antony looked away from him. 'I bumped into her while I was picking up hay in Lyndhurst. She was parked up nearby while I was loading it into the car and she came to talk to me. I was . . . I was bowled over by her. She was this beautiful, strong, smart woman. So different from anyone I'd dated. And I just asked her, on a whim, if she'd like to go and do something that night. I had a night off, and nothing to do.'

'You didn't get a lot of nights off, did you?' O'Malley asked. 'We've been given the calendar from the stud farm from those months. Only a handful of evenings to yourself.'

'It's hard to take time off when you're trying to please someone who's never happy.' Antony's jaw worked for a moment before he continued. 'Anyway, Jacqueline said, well, there was a gig on she wouldn't mind seeing.' Antony gave a laugh. 'I should have known, when she said that, that it wasn't going to work. But, right then, I was taken in by her, so I agreed. I met her there, and at first it was amazing. She made me feel . . . I don't know. Like I was worth something. But then the headline band started, and the real Jacqueline came out.' His brow furrowed. He looked angry. 'She was just watching this musician instead of me, with . . . a kind of hungry look. It was humiliating. I said we should go, and suddenly she was laughing at me. Telling me not to over-react. She said I was being pathetic.'

Jonah found himself wondering about this. Had Jacqueline taken out some of her anger at her ex-husband on Antony? Her daughters had explained how difficult their relationship had been. Was this more of the same behaviour? And had it just met Antony's feelings of inadequacy head-on, unfairly and with terrible consequences? Or was he trying to invent reasons for having done something unthinkable?

'I managed to get her to leave, in the end, but then I was driving her home, while she was just telling me over and over how ridiculous I was. How we'd just met, and it was controlling and weird and childish. She asked if that was why I was single. And I just couldn't do it. I pulled over and told her to get out. And she – she launched herself at me. And I just . . . I squeezed.' He looked away.

'How did you feel then?' O'Malley asked gently.

'Terrified,' Antony said immediately. 'I knew they'd think

I'd murdered her, when that wasn't what . . . And, god, what would my dad say?' His voice cracked, and he cleared his throat. 'I thought about that pyre I'd made for Mum, and it seemed like the only thing I could do. I knew I could get supplies from the farm. So I drove into the woods, and left her in the trees, and came back with a can of kerosene and a load of firewood. Everyone else was sound asleep.'

'So you did it alone?' O'Malley asked.

'Yes,' Antony said. 'I couldn't let any of them see. Can you imagine what would have happened if Dad had realised?' He gave a convulsive shudder, and wrapped his arms around himself. His jaw was shaking as he said, 'It took a while. I knew I had to do it a long way from the Land Rover. The whole time I thought I'd be found, but then it was alight.'

'So none of this was premeditated,' Jonah said.

Antony shook his head. 'No,' he said. 'Of course it wasn't. I thought I loved her. And Lindsay . . . I actually . . .' He stopped, looking upwards. And then something changed in his expression. It hardened before he looked back down. 'But they all turned on me in the end. All of them.'

Jonah watched the change, and for the first time saw in this man someone who could kill a woman. Three women. A man who had come to think that everyone would betray him, and had turned vengeful.

'I learned my lesson after Jacqueline,' Antony continued quietly. 'When I went out, I started taking ketamine with me. It meant I could soothe them. Stop things getting out of hand.'

'You wanted to incapacitate these women?' Jonah asked.

'No,' Antony insisted. 'Just . . . stop them from turning cruel.'

Jonah found his heart beating in his throat. 'Were there . . . others?'

Antony stared at him for a moment, and then slowly shook his head. 'One who – she rang a friend to take her home. She didn't feel well . . .' He glanced up again, with that hardness still partly there, and Jonah wasn't sure he believed him when he said, 'I wouldn't have hurt her.'

Jonah thought back to their inquiries about drugging. Had someone called in about that failed attempt, in the dozens and dozens of reported instances of drugging that had come in? Could they track it down and build it into their case?

He could see O'Malley making a note with the same thought, and he nodded, and continued.

'You drugged Lindsay too, didn't you?' he said.

Antony nodded slowly. 'Only . . . a very little at first. It seemed to be going well. Then I had this idea we could sit and watch the fireworks and the Quadrantids. On the heath. I'd been going to head out there myself after a few drinks. It was going to be so much better having her there, that's what I thought.' He gave an empty smile. 'I didn't want her suddenly changing her mind, so I put a bit more ketamine in the hot toddy. Just in case.'

'But something still went wrong,' O'Malley said quietly.

Antony's face twisted. 'I'd – figured I'd make myself a fire, and I'd got quite used to bringing wood and kerosene with me. I'd set a few fires since – since Jacqueline. It made me feel better, somehow, sitting and watching them burn. But anyway, Lindsay saw all the wood and the can of fuel. She pretended she hadn't, but it was so obvious she was freaking out. And then when I stopped the car, she hit me with a piece of wood, then opened the door and ran for it.'

There was a pause, so Jonah said gently, 'And did you pursue her?'

Antony's jaw worked for a moment. 'I had to. I was fucked

if I didn't. I'd told her everything about myself, and she'd seen the wood. We'd driven past Matthew Downing and his stupid band, and if she'd managed to reach them somehow . . .' He started to shake, a shudder running through him. 'I was so scared. And she'd – she'd betrayed me . . .'

Jonah had to look away. He could imagine Lindsay Kernow's fear too. How terrified she must have been in her final moments.

Part of him badly wanted to confront Antony with what he'd done, in spite of the plan. He wanted to ask whether Antony really thought his freedom was worth more than the life of a vibrant woman and mother. Whether her attempt to save herself had made her deserve death. And whether he'd really been afraid, or whether he'd wanted to prove that he was more powerful than Lindsay thought.

But Jonah wanted that guilty plea. For the sake of Pippa and Rosie and Dylan.

'I didn't let her suffer,' Antony said quietly, as if he could read some of Jonah's thoughts. 'I forced the rest of the ketamine into her mouth. She slipped off to sleep before I . . . you know.'

Jonah watched him for a moment, wondering at the strange contradictions that made up this man. The rushes of tenderness that seemed to fight with the coldest desire for revenge. The fact that he'd wanted to drug Aisling Cooley, and then in the end decided to let her go.

'And the blood?' Jonah asked quietly. 'Did you cut yourself?'

'It was when she hit me,' Antony said. 'I didn't realise I was bleeding. I guess there was too much adrenaline. I only felt the wound on my head later. It never occurred to me that I'd left blood.' He raised a hand up to his thick blond hair. 'It would have been OK if that helicopter hadn't come over. I could have burned the pyre. I wasn't going to go near any more women.'

Jonah tried not to react. He knew that O'Malley, alongside him, would be finding that as hard to believe as he was.

There was quiet for a while, and then O'Malley asked, 'But what about Merivel?'

Antony shook his head, his sadness mounting into a confused sort of anger. 'She – she rejected her foal. She tried to kill it. It was awful to watch. I was so angry with her.' He looked between Jonah and O'Malley. 'It was the right thing to do, for the sake of the foal. Wasn't it?'

Jonah gave it a moment, and then asked, 'What about your recent behaviour?' He lifted his chin slightly. 'Have you been following our team? Keeping tabs on us?'

Antony blinked at him blankly. 'What? I don't know what you mean.'

'You were watching us work at some of the sites, weren't you?' O'Malley asked. 'At Lyndhurst Heath, and some of the other pyres.'

Antony frowned, and then said, 'I only went to see at the farm. Where I'd – where I'd left Merivel. I thought I might watch you work, but I was too scared of you finding something. I had to leave.'

'Did you go to get coffee?' Jonah asked. 'Coffee for our team?'

'What? No,' Antony said. 'No, I shut myself in my flat and put the TV on.'

Jonah watched him, wondering whether he was denying this for a reason. Whether his confusion might be genuine.

'How about at the site where you killed Lindsay?' he tried. 'Did you leave something for us there? For one of us in particular?'

Antony shook his head slowly, and then more vigorously.

'I don't – do you mean the blood? I didn't leave anything else.'

'You wouldn't describe yourself as a guardian angel?' Jonah pressed.

Antony looked at him with that same confusion, and then said dully, 'I'm nobody's angel. My mum used to call me a spawn of the devil, you know? Maybe – maybe she was right.'

Jonah and O'Malley left him a while later. They wanted to persuade Danny Murphy to stop covering for his brother.

'DNA will be our friend now,' Jonah told Danny gently, after explaining that Antony had confessed to everything. 'We've taken a blood sample and will be able to prove that he's a match for the blood we found. We also have evidence from Henning Andersen that you were at an out-of-hours clinic being seen for complications of influenza the evening Jacqueline Clarke died. Antony, on the other hand, had a night off, and was out early enough that he didn't know you'd become very unwell.'

Danny sat in silence for a few moments, and then exhaled long and loudly. 'All right,' he said. 'All right.'

He went on to admit that he'd lied, because he'd felt that Antony had never had a chance in life.

'I know what he's done is awful,' he said. 'But what's happened to him has been awful too. When I ran, I just thought of him in prison, and it breaking him. It seemed like I had to save him again. It felt like fate had handed me this duty, with the blood.' He looked up at Jonah, steadily. 'Why else would the help I gave him before have made it look like it was me?'

'It was your life,' Jonah said, gently.

Danny gave a shrug. 'I don't think it would have broken me. I'd get through it. I'd never been made to believe I was worthless.' His expression turned pleading. 'And whatever he's done, there's a good man in there. I thought, maybe, with me gone and Dad giving him respect at last . . .'

'He needs more help than that,' Jonah told him gently but firmly. 'Prison may not seem kind, but he'll see psychologists. Really good ones. He'll be able to start dealing with all the things that happened to him in his life.'

He didn't add that even that might not be enough.

Danny nodded. He went on to answer all their questions in full, including whether Antony could have been following his team around. Danny wasn't convinced he'd have time to do such a thing, but admitted that he might be sneaking out while others were asleep.

By the end of it Danny looked older and more fatigued than Jonah had seen him. And then he was released to go home, which he did slowly. Reluctantly.

Aisling Cooley and her sons were due in the next afternoon to give their statements. Michael Murphy was being treated for ketamine poisoning from the tea Antony had fed him. He'd suffered possible damage to his bladder but he would live to tell the tale, and Jonah was relieved about that, among many things. He'd been more than a little afraid, as they'd arrived at the Murphy farm and seen the cars drawn up, that they would find both Aisling and Michael past help.

Instead Aisling and Finn had been sitting with Antony, each with an arm round him. They'd waited like that until Jonah and the constables had come to arrest him. Ethan and Hennning Andersen had been close by them, and the lot of them had reeked of kerosene.

'It's OK. I'll come with you,' Antony had said, before Jonah could say a word.

Jonah had been surprised to see Aisling Cooley's tears, and wondered how it was possible for her to cry over a man who had come close to ruining all three of her sons' lives.

'Please look after him,' she said, as they led him to the car. 'He chose not to hurt me. He – he's my half-brother, you know.'

'I do,' Jonah said. 'It just took me a while to figure it out.'

It had only been on the drive over that that last piece of information from Antony's DNA had clicked into place: that he had been related to the owner of the blood at the crime scene.

Aisling and Antony would be able to get a formal DNA test if they felt it necessary, but nobody really thought that it was. Antony Murphy looked the spit of a young Dara Cooley (or Patrick Horan, as he'd been known then). Jonah wondered whether it was Anneka's pregnancy that had been the final thing to tip Dara Cooley over the edge, making him choose the long, cold drive into Ullswater.

Jonah informed Jacqueline Clarke's daughters of the arrest at eleven thirty in one of the relatives' rooms, and then spoke to Dylan Kernow directly afterwards to tell him the same news. And if he'd had any doubts about the rightness of prosecuting Antony with the full weight of the law, they were squashed when he saw those three once again. He could well understand the sagging relief of closure. Of knowing that there would be justice.

He eventually emerged from the relatives' room into a CID that was almost empty. Only his team and four constables from the Red Desk who had assisted with the arrest occupied the main floor. They were talking in a big group, clearly feeling the need for a debrief after the events of the day.

It was gone midnight, and Jonah was more than tired. The paperwork could, he felt, wait until the morning. Everyone needed home, and sleep.

Though Jonah had to admit that there was a part of him that didn't want to go home. That didn't want to have to confront the new, more depressing reality he now found himself in with his partner.

It was while he was standing there, dreading the thought of trying to curl up in bed with Michelle that his phone rang. It was her number, and he didn't know what to feel as he answered.

'Hey,' he said, trying to sound neutral.

'Jonah.' He could hear traffic in the background, and realised that she'd gone out again. Rhona must be looking after Milly, but Jonah hadn't had a clue that Michelle had decided to go out, even though he'd messaged her his schedule. And it gave him a pang of hurt.

There was silence except for the traffic, and distant loud conversation.

'Is everything OK?' he tried. 'You need a lift?'

'No, I'm . . . I'll be a while.' He could hear it now. The unsteadiness in her voice. She was very drunk. Perhaps more so than she'd been last night. She took a noisy breath. 'Just out with Siobhan.'

'OK.'

There was another pause, and then Michelle said, 'I think we made the wrong decision.' There was a sniff, and she said, 'We shouldn't have . . . tried again.'

Jonah felt it like a gut punch. In spite of the day's emotional drain, it still hurt hugely. Physically.

'I . . . I'm really sorry if you're not happy,' he said.

'I'm not,' Michelle said. 'And it's not your fault. We're just . . . I don't love you like I should. I'm sorry, Jonah.'

And then, before he could reply, she'd hung up.

For a few moments all Jonah could do was to sit where he was and try to breathe in and out. He wanted to dismiss this as postnatal depression. As drunkenness. But he knew that it wasn't.

How was he supposed to fix it?

At the end of ten minutes, he realised that he didn't know. That the only thing he *could* do was what he *needed* to do right now.

Taking a breath, he walked out into CID.

'It's twelve twenty,' he said loudly. 'What the hell are you all still doing here?'

There was a collective laugh, and everyone began getting themselves packed to go.

Jonah went over to Hanson, and said, in as together a voice as he could manage, 'It's not entirely clear that Antony Murphy was the one leaving you those gifts.' He watched her blink twice, and then look away from him, her expression worried. 'It might be that he's denying it because it makes him look much more like a methodical stalker than a man who just lost control. But until we're sure, just . . . maybe stick with making sure you're in company, all right?'

Hanson nodded slowly, and then gave a melodramatic sigh. 'This is going to get right in the way of my incredibly packed social life.'

Jonah grinned at her, an expression that faded as he saw Antony Murphy appearing from the door to the interview suite flanked by two uniformed constables. He was on his way to spend a first night in the cells at the station, and Jonah was hopeful that there would be many more days of incarceration before he was released.

'It's awful, what he did,' O'Malley said, coming to stand next to him. 'But, Jesus, did life deal him a bad hand. And by "life" I mean people. Can society agree to stop fucking each other up?'

Jonah wasn't quite sure how he felt about that. Jacqueline

and Lindsay had deserved long, full lives. But then perhaps Anneka and Antony had as well. And they'd never stood a chance. Either of them.

He turned away from Antony with a wave of hopelessness, and started to make his way home.

75

21 January

Aisling found herself waking to another morning with Jack O'Keane, and this time there had been no need for her to pad her way down to the spare room to find him. Despite everything, she felt pure joy as she moved her head and saw him next to her, his sturdy chest bare in the morning light. How had she done without him for thirty years?

Jack had, admittedly, been what Ethan would have called 'salty' the night before. He'd arrived at the stud farm in a fury, asking her what the hell she'd been thinking of, going to the farm on her own.

Her two younger sons – a phrase she was going to have to get used to saying – had belatedly felt a trace of concern that their mother was off visiting Danny's family alone. Having failed to raise her on the phone, they'd eventually decided to call Jack, whose number they'd had to google.

Jack had told them to get down there in Ethan's car, and to keep him updated. He'd then got off the train, and paid a small fortune for a cab to take him straight back to the farm.

He had, of course, missed all the fun. He'd arrived, anxious and furious, to find the three of them being given tea in the farmhouse kitchen – pure, unadulterated tea this time, without the ketamine.

'Jesus,' Jack had said on being shown in. 'I just walked past a fucking ambulance and thought . . .' He'd stopped, staring at Aisling, his chest moving up and down in an exaggerated motion. 'What were you thinking?'

Aisling had felt a rush of contrition, but also a strong surge of gratitude for this man who still seemed to care about her. She'd risen, and gone to take him by the hand. She'd almost finished apologising to him profusely by the time he'd leaned down and kissed her – right there, in front of her sons, a detective and a constable.

'Jeez, get a room!' Ethan had called.

'Don't be such an unromantic twat,' Aisling shot back, having extricated herself.

They had, in the end, got a room – this room – though Aisling had at first made the effort of setting up the spare room for Jack to stay in. Neither of them had, it emerged, felt like sleeping once they'd got home, and so a long, far-reaching chat – covering everything from their lives over thirty years, to Aisling's hopes for her new game, to thoughts on *Halo 5* – had turned very slowly into contact, and kissing, and then a firm move upstairs to her bedroom.

Aisling had a good ten minutes to watch him this morning before he woke up, something that was rendered a little less romantic by the fact that she needed to creep out and pee. But these were moments she was determined to hang on to. She slid back in next to him and put her arm over him lightly, keen not to wake him just yet.

But Jack eventually seemed to feel her gaze on him, and opened one eye enough to take her in.

'OK,' he said. 'I think it's your turn to make coffee.'

'Ahh, my visions of a live-in maid have just died a death,' she said. But she kissed him before she got up.

Neither Finn nor Ethan seemed at all bothered about having Jack at the breakfast table, and it was disconcerting how easily he seemed to fit into their strange routine once again. Barks was still a fan, managing to scramble his way onto Jack's lap despite him being tucked half into the table, and then standing to lick his face as he was trying to eat a plate of eggs.

'I can't believe he's choosing your face over food,' Finn said.

'My face is obviously delicious,' Jack retorted.

Nobody said anything about the fifth place Aisling had laid. It was for Danny, who she'd messaged last night, asking him to come and see them if he could.

They hadn't had to talk about the fact that Danny was welcome here. It was a given for Finn and Ethan somehow. They were fascinated by their brother, as desperate to find out about his life as she was.

'He should move in,' Finn had suggested, while laying the table. 'He could pay a bit of rent, and you'd be able to keep the place.'

'I think he'd find it a bit of an arse driving to look after the horses every morning,' Aisling retorted. But she'd still hoped that he might at least become part of their lives. It would take time and effort to get to know their son, but she was willing to put that in.

'Guess I'd better move closer,' Jack said, around a mouthful. 'Which is embarrassing, as you might think I'm keen on you as well.'

'Ha, I know you are,' she said, whacking him on the arm. 'You've always been a man of taste.'

For some reason the speed with which they were becoming an item once again didn't worry her at all. It was happening like this in some ways because of Danny, but also in some ways because of them. In spite of the mess of life that had come in the middle, there was still that pull towards each other. That sense that the two of them worked. That they worked, in fact, as nothing else ever really had.

Her mood dropped as breakfast continued and Danny's place remained empty. He had only messaged 'Thank you' in reply to her invitation, and she'd hoped he meant he would come.

She eventually had to admit to herself that she'd been wrong, and began to stack plates. As she was rinsing them in the sink, she felt a pair of strong arms round her, and Finn's chin rested on her shoulder. 'I'm sure he'll come some day. It's a lot to, you know, adjust to. New fam . . . awesome younger brothers . . .'

She ruffled his hair. 'Thinks, Finny.'

'Now are you going to show us the game you've been working on? I think we've been patient enough.'

'You weren't supposed to know about that,' she told him, outraged.

'Oh, come on. You've had it up on your screen when I've come in about fifteen times, and I do see things when I organise your desktop, you know.'

'All right,' she said. 'But be nice. I'm not ready for brutal feedback just yet.'

Danny hadn't meant to be an hour late to breakfast at the Cooley house. He'd known it would be difficult to fit in around the morning routine – particularly with his father now moving at a slow drift instead of his usual stamping limp. But he'd been determined to make it for ten o'clock anyway, and had got up twenty minutes early so he could do the feed, speak to his father and perhaps the vet, and shower before driving over.

It had been Henning who had slowed him down, an unusual event. But things were unusual today. More than unusual.

Danny was no longer Michael's son, and Antony was no longer his brother. Antony was also no longer slumbering in bed while the morning began, but sleeping – or perhaps not sleeping – in a cell at Southampton Central Police Station. Knowing that had made it hard for Danny to focus. Hard for him to keep momentum at times.

He'd thanked his stars for Henning all over again when the Dane had emerged at six, all ready to help. Without fuss, he'd taken on task after task, and picked up the slack whenever Danny had faltered. They were ahead of schedule by the time the vet had arrived, and when the two of them had gone to the far stable to lead the non-foaling mares out, Danny had paused just inside the doorway.

'I should have thanked you last night,' he said. 'For helping me to get away. And for trying to defend me, even when I didn't want you to.'

Henning moved just inside the door, and then gave him a wide grin. 'I'm sorry for doing exactly what you didn't want me to,' he said. 'But I'm also not sorry.'

Danny nodded. 'I keep thinking back to before you were here, and . . . I don't know how I did without you.'

Henning gave a shrug. A half-laugh. 'I'm sure you did just fine. I just like to interfere.'

'No,' Danny said, and put a hand out to touch Henning's arm. 'No, I . . . I'm glad you're here.'

Henning nodded, a considering expression on his face. 'You know, I'm . . . not glad you're here.' Danny winced, but Henning raised a hand. 'I don't mean like that. I'm glad to be around you. It's just . . . the one thing I really want is for you to realise that you don't owe anyone a life spent in a cage. Not a prison cell for your brother, or this place for your dad. Your . . . sort of dad.'

Danny let out a long breath. He felt the rightness of what

Henning was saying. He felt as though he could just . . . leave. He would stay for a short while for his father, while he dealt with Antony's imprisonment, sure. And then he could *not* be here. And his father would cope. Maybe even thrive.

'Maybe I don't,' he said, nodding. 'But . . . I'd miss you all if I left.'

He looked steadily at Henning, who gave him a grin. 'Maybe the rest of us might like to travel too.'

'That would be . . .' Danny said. 'That would make it all a lot more fun.'

And somehow, as the two of them went on to complete the rest of the farm's duties that morning, it was with such a sense of lightness that he didn't notice the time passing, and he was astonished to realise that he'd missed breakfast entirely.

'It's fucking brilliant, *Mutter*,' Ethan said. 'It's going to be . . . huge.'

It was just her son saying it. Not an unbiased review. But Aisling still felt like laughing, and jumping, and crying.

'It is, isn't it?' she said. And Jack laughed at her.

'I second that,' he said. 'It's . . . it's another *Survive the Light.*'

She looked over at him, slightly startled. 'Yes, I . . . I didn't think you knew. That that was me.'

'Let's just say that I have not only played more games than most teenagers over the last ten years,' Jack said, 'but that I also did some fairly extensive googling of you after I saw you in the office on Monday.' He tutted. 'I was so, so convinced that it was you. Which made me feel like I was going mad when he said that you were Aisling Cooley. And I did vaguely know that you'd created that game. I just hadn't seen any pictures.' He shook his head. 'I must have looked at every photo of you ever taken, trying to figure out if I was going mad, or if you really were Martha.'

'God,' Aisling said, taking his hand. 'Sorry.'

'Well, I think your game's shit,' Finn said loudly. And then, at Aisling's gasp, he said, 'Joooooke. It's brilliant. And I now see why you didn't think we needed Dad and his flash cash.'

'Well, it may not make me an instant millionaire,' she said, a little more soberly. 'But I think we can do without his help if we're lucky.'

'Except the three grand,' Finn added.

'Except for that. Five-second rule. It's ours.'

'Mum,' Ethan asked suddenly, using her actual title for once in a way that was immediately disconcerting. 'You said you'd go and see Antony. In prison and stuff. Are you actually, like, going to do that? Even though you don't have to?'

'I have to,' Aisling said simply. 'He's my brother.'

'But he's a serial killer too,' Ethan said. 'Just saying.'

Aisling shook her head, thinking again of what she'd read about Lindsay Kernow. About Jacqueline Clarke. About what he'd taken from them.

'He's going to pay for what he's done for a very long time,' she added. 'And I think . . . that he isn't just a bad person. At the end he was letting me go. He didn't want to hurt me. And while he's in prison, he's going to get the help he should have had before, I hope, and come out remorseful and patched up and . . . someone who would never, ever harm someone again.'

'And if he doesn't?' Ethan asked.

Aisling made a noise of frustration. 'I don't know. It's . . . complex. Families are fecking complex, in my experience.'

'I'm not,' Finn said, beaming. 'I'm beautifully straightforward.'

'Of course you are, darling,' Aisling replied.

There was a knock at the door then, and Aisling was filled with a singing hope at the thought that it might be Danny.

She knew that it would be hard folding him into her family. The quiet, outdoorsy man who didn't banter away like her sons, or spend half his life in front of a screen. He didn't play tennis either, as far as she knew. Or have a band. Or enjoy ordering pizza with banana and chilli and six extra cheese.

But they'd make it work somehow. They'd flex to find some middle ground. And it'd be good for all of them.

She was smiling as she swung the door open.

76

Going to the pub as a team after successfully charging someone was a tradition, and one that felt important to Hanson. Without it there was an uncomfortable sense of anti-climax. A trip home to a bed that you'd barely seen in days, and, at times, a sense of the futility of it all.

They'd missed their chance the night before, having finished up after midnight. But now, after a full day spent assembling evidence, she, Ben and Domnall had made it to their regular haunt down the road, with the chief set to follow. And it seemed that the chief's invitation had brought half of CID down there with them, including a lot of the Red Desk who had helped apprehend the two Murphy brothers.

'It's rammed,' Hanson said with a laugh, as she stepped inside. It was also hot and loud and strangely comforting.

'I'm going to fight that constable for a table,' O'Malley said, beginning to move towards a four-seat spot. 'You two get the drinks in.'

'Roger that,' Lightman said, and the two of them squeezed towards the bar. They ended up tightly packed next to it, and when Ben suddenly turned towards her, Hanson found herself very close to him. Almost as close as she'd been the time she'd hugged him.

There was something disconcerting in his expression as he said, 'So we made it.'

'We did,' she agreed. 'At least to the pub, if not to the drunken crap-talking bit.'

'I'd say we'll get there after fifteen minutes and a couple of pints drunk too quickly,' he said. 'So I recommend we get double-parked for this first round.'

Hanson felt her phone buzz in her coat pocket, and she wasn't sure whether she was relieved or not. She managed to extricate it, and saw a mobile number she didn't recognise. 'Hmm. Could be one of the Red Desk, I guess?'

Ben glanced towards the bar. 'I can get the drinks if you need to get it.'

'Sure,' she said, a little torn. She hesitated, and then said, 'OK. Sorry. Won't be a sec.'

She pressed the button to answer, and said, 'Juliette Hanson,' but then could hear only speech-like sounds. It was too loud in there. 'Sorry, hang on. I'm just going outside. I can't hear.'

She fought her way the few feet back to the door, realising that the DCI was on his way in. He waved at her, and she gestured at the phone.

She emerged into the icy night. It was only once outside that she could hear something more down the line. It sounded like an engine.

'Hello?' she asked, to be met with nothing but that noise.

Someone had pocket-dialled her while driving.

And then, in an odd echo, the sound cut across the phone call in real life. She turned to see a pair of X-ray bright LED lights coming along the road towards her. And she knew, before she really should have known, that they were coming *for* her, not just towards her.

With awful speed, the black shape of the car hit the kerb on its near side and kept coming. There was nowhere to go. No time.

Roll, she thought. *Jump and roll.*

She knew it was her only chance. To get up and onto the bonnet on her thigh and shoulder. She'd seen this in videos.

Knew it. Though none of those cars had been travelling like this one. None of them had been going so relentlessly fast.

Somehow, she timed it right, and left the ground just before the car hit her legs. She felt a moment of lightness as the car's bonnet caught her, and she slid on it, trying to brace for the impact with the windscreen.

When it came it was with the sound of rending metal, and a force that sent her into the air. She knew, as she lifted up and off to the side of the car, that she was in trouble. That she was going too high. That the drop would be too hard.

She had no chance to turn or right herself. There was nothing she could do except let the fall begin, bringing her towards the hard edge of the road.

The sound was like an explosion in the pub itself. Suddenly the wall near the door was bulging inwards. The three nearest customers threw themselves away from it.

Jonah was running for the door before he'd stopped to think. He half heard Ben's sharp call of 'Juliette!' before he barrelled outside, through a door that was now half off its hinges.

He almost ran into the side of a black BMW. The rear half of it was across the doorway. His mind threw back at him immediately that this was Damian's car. Hanson's ex's car. But he was still moving round it, shouting out her name.

He saw her legs first, and felt a strange, disconnected feeling. She was on the ground, next to it, and as he rounded the end of the car fully he saw that she was on her back, half on the kerb and half off it, her chest moving in gasping jerks.

He could hear O'Malley behind him, calling for an ambulance, as he dropped down next to her.

'Juliette,' he said.

She looked up at him, a turn of her eyes without anything

else. She was still gasping, and he didn't know what he should be looking for. How to help her.

He took her hand gently, and said, 'Ambulance is coming. Ambulance is coming. It's OK.'

And then suddenly Ben was there, flinging himself in a sliding run over the car and crouching down next to her. And cool, calm, emotionless Lightman looked anguished.

Jonah rose then, letting Ben take his place. And he turned and went towards the car.

A man's form was visible behind the wheel, his face obscured by the airbag that had inflated on impact.

Damian was groaning but moving, as Jonah wrenched the door open.

'Fuck,' Damian said.

Jonah knew the drill. Knew that he shouldn't move him. That he should wait for help.

But he leaned in, undid the seat belt, and then grabbed Damian by the back of the neck. With a feeling of greater anger than he could ever remember experiencing, he wrenched him out of the car and into the road.

There were other cars pulling up now. And people emptying out from the pub. And Jonah cared not one bit as he turned Damian onto his front, dragged his arms up behind him and cuffed him with as much force as he could.

Damian gave a short laugh the moment the cuffs were clicked closed.

'That's why you don't fuck with your guardian angel,' he said. And then he spat a dribble of blood onto the tarmac.

Hanson knew something was wrong. Really, badly wrong. She could see fear in Ben's eyes as she tried again and again to draw breath properly. There was pain, but pain she somehow couldn't feel fully. As if she wasn't quite part of it.

'I – I'm–' she said.

Ben leaned close to her. Close enough for her to see that his eyes were swimming. He put his hand up to her hair with the lightest pressure and said, 'I'm here. I'm staying. I'm here.'

And she half smiled at him, hoping she was staying too.

Author's Note

Forensic genealogy has fascinated me ever since it made headlines with the identification of the Golden State Killer. Although by that time DNA evidence had already become a key part of building successful cases against criminals of all kinds, this was a totally new method. Commercial companies such as GEDmatch and Family Tree DNA had begun including a clause about consent to the use of DNA by law enforcement in their terms and conditions. This meant that these companies had become active in helping to catch murderers.

Once the police and FBI can upload their matches to a database containing hundreds of thousands of DNA records, experts are able to use them to pinpoint specific suspects – or, at times, just a single suspect. It was this method that led to Joseph James DeAngelo's eventual arrest for his crimes as the Golden State Killer. Federal detectives led by Paul Holes uploaded his DNA to GEDmatch, created a family tree of over 1,000 people, and then narrowed it down based on age, sex and location.

They ended up with two suspects, one of whom they were able to exclude by a familial DNA test. Which left the real Golden State Killer, who was able to be linked conclusively to the crimes by his DNA and sentenced to life imprisonment, forty-four years after he first committed rape.

Like a lot of other people, I was immediately intrigued by the possibilities this raised for solving crimes. So many murders have gone unsolved over the years, and this is a trend that is only increasing here in the UK with cuts to policing.

Where 90 per cent of murders within London were once solved and a conviction secured, current rates are down to 72 per cent after the disbandment of specific murder squads. Without time and resources, it's no surprise that murders have gone unsolved, with as many as a quarter nationally never ending in a conviction.

The picture is equally bleak in other nations. Even in countries with low rates of unsolved crime, like Switzerland and Finland, more than one in ten murders will not end in justice. And the figures are starkest in the US, where a third of homicides will never result in a successful prosecution. Again, for US police officers, the problem is one of numbers. There aren't enough officers or resources to manage the very high number of killings committed, and even high-profile serial killers have been able to evade justice for years as a result.

Of course, there are other reasons for killers never being brought to light. As in *A Killer in the Family*, killers can be both careful and lucky. Preying on victims who are not well known, at the right times, can allow them to go undetected. They might never walk past CCTV, or have no DNA on record. Whatever the cause, that lack of a conviction is inevitably devastating for the family and friends of the victim.

The two most exciting parts of forensic genealogy struck me as stopping serial killers before they could strike again and bringing closure by solving cold cases. But there are downsides to this approach. The idea of *any* individual's DNA being searchable, whether or not they've committed a crime, is problematic. For Parabon, the US genealogy agency that made headlines by solving a number of cold cases, privacy concerns became very pressing after they used GEDmatch data to solve an assault. This was not something users had allowed their DNA to be used for; the terms and conditions mentioned only rapes and murders. The outcry resulted in GEDmatch CEO Curtis Rogers swiftly changing company policy to one where users had to opt *in* to having their data used for law enforcement purposes instead of opting out.

The other side to forensic genealogy that I found fascinating, but which could be troubling, was the way those who have become expert in it are not geneticists or detectives. They are instead amateurs (or professionals of other kinds) who have devoted huge amounts to time to understanding exactly how a genetic report from any one of these databases could guide them to the right culprit. This is both wonderful and potentially worrying when you consider how much information is being given to these people acting outside any legal framework.

I was particularly drawn to profiles of the brilliant CeCe Moore. Despite coming from a background in theatre and commercials, having researched genealogy in order to produce a commercial for Family Tree DNA, she became fascinated by the subject. This led to her handing over her business to be run solely by her husband and partner, and instead focusing only on using genetic data from these sites to identify people. Her initial work was with swapped or missing babies, and in helping an amnesiac recover her identity. But by 2018, she received permission from GEDmatch and Family Tree DNA to upload crime scene DNA to their databases.

The results were astonishing. CeCe Moore helped solve more than fifty crimes in a year by giving her information to law enforcement agencies, establishing herself as the first entrepreneurial forensic genealogist. The character of Cassie Logan in *A Killer in the Family* inevitably owes a great deal to her. And I'm definitely bearing in mind the option of going into actual crime-fighting for a living instead of just crime-writing as a result.

Given all the fascinating sides to forensic genealogy, there was no question I wanted to write about it. But I discovered that this technique was not a technique that would immediately be arriving in the UK. Existing British laws here prohibit the use of data from genealogy websites for the purpose of crime prevention. Privacy concerns have, here, outweighed the perceived benefits. And yet so many crimes could be solved using these methods, without the use of huge numbers of officers. It could be a solution to many policing issues.

So I decided that I'd like to put forward a situation we might find ourselves in a few years down the line: one where we have our very own equivalent of GEDmatch where users can opt in to have their data harvested for the prevention of crime, where the law has subtly changed, and where the crown prosecution service is actively looking for a test case to prove that this can work. If I had to choose anyone to manage that test case, I think it would be Jonah and his team.

I was envisaging how this would work, when another angle to all of this struck me, as often happens in creating stories. I thought quite suddenly about all those real-life family members who had uploaded their DNA, only to discover that someone related to them had committed a crime. It had in many cases been a distant cousin, niece or nephew. So for anyone uploading their data, if they made this awful discovery, the killer might be someone from a branch of the family they barely knew.

But it might also be a son or a daughter, or a sibling. A father, mother, husband or wife.

That, I realised, was the story I wanted to tell more than any other. The story of someone searching for their lost father, and instead being told they had a killer at the heart of their family.

For Aisling, violence really did lie close to home, as it has done for many others. But in the ties of blood and genetics, there also lay a form of justice.

Acknowledgements

I have so many thanks to give to the amazing people at Penguin Michael Joseph who actively support me in keeping on doing this writing thing. They are the most incredible team. Joel Richardson, Grace Long, Jen Breslow, Jen Harlow, Ella Watkins, Kelly Mason, Nick Lowndes, Jennie Roman, Gray Eveleigh, Rachael Sharples and the brilliant rights team – you rock my world. I can't thank you enough.

And of course, without Felicity Blunt and Rosie Pierce – the most wonderful agents any human could wish for – none of this would ever have been possible. Thank you, thank you, thank you.

I also owe a huge debt of thanks to my wonderful international publishers, who help spread the word far and wide.

There are also a lot of people who helped with this book from beyond that pool, too. I want to thank Laura McKinlay for all the fabulous and fascinating knowledge and insight into the running of a stud farm. I'm only sad I couldn't fit more of it in! A whole book set in the world of horses is clearly on the cards. And equally Gwyneth Horscroft for her sharing of Tinder hilarity, which I shamelessly stole. You are both also excellent humans, which needs mentioning.

Chris Haines gets big thanks, as always, for telling me brilliant police procedure for me to geek out over, and for being so patient and great. Any and all errors are once again my own!

And Tariq Joyce needs huge thanks for as always responding to my emergency 'I need plot help!!' requests for zooms, as well as for never failing to make me laugh. I'm so glad

I have you in my corner (and not just for when the zombie apocalypse comes).

To the fabulous Cambridge writers, and in particular to Victoria Brown and Holly Race for being constant, utterly lovely rocks to rely on, and also to Gilly McAllister for being my unbelievably welcome source of advice via WhatsApp. You are all wonderful.

To my fabulous friends, too, who have been an incredible support this year during all the ups and downs. There are genuinely too many of you wonderful humans to name, but I couldn't let this opportunity go by without mentioning Naomi Morris and Melanie Staley, who respond tirelessly to my whinges, and to Sarah Durand, Sarah Wordsworth, Liz Stevens, Alison Stockham, Kathryn Brown, Livia Oldland and Jo Shadbolt for being just fabulous at all times.

And finally to the LKs, that incredible bunch of gorgeous and talented ladies who constantly overwhelm me with their marvellousness. Huge, huge thanks.

Seven friends went into
the woods.
Only six came back. . .

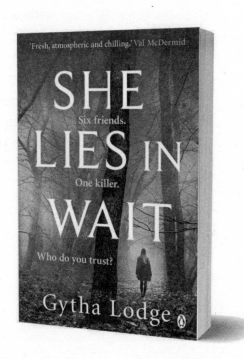

'Fresh, atmospheric and chilling.' Val McDermid

SHE
LIES IN
WAIT

Six friends.

One killer.

Who do you trust?

Gytha Lodge

'An engaging tale of lust, rivalry
and murder'
Sunday Times

WHICH BOOK WILL YOU READ NEXT?

The worst thing you can imagine.
And all you can do is watch. . .

'A satisfyingly complex whodunnit'
Daily Express

WHICH BOOK WILL YOU READ NEXT?

What do you do when the man in your bed isn't your husband. And isn't breathing. . .

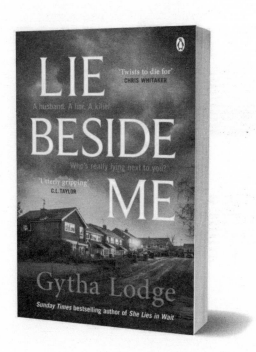

'A killer premise, razor-sharp writing, and twists to die for'
Chris Whitaker

WHICH BOOK WILL YOU READ NEXT?